THE HEALING JAR

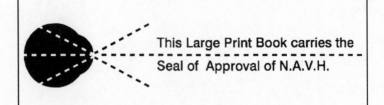

This Large Print Book carries the
Seal of Approval of N.A.V.H.

THE HEALING JAR

WANDA E. BRUNSTETTER

THORNDIKE PRESS
A part of Gale, a Cengage Company

Farmington Hills, Mich • San Francisco • New York • Waterville, Maine
Meriden, Conn • Mason, Ohio • Chicago

LIBRARY OF CONGRESS CIP DATA ON FILE.
CATALOGUING IN PUBLICATION FOR THIS BOOK
IS AVAILABLE FROM THE LIBRARY OF CONGRESS

ISBN-13: 978-1-4328-6744-7 (hardcover alk. paper)

Published in 2019 by arrangement with Barbour Publishing, Inc.

Printed in Mexico
1 2 3 4 5 6 7 23 22 21 20 19

To my dear friends Delbert and Mary.
Your ministry to hurting souls
is a blessing.

He healeth the broken in heart, and
bindeth up their wounds.

PSALM 147:3

PROLOGUE

Lancaster, Pennsylvania

Tears sprang to Lenore Lapp's eyes as she stood with the others who had come to witness this special English wedding. Her cousin Sara walked up the aisle behind Darlene Koch, her maid of honor and a childhood friend. Sara looked radiant in her beautiful, floor-length wedding gown. Because Sara's stepfather had died from injuries sustained in a car accident, and she didn't know who her biological father was, she had asked her half brother, Kenny, to escort her down the aisle.

Brad waited at the front of the church beside his best man, Ned Evans, and the pastor.

"Who gives this woman to be wed?" the clergyman asked.

"I do." Kenny stepped aside as Brad took Sara's hand.

The minister gestured for everyone to be

7

seated, and then he, Sara, and Brad stepped up to the altar area, where they took their places in front of a small table draped with a white linen cloth. An open Bible and three candles sat on the table. The larger one, Sara had previously told Lenore, was called a unity candle. At some point during the ceremony Sara and Brad would pick up their lighted candles and light the bigger one in unison to signify the two becoming one. It was a different custom than anything done in an Amish wedding, but a lovely gesture nonetheless.

As Lenore took her seat next to her Amish grandparents, Grandma sniffled, then dabbed her eyes with a handkerchief. Although Lenore was Amish and Sara was not, Grandma and Grandpa Lapp loved both granddaughters equally.

If Sara's mother hadn't run away from home when she was eighteen, Sara might be Amish too. Lenore shook her head. *What a shame Sara's mother passed away and couldn't see her daughter get married today. It would have made Sara's day even more special.*

As Brad and Sara repeated their vows, Lenore glanced across the aisle at Michelle and Ezekiel King. It was hard to believe they'd been married a year already. It was even more difficult to imagine that Michelle used to be English and had pretended to be Sara for a time. But Michelle found forgiveness when she sought God and accepted His Son as her Savior. Not long after, she made the commitment to be baptized and join the Amish church.

So two of my dear friends are now happily married. Lenore glanced down at her simple blue Amish dress and white apron. *I wonder if my chance at love will ever come.*

CHAPTER 1

Six months later
Strasburg, Pennsylvania

Lenore sat on the top step of her grandparents' front porch, barely noticing the summer flowers as she stared into the yard. Her gaze took in the stately old barn, weathered chicken coop, and Grandma's lovely flower garden. She could smell the sweet perfume of the fragrant lilac bushes not far from the house and heard the hiss of a running sprinkler, helping to keep the lawn growing and green. A slight breeze ruffled the leaves on the huge maple tree, and she heard the flutter of wings as several birds jostled for space on one of the many feeders, completing the peaceful picture. Unfortunately, Grandpa and Grandma's home and yard were not as serene as they used to be for Lenore. She still enjoyed being here, but now she saw everything through a new perspective — one that

11

included stress that no tranquil yard could eradicate.

Grandpa's collie, Sadie, lay beside her with one paw on Lenore's lap. That too used to be comforting. Now it was just a reminder that Grandma and Grandpa's pet was in need of love and assurance.

A lump formed in Lenore's throat. How could so many unexpected things happen in six short months — some good, some bad? Brad had accepted a call to pastor a church in Lancaster, and Sara, in addition to running her flower shop, now played the role of a minister's wife. Ezekiel still worked in his parents' greenhouse, and Michelle helped out there sometimes too. Unfortunately, Michelle's husband did not enjoy working with flowers, bushes, and various other plants. He'd made it clear he was looking for some other type of job.

Lenore had accepted a teaching position at a school in Strasburg this year and would begin her new assignment in two months. She looked forward to getting to know her young students and hoped her first year of teaching here would go as well as it had when she'd taught school in Paradise, not far from her parents' home.

With a heavy sigh, Lenore turned toward the front window, where Grandpa Lapp sat slumped in his wheelchair, peering out with a distant, almost empty stare. It tore at her heart to see him looking so forlorn. Three months ago, Grandpa had a stroke, leaving the left side of his body paralyzed. Even with therapy, he hadn't improved much.

Despite his inability to take care of the farm anymore, Grandpa refused to move, announcing in slurred words that he would live in this home until the day he died, and no one could make him move. Not wishing to cause him further anxiety, Lenore's father agreed to let his parents continue living on their own, but only if Lenore agreed to move in with them and help out when she wasn't teaching. With all the added responsibilities on Grandma's shoulders, Lenore had willingly settled into one of Grandma and Grandpa's upstairs guest rooms. She loved her grandparents very much and would do anything to help them during this challenging time.

Grandpa could no longer raise hogs and it was doubtful he'd ever be healthy enough to care for them, so they'd been sold. He also couldn't preach due to his speech impediment, so unless a miracle occurred, he would resign from his ministerial position, allowing someone else to take his place. Even if the stroke hadn't happened,

Grandpa and Grandma were getting older and less able to perform all the chores they'd previously taken on.

It was difficult for Lenore's grandparents to be faced with so many changes. Some decisions were hard to make.

Sadie grunted as Lenore shifted on the unyielding porch step. *Why must good people like Grandma and Grandpa Lapp face so many trials? It doesn't seem fair.*

Lenore's parents had been affected by Grandpa's failing health as well. Either Dad or one of her brothers came over several times a week to check on Grandpa and take care of any of the heavier outside chores needing to be done. Mom dropped by whenever she could too, and often helped Grandma with baking. Sometimes when Lenore had to be away from the house, her mother stayed with Grandpa so Grandma could get away for a while to grocery shop, meet a friend for lunch, or simply have a little time to herself.

"My faith has weakened of late," Lenore murmured, reaching over to stroke Sadie's head. "Sometimes I wonder if God even hears my prayers."

"Of course He does, dear one. We just need to be patient and wait for His answers."

Lenore jumped at the sound of her grandmother's voice. She hadn't heard the screen door open or shut.

Grandma took a seat on the porch swing, and Lenore joined her.

"I don't understand why bad things happen to good people." Lenore pushed her feet against the wooden boards beneath them to get the swing moving. "My heart clenches every time I see the pained look on Grandpa's face."

Grandma reached over and patted Lenore's hand. "We must learn to trust the Lord, even with things we don't understand. As we go through troubled waters, it should strengthen, not weaken, our faith. And remember, dear one, prayer is not a business transaction. We don't give something to get something in return."

Lenore sat quietly, reflecting on her grandmother's words as the swing moved gently back and forth. *Regardless of the hardships she and Grandpa are facing right now, Grandma's faith is a lot stronger than mine these days. Maybe I need to pray harder and try to keep a more positive attitude, like I used to have. No one likes to be around a negative person, so I'll do my best to look for things to rejoice about and remember to thank God for His blessings.*

After Grandma went back inside, Lenore headed for the barn to groom her horse, Dolly. She would be using the mare to pull the buggy when she and Grandma went to church tomorrow morning. Since it was an off-Sunday for the church district Lenore's parents belonged to, they would come over to be with Grandpa while Grandma and Lenore attended church.

When Lenore entered the barn, the first thing she noticed was a creamy white cat curled up on a bale of straw. Grandma had named the cat Precious. The feline was her favorite of all the barn cats and often tried to sneak into the house. Grandpa would have none of it, though, so Grandma never allowed the cat to come in.

"You've got life made. You know that, don't you — you lazy old *katz.*" She paused and stroked the cat's soft fur, and Precious responded with a contented purr.

The rustle of hay drew Lenore's gaze up to the loft where two more cats lay close to the edge, cleaning their paws. Grandma's favored cat wasn't the only critter on the farm that had life made. All the animals were treated well, but Grandma liked to give

Precious a little more attention than the others.

Lenore remained in place, listening to the muffled thump of the hooves of horses moving around in their stalls. Grandpa's horse, Bashful, snorted from the nearest stall. No doubt he missed his master's daily treks to the barn.

She drew a deep breath and blinked against invading tears. *Poor Grandpa. He used to love spending time out here with the animals. Now he mostly sits and stares out the window. Oh, how I wish things could be different. Maybe if he had taken better care of his health, he wouldn't have had the stroke.* But her grandparents had always seemed healthy to her. They'd worked hard, eaten well, and gotten enough rest. Even so, there might have been more Grandpa could have done to prevent the stroke.

Whenever Lenore offered to bring him out to the barn in his wheelchair, Grandpa always shook his head and mumbled, "No good. No good." She wasn't sure what he meant by that. Was Grandpa saying the idea of going to the barn was no good, or did he believe he was no longer any good?

Lenore's vision blurred as she released a lingering sigh. *I wish there was something I could do to lift Grandpa's spirits — and mine too, for that matter.*

Rising from her seat and heading toward Dolly's stall with renewed determination, Lenore heard buzzing overhead. She looked up and saw a wasp nest attached to one of the rafters. *I'd better climb into the loft and get rid of that right away. Sure don't need anyone getting stung while they're out here in the barn doing chores or getting one of the horses out.*

Lenore glanced around, searching for some spray to kill the wasps and douse the nest. She spotted a spray can on a shelf along one wall and went to get a ladder.

Positioning the ladder in front of the shelf, Lenore climbed up and reached for the insecticide. In the process, she noticed several antique canning jars. A blue-green one was partially hidden, and when she pulled it away from the others, she realized it had been filled with a bunch of folded papers. Curious to see what they were about, she set the wasp spray aside, picked up the canning jar, and climbed down from the ladder.

Taking a seat on a wooden stool, Lenore opened the jar. After removing the paper closest to the top, she unfolded it and read it out loud. "Dear Lord, I know I'm not worthy, but please answer my prayers."

18

Lenore sat silently, pondering the words. *Who wrote this, and why did they hide it in an old jar out here in the barn?*

She pulled out another slip of paper and read it too. "Lord, I need Your direction. Show me the right path." *I wonder if Grandma knows about this jar full of notes. Think I'll go ask her.*

Lenore was almost to the barn door when Michelle stepped in.

"*Ach,* you startled me!" Lenore jumped back. "I didn't hear your horse and buggy come into the yard."

"Sorry. Didn't mean to frighten you." Michelle pushed a wisp of auburn hair back under her *kapp.* "I walked over this morning. Figured I could use the fresh air and exercise after all that birthday cake I ate at my party last night."

Lenore smiled. "It was a fun evening. I'm glad Ezekiel's mom invited me."

"Too bad your grandparents couldn't be there." Michelle's eyes darkened. "But I can understand why your grandpa doesn't leave the house much anymore."

"Did you come here to see him today?"

Michelle nodded. "I went into the house, but he was napping, so I visited with Mary Ruth for a bit. When she mentioned you were out here, I decided to come say hello before I headed for home."

Lenore smiled. "I'm glad you did."

Michelle pointed to the jar in Lenore's hands. "I see you found my hope jar."

Lenore tipped her head. "Hope jar?"

"Yeah, some of the scriptures, prayers, and notes gave me hope during the time I was living with your grandparents and pretending to be Sara."

"Did you put the notes in the jar?"

Michelle shook her head. "I have no idea who wrote them or why they put notes in this jar or the one I found in the basement."

Lenore's brows lifted. "You mean there are two jars?"

"Yeah, and for all I know, there could be more, but those are the only two I found." Michelle placed her hand on the jar. "Sara knows about the jars too. She discovered both of them while she was living here."

"How interesting. I wish I knew who owned the jars and why they put notes inside."

"I've always suspected it might be your grandma."

"Have you asked her about it?"

"No, and to my knowledge, neither has Sara. We were afraid if it was Mary Ruth, she might not want to talk about it. Some of the notes are personal, and I have a

20

hunch that whoever wrote them didn't want anyone else to know. That must be why the jars were hidden."

"Guess that makes sense." Lenore tapped the side of the jar. She needed to tend to the wasp nest, and when she went back to the house, she wouldn't mention finding the old jar to Grandma. Next week on washday, she'd look for the jar in the basement. Perhaps one of the papers would give her a clue as to who had written the notes. If Lenore didn't unravel the mystery soon, she might ask Grandma after all.

CHAPTER 2

"It's a beautiful Sunay morning, *jah?*" Lenore glanced at her grandmother, sitting straight and tall on the buggy seat beside her. Grandma hadn't said more than a few words since they left home. She appeared to be deep in thought.

Lenore reached over and touched Grandma's arm. "Did you hear what I said?"

"Umm . . . yes, it is a nice day, but going to church isn't the same without your *grossdaadi* along. I wish we could have loaded up his wheelchair and brought him with us today. He's missing so much by not going to church." She sighed. "Others in worse shape than him are brought to church, but he's too embarrassed by his condition to be seen in public settings. Guess he doesn't want anyone's pity."

"Grandpa doesn't look bad; he's just not able to use his left arm or leg as he once did, and his mouth still sags a bit — especially when he talks."

"But he's in a wheelchair, and that really bothers him." Grandma lifted her hands, then let them fall into her lap with a sigh. "I've reminded him often that many people are praying for him and he shouldn't worry about being seen in a wheelchair, but nothing I say gets through to him."

Lenore nodded. "I've tried talking to him too, and so has my *daed.* I sure wish God would give us a miracle and heal Grandpa's body."

"He will be healed someday, when he is ushered into heaven. As much as your grandpa wants to be here with his family, he's said many times how he longs to see Jesus."

Lenore pondered Grandma's words. *Am I as eager to see Jesus as I am to remain here with my family? Shouldn't all believers look forward to leaving their earthly home and spending eternity in heaven?* It was a question she'd asked herself on more than one occasion. In fact, every time she attended someone's funeral, Lenore pondered this thought.

Grandpa had said several times during sermons he'd preached to their congregation that a Christian's reward was leaving the mortal body so the immortal soul could dwell with the Lord. While Lenore wanted to be transported to heaven someday, she still had a good many things she wanted to do here in this life. She hoped God was in no hurry to take her, or her grandparents, home to be with Him.

Lenore guided her horse and buggy up the lane leading to their bishop's home where church was being held this morning. When she pulled onto the grassy area where other buggies were parked, Lenore gave Grandma the reins while she got out and unhitched her horse. "You can go up to the house while I hook Dolly to the line with the other horses."

Grandma turned and gave Lenore a wave. "Okay. I'll see you outside the bishop's buggy shop before we all file in for church."

As Lenore sat on a backless wooden bench beside her friend Hannah Stoltzfus and several other young women her age, she gave a quick glance at the men's section. Michelle's husband, Ezekiel, sat beside a dark-haired, bearded young man who held a baby girl. Lenore didn't recognize him and wondered if he was here visiting someone or might be new to their district. The baby was sure sweet — didn't look to be more than six or seven months old. The little girl wore a dark green dress and white bonnet. Lenore assumed the man's wife must be present too, but she didn't want to bring attention to herself by turning around to see. Perhaps after church was over she'd meet the baby's mother.

Lenore's musings ended abruptly when two barn swallows flew in and circled the building several times. Some of the elderly women ducked as the birds swooped close to their heads.

One of the ministers got up from his seat and opened both barn doors as wide as they would go. One swallow flew out, but the other bird circled a few more times, left its mark on Vernon King's shoulder, and flew out the door. Looking more than a bit perturbed, Vernon slipped out quietly and shut both doors.

Lenore fought the urge to laugh as she thought about something Grandpa had said once when a bird left its droppings on the porch. *"It's a good thing cows can't fly."*

She slumped on the bench. *Oh, how I long to see the humorous side of Grandpa again.* Lenore closed her eyes briefly and offered a prayer. *What can I do to bring some joy into his life?*

"Would you like me to hold the *boppli* while

you eat?"

Jesse Smucker smiled at the elderly Amish woman who'd spoken to him as he held his daughter firmly on his knees.

"Umm . . . that's okay, I can manage."

"All right, but don't hesitate to let me know if you change your mind." Smiling, the woman extended her hand. "My name is Mary Ruth Lapp."

"Nice to meet you. I'm Jesse Smucker, and this wiggle worm is my daughter, Cindy. She recently turned six months." He clasped Mary Ruth's hand, but released it quickly when Cindy reached up and pulled on his beard.

"I don't believe I've seen you at any of our services before. Are you and your wife here visiting someone today?" Mary Ruth questioned.

He shook his head. "I'm new to the area, and my wife, Esther, passed away during childbirth."

"That's a shame. I'm so sorry for your loss." Mary Ruth placed her hand on his shoulder. Her kind words and soothing tone put a lump in Jesse's throat. He'd thought a new beginning in a new place would help his heart to mend, but he still missed his precious wife so much.

"Where are you from?" Mary Ruth questioned.

"I grew up in Christian County, Kentucky, not far from Hopkinsville." Jesse picked up his cup of coffee, being careful not to spill any of it on Cindy. "When my wife's uncle Herschel Fisher, who lives in Gordonville, lined me up with a job at a furniture store here in Strasburg, I jumped at the chance to leave Kentucky and start over. The memories there were too painful."

"I understand." She gave his arm a light tap. "Welcome to our community. I hope we will see more of you and your precious daughter."

Danki." Jesse watched as Mary Ruth walked away and joined a young woman who appeared to be in her late twenties. From what he could tell, her hair was brown, but she was too far away for him to make out the color of her eyes. What Jesse noticed most of all was the group of boys and girls who had gathered around her. Since they all looked to be close in age, he assumed they weren't hers. Perhaps she had a special way with children. In some ways, the woman reminded him of Esther — not so much in her looks, but in her easy smile and laughter and her attentiveness to the children.

Jesse closed his eyes for a minute, conjuring a picture of Esther in his head. When he'd first met her, before they started courting, Esther had taught school. Her love for children had been evident, and her students sought her out after their biweekly church services, as well as every event they attended. Sometimes Jesse had even felt a bit jealous of all the attention she paid the children while he stood on the sidelines watching.

Jesse's thoughts were pulled aside when Cindy gave another tug on his beard. It wasn't easy being both mother and father to his little girl, but Jesse wasn't ready to even think about remarriage. With the help of his wife's great-aunt Vera, Cindy was taken care of while he was at work. So Jesse could manage fine for now. Should the time ever come that he felt Cindy needed a mother, he might consider getting married again. But no one would ever take Esther's place in his heart. He didn't think it was possible.

"It felt good to be in church today," Grandma said as they began their return trip home.

"Jah." Lenore gave a slow nod, keeping her eyes straight ahead. There seemed to be more traffic than usual for a Sunday afternoon. *Must be all the tourists,* she thought when a car came alongside their buggy going extra slow. A few seconds later, the woman in the passenger seat held up a camera and snapped a picture.

Lenore was tempted to say something about the woman's rude behavior, but she held her tongue. Some tourists took pictures of Amish folks no matter what anyone said. Lenore didn't mind if people took photos of their farms, homes, horses, and buggies, but when they got right in her face with a camera, it ruffled her feathers.

When the car moved on, Grandma gave Lenore's arm a tap. "Guess we Amish will always be a curiosity to some people. That's why they like to take our *pickder.*"

Lenore sighed. "I should be used to it by now, but it still seems rude when someone is as bold as the lady in that car. I bet she wouldn't like it if a stranger snapped a picture of her."

"You're right, but since we can't stop people from photographing us, the best thing to do is ignore it or simply look away. While we might be tempted to say something unkind, it would be wrong. You heard the visiting minister quote James 1:12 this morning: 'Blessed is the man that endureth

29

temptation: for when he is tried, he shall receive the crown of life, which the Lord hath promised to them that love him.' "

"I remember." Lenore was amazed how calm her grandmother was about most things. She rarely got herself worked up over anything. Even when Grandma had a bad day, she managed to keep a positive attitude. *I wonder if she holds any negative feelings inside.*

Lenore reflected on how both Grandma and Grandpa had responded when the truth came out about Michelle pretending to be their granddaughter. Even though they'd been hurt by her deception, they forgave Michelle and welcomed her into their home a second time. Lenore, on the other hand, had been quite put out with her pretend cousin. She was annoyed that Michelle had taken advantage of Grandpa and Grandma's good nature. But after a time of thoughtful prayer and reflection, Lenore had also forgiven Michelle, who was now one of her friends.

"Who was that young man you were talking to while the men were being served their noon meal today?" Lenore asked, moving her thoughts in a different direction.

"His name is Jesse Smucker, and he's new to the area."

"I noticed him during church, holding a baby on his lap. I didn't see who his wife was though."

"Jesse is a widower. He moved here from Kentucky when his wife's uncle lined him up with a job. His baby's name is Cindy, and she's sure a cutie pie." Grandma gently elbowed Lenore's ribs. "Maybe it wasn't just a job he came here for."

"What do you mean?"

"Could be God sent him to Strasburg to find a new *fraa*."

Lenore lifted her gaze as she drew a quick breath. "Now please don't go getting any ideas that I might end up becoming the man's future wife. I am sure he did not come to Strasburg with courting on his mind."

"You never know. Once you two get acquainted, you might hit it off quite well."

"Now you sound like Ezekiel's mother. Until Michelle came along, and even some after that, she tried to get her son to pay attention to me."

"Would you have been interested in him if he had?"

Lenore shook her head. "Ezekiel and I are nothing more than friends. It was never anything more than that."

A motorcycle roared past, coming much

too close to Lenore's horse. Dolly had never liked loud noises, and today was no exception. With a piercing whinny, she picked up speed and bolted down the road.

Lenore gripped the reins tighter and pulled back. "Whoa, girl! Hold steady."

But the horse refused to halt. She raced down the road at lightning speed.

Lenore saw the stop sign up ahead and feared she would never get Dolly stopped. This was always a busy intersection, and if she couldn't get her horse under control before they reached the fourway stop, there was no telling what might happen.

CHAPTER 3

Sweat poured off Lenore's forehead and ran into her eyes as she tried to regain control of her horse.

"Let me help." In a surprisingly calm voice, Grandma reached over and grabbed hold of the section of reins above Lenore's hands. "We can do this. With God's help we can."

They both pulled and shouted, "Whoa!" until Lenore thought the reins might break. Then, a few feet from the intersection, Dolly came to a stop.

"Thank You, Lord. Thank You for watching out for us." Grandma let go of the reins.

Lenore breathed a sigh of relief. Was it Grandma's faith that had made the horse stop running, or her extra pair of hands trying to hold Dolly back? For the moment, it didn't matter. All Lenore cared about was that they were safe. So many accidents had occurred in their area within the past few months — most of them involving horses and buggies.

"If only drivers would be more courteous. That fellow on the motorcycle didn't care the least little bit about frightening our horse," she muttered.

Grandma reached over and patted Lenore's arm. "It's okay. God was watching over us. We're both fine, and so is your horse."

By the time she guided Dolly up her grandparents' driveway, the peacefulness Lenore had felt during church and afterward had disappeared. Even though she and Grandma were okay, she still shivered at the thought of what could have happened if Dolly hadn't stopped.

As they approached the house, Grandma squealed. "Well, forevermore. Would you look at that?"

Lenore looked in the direction her grandmother pointed. What a surprise to see Grandpa sitting in his wheelchair on the front porch, with one of the barn cats in his lap.

"Looks like Grandpa's enjoying a little time in the sun." Lenore looked at Grandma and smiled.

"And with a fluffy gray katz in his lap, no less." Grandma snickered. "Never thought

I'd see the day. As you well know, your grossdaadi is a dog lover and doesn't have much use for any katz."

Lenore nodded. "I'm surprised Sadie hasn't discovered the cat and chased it away."

"She must have found something else to keep her occupied." Grandma climbed down from the buggy. "I'll secure your *gaul* to the rail. Then I'm going to join my husband on the porch. After you've put Dolly away, we can all sit outside and enjoy lemonade and cookies."

"Sounds good. I'm sure my folks will want to join us." Lenore glanced at Grandpa sitting by himself and wondered why neither Mom nor Dad was with him. Surely he hadn't wheeled himself out the door. Well, Grandma was with him now, so he would be okay.

Lenore unhitched Dolly and led her to the barn. Once she got the mare inside her stall, she brushed her down and made sure she had food and water.

"See you later, girl." She patted the horse's flank and stepped out of the stall. If it weren't for wanting to spend some time with her family, Lenore would have taken the old jar down and read a few more notes. But she could do that another day when she had some free time.

By the time Lenore joined Grandma and Grandpa on the porch, her parents were there as well. Mom held a tray of brownies and some chocolate chip cookies. Dad had a pitcher of lemonade in his hands. Lenore figured the reason they hadn't been on the porch earlier was because they'd gone into the house to get the snacks. Most likely they figured Grandpa would be okay for the few minutes they'd be gone.

Dad smiled and set the cold drink on the small serving table when Lenore stepped onto the porch. "How was church?"

"It was *gut.*" She gave him a hug, then did the same with her mom. "How have things been going here?"

"Very well." Mom gestured to the Bible lying on the table. "Since it's such a beautiful day, we all came out here to do our devotions."

Grandma stood with one hand on Grandpa's shoulder. "Would you like a brownie, Willis?"

He nodded.

Grandma scooped one off the plate and put it in his right hand. "When you finish that, I'll give you a cold drink."

"Okay."

They all found seats and everyone ate

Mom's delicious brownies, as well as some of the cookies Lenore and Grandma had baked two days ago. Lenore had mixed up a batch of brownies many times using the same recipe as Mom's, but they never tasted quite as good.

About that time, Sadie showed up and the cat made a quick exit, jumping off Grandpa's lap and bounding across the yard.

Woof! Woof! Sadie put her paw on Grandpa's knee. "You are loved." Grandpa gave a crooked smile and patted the dog's head.

Lenore looked at Grandma and noticed tears in her eyes as she patted Grandpa's shoulder. It was a joy to see the love Grandma had for her husband.

Lenore blinked against the sudden dampness in her own eyes. *If I ever get married, that's the kind of love I want to have for my husband.*

Jesse meandered around the living room in the small two-bedroom house he'd rented from his wife's uncle. Cindy was asleep in the room where he'd set up her crib, and Jesse needed something to occupy his time that didn't involve work.

I wonder if Herschel ever lived in this home. Did he buy the place with the intent of renting it out?

Jesse flopped down on the well-worn leather couch that stuck to his skin. He glanced around at the few pieces of furniture and shook his head. In addition to the couch, seating included two straight-backed chairs and an old rocker that had seen better days. The wooden floor had scuff marks in several places, and the brick front of the fireplace was stained with soot. The only source of light was a gas lamp that hung overhead. But Jesse couldn't complain. He and Cindy had a roof over their heads, and the rent was cheap. This house would have to do until he could afford to buy a place of his own.

Arms pulled back and hands against the base of his head, Jesse mulled things over. He needed to find someone else to take care of Cindy while he was at work. He couldn't keep hiring a driver every day to take him to Gordonville five days a week so Herschel's mother could watch Cindy. Vera Fisher was getting up in years and lacked the energy needed to care for a baby.

"Should have asked around when I was at church yesterday," Jesse mumbled. "Maybe one of the young women there would be willing to watch Cindy for me."

Jesse had visited with several people during the course of the day and was pleased with the warm reception he'd received after the service. Many of the older women, like Mary Ruth Lapp, had been especially attentive to his baby girl. *And why wouldn't they be? Cindy is as pretty as a rose, and sweeter than a bowl full of sugar. She takes after her precious mamm.*

Jesse blinked a couple of times. His eyelids felt gummy and hot. He could not allow himself to give in to grief or self-pity. He'd done enough of that since Esther died, and it was time to move on.

Move on to what, though? he wondered. *Cindy needs a mother, but it's too soon for me to think about looking for a suitable wife. Even if I were to get married again, it would only be for Cindy's sake. I could never love another woman the way I loved Esther.*

He bent forward, still clasping both hands around the back of his head. It wasn't fair to his daughter to be raised without a mother, but then, nothing in life was fair.

Jesse raised his head and picked up the Bible lying on an end table next to the couch. With a shaky hand, he held the book against his chest. *Lord, help me to be a good father to my sweet baby girl. And if I am meant to get married again, then please show me that too.*

■ ■ ■ ■

Lancaster

Sara took a seat next to Brad on the living-room couch in the cozy three-bedroom parsonage their church provided for the ministerial family. "After church today, I heard a lot of positive comments about your sermon on prayer." She clasped Brad's hand and gave his fingers a tender squeeze. "I can tell the congregation is pleased that they hired you as their pastor."

"I hope so, but they're equally glad you're here." He leaned over and kissed her cheek. "And I, my sweet wife, wouldn't know what to do without you. Besides the fact that I love you very much, you're an amazing asset to my ministry. In the short time we've been at the church, you've started teaching one of the kids' Sunday school classes — not to mention keeping the table in the entrance foyer well supplied with beautiful bouquets from your shop."

"I am more than happy to do both." Sara thought back to the way things were when she and Brad first started dating. She'd pretended to be a Christian so he wouldn't stop seeing her, but the ruse had backfired in her face when he'd found out the truth.

40

Then after her stepfather died, she'd found the Lord, and everything in her life changed for the better. Marrying Brad was the best decision Sara had ever made — that and going to meet her grandparents for the first time after Mama died.

Sara was thankful Brad didn't object to her keeping the flower shop in Strasburg. It was a short commute for her five days a week. Sara enjoyed her work, and sometimes being able to minister to those who came into the shop was an added bonus.

Brad yawned, cupping a hand over his mouth. "Sorry, hon. Guess I'm more tired than I thought."

"It's fine. Why don't you take a nap while I drive over to see my grandparents?"

"No, that's okay. It's been a while, and I'd like to go with you to see how Willis is doing — Mary Ruth too." He rose from the couch. "Caring for Willis and helping him deal with his stroke has been hard on her."

"You're right, and my dear, sweet grandma needs all the support she can get." Sara got up and started for the kitchen. "Think I'll take some of Grandpa's favorite cookies with us."

"I thought all cookies were his favorites." Brad chuckled. "Willis Lapp is a man with a definite sweet tooth."

41

Sara smiled. She couldn't deny it. During the months she'd lived with her grandparents, she'd witnessed Grandpa enjoying his wife's homemade goodies many times. *Of course,* Sara thought as she entered the kitchen, *I ate my fair share of Grandma's delicious desserts too.* She grabbed a plastic container and filled it with peanut butter cookies. *I'm thankful Brad's first church is close enough that we can visit Grandma and Grandpa as often as possible.*

Strasburg

"Look who's here, Willis." Grandma pointed as Brad's van pulled into the yard.

Lenore smiled. It did her heart good to see Grandpa's face light up when Sara and Brad climbed out and walked toward the house.

He looked at Grandma and gave her arm a nudge with his good hand. "Rhoda's *dochder.*"

"Jah, Willis." She bobbed her head. "Rhoda's daughter, Sara, has come to see us, and her husband came along too."

Poor Grandpa, Lenore thought. *Since the stroke, his memory isn't as sharp as it used to be, and Grandma sometimes has to remind him of things and give detailed explanations.*

42

When Sara stepped onto the porch, she gave Grandma a hug, then leaned down and kissed Grandpa's cheek. "It's good to see you, Grandpa. How are you feeling today?"

"I be better if not in wheelchair."

Although Grandpa's words weren't spoken with clarity, Lenore understood what he'd said. Apparently Sara did too, for she knelt down in front of Grandpa's chair and took hold of his paralyzed hand. "Just keep doing what the physical therapist says, and in time you'll get better."

Tears welled in Grandpa's eyes as he slowly nodded.

"Lots of prayers are being said on your behalf." Brad shook Grandpa's right hand. "Whatever you do, don't give up. Just keep trying."

"That's what we all keep telling him," Lenore's dad spoke up. "Many people with partial paralysis get better after a stroke."

And some don't. Lenore kept her negative thoughts to herself. She would never deliberately dampen Grandpa's spirits or take away his hope of getting better. *I need to keep praying for his healing,* she reminded herself. *If it's God's will, and Grandpa keeps a positive attitude, maybe he will get out of that wheelchair and walk again.*

CHAPTER 4

"Would you like to take a walk with me?" Lenore asked Sara after everyone else had gone inside Grandpa and Grandma's house.

Sara nodded. "That sounds nice. Should we walk out back near the pond?"

"Actually, I was thinking we could go out to the barn."

Sara tipped her head. "Why the barn?"

"There's something there I want to talk to you about."

"Oh, okay." Sara rose from her chair and the two cousins headed toward the barn.

When they opened the double doors and stepped inside, three cats darted in front of them, chasing each other. Lenore groaned as the dry taste of chaff from the straw being stirred up touched her lips.

Sara flicked a few pieces of straw off her blouse. "Were the cats really chasing each other, I wonder, or could they have been after a mouse?"

"Who knows? It could have been either, I suppose." The floorboards creaked as Lenore motioned for Sara to take a seat on a bale of straw. "When I was in here the other day, I discovered an old jar filled with prayers, scriptures, and sayings." She pointed to a shelf on the wall opposite them. "Michelle showed up while I was holding the jar, and she said both of you had found it too."

"Yes, we did. And each of us was helped by some of the verses and prayers."

"Who do you think wrote the notes?"

Sara shrugged. "I have no idea. Michelle thinks Grandma may have written them."

"I thought of that too." Lenore flicked a piece of prickly straw off her dress. "But neither of you have asked her about them?"

"No." Sara shifted on the bale. "If it was Grandma who wrote the notes, she might be embarrassed if we were to ask about the jars. Many of the notes are very personal."

Lenore pursed her lips. "I'm the curious type, and I'd really like to know who the author was. Do you think I dare ask her?"

"Ask who what?"

Lenore jumped at the sound of Grandma's voice. "You startled me, Grandma. I didn't hear you come in."

"That's probably because you two were

deep in conversation." Grandma took a seat on a wooden stool across from them. "Do you mind answering my question about whether you dare ask someone something?"

Lenore looked at her cousin, hoping she would say something, but Sara just sat with a placid expression. *Oh, great. How am I supposed to respond?*

"Is it a secret? Something you don't want me to know about?" Grandma leaned to one side with her head slightly tipped.

Lenore felt like a mouse caught in a trap. She could either tell her grandmother the truth or make something up, but that would be a lie. She glanced at Sara again, and when she gave her a nod, Lenore decided to proceed.

"I'll show you exactly what we were talking about." Lenore rose from her seat and went to get the ladder. After she took down the old jar, she handed it to her grandmother.

Grandma's brows furrowed as she studied the jar with a quizzical expression. "What is inside this antique-looking canning jar?"

Lenore explained about the slips of paper with prayers, scriptures, and written notes. "There's another one in your basement."

"Michelle was the first person to find them," Sara interjected. "When I came to

46

live here, I found both of the jars too."

Grandma's eyebrows rose, and she blinked a couple of times.

"I — I had no idea this was here or that one was also in my basement."

"So you're not the person who wrote the notes?" Lenore questioned.

Grandma shook her head. "May I please look at one of the notes?"

"Of course."

Lenore held her breath as Grandma reached inside and pulled out a slip of paper. She stared at it several seconds, then slapped one hand against her flushed face. "Oh Sara, your mother wrote this note. I would recognize her handwriting anywhere."

"What?" Sara's brows pulled inward. "Are you sure about that, Grandma? The notes are all printed, not written in cursive. How can you tell Mama wrote them?"

"I recognize her style of printing." Grandma pointed to the note in her hand. "See here, she wrote in bold block letters. I'm surprised you didn't recognize it too."

Sara shook her head vigorously. "I never saw anything my mother printed. Everything she wrote was always in cursive."

Tears sprang to Grandma's eyes and dribbled down her wrinkled cheeks. "Do you know what this means, girls?"

Lenore and Sara's heads moved slowly from side to side.

"It means she may have mentioned something about the identity of your father in one of her notes."

"I don't think so. I've read all the notes in both jars and nothing was mentioned about my father, or even gave me a hint that it was Mama who'd written the notes." Sara swiped at the tears that had dribbled onto her reddened cheeks. "I doubt I'll ever know who my real father is, and I need to accept that fact. But knowing what I do about my mother's past, I understand now what many of those scriptures and notes were about. Mama was looking for hope when she thought there was none. She also sought forgiveness for the things she had done to hurt others."

"Perhaps my Rhoda was searching for healing too." Grandma sighed. "Healing for her wounded soul."

Lenore tried to imagine what it must have been like for her aunt when she left home all those years ago, knowing she was expecting a baby and feeling like she couldn't tell her parents. She stared down at the stubble of straw beneath her feet. *If I had been in Aunt Rhoda's place, would I have run away*

48

from my family and never contacted them again?* She curled her fingers into her palms. *I think not. No matter how humiliating it might have been to admit the truth, I would have told Mom and Dad and sought their forgiveness. And I would not have run away and never contacted my family again. They mean too much to me.*

"Now that I know about this, I'd like to take the jar into the house and show Willis." Grandma stepped down from the stool. "He has the right to know what our daughter has written here too."

Sara took a seat on the couch in her grandparents' living room, ready to listen and watch as Grandma read some of the prayer-jar notes to Lenore's parents and Grandpa, explaining that they'd been written by Sara's mother. Grandma read one note that said: *"If I could turn back the hands of time and do things differently, I surely would. I've done so many things I now regret."*

Grandpa moaned, and he lowered his chin to his chest but said nothing. Sara could only imagine what he must be thinking. He probably wondered if he and Grandma had done something wrong when they raised their wayward daughter.

Brad sat beside Sara, holding her hand.

She was ever so thankful for his love and support. Her throat clogged as she thought about all the times she had read the scriptures, prayers, and personal notes she'd found in the jars, never suspecting her mother had written them.

Sara closed her eyes, trying to hold back tears of frustration. *Oh Mama, why couldn't you have mentioned in your notes who my biological father was? Were you trying to protect his identity for a reason? Did your parents disapprove of him? Or could he have been a married man, and you were ashamed to admit it?*

So many questions ran through her mind as she tried to come to grips with everything. Sara's life hadn't been the same since, as an adult, she'd first learned she had grandparents, and she felt grateful for the opportunity she'd been given to get to know them. Because Sara had come here to Lancaster County, she'd met Brad, her soul mate. Even if she never learned who her father was, Sara's life would be filled with many blessings and the pleasant memories she'd made here in Amish country. She hoped things would work out at the church her husband had been called to pastor so they would never have to move out of the area. Sara couldn't imagine life without

Grandma and Grandpa, as well as her other family members, including Lenore, who was not only a cousin but also a good friend.

CHAPTER 5

Paradise, Pennsylvania

As soon as Lenore entered her parents' general store late Monday afternoon, she knew something had changed. The shelves near the front door, normally filled with stationery and greeting cards, now housed a variety of books — most about the Amish way of life.

This is so strange. She pulled one off the shelf and read the back cover. *"What is the reason Plain people live the way they do? Why would anyone shun the modern way of life? You will find answers to these questions and more within the pages of this book."*

Lenore groaned. *Since when did Mom and Dad begin selling books in their store, much less this type that will no doubt cater to the tourists who come in?*

From behind the counter, her mother greeted her with a smile. "It's good to see you, Lenore. How's your grandpa doing today?"

"Same as usual. I try to do some things that will bring a little joy into his life, like reading him a story or telling him some funny things that happened during my day, but it doesn't seem to help his mood much."

"Sorry to hear that. Maybe in time things will get better."

"I hope you're right."

"So what brings you by the store this afternoon?" Mom asked.

"I came to get a few things for Grandma." Lenore motioned to the shelf full of books. "Since when did you start selling books?"

"We got them in last week. Your daed thought it was a good idea, especially since so many tourists have been visiting the store lately, asking questions about us Amish, as well as other Plain communities." Mom smiled. "Now we can just point them to the books and won't have to answer so many inquiries."

Lenore's toes curled inside her black leather shoes. "I wish folks weren't so curious about us."

"It's understandable, since we dress differently and live a simple lifestyle compared to most English people."

"I hope whoever wrote those books knows

what they're talking about. It wouldn't be good to be giving out misinformation."

Mom clicked her fingernails against the countertop. "No need to worry, Lenore. Your daed looked over all the books and only put out the ones he felt were true." She looked in the direction of the bookshelf again. "In case you didn't notice, there are also plenty of *bicher* for our Amish patrons as well."

"What kind of books?"

"We have copies of our church hymnals, some Bibles, devotionals, and the directory for our community. We will also be getting in some teachers' resources soon, as well as some quality books for children."

Lenore was about to respond when a tall man with dark brown hair entered the store. He was the same man she'd seen at church, only today he wasn't holding his daughter. As he moved toward the counter, she stood with lips slightly parted, eager to know more about the newcomer to their community.

"Good afternoon." He glanced briefly at Lenore, then turned to face her mother. "I was wondering if you carry any gluten-free products here."

"As a matter of fact, we do." Lenore's mother pointed toward the back of the store. "You'll find a whole section with gluten-free items." She glanced at Lenore. "Would you please show him where they are located?"

Lenore pursed her lips. *Why's Mom asking me to do this? How come she doesn't show him herself?*

When Lenore hesitated, he moved away from the counter. "It's all right. I'm sure I can locate them."

"I don't mind showing you," Lenore was quick to say. Before he could respond, she began walking in that direction. When she reached the gluten-free section, she turned to him and said, "I saw you at church yesterday, and my grandma spoke to you after the service let out. She mentioned that you're new to our area."

He nodded. "I used to live in Kentucky, but after losing my fraa, I decided it would be good for me and my dochder to move here for a new start."

"How old is she?"

"She's six months." He tapped the heel of his left shoe against the wooden floor. "It's hard to accept the idea that Cindy will never know her *mudder.*"

Lenore resisted the urge to give his arm a gentle pat. Instead, she said, "I'm sorry for your loss." The grief he felt was evident in the drooping of his shoulders and his monotone voice.

"Thank you." He lowered his gaze. "It's been hard trying to imagine how my little girl's future will be without her mother to guide her. And I . . . Well, I'm doing some better now, but when Esther died during childbirth, I felt as if my life ended too."

Lenore swallowed hard. She could almost feel this poor man's pain. Thinking a change of conversation might help, she held out her hand. "My name is Lenore Lapp. My parents own this store, and the woman at the front counter is my mamm."

He shook her hand. "I'm Jesse Smucker."

Lenore wasn't about to admit that Grandma had told her his name. There was no point in Jesse knowing that they had talked about him.

His gaze met hers. "I saw you after church — with several *kinner* gathered around you. Figured you were too young for them all to be yours."

She gave a small laugh. "No, I'm not married. I am a schoolteacher, and some of the children I was visiting with will be in my class when school starts in August." She smiled. "That's why they were so eager to talk to me."

"Ah, I see."

"Where is your baby today?" Lenore asked.

"My wife's great-aunt has been watching Cindy while I'm at work, but it's too much responsibility for a woman her age. Eventually I'll need to find someone else to watch Cindy."

Lenore almost offered to take care of Jesse's daughter until school started, but she caught herself in time. She barely knew the man, and he might not appreciate her being so forward. Besides, with all the things she needed to do to help Grandma, there wasn't time for much else. Surely someone else in their community would be available to watch Jesse's baby.

After Jesse left the store with two sacks full of gluten-free items, plus a few other things, he thought about the young woman he'd met inside. She seemed friendly, and her eyes were filled with kindness. There was truly something about Lenore that reminded him of Esther. The compassion she felt for him had shown in her soothing tone and thoughtful expression. In some strange way Jesse felt drawn to Lenore — not romantically, but as more of a kindred spirit. It was too soon for him to be seeking — or even thinking about — a romantic relationship. Besides, he was sure no one could ever replace Esther or fill his heart with the kind of love he still felt for her.

Pushing his troubling thoughts aside, Jesse unhitched his horse, Restless, and climbed into his buggy. Eager to pick up his daughter, he guided Restless out of the parking lot and toward Gordonville, where Esther's great-aunt and great-uncle lived.

When Jesse arrived a short time later, Vera opened the door, peering at him through her thick-lensed glasses. "Cindy is sleeping," she whispered. "So unless you're in a hurry to get home, why don't we sit out on the porch until she wakes up?"

Jesse gestured to his buggy. "I do have some bulk food items to put away, but nothing perishable, so I can hang around for a while at least. No point waking my daughter and then listening to her fuss all the way to Strasburg."

"Indeed." Vera lifted the glasses from her face and rubbed the bridge of her nose. "Why don't you stay for supper? Milton's in the barn, checking on one of our pregnant cats, and Herschel will be coming by soon to eat with us." She set her glasses back in place. "Now there's plenty of scalloped potatoes in the oven, so there is no point in you going home and having to cook something for your evening meal when supper's close to being ready."

Jesse's mouth watered at the thought of eating a nourishing, home-cooked meal. Since Cindy wasn't old enough for grown-up food, Jesse often got by eating a sandwich made with gluten-free bread. It would be nice to sit down and enjoy some adult conversation as he ate his meal. "Danki, Vera, I gratefully accept your invitation. Is there anything I can do to help?"

"Not a thing." She smiled and pointed a bony finger at the two wicker chairs sitting nearby. "Now let's take a seat and visit while we wait for my menfolk to get here."

Jesse did as she suggested, and while he listened to Vera talk about her garden and how it had become neglected since she'd volunteered to care for Cindy, a sense of guilt crept in. Esther's great-aunt was in her late sixties — too old to be caring full-time for a baby. Her back was touchy, and she sometimes used a cane when she was in pain. In all good conscience, Jesse couldn't keep bringing Cindy here every day while he went off to work to earn a living.

Jesse was about to speak to her about the situation when Vera's husband, Milton, came out of the barn and joined them on the porch. "No kittens yet, but I'm thinking sometime tonight or by tomorrow morning." He looked over at Jesse and smiled. "How'd things go at the furniture shop today?"

"Pretty well. We're keeping busy, that's for certain. Several English people came in today, saying they'd heard the furniture was made by Amish, and for that reason, they felt sure it was of the finest quality. One man even mentioned that he chose to buy Amish-made furniture because it was hand-crafted and locally made."

"Good to hear the business is doing well." Milton turned his attention to Vera. "How soon till supper's ready?"

"About twenty minutes. We won't eat until Herschel gets here though."

"Then I have time to take a shower?"

She gave a nod. "Oh, and please be quiet when you go inside. Cindy's still sleeping."

"No problem. I'll be *mauseschtill.*" Milton opened the screen door and stepped into the house.

Vera looked at Jesse and rolled her eyes. "Can't remember when my husband's ever been quiet as a mouse."

Jesse snickered. He could almost picture Milton tiptoeing around the house.

A few minutes later, a horse and buggy pulled into the yard and up to the hitching rail. Herschel got out, secured his horse, and headed for the house. "Sorry I'm late. Hope I didn't hold up supper, Mom." He leaned over and gave her a hug.

"Not a problem. Your daed's in taking a shower, so we weren't gonna eat till he was ready anyhow." Vera rose from her chair. "I'm going inside now to check on things, but you two can sit out here and visit till I call you for supper."

"Are you sure there's nothing I can do to help?" Jesse asked.

She shook her head, then turned to Herschel again. "How come you didn't put your gaul in the barn? Your daed will probably want to challenge you to a game of checkers after we eat, and I've made a strawberry pie for dessert, with a gluten-free crust for Jesse's benefit. So if you're planning to hang around for pie, you may be here a while."

Herschel moistened his lips with the tip of his tongue. "That does sound good, but I won't be staying for dessert or any board games. I need to take care of a few things at my place before it gets dark."

Vera shrugged, then turned and went into the house.

Herschel took a seat beside Jesse. "How ya doin'?"

"As well as can be expected, I guess." Jesse

61

dropped his gaze to the wooden planks beneath his feet. "I'm adjusting to my new job, and the house you're letting me rent is comfortable." He tugged his ear. "But even though some things seem to be working out, I still miss your niece something awful."

"That's to be expected." Herschel reached over and gave Jesse's shoulder a squeeze. "It takes a long time to get over losing someone you care about. No one knows that better than me. I've had to do it twice, and the pain still lingers."

Surprised by Herschel's comment, Jesse tipped his head. He had no idea the man had been married twice. Of course, there was a lot about Herschel he didn't know or understand. Vera and Milton's oldest son had always been somewhat aloof and kept pretty much to himself. When Jesse first met his wife's uncle, he thought Herschel might not care much for him. But Esther explained that her uncle had been withdrawn since his wife died. The poor fellow had no children — just his elderly parents and two brothers, as well as a few nieces and nephews — none of whom he appeared to be close to. From what Esther had said, her uncle had no close friends either.

Jesse pushed his shoulders back. *I can't let that happen to me. I'll always be close to my*

*precious little girl, and even if I don't feel
social, I will put forth the effort to make some
friends while I'm living here in Lancaster
County.*

Lancaster

"You've been awfully quiet since we returned from your grandparents' house
yesterday." Brad pointed to Sara's plate.
"And you've barely touched your supper. Is
everything all right?"

Sara looked at Brad from across the
kitchen table. "I can't stop thinking about
the notes my mother wrote in those prayer
jars that Lenore, Michelle, and I found."
Her stomach tightened as she stared at her
half-eaten tossed salad. "All this time I
thought it may have been Grandma who
wrote the notes and hid the jars. Never once
did I suspect it was Mama. But now that I
reflect on some of the things she wrote, I
should have guessed it was her." Sara turned
her gaze on Brad. "How could I have been
so blind?"

"Sometimes the most obvious things
escape us. That was true for me before I felt
God's call on my life."

She tipped her head. "Really?"

Brad nodded. "Before it became clear to
me that I should study to become a minister,

I imagined myself learning to fly a plane and eventually becoming an airline pilot."

"What made you change your mind?"

"A note I found in my grandfather's Bible." Brad paused and took a drink of water. "It said: 'What is God calling you to do? If you don't know, you need to pray about it.' " He grinned at Sara. "So I did."

"And God revealed to you that He wanted you to go into the ministry?"

"Yes. It seemed like every scripture I read pointed me in that direction."

Sara forked a cherry tomato and popped it in her mouth. "I can't say for sure that it was God's will for me to buy the flower shop, but the way things worked out, I can't help but believe He approved of my decision."

"I agree. And you're doing an excellent job running it, while still finding time to help me in my ministry." Brad's face broke into a wide smile. "You're an amazing woman, Sara, and I'm thankful God brought you into my life."

She got up from the table and came around to give him a hug. "I love you so much. You're everything I could ever want in a husband. Someday when we have children, I hope they'll grow up to be just like their dad."

CHAPTER 6

Strasburg

A bee buzzed overhead, and Michelle tried to ignore it as she pulled a handful of stubborn weeds. At least it wasn't the irritating gnats that usually plagued her. If she didn't bother the bee, it would probably leave her alone.

The home she and Ezekiel rented was small, and so was the yard, but at least she had found a place for her garden. After Michelle and Ezekiel got married, his parents had invited them to move in with them until they could afford to purchase a place of their own, but Ezekiel declined the offer. Michelle was relieved. She wouldn't have felt comfortable living in the same house with Ezekiel's mother, even though she and Belinda got along better now than they did when Michelle and Ezekiel first began courting. Also, they had more privacy in the rental than what they would have had with just a single bedroom to call their own at the Kings' house.

As the sun beat down on Michelle's head, a trickle of sweat ran down her face. It was normal for the end of June to be warm and humid, but the last week had been almost unbearable. On a day such as this, Michelle couldn't help wishing they had air-conditioning in their home. The battery-operated fans Ezekiel had bought did nothing but blow warm air around wherever they were placed.

Despite her occasional longing for some of the modern conveniences she'd given up to become Amish, Michelle had no regrets about her decision to join the church and marry Ezekiel. He was a good husband, and she loved him very much. The only thing that would make her life more complete would be the addition of a baby. Michelle and Ezekiel had been married a year and a half, and she wondered why she had not become pregnant yet. The doctor assured Michelle that both she and Ezekiel were healthy and there was no reason she couldn't conceive. He advised them not to worry about it and said stress might be the problem.

Michelle had dealt with her share of stress over the years, beginning with the dysfunctional home she'd grown up in. Bearing the brunt of her parents' physical and emotional abuse during her early childhood had taken a toll on her, as well as on her younger brothers. Living with foster parents had also caused some stress, since she never really felt accepted by her foster family.

Gritting her teeth as she grasped another clump of weeds, Michelle reflected on the years she'd been out on her own, struggling to keep a job and pay the rent on whatever run-down apartment she had managed to stay in. A stream of boyfriends, some abusive like Jerry, had left her feeling as if she had no worth. At least that's how it was until Michelle met Willis and Mary Ruth Lapp. Even after they'd found out about her deception — pretending to be Sara — they had treated her with love and kindness. It was almost as if she was actually one of their granddaughters.

Michelle loved Mary Ruth and Willis, and she wished only good things for them. Tears welled in her eyes, nearly blinding her vision. "Dear Lord," she murmured, "please heal Willis's body and help him recover from his stroke."

Sara stood near the front of her flower shop, studying the display she'd recently set up in the front window. With the Fourth of July less than two weeks away, she'd used red, white, and blue as her color theme. The focal point was a child's red wagon she'd found in a local antique store. Sara had put a bouquet of red, white, and blue carnations inside the wagon, which she would change out as needed. A few vases full of red-and-white roses surrounded the wagon, along with several small American flags tied together with red bows and scattered in strategic locations.

Sara knew the importance of creating an eye-catching window display, representative of the flowers and plants she sold, many of which she purchased from the Kings' greenhouse. This display, she hoped, would draw potential customers into the shop. She had learned from the previous owners that it was a good idea to create window displays representative of the season. She'd also made sure to use good lighting in effective ways. When the Fourth of July holiday was over, Sara would change the decorations in the window to another creative summer scene.

In the short time Sara had owned the store, she had established a personal connection with her regular customers, always striving to be honest and sincere. And she tried to send a handwritten note or make a personal phone call to thank new customers for their orders.

As she headed to the counter where she waited on customers, the front door opened and Herschel Fisher walked in. It had been several months since he'd visited her shop, and Sara had begun to think she might never see him again.

"May I help you, Mr. Fisher?" she asked.

He gave a quick nod. "Came to buy a dozen red roses. And there's no need to refer to me as Mr. Fisher. Just call me Herschel, okay?"

"All right." Sara combed her fingers through the ends of her long hair. "Are they for your wife's grave?"

He shuffled back a step or two. "H–how did you know about that? I don't recall saying anything to you about my wife having died, much less that I'd been buying flowers to put on her grave."

A wave of heat crept across Sara's cheeks. "Actually your mother mentioned it to me. I'm sorry for your loss, Herschel."

"My mother came in here?"

Sara nodded.

With whitened knuckles, Herschel reached up to rub the back of his neck. "What business did she have telling you such a personal thing?"

Sara felt like she was caught between a rock and a hard place. If she told Herschel that his mother had come into the store, demanding that she stop selling him flowers, it would not go over well. But she had to tell him something.

Leaning against the counter for support, she swallowed hard. "Your mom was concerned that you might get in trouble with the church leaders for placing flowers on your wife's headstone."

"I don't do that anymore, so she has nothing to worry about." He let go of his neck and pulled his fingers through the sides of his blond hair, steaked with gray. "And in fact, the flowers I want today are for my mother's birthday, which is tomorrow."

Sara smiled. "I'm sure she will appreciate the gift."

"I hope so. She works hard, despite her aches and pains. For the past few weeks she's been babysitting her great-niece while the baby's daddy is at work." Herschel grimaced, slowly shaking his head. "Personally, I think it's too much for a seventy-year-old woman. At least that's how old Mom will be as of tomorrow."

"She must be energetic if she's watching a

little one."

Herschel shook his head. "She's not really up to the task, but you can't tell her that. Whenever Mom sees a need, she jumps right in and tries to help."

"You must take after her then."

"What do you mean?"

"Do you remember some time ago when you rescued me and my friend Michelle after my car got stuck in a ditch?"

He tipped his head to one side and tugged his right ear. "Oh yeah . . . now I remember. I ended up with muddy feet, and my back hurt a bit, but I was glad that I came along when I did."

"So were we. Your kindness and willingness to help out left an impression me. It was a reminder that there are good people in this world who put themselves out for others when there's a need."

He nodded. "I only did what I'd want someone to do for me if I had a problem out on the road."

Sara motioned to the display cooler where several vases of flowers had been put earlier. "Shall we see about getting a bouquet of roses put together for your mother?"

"Yes, and since it's a special birthday, let's make it an even dozen."

Sara hoped Herschel's mother knew what

a kind, considerate son she had. Not every man cared that much about his mother. No doubt he'd been a good husband too.

"You have a dandy crop of *aebier* this year, Grandma." Lenore placed a handful of the strawberries she'd picked into a plastic container.

Grandma smiled and popped a berry into her mouth. "You are so right, and these aebier are *appeditlich.*"

"Jah. In fact, they are so delicious they won't need much sugar for sweetening."

"But don't forget, your grandpa likes plenty of *zucker,* even on the sweetest of berries."

Lenore couldn't resist the temptation to roll her eyes. Too much sugar wasn't good for a healthy person, let alone someone in Grandpa's condition. But she kept silent, knowing Grandma had been giving in to Grandpa's every little whim these days. Lenore thought her grandmother sometimes tried too hard to do things that would make him happy. Unfortunately, many of those things that went way beyond her duty as a wife had little or no impact on Grandpa. Instead of saying thank you, or even conjuring up the tiniest of smiles, he would often simply sit and stare. There was no question about it — the dear man was depressed.

The tinkling of the wind chimes hanging under the porch eaves pulled Lenore's thoughts back to the present. The day was too pleasant to let worry or negative thoughts take over.

"Since there's only one row of berries left to pick, would you mind if I went inside to check on your grandpa?" Grandma asked. "He may have woken up from his nap by now. If so, he will need my help getting up from the bed."

"I should go so you don't end up straining your back." Lenore started to rise from her kneeling position, but Grandma held out a hand to stop her.

"I can manage, dear. There's still some strength left in these old bones."

"Okay, but please give a holler if you need my help with him."

"I will." Grandma rose to her feet and started for the house.

Several minutes later, a ruckus broke out in the barnyard. Lenore looked over. One of their feisty roosters had his head stuck in the hog pen. The poor thing looked like it was doing a dance as it squawked and flapped its wings.

It's a good thing we don't have hogs in the pen anymore, Lenore thought as she made her way across the yard. *They might have attacked.*

With little cooperation from the rooster, Lenore managed to free it, but she'd stepped in some manure. Setting the rooster down near the coop, she turned on the hose to wash off her gardening clogs. Only sheer willpower kept her from spraying the now strutting old rooster for all the trouble he'd caused. "I could've been nearly done picking berries out here in the hot sun if it wasn't for you," she muttered, shaking her finger at Big Ben — a name Lenore had given the troublesome rooster.

Big Ben turned to look at her, and as if in response, he let out an ear-piercing squawk.

Lenore chuckled, in spite of her aggravation. With all the negative things going on around her these days, it was good to have something to laugh about, even if it was at the rooster's expense.

CHAPTER 7

Gordonville

"*Hallich gebottsdaag,* Mom." Herschel handed Vera a bouquet of red roses and gave her a hug. Jesse had given her a box of pretty notepaper with matching envelopes, but it paled in comparison to the roses.

"*Danki,* Son, for the birthday wishes and lovely gift." She placed the flowers in a vase and set it in the center of the dining-room table. "You went all out getting me twelve roses. I'm sure it was expensive."

"Not too bad. I bought them at the flower shop in Strasburg, and the nice woman who owns the place gave me a good deal." He puffed out his chest a bit. "Besides, you're worth it."

Vera's cheeks reddened as she flapped her hand at him. "Go on with you now. I don't need any praise."

Jesse, who'd been sitting in a rocking chair holding Cindy, thought it was time for him to speak up. "Herschel is right, Vera. You've done a lot to help out with Cindy since I moved here, and I want you to know how much I appreciate it."

She shrugged. "It's nothing, really. I enjoy helping others whenever I can."

"Even so, I'm still on the lookout for someone else to watch Cindy while I'm at work. I've asked around, but all the young Amish women in my area are either married with families of their own to care for, or they already have a job." Jesse stroked his daughter's soft cheek as she nestled against his chest.

Vera took a seat on the couch next to her husband. "There's no hurry for you to find someone else, Jesse. I am willing to do it for as long as you need me."

Milton snorted, turning to face her. "You'd work yourself right into the grave if someone didn't stop you." He looked at Jesse. "My fraa means well, but it's hard for her to say no, even when she's tired, stressed, or in physical pain. So my advice to you, young man, is if you can't find a *maud,* then look for a wife."

Milton's bluntness caused Jesse's skin to tingle. He'd never expected such a bold statement. "I — I'm not ready to get married again," he mumbled, keeping his focus on Cindy. "But I will keep looking for a maid to watch my baby girl and keep the house running while I'm at work."

Herschel sauntered over and stood beside Jesse's chair. "Why don't you leave Cindy with my mamm right now and come outside with me for a bit? There's something I'd like to show you." He looked at his mother. "Would that be okay with you?"

"Of course." She held out her arms.

Although a bit hesitant after Milton's previous remark, Jesse stood and placed Cindy in Vera's lap. Then he followed Herschel out the front door.

Outside, Herschel led the way to the barn. Jesse had no idea what could be in there that Vera's son wanted him to see, but he went willingly.

Once inside the building, Herschel pointed to a pair of wooden stools sitting close to one wall. "Go ahead and take a seat."

Once again, Jesse obliged. "What did you want to show me?"

"Nothing in particular. I wanted to talk to you in private."

"About what?"

"My daed's offhanded remark." Herschel folded his arms and leaned against the wooden planks. "He's worried about my mamm, but that didn't justify his suggestion that you find a new wife."

"It's okay. I'm sure he didn't realize how impossible that would be."

"You still love your fraa, jah?"

Jesse nodded. "What Esther and I had was special. I don't think I'll ever stop loving her."

"I understand. My heart still lies with Mattie, which is why I never remarried."

"It's too bad you don't have any kinner. Cindy is the joy of my heart. Every day I am reminded how blessed I am to have her."

Herschel rubbed a hand across the middle of his chest. "Mattie and I wanted children, and she gave birth to a son a few years after we got married." His posture slumped as he paused and cleared his throat. "I would have given most anything to be a father, but I guess it wasn't meant to be, 'cause our boppli died a few hours after he was born." He heaved a sigh. "Mattie was never able to conceive after that."

Jesse stood and put his hand on Herschel's shoulder. "I'm sorry for your loss," he said gently.

"Danki. Even after all these years I still think about it. I'm not one to easily let go of things that have touched me on a deep emotional level."

Remembering the conversation he'd had with Herschel a few weeks ago, Jesse realized that it must have been the memory of losing his child that caused Herschel to say he'd suffered a loss twice. No wonder the poor man always seemed so withdrawn. After all these years, he still grieved for what he'd lost.

Jesse closed his eyes briefly. *I am ever so grateful for the privilege of raising my precious daughter. The memory of my dear Esther will never die, because Cindy is a part of her. I'll cherish every day we have together, and if by some chance I do end up getting married again, I'll make sure Cindy knows all about her mother.*

Strasburg

"How did you get that nasty-looking *gwetsche*?" Grandma pointed to the bruise on Lenore's forearm, where she'd rolled up her dress sleeve to wash their supper dishes.

"When I put my gaul away in her stall this afternoon, one of the *katze* ran in front of her. Dolly got a bit frisky, tossing her head from side to side, and as I tried to calm her, I ended up bumping into the wooden post outside her stall."

"Better watch yourself around the horses," Grandpa mumbled from where he sat by the table in his wheelchair. "They can't be trusted, and you never know what they're gonna do if something spooks them."

With eyes open wide, Lenore turned to look at him. It was the clearest he'd spoken since his stroke. Apparently the speech therapy he'd been having weekly was beginning to take effect. What a joy to see this measure of improvement. Here she'd been looking for ways to bring more happiness into his life, and today, he'd brought some unexpected cheerfulness into hers.

"Jah, Grandpa, I'll try to be more careful." Lenore glanced at Grandma and noticed the sweet smile on her face. No doubt, she too was pleased with Grandpa's progress.

"Now about that bruise . . . Have you put anything on it?" Grandma questioned.

"Just some ice after I came in the house."

"Arnica. That's what you need." Grandpa spoke again.

"He's right." Grandma reached for a clean dish to dry. "There's a tube of *Arnica montana* lotion in the bathroom medicine chest. Apply a thin layer to the affected area three times a day, and it should help. You should also take some of the arnica tablets in my homeopathic medicine kit. Just follow the instructions on the container."

Lenore smiled. "Danki. I will do that as soon as I'm done with the dishes."

It seemed like Grandma had holistic remedies for a good many things. Too bad she didn't have one to keep Grandpa from having another stroke. But hopefully with him watching his diet, taking a blood thinner, and doing everything the doctor said, it would never happen again. Lenore wanted her grandparents to be healthy and live many more years. She'd lost her mother's parents when they were tragically killed in a buggy accident six years ago. The thought of losing either Grandpa or Grandma Lapp put a lump in her throat.

"Want to join me in a game of Scrabble?" Ezekiel asked, stepping into the kitchen where Michelle sat at the table.

"Maybe later." She gestured to the pen and paper lying before her. "I'm working on my grocery list right now, for when I go shopping tomorrow."

"You came in here more than thirty minutes ago to do that. Thought you'd have it done by now."

She shook her head. "I haven't decided what all we need."

He moved closer to the table and looked down at the list. "We went over all the items we both need during supper, but you only have a few things written down. How come?"

"I don't know." Michelle didn't look up at him.

Ezekiel pulled out a chair and sat beside her. "Okay, what's the problem? You're depressed about something, aren't you?"

Slowly, she nodded.

"Is it your brothers, because you haven't heard from them in a while?"

"No, it's not that. In fact, I heard from Ernie a few weeks ago."

"What then?" Ezekiel cupped Michelle's chin with the palm of his hand, turning her head to face him.

She drew a quick breath before speaking. "I've been sitting here wondering why God hasn't answered my prayers about having a baby."

He gently stroked her arm. "We've had this discussion before, and I thought we'd both agreed that if it's meant to be, you'll get pregnant in God's time, not ours."

"I know, but —"

"Have you ever thought how worrying over this might be causing you stress, and that the stress could actually be keeping it from happening?"

"I have considered it."

"Then stop fretting, try to relax, and put your focus on other things." Ezekiel put his hand on Michelle's shoulder. "Philippians 4:11 says, 'I have learned, in whatsoever state I am, therewith to be content.' "

"Danki for that reminder, Ezekiel. You're so full of wisdom I wouldn't be surprised if someday you get chosen by lot to become a minister."

Ezekiel's eyes darkened. "I hope not. A lot of responsibility is put on a man's shoulders when he is selected to be one of the church leaders."

"It's not something you need to worry about, for now at least." Michelle reached up to stroke the side of her husband's bearded face. "I love you, Ezekiel, and I don't know what I'd do without you."

"You'd have a lot less dishes to wash." Grinning, Ezekiel leaned over and kissed her cheek. "Now hurry up with your grocery list so you can beat me at Scrabble."

Michelle chuckled. Just a few words of encouragement from the wonderful man she'd married, and already she felt better. There might be times in the days ahead when she would think about her desire to have a baby, but Michelle would try to remember to be content, even if she and Ezekiel were never blessed with children.

CHAPTER 8

Sara was about to leave the flower shop to meet Brad for lunch a little before noon on Saturday when her part-time employee, Cynthia, called out, "What should I do after I've washed all the plastic buckets in the back room?" Cynthia worked three days a week, mostly cleaning. She was also being taught how to make floral arrangements.

Sara didn't understand why Cynthia had asked her that question when Misty, her new full-time floral designer, was behind the counter filling out some paperwork. Misty used to work at a flower shop in Lancaster before coming here, after Sara's previous designer, Peggy, had moved away. So Misty pretty much knew how to run the place. Sara always felt comfortable leaving Misty in charge whenever she left the store for any length of time.

"Once the buckets are cleaned and put away, you can help Misty in the back room, and work on the orders that came in this morning." Sara nodded in that direction.

"Oh, okay." Cynthia gave Sara a hesitant nod and retreated to the back room.

Sara looked over at Misty and winked. "I'll be back in a few hours."

"No hurry. Take your time. With any luck, we'll have most of those new orders already filled when you return."

Sara left the shop and headed down the sidewalk in the direction of Isaac's Famous Grilled Sandwiches. About half a block down, she spotted Herschel Fisher heading her way.

"Hello, Mr. Fisher," she said when he drew near. "How did things go for your mother's birthday? Did she like the roses you bought her?" When he looked at her strangely, Sara paused. "Oh, I forgot . . . you prefer to be called Herschel, right?"

He gave a brisk nod.

She smiled. "I'll try to remember."

"In answer to your question: Yes, my mother liked the bouquet. Her birthday turned out well, even though she insisted on cooking the meal."

Sara remembered the time Herschel's mother had come into her shop to chew Sara out for selling flowers to her son, which he'd put on his wife's grave. Vera struck her as a woman with a lot of spunk.

They talked for a minute about the unusually warm weather they'd been having, before Herschel said he needed to be on his way.

"I hope to see you again soon." Sara waved and headed for the restaurant to meet up with Brad. It had been nice to see the gleam in Herschel's eyes when he talked about his mother. Sara wished, once again, that her own mother was alive. She had so many unanswered questions that she would never get the chance to ask her. All Sara had left of her mother were the messages she'd left in the prayer jars. Some she understood, but others were a mystery. It seemed like Mama had left out an important piece of the puzzle of her young life — the piece she wanted no one to know about.

Sara sighed. *I wish Mama had told me about the notes before she died. There are so many things I would have asked her.*

Ronks, Pennsylvania
Lenore had been running errands on Grandma's behalf for most of the morning, and she still had a few more stops to make before going home. Since it was almost noon, she decided to have lunch at Dienner's Country Restaurant, where Mi-

chelle used to work as a waitress. She quit when she married Ezekiel, but she'd said many times how much she enjoyed working there and how busy the place was because everyone liked the food.

Upon entering the building, Lenore was greeted by a middle-aged hostess who took her to a table near the window. She had only been seated a few minutes when the waitress came to take her order.

"I'd like a chicken salad sandwich and a glass of unsweetened iced tea with a slice of lemon, please."

The young woman smiled and wrote Lenore's order on her pad. "I'll bring your beverage right away, but it may be several minutes before your sandwich is ready. We're really busy today and the kitchen is shorthanded."

"No problem. I'm not in a hurry."

After the waitress left, Lenore dug in her purse for the list Grandma had given her this morning. The two stops she had left were the post office to mail some letters and the pharmacy to pick up a prescription for a refill of Grandpa's blood thinner. Those stops shouldn't take long, so hopefully she would be back in plenty of time to help Grandma fix their supper.

Lenore felt concerned about how her

grandmother would manage all day once school started in August. At one point, she'd considered resigning from her teaching position to stay home and help, but Grandma insisted she could manage on her own and didn't want Lenore to give up a job she enjoyed. If things got to be too much, Grandma would call on a friend or neighbor for assistance.

Lenore had returned the list to her purse when she heard a baby fussing. What began as a mild form of crying soon turned into fretful sobbing. She glanced across the room and saw Jesse Smucker at a table, holding his little girl in his lap. The baby's creamy complexion quickly turned red as she flailed her chubby arms and kicked her feet. Her daddy's face was equally red. No doubt he was embarrassed and at his wits' end.

Without hesitation, Lenore got up and moved swiftly across the room. "I don't mean to intrude, but would you like me to see if I can settle her down?"

Sweating profusely, he nodded and held the child out to Lenore.

A few pats on the back and some gentle strokes of the little girl's tearstained face, and all was quiet.

Jesse shook his head slowly as his mouth fell open. "If I hadn't seen it for myself, I wouldn't have believed it. Either you have magic in your hands or you're just plain good with kinner."

Lenore's chin dipped a bit as a warm flush crept across her cheeks. "I've been told that I do have a knack with children, which I suppose is the reason I enjoy teaching school."

Jesse stared at her with a curious expression. "I'm surprised you're not married and raising a family of your own by now."

His comment caught her off guard, and she lowered her gaze even further. "I would like to get married someday, but God hasn't brought the right man into my life."

A few moments passed with neither of them speaking, and then Jesse asked another question. "Would you like to join me for lunch? We can take turns holding Cindy, and hopefully with you here she'll be quiet for me."

Lenore lifted her chin to look at him, wondering how to respond. As much as she relished the idea of sitting at Jesse's table and holding his precious daughter, Lenore didn't want to start any gossip going around. If anyone they knew saw them eating lunch together, they might get the idea that Jesse was courting her. But if she didn't take him up on his offer, little Cindy might start howling again, and Jesse might not get to eat his lunch at all.

When Cindy burrowed her perky nose against Lenore's shoulder and gave a little whimper, Lenore made up her mind with no hesitation. "I'd be happy to eat my lunch here and take turns holding your baby."

When Lenore, still holding his satisfied daughter, walked away to ask the waitress to bring her lunch over to his table, Jesse mulled things over. *I wonder if Lenore would agree to watch Cindy until she starts teaching school again. That would give me more time to look for a full-time maid.*

"The waitress said it won't be a problem to bring my order over here when it's ready," Lenore said after she returned to Jesse's table.

"Okay, good."

When Lenore sat down with Cindy, Jesse continued to eat his meal. After her order came, it was Jesse's turn to hold Cindy. He was surprised his little one remained quiet, although fixated on Lenore as she ate her sandwich.

Bouncing Cindy on his knee, Jesse threw caution to the wind and blurted out the question on his mind. "I was wondering . . . Would you be interested in watching Cindy for me while I'm at work, until you start back teaching *schul*?"

She set her glass of iced tea on the table. "Well . . . uh . . . I suppose I could do it, but it would have to be at my grandparents' house, where I'm living right now to help out."

"Not a problem. Right now my wife's great-aunt is watching Cindy, and since she and her husband live in Gordonville, it means I have to take Cindy there every morning, then come back here to Strasburg to my job at the furniture store, and then return to Gordonville at the end of the workday. Also, Vera's really not up to watching the baby five days a week, although she won't admit it." He leaned forward, resting his elbows on the table. "Since you live in Strasburg and we are in the same church district, it will be much closer for me to bring the baby to your grandparents' house."

Lenore wiped her mouth with a napkin, then reached into her purse and took out a small notebook. "I'll write down my grandparents' address for you."

"Thanks. I'll be by on Monday morning around seven."

"Will I see you at church tomorrow morning?"

91

"I won't be attending church in our district this Sunday. I promised Vera and Milton I'd bring Cindy to church in their district this week." Jesse grinned. "I think Vera wants all her friends to see how much my little girl is growing."

"It's understandable. When children are young they grow so quickly. I taught some of my older students when they first started school, and whenever I see them now I can't believe how much they've grown."

Jesse kissed the top of Cindy's head. "I hope she doesn't grow too fast. I appreciate the innocence of her youth."

"I know what you mean." Lenore glanced at the clock on the far wall. "I suppose I should get going. I still have a few more errands to run for my grandma." She stood and moved to Jesse's side of the table. Reaching out to touch Cindy's chin, she smiled and said, "See you Monday morning, sweet girl." She looked at Jesse. "I hope the rest of your day goes well and Cindy remains as happy as she is right now."

Jesse nodded. "Danki again for getting her settled down."

"It was my pleasure."

When Lenore left the restaurant, Jesse worried that his daughter might start fussing again, but she seemed totally relaxed in his arms.

He looked down at her and gulped. *I hope I did the right thing asking Lenore to watch my baby. Sure hope Vera won't mind. I don't want to ruffle her feathers.*

CHAPTER 9

Gordonville

Throughout the Sunday service, and even during lunch, Jesse thought about his encounter with Lenore the day before. Now that he and Cindy were at Vera and Milton's house, it was time to tell Vera of his decision about his daughter.

Cindy had fallen asleep and lay curled up on the living-room floor on a thick blanket, while Milton slept in his recliner nearby. Since Vera had gone to the kitchen to make coffee, Jesse determined this was a good time to speak with her.

When he entered the kitchen, the spicy aroma of gingerbread made his mouth water. A plate filled with several pieces of the thickly cut bread had been placed on the table.

Vera smiled at him and gestured to the plate. "I thought you and Milton might like a treat to go with your *kaffi.*"

94

Jesse smacked his lips. "A cup of coffee sounds good, and that gingerbread looks awfully tempting, but your husband is sleeping as soundly as my little *maedel* right now."

"He can have some when he wakes up." Vera pulled out a chair at the table. "Pour yourself a cup of kaffi and take a seat."

Jesse obliged, and after she joined him, he jumped right into the topic on his mind. "I've found someone else to watch Cindy while I'm at work."

Vera blinked rapidly. "Oh? Who is she?"

"Her name is Lenore Lapp, and —"

"Where is she from? Does she live here in Gordonville, or someplace closer to you?"

"Lenore lives in Strasburg, and she's a schoolteacher. But she's not working right now and has agreed to watch Cindy until she starts back to school toward the end of August."

Vera rested both arms on the table, looking at him intently. "If she can only care for your daughter a short time, what's the point? I mean, what is the reason you chose her?"

"Lenore is good with kinner. In fact, when I had no success getting Cindy to quiet down at the restaurant yesterday, Lenore got my little girl to stop crying almost as soon as she picked her up."

"She's never cried much for me." The wrinkles around Vera's mouth deepened as she pursed her lips. "And I told you before that I don't mind watching her."

Jesse squirmed in his chair. Although he didn't want to offend Vera, Jesse felt his decision was best, not only for Cindy, but for Vera as well. He hoped he could make her understand and that there would be no hard feelings.

"You're right — you are good with Cindy, and I appreciate all you have done to help out. But you need a break and more time to do some of the things you like. Caring for a young child is a full-time job."

She nodded slowly. "All right, I accept your decision, but once Lenore returns to teaching, if you need me to watch Cindy again, I'm willing."

"I appreciate that, but maybe by then I will have a full-time maud."

Vera's eyes twinkled as she pointed at him. "Or a fraa."

He shook his head. "That's not going to happen."

"Never say never, Jesse." Vera snapped her fingers. "Say, I have an idea. Why don't you ask Lenore Lapp out for supper some evening and see where things go from there?" She gave him a toothy grin. "You can't be sure till you get to know the young woman, but Lenore might be the one for you."

"No, I don't think —"

"If she handles your daughter well, she might make a good mudder, and good mothers are usually good wives."

Jesse fought the urge to roll his eyes. "I appreciate your concern, Vera, but I'm not planning to get married again." He quickly reached for a piece of bread and took a bite. *No woman except Esther is the one for me. But God took her to heaven and left me and Cindy alone, so I guess that's how it's meant to be.* Jesse would say no more to Vera on this topic. He preferred to keep his thoughts to himself.

Strasburg

Mary Ruth sat on the couch, watching Willis sleep in his favorite reclining chair. She tried not to worry about him, but sometimes her thoughts ran amuck. If her dear husband had another stroke — or even a heart attack as their doctor had warned — she didn't know what she would do. In less than two months Lenore would resume her teaching duties, and Mary Ruth would be left alone all day to care for Willis and do all the chores around the house.

Maybe we should have taken Ivan up on his offer to move in with him and Yvonne. Of course, with them both working at his general store, I'd still be alone with Willis all day. But at least they'd be close enough to come home for lunch and check on us. Mary Ruth shifted on her chair, sucking in a breath. She knew what Willis would say if she again suggested moving to Paradise to live with Ivan and his family. His response would be a resounding no.

It's best if I don't dwell on this too much, Mary Ruth admonished herself. *Even though I'm not as young as I used to be, as long as Willis doesn't get any worse, I'm sure I can manage when Lenore is not at home.*

Lenore sat on the edge of her bed, thinking about Jesse and his baby girl. Holding the child yesterday had felt so good, and the fact that Lenore had easily calmed Cindy down surprised her as much as it apparently had the baby's father.

She hadn't told her grandparents yet that she'd agreed to watch Cindy during the days her father worked. She hoped they wouldn't object.

Lenore tapped her chin. *I should have asked them first before agreeing to Jesse's request. If either Grandma or Grandpa has any qualms, I'll have to let Jesse know right away so he can find someone else.*

She got up and moved over to the window to watch several birds carrying on in the trees closest to the house. It was hard to stay focused on the birds, though, when her mind was somewhere else. *Having a baby in the home might be too much for Grandpa. If Cindy gets fussy, it might disrupt Grandpa's peace and quiet.*

Lenore moved away from the window, walked over to the bed, then paced back again. *This is what I get for being so impulsive. The decision I made yesterday at the restaurant was hasty, and I didn't think things through well enough.*

A soft knock sounded on the door, diverting Lenore's attention. "Come in," she called.

Grandma entered the room and joined Lenore at the window. "You've been up here since you got home from church. I thought you might be napping."

"No, just thinking."

Grandma took a seat on Lenore's bed and patted the quilted cover. It was a simple nine-patch quilt like the one Grandma had taught Lenore and Sara to make some time ago. "Why don't you sit here and tell me what's on your mind?"

Lenore sank to the bed. "There's something I need to tell you."

Grandma's eyes darkened. "You look so serious. Is there a problem?"

"No. Yes. Well, I guess there could be. I agreed to do something without checking with you first."

"What do you mean?"

Staring at her hands folded in her lap, Lenore explained about Jesse's request for her to watch Cindy here at the house. "I shouldn't have agreed to it without getting your approval, but I got caught up in the moment of holding the adorable child, and then before I knew it, the word *yes* came out of my mouth."

"It's okay, dear one." Grandma clasped Lenore's hand. "It might be kind of nice to have a little one around for a while. Things have been way too serious here at the house since your grossdaadi's stroke. A sweet little boppli, no doubt full of lots of cute antics, might be just what we all need to bring some joy and laughter into our home again."

Lenore leaned close and gave her grandmother a hug. "Danki for being so understanding. But I want you to know, if it doesn't work out and the boppli gets on Grandpa's nerves, I'll ask Jesse to make

100

some other arrangements for his daughter."

Grandma gave Lenore's back a few gentle pats. "Not to worry. I'm sure it'll be just fine."

Lenore hoped the babysitting would go well, because she looked forward to watching Cindy. Getting to know the baby's father a little better would be nice too. No doubt he'd been lonely since his wife died. Perhaps there would be some evenings when he could join them for supper. Lenore was almost sure her hospitable grandma would extend some meal invitations.

CHAPTER 10

As Jesse pulled his horse and buggy up to the Lapps' hitching rail, Cindy began to fuss. She'd dozed off on the way over here, which had given him the peace and quiet he needed to concentrate on the road and try to relax. He still felt a bit apprehensive about leaving Cindy with Lenore, but they were here now and there was no turning back.

Once Jesse got the horse secured, he took Cindy out and carried her and the canvas bag full of necessary baby items up to the house. Before he had a chance to knock on the door, it opened and Lenore greeted him with a dimpled smile.

"Come in. We have everything set up for Cindy."

Jesse wasn't sure what Lenore meant by that, but when he followed her into the living room, he was surprised to see a playpen sitting near the rocking chair.

"My aunt Rhoda used it when she was a baby," Lenore explained. "When Grandma told me it had been stored in the basement, I went down last night and brought it up. I thought it would be better than putting a blanket on the floor for Cindy to lie on." She motioned to the playpen. "It's all cleaned up and ready to use when needed."

"Good idea." Jesse glanced across the room, where a man's straw hat lay on an end table. "Are your grandparents okay with you watching Cindy here in their home?"

Lenore nodded. "They're fine with it. Grandma even said having a boppli in the house would give us all something to smile about." Lenore held out her arms. "And I'm definitely looking forward to spending time with your sweet baby girl."

Jesse handed Cindy over to Lenore and set the satchel on the couch. "Everything she might need is in here." He stepped forward and kissed the top of Cindy's head. "Be good for Lenore, little one. Daadi will see you this evening."

He turned and was almost to the door when Lenore called out to him. "If you have no plans for supper this evening, we'd like you to join us. Grandma plans to make stuffed cabbage rolls, and there's bound to be more food than the three of us can eat."

Jesse's mouth watered at the anticipation of eating a good home-cooked meal. "I would be pleased to join you. Danki for the invitation."

When Jesse left the house and started across the yard, he stepped a bit livelier than usual.

"I see the boppli has arrived." Upon entering the room, Grandma gave a wide smile.

"Jah. Cindy's daed dropped her off about fifteen minutes ago." Lenore sat in a rocking chair, tenderly patting the baby's back. "She's real *schee*. Don't you think so, Grandma?"

"Yes, but then, I think all *bopplin* are pretty."

"Me too." Lenore heaved a sigh. "I would like to have a child of my own someday, but at the rate things are going, it looks doubtful that I'll ever fall in love and get married."

Grandma clicked her tongue. "Never say never. The right man will come along someday. Maybe he already has."

Lenore tipped her head. "What do you mean?"

"Could be this pretty baby's father will take an interest in you. He is without a wife, you know."

Lenore lifted her gaze to the ceiling. "Oh Grandma, I'm sure Jesse has no interest in me other than as someone to care for his daughter."

"He may not now, but he could develop feelings for you in the future. And the same goes for you."

Lenore had to admit, even in the short time she'd known Cindy's father, she found him appealing — not just his good looks, but his gentle voice and the kindness she saw in his eyes. Of course, she wasn't about to admit it to Grandma or anyone else for that matter.

She rose from her chair and put Cindy in the playpen. "The baby is sleeping now, so I'm free to help with any chores."

Grandma shook her head. "The chores can wait. Your grandpa's still reading the newspaper at the kitchen table. Why don't we join him for a cup of coffee, and then we can plan out our day."

"Okay." Lenore covered Cindy with a lightweight blanket and followed Grandma out of the room.

That evening when Jesse came back to the Lapps' after work, as soon as Mary Ruth led him into the house, he was greeted with the tantalizing aroma of cooked cabbage and tomato sauce. His stomach growled at the prospect of eating cabbage rolls, which he hadn't had since Esther died.

"How'd my little girl do today?" His question was directed to Lenore, who sat in the living room holding Cindy.

"She did very well." Lenore smiled, raking her fingers lightly through Cindy's shiny hair. She gestured to the gray-haired man sitting in the recliner next to her. "Cindy's cute smile and giggle kept Grandpa well entertained."

"Good to hear." Jesse moved toward the man and extended his hand. "I'm Jesse Smucker. It's nice to meet you, Mr. Lapp."

"Nice to meet you too, and you can call me by my first name. It's Willis." He held out his right hand. "*Ich schlaag hot ihn gedroffe,* and it left me partially paralyzed."

"I'm sorry to hear you had a stroke." Jesse gave an understanding nod. His paternal grandfather had suffered one too, followed by a massive heart attack that had taken his life ten years ago. *The world would be so much better if it were free of death and suffering,* he thought.

Jesse gave Willis's shoulder a light tap. "I hope you will experience a full recovery."

"He's doing much better than a few months ago," Mary Ruth spoke up. "His speech has improved and he's even able to walk a little when he's out of his wheelchair. Although he does have to use a cane or a walker," she added. "I do believe his physical therapy sessions are finally paying off."

"That's great. Keep up the good work, Willis." Hearing familiar baby noises, Jesse glanced at Cindy. She'd begun pulling on Lenore's dress sleeve and kicking her bare feet.

"Looks like my *dochder* is full of energy this evening," Jesse commented. "Did she get a good *leie* today?"

"Jah. In fact she took two naps."

Mary Ruth chuckled. "I think you wore Cindy out with all the games you played with her."

"What kind of games?" Jesse directed his question to Lenore.

"Let's see . . ." Lenore tickled Cindy under her chin. "We played the *kitzle* game. I tickled Cindy under her chin, and she would laugh. Then I tickled her toes, and even her nose." Lenore grinned. "It was so cute when she tried to tickle herself."

Jesse rubbed the back of his head. "I've never tried anything like that with her."

"Willis had your little girl laughing with all the silly faces he made too," Mary Ruth interjected.

"Jah," Willis chimed in. "When I made a growling noise, she growled right back at me."

"Sounds like you folks know how to keep a boppli entertained." Jesse laid a hand against his chest. "I should be doing those kinds of things with Cindy when I come home from work, instead of just sitting and cuddling her."

"That's important too." Lenore bounced Cindy on her knee. "I'm sure as time goes on, you'll find many ways to keep her entertained and help her senses develop."

Jesse nodded, although he wasn't sure he possessed the skills to be everything his daughter needed. *Maybe Vera was right when she offered her opinion the other day. Could be that I do need to find a wife so my little girl isn't deprived of having a mother.* He glanced in Lenore's direction again. *She's good with Cindy. I wonder if she might be a possible candidate for marriage.* Jesse shifted on his chair. *Of course, I'll have to get to know her better before I bring up the topic. And she would need to understand that our marriage would only be one of convenience, since there could never be any love between us.*

"Should we all go out to the kitchen and eat supper now?" Mary Ruth's question drove Jesse's irrational thoughts aside. And they were irrational, because the day Esther died he'd made up his mind that he would never get married again. It didn't even make sense that the crazy notion of marrying Lenore had popped into his mind. Jesse barely knew the young woman, and he certainly wasn't in love with her. *Maybe after I've had a good meal, I'll be thinking more clearly.*

CHAPTER 11

"Are you sure you don't want to do anything special tonight?" Ezekiel asked as he and Michelle sat at their kitchen table eating supper. "If we can find a driver to take us there, we can go up to the Fourth of July celebration in Lititz tonight." He grinned at her from across the table. "It's always fun to watch the fireworks."

She shook her head. "I'm content to stay here with you all evening. When it starts to get dark, we can sit outside and watch the *feierveggel* rise up from the grass."

His forehead creased as he reached for a slice of Michelle's homemade bread. "There's nothing exciting about watching fireflies. I might have thought so when I was a boy and caught them to put in a jar, but not anymore." Ezekiel chuckled. "I need a little more action than that."

"I suppose you're right, but I'd rather stay home tonight," Michelle repeated.

Ezekiel slathered the bread with a little butter and plenty of honey from his beehives. "We're just an old married couple now, jah?"

She snickered. "Not old, but we've definitely settled into the routine of married life. The only thing missing is . . ." Her voice trailed off. Michelle had almost broken the promise she'd made to herself not to bring up the subject of children again. It did no good to talk about her inability to conceive. And if she voiced her thoughts, it could put a damper on an otherwise pleasant meal.

"Would you please pass the lentil casserole?" Michelle said. "It turned out so well, I'm ready for seconds."

Making no comment on her dropped sentence, Ezekiel pushed the casserole dish on its oversized potholder closer to Michelle.

"Danki." Michelle put two heaping tablespoons on her plate and picked up her fork. But before she could take a bite, Ezekiel spoke again.

"I've been mulling something over in my mind for the past few weeks, and wanted to talk to you about an idea I have."

She took a quick bite and swallowed. "What's it about?"

"I'd like to leave Lancaster County and

move to New York."

Michelle's head jerked back. "New York?"

"Jah. There's a newly established Amish community there, and I saw an ad in *The Budget* recently, placed by a man who lives in that community."

"An ad for what?"

"He makes beekeeping supplies and will be getting ready to retire from the business this spring."

"But you don't make beekeeping supplies. You keep bees for their honey, which you sell to people you know and places of business here in our area," Michelle reminded.

He nodded. "True, but I'd like to learn how to make bee boxes and many other things that are used for raising bees. I could continue selling honey from my beekeeping business too."

"You have never before mentioned wanting to make the supplies you use for beekeeping."

"Didn't realize it till I saw the man's ad saying he's willing to teach the person who buys his business how to make and/or sell the supplies one needs to be a beekeeper." Ezekiel leaned closer to Michelle. "As you know, I've never been happy helping in my folks' greenhouse. This would be a chance for us to start over, and I would finally be doing something I'd really enjoy."

"How do you know you'd like it, since you've never done it before?"

"Just do." He tapped his chest with the palm of his hand. "I feel it right here, and I'm hoping you'll be willing to make the move."

Michelle sat silently, staring at her plate. The desire to eat more casserole had disappeared. Strasburg and people like Willis and Mary Ruth, whom she'd become close to, were like family. She couldn't imagine leaving them and living someplace where she didn't know a soul.

He reached over and patted her arm. "You don't have to give me an answer right now. Just think about it, okay?"

Michelle forced a smile she didn't really feel and slowly nodded. In addition to thinking over Ezekiel's idea, she would need to do some serious talking to God.

Lancaster

"How soon till you're ready to go to your grandparents' house?" Brad asked when he entered the kitchen where Sara stood working near the sink.

"Within the next thirty minutes or so." She turned to look at him. "Too bad your folks had other Fourth of July plans. It would have been nice if they could have driven down from Harrisburg and joined us."

"Yeah, but by the time I extended the invitation, they'd already agreed to spend the day with some close friends." Brad stood behind Sara and put his arms around her waist. "The fruit salad you're making looks delicious."

She reached back and swatted his hand. "Don't get any ideas about sampling some now. This is to share with the others who'll be at Grandma and Grandpa's today."

"Okay, I'll leave the salad alone." Brad reached for a piece of cut-up watermelon that hadn't made it into the bowl and popped it in his mouth.

Sara's brows pinched together. "You're incorrigible."

Brad chuckled and leaned over to give her cheek a wet kiss. "Not to change the subject or anything, but are you sure you're okay with me hosting a Bible study here in our home for new Christians?"

"When were you thinking of starting the study?" she asked.

"Maybe next Friday night, or the week after."

"I'm fine with it, Brad. Since it wasn't that long ago that I became a new Christian, I'll probably benefit from the class too."

"Christians — old or new — can always take something away when they study the Bible. What I'm mainly concerned with, though, is whether you're okay with having it here." Brad leaned his back against the counter. "With you working all day at the flower shop, it might be too much to have to come home, cook supper, and get ready for the class."

She stepped in front of him and tweaked his nose. "I thought maybe you'd do the cooking on Bible study night."

Brad's eyes widened as he slapped both hands against his cheeks. "What? You expect me to cook supper?" Before Sara could respond, he winked at her.

She poked his chest playfully. "What am I gonna do with you? You're nothing but a big tease."

"Of course, and that's one of the things you love about me." He wrapped Sara up in a big hug. "Now you'd better hurry and get the lid on that salad bowl before I lose all self-control and eat the whole thing."

Sara smiled. How grateful she was that God had brought her and Brad together. She looked forward to many years of serving the Lord as her husband's helpmate.

■ ■ ■ ■

Strasburg

"Oh, what a cute baby. What's her name, and who are her parents?" Sara asked when Lenore met her on the front porch, holding Cindy.

"Her name is Cindy Smucker. She and her daddy are fairly new to our church district, and I recently began watching her while her father, Jesse, is at work."

"She's adorable." Sara reached out and stroked the little girl's cheek. "Her skin is soft like silk."

Lenore nodded. "She's such a good baby and so smart. I'm going to miss her when I start teaching again next month."

"I assume Jesse's wife is not able to watch the child?"

"Cindy's mother died while they were living in Kentucky, and Jesse brought his daughter here for a new start." Lenore took a seat on the porch swing. "Would you like to sit with us? Cindy loves the rocking motion of the swing."

"Sure." Sara sat beside Lenore, and they both pushed against the wooden boards beneath their feet. In a matter of seconds, Cindy began to giggle.

Lenore looked at Sara and grinned. "See what I mean?"

Sara bobbed her head. "Does Cindy's dad have any family members living in Strasburg? Is that why he chose to move to this area?"

"He has no blood relatives living nearby, but his wife's uncle, Herschel Fisher, lives in Gordonville, and so do Herschel's parents." Lenore paused to wipe a blob of drool off Cindy's chin with a tissue. "It's my understanding that Herschel owns a house here in Strasburg and he's renting it to Jesse."

Tipping her head to one side, Sara tapped her chin. "Hmm . . . I wonder if it's the same Herschel Fisher who comes into my flower shop sometimes. Herschel is not a common name, and if I remember right, according to the invoices for some of his floral purchases, Herschel's home is in Gordonville."

"It's probably the same man then." Lenore glanced in the direction of the barn, where she'd seen Sara's husband go after their van pulled into the yard. Lenore's parents had gone into the house to visit Grandma and Grandpa when they'd first arrived, but her brothers had gone out to the barn. Lenore figured Brad must have caught sight of them when he arrived and followed to see what they were up to. It was a good thing, because Lenore's cousin's husband had a level head and often offered spiritual counsel that any young man — Amish or English — could benefit from.

"Will Jesse and Cindy be joining our Fourth of July gathering?"

Sara's question cut into Lenore's thoughts.

"Yes. I invited him when he brought Cindy here yesterday morning, and he accepted without hesitation."

"I'm surprised he doesn't have plans to spend the evening with his wife's relatives."

"I asked that question, and Jesse said neither Herschel nor his folks do anything to celebrate the Fourth." Lenore snickered. "I think the fact that we'll be having a barbecue with plenty of good food may be the main reason Jesse's coming. He admitted that he's not much of a cook and usually ends up fixing sandwiches on gluten-free bread for his meals."

"Maybe he ought to seek another wife." Sara placed her hand on Cindy's leg. "His precious daughter needs a mother too." She looked directly at Lenore. "Maybe someone like you."

A warm flush crept across Lenore's

cheeks. "Now don't be silly. I barely know Jesse, and I'm sure he has no thoughts about getting married again — especially not to me."

Sara elbowed Lenore gently. "You never know what the future might hold, Cousin. When I first met Brad, I never dreamed we would fall in love or that I'd end up becoming a pastor's wife."

Cindy began to fidget, so Lenore patted her back, which was a sure way to make the little girl relax. "What's it like, being married to a minister? Are there many duties you must fulfill?" Lenore figured the change of subject would get Sara's mind off the unlikely event that she would end up marrying Jesse.

"Not too many. Brad made it clear when the church hired him that I had a business to run and would continue to be responsible for that. Of course, I try to be involved in the church as much as I can. In fact, he and I will be hosting a Bible study in our home soon, for people in the congregation who are new Christians." Sara shifted her position on the swing. "I'm actually looking forward to it. In addition to delving into the scriptures on the topic of a Christian's growth, it will give both Brad and me the opportunity to get to know some of the people in a more personal way."

"I hope it works out well for everyone who comes." Lenore glanced toward the road as she heard the unmistakable sound of a horse's hooves against the pavement. A few seconds later, a horse and buggy pulled in. "Looks like Cindy's father is here. I'm sure he will enjoy meeting you and Brad." *And I will enjoy getting to spend more time with him,* she silently admitted.

CHAPTER 12

"Your little girl is adorable." Sara gestured to Cindy sitting contently on her father's lap.

Jesse smiled. "Thank you. She takes after her mother in many ways."

"Would you mind if I held her?" Sara hesitated. "That is, if you think she will come to me."

"Cindy's usually fine with strangers. I'm sure she won't mind if you hold her." When he handed his daughter to Sara, she was pleased that the little girl made no fuss. In fact, Cindy leaned her head against Sara's shoulder as she popped a thumb into her mouth.

"Aw, so she's a thumb sucker, huh?" Sara chuckled. "My little brother sucked his thumb until he was nearly four years old. I remember how Mama fretted about it, worried that Kenny might be doing that by the time he started kindergarten."

Jesse grunted. "It makes no sense to me, but Cindy prefers her thumb to a pacifier."

"Every child is different," Grandma said as she took a seat on the picnic bench beside Sara. "When your mother was a little girl, she sucked on the end of the little blanket I had made her." A faraway look entered her eyes. "I can remember the way she clung to that blanket just like it was yesterday."

Sara's throat tightened. *Poor Grandma. The whole time she and Grandpa were raising their children, I'm sure they had no idea their daughter would run away from home when she grew up, never to be seen or heard from again. If only Mama would have contacted them before she died. What was Mama thinking? Didn't she realize how much she'd hurt them? For that matter, she hurt herself by severing all family ties.*

Sara hated rehashing this scenario in her mind. She had gone over it so many times in the past. When she had finally forgiven her mother, Sara thought she'd come to grips with it once and for all. It was frustrating how a person could think they had worked through a situation, even felt peace about it, and then out of the blue, the pain of it all came right back to haunt them.

I won't allow my mind to dwell on it, Sara told herself. *Tonight is a special time to be with our friends and family, and I refuse to let anything spoil the evening. Maybe Mama did what she thought was right, so I need to give it to God again and let it rest.*

Lenore sat silently on the other side of the picnic table, observing Sara as she held Cindy. No doubt, Sara and Brad would become parents someday. Judging from the way Jesse's baby responded to Sara's gentle voice and touch, Sara would make a good mother.

It was wrong to envy, but little seeds of jealousy crept in every time Lenore saw a mother — or even a potential one — with a child.

A light breeze lifted the ties on Lenore's covering, and she tied the ends to keep them from swishing across her face. *What if I never get married or become a mother? Can I be satisfied teaching children all day but never nurturing any of my own?*

"Oh, look, there are fireworks over in that direction! I wish we had some we could set off."

Lenore smiled at her brother Peter's enthusiastic tone. She looked toward the area where he pointed. Sure enough, the sky was full of shimmery light, falling toward earth like a shower of red, white, and blue fiery sparks.

"It's pretty, but in my opinion, fireworks are a waste of money that could be spent on more practical things." Dad's forehead wrinkled as he looked at Peter. "When you've worked as hard and long as me, maybe you'll understand the value of a dollar." He pointed to another set of fireworks going off. "To me, that's just a lot of money going up in smoke."

Lenore's mother reached over and gave him a nudge. "Now, Ivan, don't be such a stick-in-the-mud."

His brows furrowed. "I'm just trying to use common sense."

Lenore remembered back to one of their Fourth of July family get-togethers when she and her brothers were young. Mom had bought balloons for them to fill with water and throw at each other. Lenore, Peter, and Ben thought it was great fun, but Dad grumbled and complained about the muddy mess in the flower bed, created by the water spigot they kept leaving on. Later, when Mom brought out a box of sparklers for the kids to light, Dad alternated between reminding them to be careful not to catch their clothes on fire and fussing about the money Mom had wasted buying the sparklers.

Of course, Lenore reminded herself, *my daed has many good attributes and has never been stingy when anyone in the family has needed money for important things.* Lenore had good parents, and for that she felt thankful — not like poor Michelle whose parents had been physically and emotionally abusive. Lenore couldn't imagine growing up in a family without love and support, or having a mom and dad who treated their children harshly. It was no wonder Michelle had struggled to forgive and rise above her circumstances. If she hadn't given her heart to the Lord and found forgiveness for her own wrongdoings, Michelle wouldn't have found peace or be where she was today.

Lenore glanced at Sara again, wondering what it must be like for her cousin not to know who her biological father was. Although Sara hadn't mentioned that topic for some time, Lenore figured she must have given up her search for him. Perhaps someday if the Lord willed it, the truth would come out.

B–boom! B–boom! B–boom! Lenore nearly jumped off the picnic bench when more fireworks went off, only this time with less color and more of an explosive sound. Lenore wasn't the only one affected, for the dog started barking and little Cindy began to howl.

"Here, let me take her inside the house where it's quieter." Lenore went around to where Sara sat with Cindy on her lap. "She probably needs her diaper changed by now anyhow."

Sara handed her the baby. "Would you like me to come with you?"

"No, that's okay. I can manage." Holding the sobbing child securely, Lenore glanced in Jesse's direction before heading to the house. She couldn't read his serious expression. Was it one of concern for his daughter, or did Cindy's father have something else on his mind?

For the next several minutes the adults chatted while Peter and Ben headed off to get firewood for the bonfire they'd both requested. Even though everyone had eaten a delicious meal of barbecued chicken, corn on the cob, and several kinds of salads just a few hours ago, the boys said they were hungry and ready to roast hot dogs and marshmallows. Jesse didn't usually eat anything much past supper, but tonight he would make an exception. It had been some time since he'd felt this relaxed and enjoyed himself so much. The Lapps were good people and had been most hospitable to him. Jesse almost felt like he was a part of their family.

When Brad stopped talking to the men long enough to ask his wife a question, Jesse glanced toward the house. *I wonder how things are going with Cindy. Maybe I should go up to the house and find out.*

"Excuse me, everyone." Jesse stood. "Think I'll go see if my daughter needs anything."

Ivan nodded. "No problem. Take your time. When you get back, maybe my boys will have the bonfire going."

"Do any of you need anything from the house?" Jesse asked.

"Not at the moment," Mary Ruth spoke up. "There's no point bringing the hot dogs out till the fire's been built and has died down a bit."

"My fraa is right," Willis agreed. "Roast the hot dogs too soon, and they'll be black as coal."

"All right then. I'll be back as soon as I find out how Cindy's doing. Hopefully Lenore's got her calmed down by now."

Yvonne smiled. "If anyone can calm your boppli down, it's my daughter."

Jesse hurried toward the house. When he stepped inside, all was quiet. That was a good sign. Upon entering the living room, he spotted Lenore sitting in her grandma's chair, humming softly while rocking Cindy. "Is she asleep?" Jesse whispered, moving quietly across the room.

"Almost."

"That's good. I think one of the reasons she became fussy is because she's tired." Jesse took a seat on the couch.

"That could be." Lenore looked over at him and smiled. "Did you get tired of watching the fireworks? Is that why you came inside?"

He shook his head. "Came to check on Cindy and to ask you a question."

"Oh?" She tipped her head. "What would you like to know?" Lenore spoke softly.

He swallowed hard and licked his dry lips. *I don't know why this is so hard for me. It's not like I've never asked a woman out to supper before. It's been a while since I thought about courting.*

Lenore kept rocking and patting Cindy's back as she looked at him expectantly.

Jesse drew a deep breath and exhaled quickly. "If you're not busy Friday evening, would you like to go out to supper with me?"

Lenore blinked and got the rocking chair moving a bit faster. "Just the two of us?"

"Jah. I checked with Vera this morning,

and she's agreed to watch Cindy while I'm gone." He tugged on his shirt collar. "I thought it would give us a chance to get better acquainted."

Lenore stopped rocking and nodded slowly. "Jah, Jesse, I'm free to have supper with you on Friday."

"Okay, good." He stood and wiped his sweaty hands on the sides of his trousers. *That wasn't as hard as I thought it would be. At least it's the first step in the right direction.*

"Guess I'll head back outside and see if Ben and Peter need any help with the bonfire. Will you be joining us soon?"

"Once Cindy is fully asleep, I'll put her down in the playpen. I will come back in periodically, though, to check on her."

"Okay. Danki for taking such good care of my little girl."

"You're welcome. It's my pleasure."

Jesse left the living room and headed out the back door. *Sure hope I didn't make a mistake asking Lenore out for supper. She might get the idea that I see her as more than a friend, and then I'd have to offer an explanation. I need to go slow and establish a solid friendship with her before I even mention the idea of marriage.*

CHAPTER 13

Michelle headed down the road with her horse and buggy Friday morning, conflicting thoughts flitting through her mind. For the last few days she had been thinking and praying about Ezekiel's desire to move to New York and learn a new trade. The thought of leaving Strasburg put a knot in her stomach, but at the same time she wanted to please her husband. It was her duty as his wife to offer support and be a good helpmate. If she put up a fuss and stood in his way, she'd feel guilty for holding Ezekiel back and squelching his desire to start over in a new place.

What Michelle needed right now was some solid advice, which she hoped to get from Mary Ruth and Willis.

Approaching the Lapps' home, she sent up a silent prayer. *Lord, please help me to be open-minded, because I am sure Mary Ruth and Willis will give me good counsel.*

Mary Ruth was surprised when she heard a horse whinny. They weren't anticipating any company. But then, friends and neighbors sometimes dropped by unexpectedly, as did family members.

Peering out the kitchen window, she saw a horse and buggy come into the yard and pull up to the hitching rail. A few seconds later, Michelle climbed down. After she'd secured her horse, she headed for the house.

Mary Ruth dried her wet hands on a towel and hurried to open the back door. "Well, good afternoon. What a pleasant surprise." When Michelle stepped onto the porch, she gave her a hug. "We haven't seen you for a while. Come inside so we can visit."

Mary Ruth couldn't help noticing the slump of Michelle's shoulders as she entered the kitchen. "If you're not busy, I was hoping I could talk to you and Willis about something."

"Willis is sleeping right now, but I'd be happy to listen to whatever you have to say." She gestured to a chair at the table. "Why don't you make yourself comfortable? I'll fix us something cold to drink."

Michelle hesitated before pulling out the

chair. She obviously had something troubling on her mind.

"Is everything all right?" Mary Ruth asked as she poured them both a glass of freshly brewed iced tea. "You look a bit *verlegge*."

"I am troubled." Michelle heaved a sigh. "Ezekiel wants us to move."

"To a home of your own?"

"Jah, only not here in Strasburg. He wants to start over in one of the Amish communities in New York."

Mary Ruth blinked. "I never expected he would move away from his family. From what I understand, they are dependent on his help in the greenhouse." She set their beverages on the table.

"I know." Michelle picked up her glass and took a drink. "I can't talk to Ezekiel's parents about this, because he hasn't told them yet. I'm sure they would not give their blessing. Ezekiel's daed has said many times that he needs the whole family's help in the greenhouse."

Mary Ruth stared at the table, pondering the best way to respond. "I'm sure there are plenty of able-bodied men Vernon could hire to work at his business."

"You're right, but they wouldn't be part of the *familye* — and their greenhouse has always been a family business."

132

"How do you feel about moving to another state?"

Michelle's face tightened. "It would be hard for me to leave all our friends, but if it's what Ezekiel truly wants, then I may not have any choice." She took another drink of iced tea, then held the glass against her reddened cheek.

"Have you prayed about the matter?" Mary Ruth questioned.

Michelle nodded. "It may seem selfish, but I've been asking God to change Ezekiel's mind and make him be satisfied to stay here. He could always look for some other job in the area if he's determined not to work in the greenhouse anymore."

"And if he doesn't change his mind?"

"Then as his wife, I'll need to go with him." Michelle's chin trembled. "It won't be easy, but I'll have to trust God that things will work out and I'll adjust."

"When would you expect to move?"

"Probably not till spring. That's if Ezekiel ends up taking over the business of some Amish man who recently put an ad in *The Budget*."

"It's a big decision, and I'll definitely be praying for both you and Ezekiel."

"Danki. I feel better being able to talk about it."

133

"Have you told anyone else?"

Michelle shook her head. "I'd rather not mention it to others yet — not till Ezekiel has made up his mind and told his parents."

"I understand, and I certainly won't repeat what you've said." Mary Ruth pointed up. "And always remember that wherever you go, whatever you do, the Lord will be with you."

Bird-in-Hand, Pennsylvania

Lenore's stomach quivered as she sat beside Jesse in his open buggy. Could his invitation to supper be considered a date, or did he merely want to get to know her better for the sake of his child, whom he'd hired her to care for?

She fidgeted nervously with the handles of her purse. *I can't imagine that Jesse would be interested in me romantically. After all, his wife hasn't even been gone a year. And Jesse's pained expression when he has spoken of Cindy's mother indicates the depth of his grief.*

"Is that the schoolhouse where you'll be teaching when school starts next month?"

Lenore turned to the right where he pointed.

"Yes, that's the one," she replied. "It will be my first time teaching there since moving from Paradise to Strasburg."

"I'm guessing you must like your job?"

She smiled. "Jah. I find teaching to be most rewarding."

"More so than being a mudder?"

Lenore's mouth opened slightly. Jesse's question was unexpected. "Well, umm . . . since I've not had the privilege of being a mother, I can't compare it to teaching, but I would like to have kinner of my own someday."

"I see." Jesse glanced briefly at Lenore, then back at the road again. They rode in silence for a while before he posed another question. "How long do you think you'll be living with your grandparents?"

She shrugged. "It depends on how well Grandpa does. If he can regain full use of his left arm and leg, I might be able to return to my parents' house. Then again, with me teaching in Strasburg, it would be better if I remained at Grandpa and Grandma's house indefinitely."

"What if you get married someday?"

"Then my place would be with my husband. But since I'm not being courted by anyone, it's not an issue I need to consider." Lenore didn't understand why Jesse was asking such personal questions. *Could he be interested in me? Would he ever consider me as a potential wife?* She gave him a sidelong glance, but he kept his gaze on guiding his horse into the parking lot of the Bird-in-Hand Family Restaurant.

Strasburg

"I hope Lenore has a nice time this evening. She works so hard around here, and it's good for her to get away for a while and have some fun for a change." Mary Ruth's knitting needles clicked as she carried on her conversation with Willis, who sat in his recliner beside her rocking chair. He'd made a few comments about what they had for supper when she'd first helped him into his chair but hadn't said much since then.

"It was nice of Jesse to invite Lenore out for supper," Mary Ruth continued. "I have a hunch he might be interested in courting our granddaughter. What do you think, Willis?"

A soft whistling sound followed by a couple of obnoxious snorts was her husband's only response.

Disgusted, Mary Ruth looked up from her knitting and shook her head. Not only had Willis fallen asleep, but now, with his mouth hanging slightly open, his obtrusive snores bounced off the living-room walls.

"Oh well," she murmured, twirling a piece

136

of yarn around her finger, "guess I ought to get used to talking to myself." These days Willis slept a lot more than he had in the past. But at least the paralysis he'd been left with since his stroke had lessened some, and for that she felt thankful.

Bird-in-Hand

"What's it like in the area of Kentucky where you are from? I've never been there, so I don't know anything at all about it," Lenore said, as she and Jesse enjoyed their meal from the bountiful buffet.

"Let's see now . . . I suppose I should start by giving you the history of the area." Jesse tapped his fingers on the table. "Christian County is named for Colonel William Christian, a native of Augusta County, Virginia. He was a veteran of the Revolutionary War and settled near Louisville, Kentucky, in 1785." He paused for a drink of water. "It might interest you to know that Jefferson Davis, president of the Confederate States of America, was born in Fairview, Kentucky, which is in Christian County."

"Interesting facts. What else can you tell me about that part of Kentucky?"

"Well, Christian County and its county seat, Hopkinsville, are located in southwestern Kentucky, a part of the Pennyroyal region. The Pennyroyal region's name comes from a branched annual plant of the mint family that can grow up to eighteen inches tall. Pioneer settlers found Pennyroyal growing throughout the area, and so they bruised the leaves and stems for use as an effective mosquito and tick repellent. Also, they discovered that a tea made from the plant was effective at treating pneumonia."

Lenore's brows lifted. "Wow, I'm impressed. You sure know a lot about the history of Christian County."

He smiled. "I enjoyed learning about our country's history when I was a boy and have read a good many history books as an adult."

"That's interesting. I'm fascinated with history as well."

"We'll have to share some historical facts we've learned about Pennsylvania some other time when we're together," Jesse said.

"Jah, that would be fun." Lenore finished eating her chicken, then posed another question. "Were you involved in woodworking when you lived in Kentucky, or is that something you took an interest in after you moved here?"

"I built a few things in a little shop on my folks' property but mostly helped my daed on the farm."

"What crops did you grow?"

"Wheat, corn, and some soybeans." Jesse cleaned his plate and wiped his mouth on a napkin. "Think I'll go back up to the buffet and get some dessert. Are you coming?"

Grimacing, Lenore placed both hands against her stomach. "Wish I could, but I ate too much chicken and mashed potatoes. I don't think there's any room left for dessert."

"Not even a small *schtick* of shoofly *boi*?"

She shook her head. "As much as I would enjoy a piece of shoofly pie, my common sense tells me I'd better not."

"Okay, guess I'll have to eat your share then." Jesse winked and headed for the buffet.

Lenore leaned back in her chair and tried to relax. *Are those fluttery feelings in my stomach from eating too much food, or am I just feeling giddy from time spent with Jesse?*

Lancaster

"Thanks for helping me do the dishes, and also for having supper ready when I got home." Sara smiled at Brad as she took the sponge from the sink to wipe the kitchen table.

He winked at her. "Not a problem."

139

She glanced at the clock and saw that it was almost seven. "Your Bible study group should be here soon. Think I'll go to the living room and make sure everything's ready."

Brad stepped over to Sara and slipped his arms around her waist. "Nothing to worry about there. I vacuumed earlier and even dusted." He wiggled his brows. "Since my folks had no girls, Mom taught me how to cook, clean, and do the dishes, so I've had plenty of practice over the years."

"I appreciate everything you do to help out around here." She turned and kissed his cheek. "Oh, and the next time I see your mother, remind me to tell her thanks for raising such a considerate man."

"Thank you, I sure will." He tweaked the end of her nose. "And now, Mrs. Fuller, let's take time for a word of prayer before our guests arrive."

They sat beside each other at the table and held hands. Brad prayed out loud, asking God to bless their time with the new believers and to give him the wisdom to say the right things and share the scriptures that would be most helpful to those in attendance.

He'd just finished praying when the doorbell rang. "Sounds like our first guest has arrived."

With sweaty hands, Sara followed Brad to the front door. She could deal with customers at the flower shop, no problem, but knowing what to say to a group of new Christians was an entirely different matter — especially when she was a fairly new one herself.

When Brad opened the door, he greeted a young couple who introduced themselves as Shawn and Arlene Campbell. He invited them to take seats in the living room, and a few minutes later two more people arrived. Becky Freemont said she was single and attended the local community college. Tim Stapleton, the young man with her, informed Brad that he used to attend Sunday school when he was a boy, but until recently hadn't gone to church regularly.

The final person to arrive was a middle-aged man named Rick Osprey.

Once everyone was seated, Brad opened with prayer and then handed out Bibles and a workbook to each person. "Before we get started," he said, "I thought it would be good if you all took turns telling a little something about yourself, along with how and when you became a Christian." Brad turned to Rick. "Would you like to go first?"

"Umm . . . sure." The man reached up and rubbed his graying sideburns. "I grew up in Lancaster County, and to be honest, I was pretty wild during my teen years and into my young adult life. For a while, I ran around with a group of Amish teenagers who lived in Strasburg — or maybe it was Paradise. They were going through a time of sowing their wild oats. I think they called it *rumspringa.* Oh, and there was this one girl named Reba. . . ." He paused and scratched his head. "Guess it could have been Rhoda or some other name that begins with *R.* Anyway, she said her folks were Christians and even tried to mention God, but I wasn't interested back then. I was having too much fun sowing my own wild oats." He stopped talking and turned to Shawn. "Okay, that's enough about me. It's your turn now."

Shawn began talking, but his words were lost on Sara. All she could think about was the name Rick had mentioned — Rhoda. *Could he have known my mother? Is it possible, by some twist of fate, that this man could be my biological father?* Sara wanted to question him further, but this was not the best time or place. She needed to wait for a better opportunity to ask him some pertinent questions. And she wanted to talk with Brad about it first.

CHAPTER 14

Strasburg

Jesse woke up in a cold sweat. He'd dreamed that Cindy was sick with a high temperature. She kept crying and crying, and nothing Jesse did seemed to calm her. He'd put a cold compress on her forehead, but it didn't bring the fever down.

Would I be able to help my little girl if she got really sick? Jesse asked himself as he rolled out of bed. If things got really bad, he would call for help, of course, but until Cindy was born, he'd never had to take care of a baby. That lack of experience always made him feel unsure of himself.

Jesse went to the window and opened the blinds to look out at the clear summer morning. The more he thought about Vera's suggestion that he find a wife, the more sense it made. If Lenore should agree to marry him, and for some reason Cindy became ill and Lenore wasn't sure what to do, between the two of them, they could probably figure it out. Lenore always seemed calm and had a level head, so she would probably think things through without going into a panic.

"There's no doubt about it," Jesse said out loud. "Two heads are better than one."

A sense of guilt took over when he thought about asking Lenore to marry him when he wasn't in love with her. *Well, I'm not going to worry about that right now. Just need to take things one step at a time.*

As Lenore stood at the kitchen sink Saturday morning, contemplating the meal she'd had with Jesse the night before, Grandma tapped her on the shoulder. "The dishes are done. How long are you going to stand there staring out the window at nothing?"

"It's not nothing. There are plenty of *veggel* in the yard." Lenore turned and smiled at Grandma. "Well, to be truthful, I wasn't really watching the birds."

"What were you watching?"

"Nothing in particular. I was mostly thinking about last night."

Grandma tipped her head. "Your date with Jesse?"

"Jah, only I'm not sure if it was an actual date. He made no mention of wanting to court me."

"What did he talk about?"

"Mostly the history of the part of Kentucky where he's from."

"Interesting, but not very romantic." Grandma's brows moved up and down.

Lenore stepped away from the sink. "I think Jesse might be lonely, and maybe he enjoys my company."

"And well he should." Grandma placed her hand on Lenore's shoulder. "In addition to being blessed with a pretty face, you're smart, kind, and quite capable, I might add."

Lenore snickered. "I believe you're a bit prejudiced because I'm your granddaughter."

"Maybe so, but the words I spoke were true." Grandma moved across the room to the stove and poured herself a cup of coffee. "Would you like some kaffi, Lenore?"

"No, thank you. Is there anything special you'd like me to do today?" Lenore asked. "Maybe pull weeds or pick some produce from the garden?"

Grandma shook her head. "You've worked hard all week. Why don't you take the day off and do something just for fun?"

Lenore tapped her fingers on the edge of

her chin. "I do have one errand I need to run."

"That's not what I would call fun."

"Maybe not, but I promised Sara I would bring in several more of my homemade greeting *kaarte* to sell on consignment in her flower shop."

"You do make some lovely cards. And they've sold quite well in Sara's shop."

"Jah. Her beaded jewelry and keychains have gone over well with her customers too."

"Sara's a busy young woman. I don't know how she finds the time to run her business, do all the duties expected of her as a minister's wife, and make up her lovely beaded items."

"From what I can tell, Sara enjoys what she does, so I'm sure that's why she is able to keep up with it all." Lenore didn't ask the question, but she wondered if Grandma enjoyed all the things she had to do these days. Since Grandpa's stroke, Grandma had more chores to do than ever before. But she'd never heard her complain — she just did what needed to be done with a smile on her face. Hard work and persistence were positive traits both Grandma and Grandpa had passed on to their children and grand-children.

"Were you planning to take your horse

and buggy out to make your card deliveries?" Grandma asked. "Or would you like to give my horse some exercise today?"

"It's such a beautiful summer day, I thought I might either walk to the flower shop or ride my scooter," Lenore replied.

"Won't that be a little difficult with a box full of cards?"

Lenore shook her head. "I'll put them in a wicker basket, and they should be easy to carry. The fresh air and exercise will do me some good."

"All right, dear. Do as you like." Grandma smiled. "Oh, and please tell Sara I said hello and that we hope to see her and Brad soon."

"I will." Lenore hugged her grandmother and hurried from the room to get the greeting cards. If Sara was free, maybe the two of them could have lunch together. It had been awhile since they'd had some one-on-one cousin time.

Outside, Lenore put her wicker basket full of cards inside the metal carrier on the front of her scooter and, using her left foot to push off, headed out of the yard and onto the shoulder of the road.

She'd only made it about halfway into town when a scraggly-looking dog ran out of a nearby field, chasing a rabbit. Lenore swerved to keep from hitting either animal, but in so doing, she lost control. The next thing she knew, the scooter tipped over and she was lying on the pavement, her greeting cards scattered all around.

Jesse whistled as he guided his horse down the road toward the Lapps' farm. Last night Lenore had left her lightweight jacket in his buggy when he'd dropped her off. He was kind of glad — it gave him an excuse to see her again today. Jesse didn't want Lenore to think he was too aggressive in his efforts to court her, but after the dream he'd had in the wee hours this morning, he'd decided that he needed to find a mother for his little girl as soon as possible. Since Cindy liked the Lapps' granddaughter and responded so well to her, Lenore was the logical candidate. Jesse still felt guilty about pursuing a woman he didn't love. The thing that concerned him the most, though, was whether Lenore would be willing to accept his terms for marriage. No pronouncement of love or physical relationship would most likely be a deterrent for her. He'd be taking a risk asking her to be his wife in name only.

He pursed his lips. *Maybe I should forget the silly notion and rely on Vera to watch Cindy for me, like she's doing today. She said she was willing to do it for as long as I needed her.*

Jesse gripped the horse's reins as he continued to wrestle with his indecisiveness. A lump lodged in his throat as a vision of his sweet Esther flashed in his mind. *What would she want me to do? If only I could communicate with her somehow.*

As Jesse drew closer to the Lapps' place, he spotted Lenore on her hands and knees along the shoulder of the road. Beside her a red scooter lay on its side.

Concerned, he guided his horse to the side of the road and stepped out of the buggy. "What happened? Are you all right?"

"A dog chasing a rabbit ran in front of me, and I lost control of my scooter when I swerved to avoid hitting them." Lenore's chin trembled as she looked at him. "The greeting cards I made and was taking to my cousin's flower shop are probably ruined." She gestured to the cards and envelopes scattered about.

Worried about her welfare, Jesse hadn't even noticed them before. "What about you, Lenore? Are you okay?"

"My legs and arms are scraped up some, but I can move them, so I'm sure there are no broken bones."

"I'll help you pick up the cards and then

give you a ride to the flower shop if you like."

"Danki. That would be much appreciated."

Jesse looked around for a place to secure his horse. Seeing a tree along the road a few yards ahead, he led the animal there and tied him to a branch, then joined Lenore in her quest to rescue the cards.

A short time later they had them all picked up. A few had been damaged, but most appeared to be fine. Jesse picked up the scooter and put it in the back of his open buggy, then he helped Lenore, holding her basket full of cards, into the passenger's seat. "Would you rather I take you back to your grandparents' house? You should probably put some antiseptic on the places your legs and arms got scraped right away."

She shook her head with a look of determination. "I'd rather go to Sara's flower shop and drop off these cards. I'm sure she has a first-aid kit on hand so I can tend my wounds there."

"All right then. Just tell me which direction to go and we'll be on our way."

As Sara took down the old window display and began putting up a new one using birdhouses as a focal point, she reflected on last night's Bible study. She couldn't help wondering if the man she'd met there might have known her mother or even her biological father.

Wish I'd had more time to talk to him, Sara thought as she placed a small ceramic bird next to one of the wooden birdhouses her cousin Ben had made. She looked forward to the next Bible study and hoped she would have a chance to speak with Rick Osprey again. She'd have to be careful how she approached the topic, though, so he wouldn't think she was being nosy or infringing on his personal life. Sara didn't want to cut into their time of reading the scriptures either or say anything of a personal nature in front of the others who attended the Bible study.

Sara's attention was captured when she looked out the window and noticed Lenore limping in the direction of the store. Jesse walked beside her, carrying a wicker basket.

Sara stepped down from the display platform and greeted them at the door. "What happened, Lenore? Why are you limping?"

Lenore explained how she'd fallen off her scooter, and said that when Jesse came along, he'd helped her pick up the cards and offered her a ride to the flower shop.

151

"I'm hoping you have some bandages and antiseptic here." Lenore winced as she held out her arm with several nasty scrapes. "My knees got scraped up too, but at least I wasn't seriously hurt." She pointed at the basket in Jesse's hand. "Some of my cards got ruined, but I brought the good ones Jesse and I rescued."

"We can look at those later." Sara motioned toward the back room. "Right now we should tend to those nasty scrapes." She turned to face Jesse. "Please place the basket of cards on the counter. I'll take a look at them as soon as I've taken care of Lenore's wounds. You can sit over there while you wait, if you want."

"Sure, no problem."

Sara gathered up her first-aid kit from her small office and found Lenore sitting in the back room. As she tended her cousin's wounds, she posed a question. "Is Jesse interested in you?"

Lenore blushed. "I — I'm not sure. He did take me out to supper last night."

Sara grinned. "That's a start in the courting process, right?"

"I'm not sure if we are actually courting, but he has been kind to me ever since I started watching his little girl."

"Where is Cindy today?"

"With the great-aunt of Jesse's late wife." Lenore looked down at her bandaged leg. "Thanks for taking care of my injuries."

"No problem. If I was the one who'd gotten hurt, I'm sure you would have done the same for me."

"Of course I would." Lenore squeezed Sara's hand. "I'm so glad you came into our lives."

"Same here. If I hadn't found that letter in Mama's Bible, I never would have discovered her wonderful family I knew nothing about. You and your folks, as well as Grandpa and Grandma, have been a real blessing to me."

Lenore smiled. "You have blessed our lives too."

Glancing toward the door leading to the front of the flower shop, Sara whispered, "And now you're a blessing to Jesse and his daughter."

CHAPTER 15

On the last Friday of July, after Michelle prayed and read her devotional book, she knew without reservation that she needed to speak with Ezekiel again about his desire to move to an Amish community in New York.

Ezekiel had gone out to the barn right after breakfast to feed their horses and Michelle's dog. When he came in and they were seated at the table, she would bring up the subject.

Michelle opened a carton of eggs and cracked four into a bowl. By the time she had them mixed up and frying in a pan, Ezekiel came into the kitchen.

"*Guder mariye.*" He strode across the room and kissed the back of her neck. "Bet those *oier* will taste mighty good."

She turned her head and smiled. "Good morning. There's some leftover sausage warming in the oven to go with the scrambled eggs."

"I'm lucky to have you, Michelle. You take real good care of me."

She smiled briefly, and when the eggs were done, she put them on a platter, along with the sausage links, and placed it on the table. "Would you prefer orange or apple juice?" she asked when he went to the sink to wash his hands.

"Apple sounds good." He took a seat at the table.

Michelle poured them each a glass of juice and sat in the chair beside him. Following their silent prayer, she passed him the eggs and sausage. "I've been thinking and praying about your idea of moving to New York."

"Have you reached a decision?" He gave her full eye contact.

Michelle gave a nod. "If it's what you really want to do, then I'm willing to go with you."

Ezekiel's face broke into a wide smile. "I'm glad. This will be a chance for us to start over in a new place, and I'll be doing something I enjoy instead of working at Mom and Dad's greenhouse." He dished up some eggs and sausage before handing Michelle the platter. "My only concern is how my folks will respond when they hear of our decision to move."

■ ■ ■ ■

As Lenore sat with Cindy on a blanket in the yard, her thoughts went to Jesse. Ever since he'd rescued her from the scooter accident two weeks ago, he'd been more talkative and attentive. She pulled her fingers gently through Cindy's curly hair as she thought more about the little girl's father. Jesse was a kind, gentle man — and rather good looking too. It was probably wrong to be thinking such thoughts when she barely knew the man, but Lenore felt drawn to him.

She reached over and tickled Cindy's bare toes. "Maybe it's you, sweet girl, who makes me think I'm attracted to your daadi. It might just be the special bond that's been made between me and you."

When a pretty butterfly floated in front of them, Cindy clapped her chubby hands and squealed.

"*Fleddermas.*" Lenore pointed as the beautiful monarch landed on a flower close by. "Beautiful butterfly."

Cindy's gaze remained fixed on the monarch, and when it flew farther away, she crawled off the blanket and started across the grass.

Lenore let her go for a little bit, knowing it was good for a child to get in touch with nature through the texture of grass on their skin. She looked up toward the blue sky with puffy white clouds. Spending time outdoors and breathing in fresh air, was good for anyone, no matter their age.

Cindy stopped crawling when a grasshopper zipped in front of her. Lenore held her breath and waited to see what the little girl would do. One hand came out, and then the other as Cindy giggled, rocking back and forth on her knees.

"Hoischreck." Lenore repeated the Pennsylvania Dutch word for grasshopper several times. After reading a book on child care recently, Lenore had learned that talking to a baby was a key part of their language development. It also stated that repetition was the key, because words spoken to a baby became stored away in the child's brain. Eventually they'd be able to use those words and respond to the adult who had spoken to them.

A few seconds went by before the grasshopper hopped away. Cindy swiveled her little body around and crawled back to Lenore. Picking the child up and caressing her face, Lenore struggled not to give in to the tears forming behind her eyes. In such a short time she had formed a strong attachment to this darling little girl. *If only . . . If only you were mine.*

"Dad . . . Mom . . . can we talk to you a minute?" Ezekiel asked when he and Michelle entered the greenhouse.

"Sure, but you'd better make it quick. It's only a matter of time before a slew of customers show up," Ezekiel's father responded. "As you well know, the summer months are our busiest time of year."

Ezekiel shook his head. "I haven't forgotten, and what I have to say won't take long." He slipped his arm around Michelle's waist as she waited nervously for him to proceed.

Ezekiel cleared his throat a couple of times. "Michelle and I have an announcement to make."

His mother's eyes widened, and she clapped her hands. "Are you two in a family way?"

"No, we're not."

Just the mention of being pregnant sent a stab of regret into Michelle's soul.

"What then?" Belinda tipped her head.

"We have an opportunity to move to an Amish community in New York, and I'll be taking over someone's business. I've already talked to the Amish man in Clymer, and the wheels are in motion. Even so, we probably won't make the move till sometime after the new year." Ezekiel undid the top button on his shirt and rubbed his neck. No doubt he felt as apprehensive as Michelle did right now. She didn't like conflict and feared there might be one between Ezekiel and his parents.

Belinda squinted as she pointed a finger at Michelle. "Was this your idea? Did you ask Ezekiel to move because you've never felt welcome in our community here? Because if that's the case, I can assure you —"

Michelle shook her head, but before she could say anything, Ezekiel spoke again. "Moving to New York was my idea, Mom. You and Dad know that I've never been happy working here in the greenhouse. I enjoy working with bees and selling my organic raw honey." He stood rigidly with his hands behind his back.

Belinda's shoulders drooped, and her chin trembled slightly. "But how will we manage without your help here?"

Ezekiel's father nudged her arm. "Didn't you hear what our son said? He's not happy working in the greenhouse."

"I know, but —"

"We'll manage without him. Our son has a right to live where he wants and work at the job of his choosing. We cannot stand in his way." Vernon looked back at Ezekiel. "What kind of business will you be taking over, Son?"

"I'll be making supplies for beekeepers. You know . . . things like hive kits, frames, foundations, and extracting equipment. I'll even be selling protective clothing, honey containers, medications for mite and pest control, as well as all the tools needed for the job of beekeeping." Ezekiel spoke in a bubbly tone. Clearly he was excited about this new venture.

Belinda's voice cracked as she said in a near whisper, "Do what you think is best, Son, and go with our blessing."

A slow smile spread across Ezekiel's face, and he gave both of his parents a hug. "Danki, Mom and Dad."

While Michelle still struggled with mixed emotions concerning their move to New York, she knew in her heart that her place was with her husband. Her throat clogged with tears. But oh, how she dreaded saying goodbye to Mary Ruth and Willis, not to mention Sara, Brad, and all of Ezekiel's family. It would be an adjustment to start over in a strange place, but with God's help they would do it.

CHAPTER 16

The first two weeks of August were busier than ever. Not only was Lenore taking care of Cindy, but she also was putting up garden produce for the winter and getting ready for the new school term. Lenore had gone out to supper with Jesse again, and at Grandma's invitation he'd eaten supper with them on several occasions — including Lenore's birthday last week. Lenore's parents and brothers had been there too, and it had been a fun evening, filled with lively banter and laughter. Sara and Brad were involved in a church activity, so they weren't able to come, but Michelle and Ezekiel had dropped by briefly to wish Lenore a happy birthday.

Grandma had given Lenore a lovely throw pillow for her bed that she'd hand-quilted. Mom gave Lenore a set of pillowcases she'd embroidered along the edges and said it was for her hope chest. Peter and Ben went in on a gift card to Shady Maple in East Earl — the largest restaurant in the area. Dad's gift was a card with some money in it so she could buy whatever she wanted. Even Jesse had brought her a gift — a book on the history of Christian County, Kentucky. All in all it had been a pleasant evening, and the more time Lenore spent with Jesse, the more she liked him. She'd quickly realized that it wouldn't take much for her to fall in love with Cindy's father. But the question was, had he begun to develop any feelings toward her that went beyond friendship? If so, he hadn't verbalized them.

Of course, Lenore reasoned as she placed Cindy in her high chair, *we've only known each other a short time. It's too soon to be thinking of anything more than having Jesse as a friend. I need to be patient and see how things go.*

Cindy slapped her chubby hand against the wooden high chair's tray, scattering Lenore's introspections. "Hold on, sweet girl, and I'll feed you some lunch."

The little girl babbled something unintelligible as she grinned and looked up at Lenore.

"That child sure likes you," Grandma said when she wheeled Grandpa into the kitchen. Even though he could walk with the aid of his cane, he often preferred to use the wheelchair.

Lenore smiled. "I like her too."

"You need a few bopplin of your own," Grandpa mumbled as Grandma pushed him up to the table.

Lenore saw where this discussion might lead, so she quickly changed the topic. "Grandma and I picked lots of *tomaets* this morning." She gestured to the plate full of sliced tomatoes on the table. "They'll go nicely on our ham-and-cheese sandwiches."

"Yum." He smacked his lips.

"Yum." Cindy mimicked him. At least it sounded like she had said "yum."

"Here you go, sweetie." Lenore placed a few pieces of cooked carrots on Cindy's tray and was rewarded with another big grin.

"Bet she won't eat those." Grandpa scrunched his nose.

"Just watch."

Cindy rolled one of the mushy carrots around on the tray a few seconds, picked it up, and popped it right in her mouth.

"See, Willis, you guessed wrong." Grandma took out a loaf of homemade whole-wheat bread and placed it on the table. Lenore opened a container of cooked squash and gave Cindy a taste. The little girl didn't seem to mind that it was cold.

She ate it hungrily and then picked up another carrot Lenore had placed on her tray.

"I'll feed her some applesauce after we've eaten our sandwiches." She glanced at Grandpa, who wore a crooked smile as he watched Cindy eat.

After Grandma joined them at the table, they bowed their heads for silent prayer.

About halfway through the meal, a knock sounded on the back door.

"It's open. Come in," Grandma called.

A few seconds later, Michelle entered the room. Instead of her usual perky stride, she walked with her head down, like she was the bearer of bad news.

"It's good to see you, Michelle. If you haven't had lunch yet, come join us for a sandwich." Apparently oblivious to Michelle's somber mood, Grandma pointed to the empty seat beside Lenore.

Heaving a sigh, Michelle sank into the chair. "I came over here to give you some news."

"I hope it's good news. We surely could use some of that these days." Grandma clasped her hands under her chin, looking at Michelle expectantly.

"Ezekiel and I will definitely be moving to New York in a few months. His parents gave us their blessing, and the business sale is going through."

Grandpa's eyes widened, Lenore dropped the spoon she'd been using to feed Cindy, and Grandma let out a little squeak.

"We'll miss you, of course, but I'm sure you'll make lots of new friends in your new community." Grandma spoke with feeling. "Please tell us a bit more about the new business Ezekiel will be involved in."

Lenore continued to feed Cindy as she listened to Michelle explain the details of the business Ezekiel would be taking over. This certainly seemed like a spontaneous decision — one she hoped they'd prayed about. But it wasn't her place to make any negative comments or throw cold water on their plans, so Lenore kept her thoughts on the matter to herself.

"Ezekiel feels that it's God's will for our lives, so it's not for me to say otherwise," Michelle continued. "We'll come back for visits whenever we can, and we hope our friends and family will be able to come see our new home too." Michelle's tone sounded overly cheerful all of a sudden, but the way she sat slumped in her seat told Lenore that her friend was not entirely thrilled about moving. Lenore felt sorry for Michelle. No doubt she felt forced to move because her husband wanted a change. Being married meant making sacrifices sometimes, and a wife's place was with her husband. No doubt Michelle would adjust to the change once they got to New York and settled in.

Lenore reached over and took her friend's hand. "As Grandma said before, we will miss you, and we'll be sure to keep you in our prayers." She looked at her grandparents. "Isn't that right?"

With a grunt sounding much like one of his previously owned hogs, Grandpa moved his head up and down. Grandma nodded too, but the tears in her eyes could not be concealed. Although Michelle was not part of their family by blood, she'd become like another granddaughter to them. This would be one more adjustment for Grandma and Grandpa to get through. *But I'll be here for them,* Lenore told herself. *And I'll pray for Michelle and Ezekiel — that the move will go smoothly and it will be an easy adjustment for both of them.*

After the lunch dishes were washed and Cindy had been put down for a nap, Lenore felt like taking a walk to the barn. She hadn't read any notes from either of the prayer jars recently and figured she could use some words of inspiration or encouragement.

Sadie greeted Lenore as soon as she entered the barn, wagging her tail and begging for some attention.

"How are you doing, girl? Did you come in here to take a nap or pester the katze?" Too many times Lenore had caught the collie running after one of the cats. She'd never hurt any of them, though — just barked and chased until the felines found a safe place to hide.

Sadie responded by nuzzling Lenore's hand. Then she flopped down with a lazy grunt.

Chuckling, Lenore stepped around the dog and went to fetch the ladder. After climbing it and retrieving the old jar, she took it outside and seated herself at the picnic table. She wanted to read the messages written on several of the slips of paper, and it was too warm and stuffy in the barn to remain there very long. The picnic table was the perfect spot because it was shaded by a huge maple tree, which offered a nice respite from the heat.

Once Lenore was seated on the bench, she opened the lid, reached deep inside, and removed a slip of paper. A verse of scripture had been written on this one, and she read it out loud. " 'Wherefore be ye not unwise, but understanding what the will of the Lord is. Ephesians 5:17.' "

Lenore reflected on the verse a few minutes before taking another note out of the jar. This one was a prayer. "Dear God, please help me learn how to discern Your will. I want to do what's right, but I am so confused."

Lenore rolled her neck from side to side. *What was my aunt Rhoda confused about? If only I would find a note in one of the jars that would explain things better. Did she know when she left home that she would never connect with any of her family again?*

"Lenore, the boppli's awake and crying pretty hard," Grandma called from the house. "Do you want me to change her *windel*?"

"No, that's okay," Lenore shouted through cupped hands. "I'll be right there."

She got up and headed back to the barn to put the jar away. The next time Lenore had a free moment, she would come back out and read a few more of the notes her aunt had written. Surely one of them would reveal more information.

CHAPTER 17

Lancaster County was in the middle of a sweltering, overly humid heat wave. Farmers across the road from Lenore's grandparents' home toiled under the blistering sun, while young barefoot children found solace in nearby ponds, where they swam, fished, and enjoyed the simple pleasure of being together in a place where it was cooler. School would be starting in ten days, and then it would be back to books and a more structured schedule. For Lenore, that meant giving up precious time spent with Cindy as she returned to her job of teaching. Since Jesse had not found anyone to replace Lenore, his wife's great-aunt had agreed to watch his baby daughter again.

"I'm gonna miss you, sweet girl," Lenore murmured, taking a seat on the porch swing and placing Cindy in her lap.

The child leaned heavily against Lenore's chest while sucking her thumb.

Sighing, Lenore stroked Cindy's silky curls, admiring the softness of the baby's pretty hair. What she wouldn't give to have a child like this. Although teaching was a satisfying profession, it didn't compare to the joy of motherhood. Not that Lenore knew firsthand what it was like to have children, but she'd witnessed plenty of interactions between mothers and their little ones to realize how much she longed to be a parent.

As she got the swing moving rhythmically, Lenore closed her eyes and listened to the cicadas singing their summer song from nearby trees.

Sara took a seat at her desk to compare the figures in the ledger of the previous month to the profit the shop had made so far in August. The flower shop had done well this summer, and as far as she could tell, word of mouth seemed to be the best form of advertising. Sara's assumption came from all the positive comments she'd received when people came into the store and mentioned they'd heard about it from a friend or relative.

Sara looked at the perpetual calendar on her desk, filled with beautiful pictures of Amish country that an English man who'd grown up in Pennsylvania had taken. Flipping the page over each day was a continual reminder of how much she loved living here. She hoped Brad would be able to continue serving as pastor to the church in Lancaster for a good many years. Sara couldn't imagine having to move away from Grandma and Grandpa.

Her thoughts went to Michelle and Ezekiel. Ezekiel had family here, and Michelle had established a good many friends. Starting over would be quite an adjustment — especially not knowing anyone in their new Amish community.

Sara tapped her pen against the ledger. Life was full of changes — some good, some not so beneficial. Certain people adjusted to change easily, while others resisted it and felt depression or anger about their circumstances.

She closed her eyes briefly. *God, please grant me the courage to accept any changes that might be in my husband's and my future.*

Sara's cell phone rang, and she was quick to answer when the caller ID showed it was her husband. "Hi, Brad. How's it going?"

"Good. I'm just calling to remind you that tonight's Bible study will begin at six, since I invited everyone for grilled burgers."

"I haven't forgotten, and I'll make sure to

pick up a couple of salads and some baked beans at the deli before I head home."

"Sounds good. See you later, hon."

"Oh, before you hang up — have you heard anything from Rick Osprey . . . about whether he plans to attend Bible study tonight?"

"No, I haven't, but since he only came to the first one and we haven't seen him at church, I'm guessing he won't be coming."

"Have you tried calling him?"

"Yes, several times, but all I've gotten is his voice mail. I don't have his address, just a cell number, or I'd drop by his house to check on him."

"That's too bad. Guess we'll have to wait and see whether he shows up or not. I'll see you in a few hours, Brad."

Sara clicked her phone off and glanced at the inspirational quote on today's calendar page: *How much better off we'd be if we learned to listen to God's still, small voice, instead of trying to do things our own way.*

"Okay, Lord, I get the message," Sara said out loud. "If it's meant for me to speak with Mr. Osprey again, it will happen in Your time."

Jesse's palms felt so sweaty he could barely hold on to his horse's reins. He was head-

172

ing to the Lapps' on a mission, and it wasn't just to pick up Cindy. Today he planned to ask Lenore if he could continue seeing her socially after she started teaching school. What he really wanted to do was ask her to give up teaching and marry him, but it was too soon for a proposal. If Jesse asked Lenore to become his wife without a proper time of courting, she might figure out that he had an ulterior motive.

Vera can't watch Cindy indefinitely, and in addition to caring for my little girl, I need someone to run my household. These were selfish thoughts, but Jesse was concerned about Cindy's need to have someone care for her on a full-time basis, not just a few hours a day. And he sure couldn't ask Lenore to move into his house without marrying her. This was a delicate situation, and he needed to proceed with caution.

The Lapps' collie barked a friendly greeting as Jesse guided his horse and buggy up the lane. Seeing Lenore by the clothesline, he headed in that direction as soon as his horse was secured to the rail.

Sadie ran beside him, barking and wagging her tail. Jesse paused briefly to give the dog a few pats.

"Need some help taking the clothes down?" He pointed to the partially filled wicker basket.

Lenore's dimples deepened as she smiled up at him and nodded. "It's kind of you to offer."

Jesse removed a bulky towel from the line. "How'd my little maedel do today?"

"Very well. She has a good appetite and is learning how to feed herself some foods."

Jesse grinned as Lenore filled him in on what Cindy had eaten for lunch. "She's growing so fast; it won't be long before she'll be ready to eat big people's food."

Lenore took down two hand towels and placed them in the basket. "Jah, babies don't stay little long enough. Just like the vegetable plants in my grandma's garden, they shoot right up, and before you know it they're ready for harvest." Lenore giggled. "Guess there's really no comparing your daughter to produce from the garden though."

He laughed. "There is in the respect that both grow quickly."

"Jah."

Jesse removed several more pieces of laundry, and Lenore did the same. She was about to pick up the basket when he stopped her. "I'll carry it up to the house for you. But first I'd like to ask you a question."

"Certainly. What do you want to know?"

"You will be teaching school again soon, and I won't be bringing Cindy over here every day anymore." Jesse paused and moistened his dry lips. "So . . . I was wondering . . . Would it be all right if we continue to see each other socially?"

Lenore's cheeks turned a pretty pink as she moved her head slowly up and down. "I would like that, Jesse."

He bent down and picked up the basket. "That's good. Jah, it's a real good thing."

Sara listened with interest as Brad shared a passage of scripture with those who had come to their barbecue and Bible study. " 'Let not your heart be troubled: ye believe in God, believe also in me.' You see," Brad continued, "as a new believer, you may be tempted to become discouraged when things don't go well. It's easy to find ourselves questioning God." He placed his hand on the open Bible. "That's why it's important to study the scriptures and seek God's will in all you do."

All heads nodded in agreement. The participants were obviously eager to learn about God.

Sara thought about Rick Osprey. As expected, he hadn't shown up. It was too bad he couldn't be here to take part in this study for new Christians. Sara hoped that nothing had discouraged him or, worse, that he'd given up on his faith. Perhaps it was the reason they hadn't seen or heard from him these past several weeks. Or could it be that the questions Sara asked him during the first Bible study had made him nervous? Did he suspect she was Rhoda's daughter? Was he trying to avoid her? But how could he know what was on her mind? Sara hadn't mentioned her mother or said anything about trying to find her biological father that evening. Yet she supposed the discussion they'd had about his teen and young adult years might have hit a nerve.

I am being paranoid, Sara told herself. *After searching and asking questions of people who knew Mama during her teen years and coming up with nothing, I'm grasping at straws. Rick may not have known my mother.*

She shifted on the unyielding picnic bench, trying to find a more comfortable position. *I need to put my obsession with finding my father aside and get on with the business of living and being a good wife.*

CHAPTER 18

Early Monday morning, August 26, Lenore entered the schoolhouse and placed her things on her desk. At the moment, her thoughts were conflicted. While it felt good to sit behind a teacher's desk again, she missed the joy of caring for Cindy and visiting with Jesse when he came by after work to pick up his daughter. But she would see them at church this Sunday, and Grandma had invited Jesse to bring Cindy to their house for Sunday evening supper. That was certainly something to look forward to. In the meantime, Lenore needed to focus on getting acquainted with the scholars who attended this school.

She glanced at the battery-operated clock on the far wall. It was eight fifteen, and school started at eight thirty sharp, so the children should be arriving soon.

Since Lenore had not taught this group of scholars before and didn't know how well

177

they conducted themselves, she hoped there would be no behavioral problems. At the last school where she'd taught, one boy in particular had been a challenge at first. She'd worked diligently to teach him, as well as the rest of the students, how important it was to practice the Golden Rule in class and during recess. But Thomas Beiler, full of mischief and a bit hyperactive, had stretched her patience several times when he teased other children or defied the classroom rules.

Lenore had learned during her years of teaching never to let things get out of control or give one of her students the upper hand. The goal of every good teacher was to teach her pupils the skills needed to lead a useful Amish life, as well as how to function and do business in the outside world. In Amish schools children were taught reading, writing, arithmetic, English, and history. All of these skills would be needed once the scholars graduated school after finishing the eighth grade. From there, some boys would go back to the farm to learn agriculture skills. Others might serve an apprenticeship to Amish shop owners or other businesspeople in the area. Girls polished their homemaker skills under the guidance of their mothers, and some might work outside the home for other Amish or to keep house for a local English family.

Lenore's thoughts were pushed aside when she heard the sound of children's laughter outside the schoolhouse.

Pulling in a deep breath, she left her desk and went to ring the bell, announcing the start of the school day and letting the scholars know it was time to come inside.

Things went well during the first part of the day, and Lenore's assistant teacher, Viola Weaver, was a big help.

At ten o'clock, Lenore dismissed the children for morning recess. They were encouraged to use the outhouse, get a drink of water, and sharpen their pencils so that these things would not need to be done during class. When those items had been taken care of, it was time to go outside and play. With thirty children in the class, ranging from first to eighth grade, it would be difficult to start an activity they all could engage in and enjoy. Lenore got a game of baseball going for the older ones, while Viola kept an eye on the younger ones as they enjoyed swinging and climbing on the old-fashioned wooden playground equipment.

The ball game was going at full speed when a young girl named Linda ran out of the girls' outhouse, hollering as though there were no tomorrow.

Lenore ran quickly to the child. "What's wrong? Are you hurt?"

"Der weschp hot ihr gschtoche." Linda's sister, Katie, pointed to the wasp nest outside the girls' outhouse.

Lenore felt immediate concern hearing that one of the children had been stung by a wasp. She would look in the shed behind the schoolhouse to see if there was any insecticide she could spray on the nest. Before she had a chance to do that, however, one of the older boys rushed up to her. "Don't worry, Teacher. I'll take care of the nest while you tend to Linda's arm."

She gave him an appreciative nod. "Thank you, Andrew." Lenore took Linda's hand. "Let's go inside and I'll put some drawing salve on that stinger."

Sniffling all the way, the little girl went willingly with Lenore across the yard. Glancing over her shoulder before stepping inside, Lenore was glad to see Viola take charge of the little ones again while the older children continued playing ball. She hoped things would go better the rest of the day.

Before recess was over, Lenore had Linda resting at her desk while the salve was doing its job. She looked over at the child, sitting at her desk with her head down. "I'll be back in a few moments, Linda."

"Okay."

Lenore opened the schoolhouse door and stepped onto the porch, looking out toward the sunny schoolyard. All the children were busy playing. She saw Andrew and called to him. "Did you take care of the nest?"

"Yes, I sprayed it real good then knocked it down after that. I even looked around the rest of the building but didn't see any more wasps or nests."

"That's good to know. Thank you for taking care of it so quickly."

"You're welcome, Teacher."

Lenore went back inside and checked on Linda. "How does your arm feel now?" she asked.

"It doesn't hurt as much as it did."

"I'm glad to hear that." Lenore lifted the child's arm and turned it gently so she could see the lightly reddened spot better. Then she carefully rubbed away the dried medicine. "I don't see any sign of the stinger in there. I think you should be all right now."

Linda grinned. "Thank you, Teacher. That was real scary being stung by a wasp."

"I'm sure it was. But don't worry anymore, because the nest is gone now." Lenore glanced at the clock on the wall across the room. "It's time to start class, so I'm going to call the other children."

Lenore rang the bell and watched as the scholars filed in and took their seats. A few of them had stopped to get a second drink of water, but soon all the children were at their desks, looking up at her with expectant expressions.

She took a seat at her desk. "Before we begin, I wanted to let you all know that Linda is doing fine after getting stung by a wasp."

The child bobbed her blond head, and many of the students smiled.

Lenore tapped the little bell on her desk. "All right now, class, grades three through eight will have reading class with me, while Viola works with the first and second grades on their numbers in their workbook."

The older students began reading their lesson for the day, preparing to answer Lenore's questions that would determine their reading comprehension. Once the children had been given sufficient time to read their lesson, Lenore called each grade in turn up to the front of the room to read some and answer her questions.

As the children read, Lenore got up and opened a few windows to bring some fresh air into the stuffy room. With summer still in full swing, the days could get rather warm. But not too far in the future, fall would arrive.

Earlier this morning, Viola had mentioned that her dad had read in the local paper's forecast that rain was on its way. Viola was anticipating the rain eagerly because it would cool things off and help to freshen the stale humid air. Lenore had to agree, but she still preferred the warmer summer weather.

She smiled to herself. Teaching again felt good, and so far she had stayed in control. She hoped the rest of the day would go as well.

"How are things here today?" Ivan asked when he entered Mary Ruth's kitchen.

"Lenore started teaching again, and it's been so quiet around here I scarcely know what to do with myself." Mary Ruth's forehead wrinkled. "I miss Jesse's sweet little girl too. If I didn't have the responsibility of caring for your daed, I may have volunteered to watch Cindy myself."

Ivan shook his head. "Watching a boppli is a full-time job, and since you have enough on your hands taking care of Dad, I'm glad you didn't volunteer to watch Jesse's baby." He glanced around. "And speaking of Dad,

183

where is he right now? Didn't see him in the living room when I first came in, and I wanted to check with him and see if there are any specific chores he'd like me to do before I head back to the store."

Mary Ruth's mouth puckered as she picked up the coffeepot to fill it with fresh water. "That's strange. After lunch, with the use of his cane, he went to the living room and sat in his favorite chair. Maybe he got up and made his way down the hall to the *baadschtubb*."

"I don't think so, Mom. When I came down the hall, the door to the bathroom was open, and I didn't see any sign of Dad." Ivan leaned on the counter near the sink. "Maybe he decided to take a nap and went to your room to lie down."

She set the coffeepot down. "He usually naps in his chair, but I'll go to our room and check, in case he decided to go there."

Mary Ruth left the kitchen and shuffled down the hall. When she arrived at their door and found it slightly ajar, she opened it a little further and stepped inside. A chill ran up her spine. Willis lay facedown on the floor near the foot of their bed. Could he have stumbled and fallen? Become dizzy and passed out?

"Willis, can you hear me?"

He lay there unmoving.

Fear gripped Mary Ruth's chest like a vise. She wasn't strong enough to pick up her husband and put him on the bed, but she needed to get him off the floor and evaluate his condition.

She cupped her trembling hands around her mouth and hollered, "Ivan! Come quick! Your daed's fallen, and I can't get him to wake up."

CHAPTER 19

Sara had just finished waiting on a customer when Brad came into the shop, wide-eyed and with deep furrows lining his forehead. "I got an urgent call from your uncle Ivan about twenty minutes ago. He asked me to come here right away and get you." He moved close to her desk. "We'll go by the schoolhouse and get Lenore next."

Sara blinked rapidly as she stared up at him. "You're scaring me. What is it, Brad?"

"Your grandma found your grandpa on the floor of their bedroom, and she couldn't get him to wake up. Fortunately, Ivan was at their house. He got ahold of me as soon as he called 911."

"Is . . . is Grandpa gonna be okay?" Her voice wavered as she clutched the pen in her hand.

"They don't know yet. He's been taken to the hospital in Lancaster. From the way Ivan talked, it didn't sound good." Brad gestured to the front door. "We'd better go now."

"Okay, just let me tell Misty I'm going." As Sara headed for the back room on shaky legs, images of what might happen flashed through her mind. She paused at the door of the other room and closed her eyes. *Dear Lord, please let Grandpa be okay, and be with my dear grandma right now. She must be so worried and afraid.*

"I am surprised to see you here. Aren't you supposed to be at your shop this time of the day?" Lenore asked when Sara entered the schoolhouse and hurried up to Lenore's desk. Most visitors didn't show up at school right in the middle of class.

"Grandpa's in the hospital, and Brad's waiting outside in the van to take us there." Sara spoke breathlessly. "Can you dismiss school early and come with us now?"

"School will be out in half an hour, and my assistant can take over for the rest of the day." Heart pounding and mouth quivering, Lenore rushed over to Viola and explained the situation.

"Of course I'll take charge of the class." Viola placed her hand on Lenore's arm. "I'm sorry about your grandfather. I'll pray that everything will turn out for the best."

187

Lenore managed a weak smile, got her purse, and followed her cousin out the door. As they headed for Brad's van, Sara slipped her arm around Lenore's waist. "Grandpa's going to be okay. He has to be."

Lancaster

"Where's Grandpa? Is he going to be all right?" Lenore drew in several quick breaths in an effort to calm herself. When she, Sara, and Brad entered the waiting room, they saw Grandma huddled beside Lenore's dad. The scene was almost too painful to bear. Her grandmother's unfocused stare and the grim twist of her mouth let Lenore know Grandpa's situation must be grave.

"My daed's suffered a heart attack, but we won't know how bad it was until the doctors have finished examining him," Lenore's father explained. "I did CPR on him before the paramedics came to the house, but I'm not sure it did any good." He leaned forward, rubbing a spot on the bridge of his nose.

Sara and Lenore went down on their knees in front of Grandma, while Brad stood behind her chair with his hands resting on her trembling shoulders. "Let's pray." Brad spoke quietly but with assurance.

All heads bowed as he prayed out loud:

"Heavenly Father, please be with Willis right now, as well as those who are caring for him. If it be Your will, we ask for complete healing. If not, then give us the grace to accept the outcome and the courage to go on without Willis should You decide to take him. We ask it all in the name of Jesus. Amen."

Grandma sniffed and wiped the tears running down her cheeks with the tissue Sara handed her. "I can't imagine my life without my dear husband, but if it's God's will to take him, then I'll have to accept it and go on. That's what Willis would want me to do."

"It's not easy to accept it as God's will when someone you love dies." Sara's tone was filled with emotion. Lenore figured her cousin must be thinking about when her mother had died. No doubt Sara had questioned God many times and perhaps had never fully come to grips with her loss.

Lenore stiffened. "We're being too negative. Grandpa is going to be fine. He got better after his stroke, and I believe he'll get better this time."

With a slow nod, Grandma sank into a chair. Everyone else took seats too and talked quietly until Lenore's mother and brothers arrived.

"How's Grandpa doing?" Peter asked, clutching his father's shoulder.

"We don't know yet. He's still being examined. They're running some tests to see how bad his heart is." Dad rubbed his eyes. "That's why we're all waiting out here." He looked over at Mom. "Who's minding the store, or did you put the Closed sign in the window?"

"I left Anna in charge, and Becky is also there to help out. The boys and I wanted to be here, and I'm sure everything at the store will be fine with our two capable employees in control."

"Okay." Dad blew out his breath with a puff of air that lifted the hair off his forehead. "I hope we hear something soon. I've never been good at waiting for things, and I'm nearly out of patience."

A short time later, a doctor came in and approached Grandma. "We did all we could for your husband, Mrs. Lapp, and I'm sorry to have to tell you this, but unfortunately, his heart gave out. Willis is gone and is now resting in peace."

Lenore's fingers touched her parted lips, and Sara stifled a gasp. Grandma, however, merely stood and said, "May I please see him?"

The doctor nodded. "Of course. Follow me."

"I'm coming too." Lenore's father got up and, pressing a fist against his chest, followed his mother out of the room.

Sara reached over and clasped Lenore's hand. "I . . . I can't believe our dear grandpa is gone."

Lenore's throat felt too swollen for her to talk. All she could manage was a nod.

Within the next three days, Grandpa's body would be laid to rest, and everything about their family's life would be forever changed. All they would have left of Grandpa were the memories they'd made with him over the years.

Mary Ruth and Ivan followed the doctor through the first set of double doors and then through another set. The doctor turned to them. "We have a little walk yet. We'll be going down a couple of floors to where he is."

Mary Ruth saw the bank of elevators and dreaded what was coming. They took the first one available, despite the busy foot traffic around them. Mary Ruth looked toward her feet as she rode the elevator down to their stop. When the doors opened, they were in front of a small nurses' station. A

191

vase with flowers stood welcoming them on the receptionist desk, but Mary Ruth barely took notice. One of the female staff members came over and led them to the room Willis was in.

Once at the doorway, the doctor expressed his condolences and apologized again that he couldn't save Willis. Then he dismissed himself.

Mary Ruth stood beside Ivan for a moment, trying to let it all sink in, while the nurse waited with a somber expression. "You may go in and see your husband, Mrs. Lapp."

Mary Ruth nodded. She reached out to her son with trembling hands and held on to his arm. "I'm so glad you're here with me, Ivan. I never imagined how difficult this part of marriage was going to be." Mary Ruth paused. "I know we need to do this, saying goodbye to your father and my dear, beloved husband, but it's taking all my strength and determination."

"I know, Mom, and we'll do this together." Ivan's eyes filled with tears. He waited until she was ready, then walked alongside her into the intensely quiet room.

She clung to his arm the whole way, while the lump in her throat grew larger. The closer they got to his lifeless form lying on the cot, the slower Mary Ruth moved. *This doesn't seem real to me. If only it was a terrible dream.* She wiped at the uncontrollable tears with the tissue she'd tucked inside her dress sleeve.

When they came up to his bed, Mary Ruth stared at Willis, then closed her eyes tightly as memories of the two of them on their wedding day began to flow, along with more tears. Their courting also came to her like it happened just yesterday, and she recalled so vividly how sweet his manner was and how often he'd made her laugh.

She also remembered with sadness the time Willis had said that he hoped when the good Lord decided to take them, they'd leave the earth together. It was a pleasant thought but apparently was not meant to be.

Mary Ruth placed her hand upon his sheet-covered shoulder and wept. *The love of my life is gone, and it didn't happen the way he had hoped. Oh, how am I going to manage without him?*

Ivan stood with his mother as she weeped. It broke every bit of his heart to hear her cry like this. His mind went back to the beginning of the day. He had never thought for a moment that his father would be gone.

Is it awful of me to wish that he was only sleeping? It seemed like Dad would simply wake up and things would be the same again. Ivan looked away from his father, swiping at his own tears. *I will miss him so much. What a good role model he was for me and Rhoda. Too bad she's not here to say her goodbyes with me and Mom.* Ivan choked back a sob. He'd missed out on a lot when his sister left home. When they were children they used to be so close. *What went wrong that she would just up and run off, never to be heard from again? What Rhoda did to Mom and Dad was unforgivable, yet they both forgave her.*

Ivan clenched his fingers into his palms, wondering if he had ever truly forgiven his sister for running away. *If my sister had stayed put in Strasburg and let Dad and Mom help raise her baby, maybe she would still be alive. She'd be right here in this room, grieving like me and helping Mom through this traumatic ordeal.*

Ivan moved closer to his mother. "It will be all right, Mom. I'm here for you, and so is Lenore and the rest of our family. You can count on us for anything you need."

Mom gave a brief nod, and Ivan's river of tears increased as he listened to her speak to his father. "I will miss you so very much,

Willis. You brought me such joy and made me feel so alive."

Ivan let go of her to grab some tissues from a box on the nearby counter. He swallowed hard and struggled to speak. "I can't believe he's gone. Things just won't be the same without him."

Mom turned her head to look at Ivan. "I feel so numb."

"I understand. This is hard for us, but I'm confident that Dad is in a better place."

"Yes, he is. Your father is free from this life and at home with Jesus now."

They stood and talked together about Dad, going over the final days and hours leading to his passing.

Mom leaned against Ivan, as though needing support. "As much as it hurts to say this, it was your daed's time to go. The Lord was ready to receive him." She dabbed at the tears beneath her eyes. "We'll need to take care of the funeral arrangements and make sure it's all done right."

"Yes, and don't worry, Mom, because Yvonne and I will take care of most of the details for you. I'm certain Lenore, Ben, and Peter will help out with a good many things that need to be done too."

"And don't forget about Sara. She's part of our family as well."

"You're right, but she is not familiar with our Amish ways and funeral practices."

"She will still want to help, and I'll tell her what needs to be done. It will be a challenge to get through the next several days, but as long as we're together, it will be easier." A fleeting smile crossed her face. "I remember how I used to leave most of the decision-making up to your father. Now I've got to try to take things over. Makes me wonder how some families get through this time of loss without help."

"Don't worry. We'll all be there for you." He gave her arm a gentle squeeze. "When you're ready to talk about it, we'll need to discuss where you're going to live."

Mom didn't say anything. She moved closer to the bed and reached out for Dad's unmoving hand.

Now's not the time or place to discuss this, Ivan thought. *But after the funeral is over, I'll talk to Mom again about moving in with me and Yvonne. She needs someone to look after her now that Dad is gone. And we are available to do it.*

Back in the waiting room, Sara waited with Brad, Yvonne, and Lenore and her brothers — everyone looking so sad.

"I think I'll get something to drink. Would

either of you like anything to eat or drink?" Brad glanced in the direction of the cafeteria.

Sara shook her head.

"No thanks. I'm not thirsty or hungry right now." Lenore's tone was dull as she sat slumped in her chair.

"I'll go with you." Peter left his chair.

"Me too," Ben said. "I could use something cold to drink."

Sara sat in silence as Brad and her cousins walked across the carpeted floor out into the hallway and disappeared from view. The waiting area had gotten quieter, which suited Sara just fine. She thought about her grandfather and the times she'd spent with him. It was hard to accept that he was really gone. It would seem so strange going over to her grandparents' house and Grandpa not being there to greet her with his contagious smile.

She squeezed her eyes shut, willing herself not to break down. If she gave way to the sob she kept valiantly pushed down, she might never stop crying. *Grandma will need a lot of support from me and the rest of the family. I will try to help her through this the best way I can.*

Lenore shifted in her chair, glancing toward the windows on the far side of the room. "Looks like it's trying to rain out there."

"I don't care if it rains." Sara looked toward the window and then back at Lenore. "It's true, life does go on."

"What do you mean?"

"Just that everyone is going through different things at the same time. We've received bad news today, while others around us may have gotten some good news."

"You're right, Sara," Aunt Yvonne spoke up. She'd been awfully quiet up until now. Perhaps she'd been thinking about the grief her husband and mother-in-law were dealing with as they viewed Grandpa's body.

Sara looked toward the double doors Grandma and Ivan had walked through a while ago. *I don't know how Grandma and Uncle Ivan could manage the strength to go see Grandpa. I'm not ready yet. I only want to remember him the way he was.*

Brad came into view with his beverage and went over to the window. He stood there and stared out for a while, as though deep in thought. Sara saw the vapors rising from his coffee and smelled the robust aroma, but she had no desire for any. The tears behind Sara's eyes nearly spilled forth as she thought about how Grandpa had always enjoyed a good cup of coffee. She remembered well seeing him looking out the living room window, watching the birds at their feeders, while slowly sipping his steaming brew. *Grandpa. Oh Grandpa. I miss you already. If only we could have had more time to spend together.*

Sara's limp hands lay loosely together in her lap as she remembered something she should have done as soon as they received the news that Grandpa had been rushed to the hospital. "Oh no — I can't believe I forgot to call Kenny." Sara lifted her hands and placed them against her hot cheeks. "He needs to know about Grandpa's passing."

"Would you like me to make the call for you?" Brad asked, moving back across the room and taking the seat beside her.

Sara shook her head. "No, I should be the one to tell him." She rose from her chair. "I'll look for a more private spot to talk to my brother. He's going to be shocked when I tell him the news." Without waiting for Brad's response, she hurried from the room.

Lenore stood up. "I need to stretch my legs." She walked over to the windows and looked out at the strip of dark clouds in the sky. It had begun to rain, and she could see scattered thundershowers as well. She stood for several minutes, trying to come to grips with all that had occurred, but her brain felt so fuzzy it was hard to think clearly. Turning away from the windows, she walked back to her chair and sat down.

Lenore teared up when Mom reached over and clasped her hand. "Are you okay?"

"Yes. No. I'm not sure anything will ever be okay again. I'm worried about Grandma. What's she going to do now that Grandpa is gone? They loved each other so much, and it's going to be ever so hard for her to go on without him."

"You're right, it won't be easy, but with all of our support, plus her strong faith in God, your *grossmudder* will make it."

Lenore glanced over at a hospital worker as he held one of the double doors open. Two figures emerged.

"They're back." She rose to her feet.

Lenore's mother stood up too, as did Brad.

Grandma came up to them, holding a crumpled tissue in one hand. "Grandpa is at rest, and I am confident that he is with the Lord."

"Even seeing him lying there, with no breath passing between his lips, I'm still trying to get used to the idea that he is gone." Dad's form seemed weakened as his shoulders slumped.

"Would you like me to pull my van up to the door?" Brad asked, looking at Grandma.

Sniffling, she nodded. "Yes, that would be appreciated."

Sara entered the room, and seeing Grandma, she pulled her into a hug. With tears rolling down her cheeks, she hugged Lenore's dad too. "We'll get through this together."

Lenore rubbed her forehead in an area that had begun to pound. It was upsetting to see the sadness in her grandmother's normally happy face. *Poor Grandma. I wish I could say or do something to take away her pain.*

CHAPTER 20

Strasburg

During Grandpa's funeral service, held in his and Grandma's home, Sara and the rest of her family sat on folding chairs a short distance from the very plain coffin made of poplar wood. She was told it had been constructed by a local Amish man who owned a woodshop and primarily made caskets for the Amish. It was wider at the shoulders than at the head and feet. The lid came to a peak. It had two parts: one that went across the lower body, and the other that had a two-part hinge so it could be folded open to allow viewing of the upper part of the deceased's body. Sara's cousin Ben had informed her that the Lancaster Amish cover the upper part of the coffin with a sheet during the funeral. The coffin had no handles or any veneer. It was simple in its construction and had no internal padding. The final resting place for the coffin would be in the local Amish cemetery.

This was Sara's first experience attending an Amish funeral, and she'd asked all three of her cousins a good many questions beforehand so she might understand better what was happening. She'd learned that usually people in the community who died were buried three days later. Their bodies were taken to a funeral home for embalming and then brought to the family's home.

Sara had also been told that family members, friends, and acquaintances would be able to view the body before the day of the funeral. When the first viewing took place, Grandpa's body had been placed in his open coffin in the dining room. When Sara and Brad had arrived for that viewing, she was surprised to see that the room the casket was placed in had been stripped of all furniture and decorations. The second viewing would take place at the end of today's funeral service.

Grandpa had been dressed in a white shirt, white vest, and white pants. No flowers or decorations of any kind softened the experience, and no eulogy was given, as in most English funerals or memorial services.

The first minister stood near the coffin. He spoke on the creation of the world, pointing out that Adam was created from dust and each person must return to dust. The minister read John 5:20–30, which spoke of the resurrection of the dead.

The second minister gave the main funeral sermon, and he read from 1 Corinthians 15, starting at verse 35 and continuing to the end, including the words, "O death, where is thy sting? O grave, where is thy victory?"

Very little was said about the deceased, because the Amish believe that God, not man, should be praised. They learned from an early age that their focus should be not so much on this world but on the world yet to come.

The reading of the obituary came at the end of the service, after the closing prayer and benediction. As in most Amish communities, the obituary included the deceased's name, age, date of birth, date of death, and number of descendants.

Sara wished Brad could have preached a sermon during Grandpa's funeral. At least then she would have understood everything being said. It had been difficult for her to listen to a sermon spoken in German, with only a few English words thrown in now and then. Sara still couldn't accept that her precious grandfather was gone. It pained her to think that she hadn't known him very long, and now there would be no more chances to spend time with him — at least not here on this earth.

I was cheated of spending more time with my mother too, Sara thought with regret. *Mama was too young when she died.*

She glanced to her left and saw her brother, Kenny, sitting on the other side of Brad. He too had been cheated out of time spent with Grandpa Lapp — he'd known his Amish grandparents for an even shorter time than Sara.

She thought of her stepfather, Dean, and how hard it had been on Kenny when his father died. She curled her fingers into her palms. Dean's death had affected Sara as well — especially once she'd come to realize how much he had actually cared about her. *So many regrets and so many unnecessary misunderstandings. Life certainly has its ups and downs, and each person must learn how to cope with them.*

Sara shifted on her chair and swallowed hard to push down the sob rising in her throat. *What's Grandma going to do now without Grandpa? They were so close, and she never seemed to mind taking care of him.*

Sara thought about the vows she'd exchanged with Brad on their wedding day: "For better, for worse, for richer, for poorer, in sickness and in health." If she were to become sick, Sara had no doubt that Brad would take care of her. And if her husband got sick or injured, she would be there for him too. A loving marriage, bound by the vows the wedding couple had made, required commitment through good times and bad. Sara's grandparents were a fine example of that, and their legacy would live on.

Her gaze went to Lenore. On the outside, she seemed to be handling things well, but no doubt she was also hurting today, as were her brothers. Sara's cousin was loving, kind, and strong in her faith, but she was also human. She had grown up spending a lot of time with her grandparents, so losing Grandpa could not be easy — for Lenore, Peter, or Ben. It had to be especially difficult for Uncle Ivan to lose his father. From what Sara had observed, he and Grandpa had a close father-son relationship.

Sara looked in Ivan's direction. *I wonder if he will insist on Grandma moving in with him and Yvonne. Or will Lenore continue to live here with Grandma? Since Jesse has begun courting Lenore, they might end up getting married. If so, maybe they'll live with Grandma, unless they decide to get their own home somewhere in the area.*

Someone sniffled. It didn't take long to realize the noise came from Michelle. From the pained expression on the young woman's face, Sara knew her friend — even though she was not a member of the Lapp family — grieved the loss of Grandpa as much as she and the other family members did.

Following the funeral service, four of Willis's friends carried his body from the house to the black, horse-drawn hearse. They traveled in a solemn procession with other buggies to the graveyard where he would be buried. These same four friends, acting as pallbearers, had dug the grave beforehand.

At her husband's gravesite, Mary Ruth, dressed in black just like the other mourners, stood between her two granddaughters. Her legs felt like they might buckle at any minute, and she was thankful Lenore and Sara had put their arms around her for support. Brad stood on the other side of Sara, and to the right of Lenore stood Ivan, Yvonne, Peter, and Benjamin. Other mourners, including Michelle and Ezekiel and all of his family, were nearby, along with many people from their church district. Because Willis had been a minister for a good many years, he would be missed by everyone in their church, as well as many in the surrounding communities.

Tears stung the back of Mary Ruth's eyes as Willis's casket was lowered into the ground. Their bishop read a hymn as the grave was covered with dirt, and he continued reading until the job had been finished. She bit the inside of her cheek, struggling to keep her emotions in check. Mary Ruth would not give in to the tears begging to be released. She had to remain strong for her family's sake. She would have plenty of time when she was alone to give in to her grief and allow the tears to flow unchecked.

Mary Ruth thought about the plain Amish tombstone that would be placed over the spot where her husband was buried. It would simply state Willis's name, his birth and death dates, and his age in years, months, and days. The plot itself would be bare, with no foliage planted or flowers placed on the grave. Children usually were buried in unmarked graves or had small headstones that lay flat on the ground.

Mary Ruth's one consolation was the assurance that Willis had gone to heaven and stood in the presence of God. Her dearly loved husband had professed Christ as his Savior and lived a Christian life in every sense of the word. Someday Mary Ruth would be reunited with Willis. Until then, she had to keep the faith and set an example to her family and friends.

As the mourners headed back to their buggies following the graveside service, Ivan paused and looked over his shoulder at the place where his father had just been buried. It didn't seem real — it felt like a bad dream, only he knew he wouldn't wake up and realize it hadn't happened at all.

Dad had only been gone three days, and already Ivan missed him. Ever since he was a boy, they had enjoyed playful banter. Dad had told Ivan corny jokes, and when Ivan told some of his own, Dad had always laughed and said, "That was a good one, Son."

"Are you okay?" Yvonne put her hand on Ivan's arm.

"No, not really, but for my mamm's sake, I have to remain strong."

"It's okay to cry. No one will think you're weak if you let your emotions out."

Ivan bristled. "This is not about me being afraid of what others might think. If I give in to my tears and Mom sees me crying, it will only make her feel worse."

Yvonne shook her head. "I don't think so, Ivan. Mary Ruth will understand, because like her, you are grieving for a man who was much loved by everyone in this family. Grief is an important part of healing. The Bible tells us that even Jesus wept when He was overcome with grief."

"Jah, I know." He reached up and rubbed a spot on the back of his neck where a muscle had tightened. "Even so, I'll shed most of my tears in the privacy of our home or when I'm alone in the barn."

Yvonne didn't say anything more, but Ivan caught her glancing at Lenore with raised brows. *My wife clearly doesn't understand where I'm coming from. After all, it's not her father we just buried.*

By late afternoon, the tables, benches, songbooks, trays, and coffee butlers had all been put back into the bench wagons and hauled to the home where church would be held the next Sunday. The barn, shop, and house had been cleaned, and all the food taken care of. Everyone headed for home, except the closest family members and a few neighbor ladies who had set out leftovers for the Lapp family's supper.

Lenore felt relieved when the funeral dinner was over and everyone had gone home. It had been a long, tiring day, and she'd made a valiant effort to hold her emotions in check. She had wanted to be strong for her grandmother's sake, but watching the expression on sweet Grandma's face when Grandpa's coffin was lowered into the ground was almost her undoing. Lenore knew her grandmother quite well, and she was not easily fooled. No matter how much of a brave front Grandma had put on today, fatigue and sadness from deep within became more evident as the day wore on.

Soon after Sara, Brad, Kenny, and Lenore's parents and brothers left for home, Lenore insisted Grandma go to the living room to rest. Then she fixed them both a cup of chamomile tea and joined her there.

Lenore's heart nearly broke when she entered the room and saw Grandma sitting in Grandpa's favorite chair, staring at her folded hands.

"Your daed wants me to sell this old house and move in with him and your mudder." Grandma lifted her head and looked at Lenore.

"How do you feel about that idea?"

"I don't like it one bit." Grandma shook her head. "This is my home, and I want to stay here as long as I'm able." She moaned. "But your daed's likely to keep pestering me till I give in and do what he says."

"You don't need to give in, Grandma. I'm

willing to keep living here with you. I'm sure that arrangement would satisfy Dad."

"Are you sure? What if Jesse asks you to marry him? I doubt he would want to move in here."

"We'll deal with that should the time ever come." Lenore took a seat in the chair nearest Grandma. It seemed so strange not to have Grandpa here, occupying his favorite chair. She still couldn't wrap her mind around the fact that he was gone. Lenore thought about how one of their ministers had reminded them today that life goes on, and although they felt sorrow, they also needed to face the future with acceptance, a quiet joy, and a living hope and faith that Willis Lapp was in a better place, spending eternity with the One he had served for most of his life.

"I don't know what I'm going to do without him. Nothing will ever be the same in this house, and I've been sitting here trying to figure out what my future holds." Grandma stroked a worn spot on the arm of the chair. "When I married your grandfather, I never expected that he would be the one to go first." She sighed once more. "Always thought it would be me, even though he said once that he hoped we would leave this earth together."

Lenore's throat had swollen to the point that she could barely speak. "As Grandpa said many times over the years, 'none of us knows what the future will hold.' "

Grandma gave a slow nod. "Getting up every morning and not having him to look after is going to take some getting used to, and I'll have a lot of time on my hands. I'm likely to feel like a horse with no buggy to pull."

"It will be difficult at first, but you'll find something to do."

"I hope so, because it's not in my nature to sit around all day and do nothing."

Lenore sat mulling over her grandmother's words until an idea popped into her head. "Say, what would you think about caring for Jesse's little girl during the day while he's at work? Or would that be too much for you?"

Grandma remained still for several minutes, staring straight ahead. Then, with one quick nod, she said, "That's a *wunderbaar* idea, Lenore. If Jesse's agreeable to the idea of me taking care of his little girl, I'm more than willing." She touched her chest. "In fact, it might be exactly what I need to keep my mind occupied and to fill this emptiness."

CHAPTER 21

Children's laughter rang throughout the schoolyard as Lenore's students headed for home. Today was Friday, and they were undoubtedly eager for their weekend to begin.

Lenore stood on the schoolhouse porch, watching them go and enjoying the wonderful cooling breeze. The heat wave they'd had since Grandpa's death a week and a half ago had finally passed, and last night light sprinkles of rain took away some of the dust. Lenore was also eager to get home. It had been difficult to return to teaching, but keeping busy helped to keep Lenore's mind active — giving her fewer chances to feel the pain of losing her beloved grandfather.

A vision of Grandpa's face flashed into her mind and she remembered an incident from before he'd suffered a stroke. Lenore had gone to the living room to tell him supper was on the table, and she'd found

214

Grandpa in his recliner with his eyes closed. "Wake up, Grandpa," she'd said, giving his arm a nudge. He didn't budge — he just lay there. When Lenore was about to call out his name again, Grandpa's eyes popped open, and he looked at her with a teasing grin. "Wasn't sleeping. I was just restin' my eyes." They'd had a good laugh.

Lenore smiled, in spite of the sharp pain of regret that penetrated her soul. Grandpa had always been good at making other people laugh. The only time she'd ever seen him succumb to depression was after he'd suffered that horrible stroke. But later, when it appeared that he was getting better, Grandpa's humorous side had resurfaced.

Lenore's thoughts turned to her grandmother. On Monday, Grandma had begun watching Cindy while Jesse was at work. Lenore looked forward to seeing how they were both doing. While it was good therapy for Grandma to have something meaningful to do, caring for an eight-month-old child was also a lot of work. But Grandma had insisted she was up to it, and according to Jesse, his late wife's aunt had seemed somewhat relieved to relinquish the responsibility.

I'm also eager to see Jesse when he joins us for supper again this evening, Lenore admitted to herself. He'd eaten the evening meal with them every night this week and would no doubt stay for some of Grandma's delicious cabbage rolls this evening. Having his company was nice, and Grandma seemed relaxed around him. It almost seemed as if she'd accepted Jesse as part of the family.

Although Lenore enjoyed Jesse's company, she never felt fully at ease with him. Maybe it was because she tried so hard to make an impression on him and was never sure what he might be thinking. Sometimes, like two nights ago, Jesse engaged her in conversation and smiled a lot. Other times, such as last evening, he said very little unless spoken to and appeared to be deep in thought. Lenore longed to know what was on his mind. *Maybe I'm overanalyzing things. It probably doesn't matter what's going through Jesse's mind when he's quiet.*

A buzzing fly circled Lenore's head, putting an end to her thoughts about Jesse. She stepped back inside the schoolhouse to help her assistant take care of a few things, and then it would be time for them both to go home.

"You've been awfully quiet today," Ezekiel said as he and Michelle worked side by side in the greenhouse that afternoon. "Are you still worried about moving to New York this fall instead of waiting till spring as originally planned? If it's a problem, I can contact the man who is selling me his business and tell him that fall is too soon for us to move."

Michelle shook her head. "It's not the move I'm having a hard time dealing with, but the fact that Willis is gone. He was like a grandpa to me — the grandfather I never had."

"I miss him too." Ezekiel's mouth turned down at the corners. "I've known the Lapps since I was a boy, and both of them always treated me kindly."

Michelle brushed some dirt off her hand after repotting an African violet. "I'm glad Lenore is living with her grandma. Mary Ruth needs someone with her — especially now. She has to be so lonely without Willis." Michelle teared up. "I can't begin to imagine how much she must miss him."

"I'm sure she does, but I guess you haven't heard. Mary Ruth began watching Jesse Smucker's daughter this week," Ezekiel's mother chimed in from the next aisle over. "I bet that little girl is keeping Mary Ruth so busy she hardly has time to think about much else."

■ ■ ■ ■

Mary Ruth's knees creaked as she knelt on the blanket she'd spread on the living-room floor for Cindy. It was diaper-changing time, and since the little girl wasn't fond of having her diapers changed, Mary Ruth decided to make a game of it. "Where's Cindy?" she asked, dropping a diaper onto the little girl's head and then pulling it off again. "Ah, there she is! There's my sweet Cindy."

Cindy giggled and kicked her feet.

After Mary Ruth put the diaper in place and fastened it, she tickled Cindy under her chin. "*Kitzle voggel* . . . Kitzle voggel . . . Here comes the tickle bird."

Cindy giggled even more, and Mary Ruth did too. Thinking back to how her son and daughter had reacted when she'd played silly games with them during their babyhood brought a smile to her face. Rhoda and Ivan had both enjoyed the "tickle bird" game. Oh, how she missed those fun-loving days when she and Willis were raising their children. If only there was some way to turn back the hands of time.

Taking care of Jesse's daughter was a joy, as well as a privilege, and it did take some of her depression away. But Mary Ruth's life would be so much better if Willis were here to share it with. There would be no fresh apple cider this year, unless Ivan made it, and there were so many other things Willis used to do as head of the house — things Mary Ruth and everyone in the family would miss.

But he's not coming back, she reminded herself, *and I need to keep busy and stay focused on the now. In time, the indescribable pain I feel will hopefully diminish.*

Mary Ruth put Cindy's pink sleeper on and had begun patting the baby's back when Lenore came in. "How was your day, Grandma? Was Cindy a good girl for you?"

"Jah, she's a sweetheart." Mary Ruth picked up the wet diaper and grunted as she pushed herself up. "Would you like to spend some time with her while I go take this disposable windel out to the garbage and wash up? Then if you don't mind, maybe you can spend some time with her while I get supper started."

"Most definitely. But not for too long. Jesse will be here soon, and I need to help you get our evening meal going."

Mary Ruth shook her head. "You've had a busy week at school and deserve a little downtime, so just relax and enjoy being with the boppli." Without waiting for a response, Mary Ruth left the room.

Lenore sat on the floor beside Cindy and played this-little-piggy. The little girl giggled every time Lenore wiggled one of her toes and said what each pretend piggy was doing. It felt nice to spend time with Jesse's daughter. She missed all the fun and games they used to have. "*Bissel seiche* — little piglet." Lenore wiggled all ten of Cindy's toes and tweaked her nose.

Lenore's attention was diverted when she heard a buggy roll into the yard. *I wonder who is here.* After a few moments, Lenore heard someone come up onto the porch and knock on the door. It couldn't be Jesse. It was too early for him to be off work yet.

The door opened and Dad walked in, awkwardly carrying what looked like quite a heavy box.

"Hello, Daughter." He grinned at her.

"Hi, Dad. I'll help you with the door." Lenore jumped up and went to close it. Then she scooped Cindy up and followed her father into the kitchen.

"This box is full of frozen beef from my English neighbor, Ron. His freezer died, so he came by earlier in a panic to see if I'd have enough room to hold all the packages before they thawed." Dad set the box on the table. "I helped Ron out, and we got all the meat inside safe and sound. And for my trouble he insisted I should keep this amount."

Lenore smiled. "That was nice of him."

"What was nice?" Grandma asked as she came into the room. "Oh, hi, Ivan. I didn't know you were here."

After giving her a hug, he gestured to the cardboard box. "I've come bearing gifts."

Grandma tipped her head. "Oh, what is all this?"

Cindy squirmed in Lenore's arms, so she patted the little girl's back. "There's frozen beef inside the box."

"Really, from who?"

"My neighbor's freezer died, and for me helping him out he gave me this."

"That's a pleasant surprise." She stepped closer to the box.

Lenore watched as Dad pulled out the packages of meat. There were some steaks, a roast, and a good amount of hamburger. Grandma's eyes seemed to brighten as she watched the packages pile up on the kitchen table.

"Since you often invite me, Yvonne, and the boys over for a meal, this will save some money from your grocery bill." He grinned.

"Thank you, Son. I'll take a look in my freezer to see if we can get all this meat inside." Grandma reached over and pulled open the freezer part of her propane-operated refrigerator.

Lenore leaned over to look inside too. "There's not a lot in there right now, so maybe it will all fit."

Dad came over with an armload of packages and began to fill up the spaces. Lenore stepped out of his way and took a seat at the kitchen table, placing Cindy in her lap.

"What are your plans for this evening?" Grandma looked over at Dad.

"I'm going back to the house after I run to the bank. Why, Mom? Did you need me to do something before I go?"

"I thought if you weren't busy you might like to join us for a cup of kaffi and some of my banana bread."

"Danki, but I really have to go. I'll take a rain check, though."

"Okay." She went to the pantry and brought out a roasting pan. "It's probably time for me to start supper, and I really shouldn't be snacking so close to the evening meal." Grinning at Ivan, Grandma thumped her stomach. "If I'm not careful, I'll end up looking like one of your daed's old hogs."

Dad laughed, but the mention of Grandpa's hogs sent a pang of regret through Lenore. She'd give anything to have him sitting here at the table right now, enjoying a cup of coffee and telling some of his silly jokes. "Grandma, why don't you take Cindy and go into the living room? I'll get supper started."

Dad patted Lenore's back. "That's my thoughtful daughter — always thinking of others."

He pointed at the cardboard box on the kitchen table. "I'll take that with me when I leave, unless you need an extra box for something, Mom."

Grandma shook her head. "There are a few empty boxes out in the barn, so feel free to take this box with you." She told Ivan goodbye and gave him a hug, then took Cindy from Lenore and headed for the living room.

Dad turned to face Lenore. "Before I go, I was wondering how things are going between you and Jesse."

"We're doing well." She smiled. "He should be here in another hour or so."

"Will he be staying for the evening meal?"

"Jah."

"What are you having for supper this evening?"

223

"Grandma made up some cabbage rolls in the tangy tomato sauce earlier today. They're in the refrigerator. All I have to do is put them in the roasting pan and pop it into the oven."

"Mmm . . . that young man of yours is in for a tasty treat. My mamm's a good cook, and you're fortunate to be living here with her. Bet she's taught you a lot about cooking."

Lenore folded her arms as she released a puff of air. "Dad, I knew how to cook when I moved in with Grandma. As you already know, I've been working in the kitchen with Mom since I was a girl."

"Of course you have. I only meant that . . ." He waved his words aside. "Oh, never mind. I'm just glad you agreed to live with my mamm, because I never would have stood for her living here all alone."

"I'm well aware." Lenore gave her dad a hug. "I'm sure Grandma appreciates the concern you feel for her too."

"Has Jesse taken you out lately?"

"There hasn't been a lot of time to do that."

"Well, I'd best get going." Dad picked up the box. "Tell Jesse I said hello, and I'm sorry I can't stay around to say it myself."

"I'll give him the message."

"Jesse seems like a nice fellow." He leaned close to Lenore. "But if you ever have any problems with him, just let me know."

Lenore lifted her gaze to the ceiling. "Don't worry, Dad, everything's going just fine between me and Jesse."

"Good to hear." He bent down and kissed her cheek. "I really do need to go. You all have a good evening." He turned and headed for the back door.

"Tell Mom I said hello," Lenore called to his retreating form.

After the door clicked shut, Lenore left the kitchen and peeked into the living room. It had gotten awfully quiet in there, and she wondered if Grandma might have fallen asleep.

Stepping into the room, Lenore realized quickly that Grandma was wide-awake. She sat in Grandpa's old recliner with his Bible in her lap. Cindy lay on the floor with her eyes closed and her thumb in her mouth.

"Isn't she cute?" Lenore whispered when she caught Grandma's eye.

"Jah, Cindy is adorable. Children are a blessing to their parents' lives. It says so right here in the Bible." Grandma lifted the book toward Lenore.

Lenore nodded and smiled. *I can't wait to*

be able to say that in the future, hopefully as Jesse's wife.

"Something sure smells mighty good in here," Jesse said when he entered Mary Ruth's house and found Lenore on the floor playing peekaboo with Cindy.

"That would be my grandma's tasty cabbage rolls." Lenore pointed toward the kitchen. "They're keeping warm in the oven while Grandma takes a shower. We'll eat as soon as she comes out of the bathroom."

Jesse smiled when Cindy reached her hands out to him. "How's my little girl today?" he asked, going down on his knees beside Lenore and scooping Cindy into his arms.

"Well, I haven't been here all that long, but from what Grandma said earlier, she and Cindy got along real well today."

"That's good to hear."

Cindy squealed when Jesse rubbed noses with her, then tickled her belly.

"She sure is a happy baby," Lenore said.

"Jah, except for when her diaper needs changing or she just wants to be held."

Jesse was on the verge of asking Lenore a question when Mary Ruth entered the room. "Oh, good, I'm glad you're here, Jesse. If you're ready to eat supper, we can all go out to the kitchen now."

He didn't have to be asked twice. Putting Cindy over his shoulder like a sack of potatoes, Jesse rose to his feet and followed the women to the kitchen.

"Why don't you sit here this evening?" Mary Ruth pointed to the chair at the head of the table. "That used to be where Willis sat, and I'm tired of seeing it empty."

Jesse hesitated at first, but after he put Cindy in her high chair, he did as Mary Ruth suggested.

They bowed their heads for silent prayer, and when everyone had finished praying Lenore passed Jesse the casserole dish filled with steaming-hot cabbage rolls covered in herbed tomato sauce.

He put two on his plate and passed the dish to Mary Ruth.

"There's also coleslaw, mashed potatoes, pickled beets, and some carrot sticks to go with the main dish." Lenore gestured to the other bowls. "Would you like me to pass those to you, Jesse?"

"I'll try some of each shortly, but right now I'm gonna sink my teeth into one of these 'bound to be special' cabbage rolls." Jesse took his first bite and smacked his lips. "These are the best I've ever tasted."

"Danki. Feel free to have as many as you

like." Mary Ruth pointed to the dish sitting between her and Lenore. "As you can see, I made plenty, so I'd be pleased to send some home with you as well."

He grinned and gave his belly a thump. "I won't say no to that."

Jesse looked over at Lenore. She hadn't said more than a few words since they'd been seated at the table and said their silent prayer. "How was your day at school?"

"It went well, but I'm looking forward to having the next two days off." She handed him the bowl of mashed potatoes. "Would you like some?"

Jesse obliged, and after he'd added a couple of spoonfuls to his plate, he passed the dish on to Mary Ruth. "Your job must be very rewarding, Lenore."

She nodded, then turned her focus on Cindy playing happily with the finger food on her high chair tray. "As much as I enjoy teaching, I have to admit, I miss spending my days with your daughter."

"I think Cindy misses you too," Mary Ruth spoke up. "She does well enough for me," she added, "but Cindy doesn't light up when I come into the room the way she does when she sees you, Lenore."

Lenore's cheeks flushed as she rubbed some food off Cindy's chin. "And I think the world of her."

Jesse almost had to bite his tongue to keep from asking Lenore right then if she would marry him. He was more certain than ever before that Lenore would make a good mother for Cindy. But this was not the time or place for a proposal. He needed to give their relationship more time before asking that question.

CHAPTER 22

By the end of September, evidence of fall could be seen throughout Lancaster County. As Lenore guided her horse toward the schoolhouse Friday morning, the scent of smoky air coming from people's chimneys drifted into her buggy. Thanks to several days of heavy winds, the heat and humidity of summer were definitely gone, and due to the chillier weather, some trees were already dropping their leaves.

Grandma's apple trees had done well this year, and Lenore's father would be coming over this evening with his cider press. Lenore looked forward to drinking fresh cider and nibbling on popcorn as she and her family sat around the bonfire that would no doubt be built.

The whole family would be there, as well as Ezekiel and Michelle. Jesse had also been invited to join them, which pleased Lenore, but Grandpa would be sorely missed. This would be the first year he hadn't been involved in making fresh cider. His absence was bound to affect dear Grandma most of all. Lenore would continue to pray for her grandma, as well as the rest of her family, and she hoped to keep a positive attitude.

As the crisp, cool air wafted into the buggy, she shivered. *Even though I do miss Grandpa, I'm adjusting to his absence more easily than Grandma is. I think it's because I've got the school curriculum to plan every week and students to keep my thoughts occupied during workdays.* Her face warmed. Jesse was consuming her thoughts during the day too, and adorable little Cindy was becoming increasingly important to her.

Lenore held firmly to the reins when her horse decided to pick up speed. "Whoa, Dolly — slow down."

Lenore was glad Grandma had Cindy to keep her occupied these days. She couldn't help feeling a bit envious though. Truth was, even though Lenore loved to teach, this year the stress of being responsible for so many children had become more difficult for her to manage. Lenore didn't feel cut out to be a schoolteacher anymore. Even little things, like finding a mouse under her desk the other morning, were setting her nerves on edge. What Lenore really wanted and couldn't stop thinking about was to be a wife and have children of her own.

Did I feel this discontented before I met Jesse and Cindy? Lenore wondered. *I need to be patient. Jesse and I seem to be getting closer. Perhaps in time he will propose marriage. But if he doesn't, I must learn to be content with whatever the Lord has planned for my life.*

When Sara entered the flower shop, she found Misty already hard at work in the back room, putting together a large autumn floral arrangement.

"That's looking really nice, Misty. I love the fall colors."

"Thank you." She added some greenery and stood back, eyeing it. "We've got a busy day ahead with orders."

Sara put her lunch away in the refrigerator and looked at the list of orders going out for today. "Yep, another full one. How's it going so far?"

"Good. I have one arrangement already done and in the cooler." Misty remained focused on her job.

"All right then. I'll let you keep working." Sara left the room and went to her desk to check phone messages. A few minutes later, her cell phone rang. Seeing it was Brad, she answered immediately.

"Hi, hon. Are you busy right now?"

"Nothing that can't wait." Sara pushed her invoice book aside and reached for a writing tablet. There'd been some tension between her and Brad this morning when she brought up the hot dog roast and apple cider pressing at her grandma's tonight. The trouble started when he reminded Sara that this evening was Bible study, so they wouldn't be able to attend her family gathering.

"Can't we cancel this one?" Sara had asked. "I don't want to miss sampling Uncle Ivan's fresh-squeezed apple cider and saying goodbye to Michelle and Ezekiel. They'll be moving tomorrow, you know."

Brad had said he didn't feel right about canceling the Bible study, but thought they might get done early enough that they could go to Strasburg for an hour or so.

"Are you still there, Sara?"

Brad's question drew her from her musings. "Yes, I'm here. What did you call about?"

"I wanted to let you know that I'd like you to go ahead to your grandma's place when you get off work. I'll join you there as soon as the Bible study is over."

"Are you sure?" Sara shifted the phone to

her other ear. "Aren't you worried about how it will look to those attending the class if I'm not there?"

"Nope, not at all. I think they'll understand when I explain why you're not there."

Sighing, Sara pressed a palm to her chest. "Thanks, Brad, for being so considerate of my feelings."

"You'd do the same for me if the sandal was on the other foot."

Sara laughed. "I doubt anyone would be wearing sandals this time of year, but I get your meaning."

He chuckled too. "I'll make sure the study is done on time tonight, and then I'll see you at Mary Ruth's."

"Thanks, Brad. Have a good day."

"You too, Sara."

After Sara hung up, she bowed her head. *Thank You, Lord, for the loving, sensitive husband You have blessed me with.*

That evening after Jesse arrived at Mary Ruth's, he secured his horse at the hitching rail and went up to the house, eager to see his daughter. Mary Ruth greeted him at the door. "Welcome, Jesse. How was your day?"

"It went well, but I'm kind of tired. It seemed like there was more work than usual at the furniture store." He stepped into the entryway.

"Well, we're glad you could join us tonight, and hopefully after some food and tasty cider, you'll feel revived."

"I'm glad to be here. I bet my daughter is too. How'd she do for you today?"

"Just fine. Cindy and I always get along well." Mary Ruth gestured toward the living room. "Yvonne, Sara, and Lenore are keeping her entertained in there."

He grinned. "I bet they are." Jesse took a few steps toward the door. "I was going to say hi to Cindy, but it sounds like she's in good hands, so I think I'll head back outside and put Restless away."

"Not a problem." Mary Ruth headed off to the living room.

Jesse stepped off the porch and walked back to his buggy to unhook his horse. Then he led the gelding over to the corral gate and put him in with the other horses.

A good-sized group of family milled around on the lawn. His gaze came to rest on Lenore's father talking to one of the men. Jesse couldn't shake the awkward feeling he had at times in Ivan's presence. Lenore's dad didn't talk to Jesse as much these days as he had before he and Lenore started courting. Lately when Ivan came by Mary Ruth's house and Jesse was there, he mostly chatted with his mother and Lenore. It almost seemed as if Ivan had a sense about how Jesse felt toward his daughter. *Does Ivan realize I'm not in love with Lenore and that I only want to marry her for convenience' sake? I wonder how Ivan might react if things don't go the way his daughter wants.*

Shaking aside his concerns, Jesse brushed at a smudge on his trousers and walked back to the house. He spotted Lenore near the entrance of the kitchen and smiled.

She stepped over to him, wearing a jacket with a woolen scarf tied over her white head covering. "Grandma is getting Cindy bundled up pretty well so she'll stay nice and warm outside."

"That's good. It's kinda nippy out this evening, jah?"

Lenore nodded. "I'm about done helping in here, so we can head outside if you'd like."

"Sure, that will be good."

They passed Ivan at the door as they were headed out. He smiled briefly as he looked over at Jesse. "Glad you could be here for the family gathering."

"Danki, I'm glad I could be here too." He followed Lenore out to the chairs.

Almost as soon as they picked out their seats, Jesse noticed the bags of marshmallows on the picnic table. "I can't wait to roast some of those." He pointed to them.

"Me too. I've been thinking about this off and on all day." Lenore picked out a skewer and grabbed a marshmallow. Jesse did the same.

They returned to their chairs and scooted them closer to the fire. Jesse put his skewer into the flame, and in no time it began to burn. "Oh no! Would you just look at my marshmallow? I don't think I'm gonna eat this one. It's a little too overdone for my taste."

Lenore leaned closer to him. "Why don't you get a new one?"

Jesse wiggled his brows. "Good idea." He grabbed another marshmallow, put it on a stick this time, and held it over the fire. It didn't take long before this one burned too.

"Oh, great. Not again." He grunted as it fell off and burned up in the flames. Jesse squinted as he glanced over at Lenore; he could hardly believe his eyes. She had roasted a perfectly brown marshmallow without a speck of black on it. "I don't know how you did that. What's your secret anyway?"

She lifted her shoulders in a quick shrug before giving a dimpled smile. "Here you go, Jesse." Lenore handed him her skewer.

He shook his head. "No, that's okay. You did a good job roasting your marshmallow, so you should be the one to eat it."

"All right, if you insist." Lenore popped the creamy morsel into her mouth. Chuckling, she smacked her lips. "Would you like me to roast you one, sir?"

Jesse felt like an incompetent fool, but as much as he enjoyed marshmallows, he couldn't say no. "Sure, if you don't mind."

"I don't mind at all."

He leaned forward with his elbows on his knees, watching Lenore roast another perfect-looking puffy treat. When it was just the right shade of brown, she handed him the skewer. "Thanks, Lenore." Jesse wasted no time in eating it and didn't even care when he ended up with sticky goo all over his lips.

Lenore laughed and handed him a napkin.

After Jesse wiped off his face, he looked toward the house and saw Mary Ruth, Sara, and Yvonne coming across the yard with his daughter. Cindy was crying, and when the women joined them at the bonfire, Lenore offered to take Cindy.

As she sat quietly on her folding chair, holding Cindy in her lap, Jesse couldn't help noticing Lenore's tender expression as she patted his daughter's back and spoke soothingly to the child. Not more than two minutes ago, Cindy had been fussing, but as soon as Lenore took her, all crying ceased. As much as Jesse loved Cindy, he didn't have the ability to soothe her the way Lenore always did. One more reason his daughter needed Lenore as her mother.

He scratched his head. *What should I do — pretend to be in love with Lenore so she'll marry me, or ask her to be my wife in name only, which she'd probably never agree to?*

Esther's death had put Jesse in a tight spot, and he didn't know which way to turn.

Mary Ruth had just entered the kitchen to make some popcorn when Michelle came into the room. "What can I do to help?" she asked.

"You can get out the coconut oil while I get the popping corn and kettle." Mary Ruth smiled.

"Sure, no problem." Michelle took the jar of oil down from the cupboard, and when she placed it on the counter near the stove, her eyes misted. "I can't believe Ezekiel and I will be moving tomorrow. We'll both miss you so much, as well as our other friends and family."

Mary Ruth set the items she'd gathered on the counter and gave Michelle a hug.

"We shall miss you too, but you'll be back for visits, right?"

"Jah, but not often enough." Stepping out of Mary Ruth's embrace, Michelle swiped at the tears trickling down her cheeks. "Ezekiel's family said they'll come visit us in New York, and my brothers said they will too. Even so, it's going to be hard to start over in a place where we don't know anyone. I don't even know what our new house looks like. When Ezekiel made the trip up to New York to look the place over and talk with the owner, I stayed home to work in the greenhouse because they were so busy and needed the extra help." She paused and blotted her face with the palm of her hand. "I wonder how Ezekiel's folks are going to get along without us."

"I am sure his parents will hire someone to work in the greenhouse after you're gone. And don't worry, Michelle — you'll make new friends, just like you did when you moved here." Mary Ruth hoped her words were encouraging. Truth was, though, she had no idea what it was like to move to a strange place where she didn't know anyone. She and Willis had grown up in Lancaster County, and during the course of their marriage they had never moved away. They'd always had the support of their family and friends.

She placed her hands on Michelle's trembling shoulders. "Remember to pray often and study God's Word. If you keep your focus on Him, He will lead, guide, and direct you all the days of your life."

Michelle nodded slowly. "I know, and I am ever so thankful that I'm not moving there by myself. I'll have my husband's love and support, and I want to be supportive of Ezekiel too." She wiped her nose on the tissue Mary Ruth placed in her hand. "And can I just say one more thing?"

"Of course."

"I feel certain I'm supposed to go to New York with my husband, even though it's hard for me to leave the only place I have ever felt at home and loved." Michelle placed one hand over her heart. "No matter where I go, or whatever I do, I will always remember the example you have shown me of what a loving, Christian wife should be. Danki, Mary Ruth, for all you have done for me."

"It has been my pleasure." Mary Ruth looked deeply into Michelle's eyes. "Remember, dear one . . . I shall be praying for you, and whenever you feel lonely or just need to talk, please give me a call."

"Danki, I will. Brad and Sara said they'd be praying for us too." Michelle dried her damp eyes and managed to smile. "Want to hear something funny?"

"Of course."

"When we were beginning to pack, my crazy *hund* started jumping into boxes and nosing around in our suitcases. Val likes it here, but I think she's afraid she might be left behind."

Mary Ruth chuckled. "Dogs have a sixth sense about things. Val will be good company for you after the move. It'll be an adjustment for her, same as you, but I bet in no time she'll get used to her new surroundings."

"You may be right. She'll probably adjust faster than I do, but it's not like I've never moved before. Only this time I won't be moving by myself." Michelle dropped her gaze to the floor. "I'm glad those days are behind me now."

CHAPTER 23

Sweat beaded on Jesse's forehead as he paced the floor with Cindy. She was cutting a tooth, and he'd been up half the night trying to calm her. The poor little thing was in obvious pain and running a slight fever. Unfortunately, nothing Jesse did seemed to ease her distress.

He glanced at the battery-operated clock on the living-room wall. It was almost two in the morning. *If Esther were here holding our baby, I bet she'd know what to do. She was so good with her nieces and nephews and young siblings.*

Jesse took a seat in the rocking chair and began patting Cindy's back as he got the chair moving. It did nothing to quiet her down. His daughter's sobs tore at his heart. *There must be something more I can do for her.*

He meandered over to the bookcase, patting Cindy's back as he went. He'd purchased a book on child care a few months ago and wondered if it might say anything about teething.

When Jesse spotted the book, he placed Cindy in the playpen and took it off the shelf. She hollered even more, of course, and Jesse felt like screaming himself as he flopped onto the couch.

Looking through the index, he found what he was looking for and turned to the section that listed the symptoms and remedies for teething.

"The signs of teething are swollen, tender gums," Jesse read out loud. "The baby may be fussy or cry, have a slightly raised temperature, drool a lot, and chew on whatever he or she can find to put in the mouth." Most of the symptoms fit Cindy, so Jesse felt confident his daughter was in fact teething. According to the book, babies began teething sometime between four and seven months, but some started even later.

Now to locate a solution to the problem. Jesse's fingers slid down the page until he came to the part about how to soothe a teething baby. The book's author suggested putting something cold in the baby's mouth, like a chilled pacifier, the end of a clean wet washcloth, or a refrigerated toy or teething ring. Another suggestion was for the baby's caregiver to dip his or her finger in cool water and gently rub the baby's gums. Jesse opted for that idea, but before he tried it, he put Cindy's pacifier in the refrigerator to chill. Then he brought a glass of cold water to the living room.

After Jesse returned to the rocker with Cindy and got the chair moving again, he dipped two fingers in the water and rubbed his daughter's gums. It seemed to help some, and as Jesse continued to rock and rub, he thought about Lenore. It would be a week tomorrow since he'd enjoyed the bonfire at Mary Ruth's place, and he'd only spoken to Lenore a few times since then. One evening when he'd gone to pick up Cindy, Lenore wasn't there. Mary Ruth explained that her granddaughter had been invited to join her parents for supper at their house that night and probably wouldn't be home until close to bedtime. Jesse had been disappointed, because he enjoyed visiting with Lenore and hearing about some of the things that went on at the schoolhouse. But he realized she had a life of her own and had every right to spend time with her family.

Thinking about Lenore's parents caused Jesse to recall a recent phone conversation he'd had with his mother. Mom had pressured him to return to Kentucky so she could help out with Cindy, but he held firm. He had too many memories of Esther in Kentucky, and Jesse wasn't ready to face them. Besides, he liked his new job and didn't want to take Cindy away from the familiarity of being with Mary Ruth and Lenore, whom she'd become attached to. Jesse was convinced he'd made the right decision by moving here, and he wasn't going back to Kentucky no matter what.

After several more minutes of rocking Cindy and rubbing her gums, she quit crying and dozed off. Eager to get some much-needed sleep of his own, Jesse put Cindy in her crib and collapsed on his bed. Before long, it would be time to get up and start another workday, but even a few hours of sleep would help.

Jesse closed his eyes, lifted a silent prayer, and fell asleep.

Lenore was getting ready to leave for school the next morning when Jesse showed up with Cindy. The dark circles beneath his eyes, in addition to his pinched, tension-filled expression, indicated that he hadn't slept well the night before.

"Is everything okay?" she asked, holding the door open for him. "You look *tired*."

"You're right, I am tired. *Ich bin mied wie en hund.*"

She bit back a chuckle. "Why are you tired as a dog?"

Jesse stepped inside, and as he stood in the hallway with Cindy clinging to his neck, he explained what had happened the night before. "It was after two before either of us got to sleep," he added with a groan. "I had no idea so many challenges came with being a parent. I'm sure glad I located a book on child care I'd bought previously. It taught me pretty much everything I needed to know about teething."

Lenore felt pity for Jesse. He was clearly exhausted from last evening's ordeal. "I'm sorry you had a rough night."

"Hopefully it won't happen again, because next time Cindy cuts a tooth, I'll know exactly what to do. 'Course, that's not saying I'll handle things well if she gets the flu or a bad cold."

"Ah, there's my precious little girl." Lenore's grandmother's arms opened wide when she joined them in the hallway.

Jesse handed Cindy to her. "My daughter's having a hard time cutting her first tooth, so I hope she won't be too fussy for you today."

"I'm sure she'll be fine. I raised two kin-

247

ner who were both fussy when they were cutting their teeth, but we got through it." Grandma gestured to Lenore. "You were only four months old when you cut your first tooth. The one thing your mamm did that seemed to help the most was soaking a clean washcloth in chamomile tea, which she then put in the refrigerator to chill. The fabric massaged the ridges of your gums while the cold numbed the pain, and the herbal tea helped to calm you."

Lenore smiled. "My mom's a *schmaert* woman, jah?"

"Yes, she is very smart." Grandma's eyes glistened with tears as a slight smile lifted her thin lips. "Your grandpa always teased and said she had to be smart because she chose to marry our son even after she found out his daed raised hogs."

Lenore and Jesse laughed. Grandpa was always full of wisecracks that made people smile. She missed him so much, and of course, Grandma did too. Probably more than Lenore could comprehend, since she had never lost the love of her life.

"I'd better get going." Jesse placed Cindy's diaper bag on the floor by the coat-tree. "Oh, and I wanted to remind you that I have a dental appointment after work, so I'll be a little late picking Cindy up."

"Not a problem," Grandma said. "In fact, if you like, you can leave Cindy here overnight. That way, if she gets fussy again tonight, you can get some good sleep."

Jesse drew in a breath, then closed his eyes briefly while exhaling. "Danki, I would appreciate that very much." He stepped forward and gave his daughter a kiss on the cheek. "I'll see you tomorrow evening, my sweet girl. Be good for Mary Ruth and Lenore."

Lenore said goodbye to Grandma and followed Jesse out the door. "I hope you have a good day at work and that everything goes well at your dental appointment."

He smiled. "I hope your day at school goes well too."

Clymer, New York

Michelle stood in front of the kitchen window, washing dishes and looking out at the fertile land surrounding their new home. With farmland being cheaper here than in Lancaster County, it was easy to understand why several Amish families from Pennsylvania, Maryland, and Ohio had chosen to pack up and move to New York State. Fortunately, Michelle and Ezekiel had joined a more progressive district than some in the area. While the home they were buying was an older two-story, four-bedroom house that needed a fresh coat of paint and a few updates, it was comfortable and provided them with all that they needed and had been accustomed to while living in Strasburg, including indoor plumbing. Michelle couldn't imagine doing without indoor plumbing and phone shacks, or driving buggies with no front windshield, like the brown-topped-buggy Amish she'd heard about who originally came from New Wilmington, Pennsylvania. It was hard enough to adjust to living where she had no friends or family, without trying to deal with hardships she'd never experienced before.

Pulling her fingers slowly through the lukewarm dishwater, Michelle thought about the phone call she'd received yesterday from her brother Ernie. He let her know that he and Jack might drive up to New York to see her before winter set in. Since both of her brothers lived in Ohio, it would be a bit of a drive, but a lot cheaper than flying. She looked forward to seeing them and finding out what was new in their lives. In the meantime, Michelle needed to concentrate on unpacking all their things and getting the house organized. Opening most of the boxes filled with household items had been left up to her, since Ezekiel had been keeping plenty busy learning all he could about running his new business.

Needing a familiar voice to talk to, Michelle had called Mary Ruth yesterday, hoping she might catch her in or near the phone shack, but all she'd been able to do was leave a message. Michelle felt certain that if she had been able to speak to Mary Ruth, she would have received some words of encouragement to help lift her depression.

Michelle finished washing the dishes and decided to let them air dry instead of drying each dish with a towel. She had better things to do, and the first item was to get some laundry done and hung on the line to dry. Later, she planned to take Val for a walk. Since the area was new to the dog and Michelle didn't want the Irish setter to run off, so far she'd kept her secured with a long leash or inside the barn. Of course, the dog managed to sneak in the house now and then too. Eventually, once Val became acclimated to her new surroundings, she'd be given the freedom to roam around their yard and all the acreage that came with it.

Michelle dried her hands and slipped into a lightweight jacket, then stepped out the back door. Drawing in a breath of fresh air, she tipped her head and listened. Other than Val's whine as she pulled on her tether, the only sound Michelle heard was the chirping of birds. "It's so peaceful here," she murmured. "Almost too quiet to suit me, though."

The dog's ears perked up, and she let out a couple of loud barks.

Michelle laughed. "Okay, okay, I can take a hint. You want some attention, don't ya, girl?"

The Irish setter wagged her tail, and Michelle bent down to pet Val's silky auburn head. "Let's go for a walk now. I can start the laundry when we get back."

Chapter 24

Strasburg

By the fourth week of November, the weather had turned frigid, and on Thanksgiving morning, Lenore woke up to the sight of snow falling from the sky. She stood at her bedroom window and watched as everything in the yard was quickly covered in white. Over in the next field, the neighbor's two horses romped around in the chilly weather. The animals followed each other like children in an energy-driven jog, and then one horse would stop while the other started kicking like it was thrilled with the new-fallen snow.

What a lovely sight, she mused. *I just hope for the sake of our company that the roads don't get bad.* Others in the area would no doubt be traveling for the holiday, and Lenore prayed for their safety as well.

Pulling her gaze away from the window, she hurried to get dressed so she could help

Grandma with breakfast and the preparations for their big Thanksgiving meal. Jesse and Cindy would be joining them, along with Lenore's parents and her brother Peter. Ben had been invited to join his girlfriend's parents, so his chair at the table would be empty. Sara and Brad were spending Thanksgiving with Brad's folks in Harrisburg. They planned to return on Saturday, as Brad needed to be back in Lancaster to preach on Sunday.

Grandpa's seat will be empty too. Lenore choked up. Last Thanksgiving had been such a fun time with all the family together. Even when the turkey ended up on the floor, Grandma had kept a positive attitude, and everyone had enjoyed a good laugh. But today would probably be quiet and uneventful.

Lenore plodded in her slippers over to the closet and picked out a frock. It was one of her work dresses she didn't mind getting dirty. She changed from her nightclothes to the dress and slipped on her comfy shoes.

Going to her dresser, she grabbed her brush and ran it through her long brown hair. "Ouch!" Lenore frowned as the brush pulled at a tangle. While she patiently worked her hair free, Lenore remembered that the dress she'd put on was the same one she'd worn last Thanksgiving while helping Grandma get things ready for their meal. *I remember Grandpa commenting on how much he liked this rose-pink color on me.* Lenore smiled. She couldn't help thinking how strange it was that the memory had simply popped into her head. Such a small thing, but a lovely reminiscence.

Lenore pinned up her hair and put her head covering in place. *No matter how hard we all try to enjoy the day, it won't be the same without Grandpa sitting at the head of the table.*

Clymer

"Just think, this is our first Thanksgiving in our new home." Ezekiel slipped his arms around Michelle and gave her a kiss. "Aren't you excited?"

She nodded. Truth was, she'd be more enthused if they were going to Strasburg to celebrate the holiday. They'd only been here two months, but to Michelle, it felt like an eternity. She missed Sara, Lenore, Ezekiel's family, and most of all, Mary Ruth. If just one of them could have come up to New York to celebrate Thanksgiving, it would have made her happy. Instead, she and Ezekiel were all alone with a fifteen-pound turkey in the oven. Michelle didn't know what her husband was thinking when he'd come home with such a big bird.

"I know it's a lot of meat," Ezekiel had said, "but we'll have plenty of leftovers for turkey sandwiches, soups, and casseroles."

Michelle didn't care about leftover turkey. She would have rather gone out for dinner than cook a big meal for just the two of them.

I'm an ungrateful wife, she scolded herself. *I should be more appreciative of Ezekiel and try to make this a special day for him. I wish I was more like Lenore, who has always seemed so peaceful, loving, and full of joy to me. I bet if she were here now, she'd say I have a lot to be thankful for, and of course she'd be right.* Michelle placed her hands against her warm cheeks. *I need to quit feeling sorry for myself.*

"The turkey will be done soon, so I suppose I should set out the dishes and silverware before I cook the potatoes and heat up the green beans." She gestured to the kitchen table. "Since it's just the two of us, we may as well eat in here."

Ezekiel shook his head. "This is a special occasion. Don't you think it would be nicer if we ate in the dining room?"

Michelle shrugged. "If that's what you would prefer."

A knock sounded on the front door, and Ezekiel cocked his head. "Now, I wonder who that could be. Why don't you answer it while I start peeling the potatoes?"

Michelle touched his forehead. "Are you *grank*? Since when would you rather peel potatoes than answer the door?"

"No, I'm not sick — only trying to be helpful." He stroked the side of her cheek and gave her a quick kiss.

"Okay, whatever. It's probably our English neighbor to the north of us. She's always asking to borrow something." Michelle left the room and made her way to the front door, in no hurry to get there. When she opened it and saw who stood on the front porch, her mouth opened wide and she let out a squeal. "Ernie! Jack! I had no idea you two were coming here today." Michelle barely took notice of the young woman standing between her brothers until Jack gave her a hug and said, "Michelle, this is my fiancée, Gina."

Her eyes widened. "You're engaged?"

"Yep. I proposed to her two weeks ago." He shuffled his feet. "I would have told you sooner, but when Ezekiel contacted me and Ernie about coming here for Thanksgiving, I decided to wait and surprise you with the news."

"I certainly am surprised, and I'm happy for you too." Michelle gave Gina a hug and wrapped her arms around Ernie.

At that moment, Ezekiel stepped onto the porch and slipped his arm around Michelle's waist. "See now why I wanted you to answer the door? Are you surprised?"

"Yes, very." She poked his arm playfully. "I knew something had to be up when you volunteered to do the potatoes. And I'm definitely getting the dining room ready for Thanksgiving supper, for us and my surprise guests."

"Now be fair, Fraa. You know I'm pretty handy in the kitchen." He chuckled and invited their guests inside.

As Michelle followed the four of them inside, her heart swelled with joy. How blessed she felt to be married to such a thoughtful, loving husband. *Thank You, God, for bringing Ezekiel into my life.*

Strasburg

"Now that we've prayed and before we begin eating, could we take a few minutes and tell what we are thankful for?" Lenore asked as she and their guests sat around the dining-room table.

"That's an excellent idea." Lenore's father looked at Grandma. "Why don't you go

258

first, Mom?"

Grandma sat up straight and folded her hands, placing them on the table in front of her. "Let's see now. . . . I am thankful for all the years I had with your daed. There are so many memories it's hard to choose one, but last year's Thanksgiving was special."

"Oh, you mean because when Grandpa handed the knife to Dad so he could cut the turkey, the bird ended up on the floor?" Peter chortled. "I'll never forget the shocked look on both of their faces."

Grandma smiled. "I have to admit, it was pretty funny."

"Jah, and let's hope after we're all done sharing what we're thankful for that I do better this year when I carve the Thanksgiving bird." Dad gestured to the golden-brown turkey sitting on the large platter in the middle of the table. "I sure don't want to make any new memories that everyone will be talking about for another whole year."

"If it happens again," Lenore's mother interjected, "it could be the last time you're given the honor of using your daed's carving knife."

Everyone laughed, including Lenore's dad, who sat at the head of the table in the chair that used to be occupied by Grandpa.

"All right — who wants to go next and share what they're thankful for?" Grandma asked.

"I will." Lenore's hand shot up. "I'm ever so thankful that I was born into a loving, caring family that can laugh together and cry together and make so many good memories. As Grandpa once said, 'Quality family time together is the foundation for a solid home.'"

All heads nodded in agreement.

Lenore's dad turned to look at Jesse. "What about you, Jesse? Would you tell us what you're thankful for?"

Jesse's ears turned a dark shade of pink. Lenore figured he wasn't used to being put on the spot.

"Go ahead," Dad coaxed. "Don't be shy. We'd all like to hear what you're thankful for."

"Well, the first thing I'm thankful for is my precious little girl." He turned in his seat and gestured to Cindy sitting in her high chair. "She's my ray of sunshine, even on dreary days." He then turned his gaze on each one sitting around the table. "I'm also thankful for the pleasure of being here with all of you today. It was kind of Mary Ruth and Lenore to invite me and Cindy to join you."

Grandma, who was sitting to Jesse's left, reached over and gave his arm a few taps. "And we are thankful you two could be here today. It's our pleasure to have you."

Lenore felt content inside, seeing everyone in good spirits. Even though Grandpa was deeply missed, the family's tradition of celebrating holidays together was being carried on.

"That was one delicious meal. Danki, Mary Ruth and Lenore, for all the work you did preparing it for us." Jesse rubbed his stomach. "Now I need to either take a nap or go outside and get some exercise."

"I vote for going outside." Peter pushed his chair away from the table. "Bet there's enough snow on the ground to build a snowman. Anyone wanna help me?"

"Count me in," Jesse said.

"Me too." Lenore gathered up a few plates. "I'll join you after the dishes are done."

"No need for that." Lenore's mother shook her head. "I'll help Mary Ruth with the *schissele*. You should go outside and have some fun."

Jesse looked at his daughter, sitting in the high chair with mashed potatoes all over her face. "Maybe I should stay inside and keep an eye on my messy little *schtinker*. She needs to be cleaned up and might even be ready for a nap."

Mary Ruth patted the top of Cindy's head. "She does look kind of drowsy, but I bet she won't fall asleep if I put her down. She seems to be awake more than asleep these days."

Jesse smiled in response and stepped over to his daughter. He grabbed a couple of paper towels and dampened them before returning to Cindy. With ease, Jesse wiped off her face and hands. His little girl smiled up at him and reached out her hands. "Not yet, little one; hang on there. I'll have you out in a minute."

He continued to clean up the tray that had some small morsels left on it. "That's better; now you're ready to come out of there." Jesse set aside the soiled paper towels and lifted his daughter from the high chair. He held her for a moment and watched the activity around the kitchen, focusing mostly on Lenore. *I do care about her.* His back stiffened as he looked over at Lenore's father. *It's just that my feelings aren't what they should be.*

"I'll keep Cindy occupied," Lenore's dad offered. "We'll go in the living room, and

I'll give her a horsey ride on my knee."

"She'll like that. Thanks, Ivan." Jesse got his jacket, hat, and gloves. "You comin', Lenore?"

"Sure, I'll be out as soon as I put on some warm clothes and my boots."

"Okay, see you soon." Jesse followed Peter out the door. As they stepped onto the back porch, Jesse's foot slipped on a patch of ice. He grabbed hold of the wooden railing and went on down the stairs to join Peter in the yard. The snow was still falling and creating a white blanket over everything. Peter began making a ball of snow, then rolling it along the ground, and Jesse did the same. Before long, he had a good-sized sphere made. "What do you think, Peter? Does this look good enough?"

"That's perfect! We'll use that one for the bottom of the snowman." Peter went back to rolling his own ball again.

Meanwhile, Jesse watched him and enjoyed the fun he was having. He soon picked up some snow, packed it, and threw the icy ball at the barn. It hit with a *thud* and stuck there. "This is some real good stuff." He made another snowball and tossed it, nearly hitting Peter.

Peter snorted. "Keep that up and we could end up having a real snowball fight."

"No way, but if this keeps up we could have enough to build a couple of snow forts." Jesse chuckled.

"I think my section is the right size." Peter tried picking it up, but it wouldn't budge.

Jesse came closer to him. "Wait, don't lift it. Just roll it over by mine."

He watched Peter work on getting the middle over next to the base. "Now you and I can lift it up together," Jesse instructed.

They both reached around and put the smaller sphere on top of the base. Jesse stepped back, looked it over, and gave a whistle. "Looks pretty good to me."

Peter shook his head. "Nope. It's leaning kinda funny." Grunting and groaning, he managed to move the giant snowball until it looked symmetrical. Then he brushed off any imperfections with his gloves.

"That's looking more like a snowman now." Jesse looked around the yard for some sticks to use for the snowman's arms. It was getting harder to see things because the snow had accumulated so fast. Peter was taking a break and messing with his hat. "I wonder if Grandma has any spare carrots we could use for his nose when we get finished."

"Good question." Jesse's nose started to run from the cold. He pulled off his dampened glove and fished around in his coat pocket. Jesse's numbing fingers found the tissue he'd put in there this morning and wiped his nose. *Ah . . . that's better.* He stuffed the wadded tissue into his pocket and was about to put his glove back on when a snowball hit him on the shoulder. "Hey!" Jesse looked up and saw Peter laughing so hard he was holding his stomach.

"I wasn't even trying." Peter snickered.

"Okay, now you'd better watch out, because I'm getting ready to throw one at you." Jesse quickly pulled on his glove.

Soon they were throwing snowballs one after the other. Jesse was out of breath and laughing so hard he could hardly pick up any more snow. "All right, that's enough, Peter!" he hollered. "We need to put the finishing touches on our snowman."

Peter dropped the snowball in his hand. "Okay, okay . . . I get it. You're too tuckered out to keep throwing snowballs at me."

Jesse couldn't deny it. Lenore's brother was younger than him, and once they'd started the snowball fight, Peter had become even more energetic. "I admit, I am kind of tired, but the truth is, we came out here to build a snowman, so let's finish the job we started."

"You're right, we still need to find something to use for the snowman's eyes." Peter looked around. "There's so much snow on the ground, we'll probably never find any small rocks to use. I'll go look in the barn and see if there's anything there that could serve as the snowman's eyes."

Peter turned toward the barn just as Lenore came out the back door. Jesse was on the verge of warning her about the patch of ice when Lenore's feet went out from under her and down she went. When she didn't get up right away, Jesse figured she must be hurt. He dropped the snowball he'd started, leaped onto the porch, and swept Lenore into his arms. He hoped she wasn't seriously hurt.

CHAPTER 25

"What happened? Is my daughter hurt?" Lenore's mother rushed forward when Jesse entered the house carrying Lenore.

Peter came in right behind them. "Is my sister okay?"

"She fell on a patch of ice on the porch. I saw it there when I went out to build the snowman and should have done something about it then." Jesse's voice was filled with regret.

"Did she break anything?" Grandma asked as Lenore clung to Jesse. It felt good to be held in the safety of his strong arms.

"I don't think so, but let's get her on the couch."

As Jesse placed Lenore down, she groaned. "My lower back and hip hurt, but I don't think it's serious. Probably just bruised really bad."

"I'll get some ice." Grandma hurried from the room.

"Or we could try alternating heat and cold." Mom's brows wrinkled. "Come to think of it, I believe a person should use ice in the first twenty-four hours of an injury. Jah, that's what our chiropractor said."

"I think we should call a driver and go to the hospital to have your back x-rayed," Dad said from across the room where he held Cindy, who was straddling his knee.

"There's no need for that." Lenore pulled herself to a sitting position and stood. "I'll just walk around for a bit and see how I'm doing."

Lenore's cheeks heated with embarrassment as everyone watched her move slowly around the living room. Each step she took caused pain, but she tried not to let on. It was a good thing the scholars had no school tomorrow, because with the way Lenore's back felt now, she would not be able to teach. Hopefully by Monday she would feel better, and in the meantime, Lenore would rest and try icing it as Grandma and Mom had suggested.

When Grandma returned to the living room with a bag of ice, Lenore took it gratefully. Then she excused herself and limped down the hall to the guest room. Her back hurt more than she was willing to admit, and the thought of climbing the stairs to her bedroom held no appeal whatsoever.

"I think Cindy and I should probably go." Jesse moved toward the baby.

"But you haven't had dessert yet," Mary Ruth said. "You really need to try some of Lenore's delicious Pineapple Philly pie."

"I'm still full from dinner, and it won't be long before Cindy's bedtime." Jesse glanced at his daughter, who still looked wide-awake. He figured all the extra attention she'd gotten today had her keyed up. Hopefully she'd sleep like a log tonight.

"Oh, I understand." Mary Ruth's slumped shoulders let Jesse know she was disappointed.

"Guess I could stay long enough to eat a piece of pie. But before I do, I need to take care of that icy porch for you. Do you have any ice melt, Mary Ruth?"

"Jah, there's a bag in the utility room. I was going to put some out earlier but got busy fixing the meal and forgot." Mary Ruth glanced in the direction of the guest room. "If I had taken care of it, Lenore wouldn't have gotten hurt."

"Accidents happen, Mom, and if I had known about it, I would have melted the ice for you," Ivan interjected.

"Your son is right," Yvonne put in. "An accident can happen, indoors or out, when a person least expects it. Why, if some water or milk had been spilled on the kitchen floor, Lenore could have slipped on that."

"That may be true," Jesse said, "but the fact is, she slipped on ice that I saw and should have taken care of. And even though it's after the fact, I'm gonna get rid of it right now." He headed for the utility room to get the bag of ice melt. *I sure hope Lenore will be okay.*

After everyone went home and Mary Ruth had given her kitchen a final inspection, she went to check on Lenore again. The last time she'd looked in on her, to offer a piece of pie, Lenore had been awake but said she wasn't hungry and preferred not to get up. She asked Mary Ruth to offer her apologies to everyone for not joining them at the dessert table.

Lenore's parents and brother had popped into the guest room to say goodbye before heading for home, and Jesse said he would drop by sometime the following day to check on Lenore.

He's such a nice man, Mary Ruth thought as she left the kitchen and headed down the hall. *Jesse seems to care about my grand-*

daughter, and I'm hoping those two might have a future together. She smiled, thinking about the way little Cindy lit up every time she was with Lenore. *That sweet little girl needs a mudder too.*

Mary Ruth had invited Jesse to join them for supper many times over the last few months — partly so he didn't have to cook, but mostly so he and Lenore could spend time together and get better acquainted. Lenore had waited several years to find a husband, and Mary Ruth hoped Jesse might be the one God intended for her granddaughter.

She paused by the guest room door. *When Lenore feels better, I'll volunteer to watch Cindy some evening so she and Jesse can go out to eat at one of the local restaurants by themselves. It might help to get them together quicker if they have more time alone.*

Harrisburg, Pennsylvania

"That sure was a great meal, Mom. You outdid yourself today." Brad yawned and stretched his arms over his head. "Eating all that turkey made me sleepy, and I bet I gained five pounds."

Taking a seat on the couch beside him, Sara looked at Brad's mother, Jean, and rolled her eyes. "I think my husband may

271

be exaggerating just a bit."

Jean chuckled and poked her husband's arm. "He gets that from his dad. Isn't that right, Clarence?"

"Maybe." Brad's father lifted his shoulders and let them drop. "But only about unimportant things."

"Food's important." Brad thumped his stomach. "And the truth is I really did eat too much today."

"I think we all did," Sara admitted. "But that's because everything was so good." She looked over at Jean. "I'll have to get your recipe for the dressing you stuffed the turkey with. It was so moist and tasty."

"I'll write it down before you and Brad leave on Saturday." Jean released a lingering sigh. "I wish you could stay longer. We don't get to see enough of you."

"I know, but it could be worse," Brad said. "I might have ended up taking a church on the other side of the country. At least Lancaster is within easy driving distance of Harrisburg." He smiled at his parents. "And you two are welcome to come down anytime you like. There are two guest rooms in the parsonage, you know."

"If the roads aren't bad, we'll try to come down for your church's Christmas Eve service." Clarence looked at his wife. "Your mother still gets nervous when the roads are icy or there's too much snow coming down."

Jean nodded. "Even as a passenger, I'm white-knuckling it during bad weather. Can you imagine what shape I'd be in if I was sitting behind the wheel?"

"I don't blame you," Sara said. "I've never enjoyed driving in snow either. And it's a good thing Brad doesn't seem to mind, because from the way the snow's been coming down today, we could have nasty roads to contend with on our trip home Saturday."

Jean's forehead wrinkled. "Oh, I hope not. Let's pray for warmer temperatures that will melt the snow."

When Sara's cell phone vibrated, she excused herself to take the call and went into the kitchen.

"Happy Thanksgiving, Kenny," she said, having recognized her brother's phone number.

"Is this Sara Fuller?" The female voice on the other end was definitely not Kenny's.

"Yes, it is. Who's this?" She couldn't imagine why someone else would be using her brother's phone or calling her. Had he lost it somewhere, and someone found it?

"Sara, I'm Lynn Moore, Kenny's girlfriend. We were on our way home from my parents' house, where we ate Thanksgiving dinner, and after traveling just a few miles down the road, we were involved in an accident."

Sara's blood ran cold. "Has Kenny been hurt?" She suddenly felt as if she was reliving the past, when she'd received a call informing her that her stepfather, Dean, had been in an accident.

"Yes, but we don't know the extent of his injuries yet."

"Were you hurt too, Lynn?"

"No, just pretty shook up. The vehicle that hit us rammed into Kenny's side of the car."

"Where are you now?"

"We're at the hospital in Philadelphia. My folks are here too." Lynn gave Sara the name and address of the hospital.

"I'll let my husband know, and we'll be there as soon as we can." Sara's voice shook and tears pricked the back of her eyes. Kenny's father had died from his injuries. She couldn't stand the thought of losing Kenny too.

Sara leaned against the wall for support. *Dear Lord, I've lost too many people I love. Please let my brother be okay.*

CHAPTER 26

Philadelphia, Pennsylvania

Sara sat in one of the hospital's waiting rooms with Brad and Kenny's girlfriend, waiting to see her brother and rubbing her clenched jaw. When she and Brad had arrived an hour ago, Lynn explained that Kenny had a concussion and some broken ribs, but the doctor was running a few more tests to be sure there were no internal injuries and that the trauma to his head was not severe.

Another half hour went by before a doctor came in and said Kenny had been admitted to a room and would remain at the hospital overnight for observation. He also gave the good news that there were no internal injuries.

Relieved, Sara inhaled deeply and blew out her breath. "Thank you for letting us know. Is it all right if we see him now?"

"They're getting him settled into his

room. Once that's been done, a nurse will come out and get you." The doctor offered a reassuring smile as he looked at each of them. "Try not to worry. Kenny's going to be fine."

Lynn sagged in her chair. "When that other vehicle came barreling toward us, I was so scared." Her chin trembled. "Then after the impact, Kenny didn't respond. I was afraid he might have died."

Sara shuddered at the thought but found comfort when Brad put his arm around her. It was hard not to think of that day when her stepfather died.

"Everything's going to be okay, Sara," Brad said in a soothing tone. "Kenny will be out of commission for a few weeks while his head and ribs heal, but I'm sure he'll be fine."

"I want to stay till he's released from the hospital, and then if Kenny is willing, I think we should take him home with us until he is fully recuperated and can return to classes at the music school."

"I don't think Kenny will want to leave Philly," Lynn spoke up. "I'm pretty sure my folks will be okay with him staying with us."

Sara didn't want to upset Lynn any further, so she chose not to voice her objections. Her only response was, "It's nice of you to offer. We'll wait and see what Kenny wants to do."

Brad clasped Sara's hand and gave her fingers a comforting squeeze. "I'll call Mom and Dad and tell them we won't be coming back to Harrisburg and that hopefully we'll see them at Christmas. It's a good thing we put our luggage in the van before we left; I had a hunch we might not be going back to my parents' house today."

Sara managed a weak smile. "Thank you. I'm sure they'll understand." She felt grateful to be blessed with kind, caring in-laws.

"I should call and leave a message for Grandma, letting her know about Kenny's accident, but I don't want to worry her."

"I'm sure once you explain that Kenny's injuries are not life-threatening, she won't worry." Brad let go of Sara's hand. "Is your phone battery holding a charge, or do you need to use mine?"

Sara pulled her cell phone out of her purse. "The battery is fine. I'll call now and leave a message, even though Grandma may not go out to the phone shack till tomorrow morning."

Strasburg

"How are you feeling?" Mary Ruth asked when she entered the guest room where

277

Lenore lay the following morning.

Lenore groaned and sat up, pushing the pillows up behind her back. "I feel as though a horse and buggy ran over me. My right hip aches some, and my back feels like it's out of whack. Don't think I'll be much help to you today, Grandma."

"It's all right. You need to rest, but I still believe you should have gotten your back x-rayed and checked over last evening."

"If it'll make you feel better, you can make me an appointment to see our chiropractor. If he thinks it's necessary, he can take an X-ray there in his office." Lenore shifted on the bed, trying to get comfortable. "Maybe all I need is an adjustment. That fall I took yesterday could have put my spine out of alignment, which might be the reason I'm in so much pain."

"You may be right. I'll go out now and call Dr. Clark before Jesse gets here with Cindy. If he's in his office today, he might be able to squeeze you in. And if that's the case, I'll call one of our drivers to take you there."

"Danki, Grandma." Lenore grimaced as she shifted again. She couldn't find a comfortable position. The ice pack and arnica lotion hadn't helped much either. If she couldn't get the pain under control by

Monday, she'd have no choice but to stay home from school and let her helper take over. *I wouldn't want to stay away too many days, however,* Lenore thought as Grandma left the room.

Mary Ruth shivered as she stepped inside the cold phone shack. She made the call to the chiropractor and was relieved to learn that he was in his office and could squeeze Lenore in at one thirty. Then she arranged for Stan, one of their drivers, to give Lenore a ride.

Mary Ruth was about to leave the phone shack when she remembered she hadn't checked for phone messages. She clicked on the answering machine and found only one. It was from Sara, and the tone of her voice when she began speaking frightened Mary Ruth. Something was wrong; she just knew it.

"Grandma, I wanted to let you know that Brad and I are at the hospital in Philadelphia. Kenny and his girlfriend were involved in a car accident on their way home from her parents' house, where they'd gone to celebrate Thanksgiving. Kenny is not seriously injured, but we would appreciate your prayers. I'll call again and give you an update on things, and please try not to worry."

Mary Ruth squeezed her eyes shut. *Heavenly Father, please be with my grandson and heal his body of the wounds he received during the accident.*

Hearing a horse and buggy come into the yard and knowing it must be Jesse, Mary Ruth stepped out of the phone shack. "Guder mariye, Jesse."

"Good morning," he responded as he hitched the horse to the rail and took Cindy out of the buggy. "How's Lenore doing?"

"Still hurting, but I managed to get her an appointment with the chiropractor. One of my drivers will be by to get her this afternoon." Mary Ruth reached in and grabbed Cindy's diaper bag, and they made their way up to the house.

Once inside, Jesse took Cindy's outer garments off, gave her a kiss, and set her on the blanket Mary Ruth had placed on the floor. "If there's anything I can do to help, just say the word. I can do a few chores after work this evening, and I'd be glad to come by tomorrow to do whatever else needs to be done."

She smiled. "Danki, Jesse. That's very kind of you. And knowing I won't have to do all the chores by myself will no doubt give

Lenore a sense of relief." Mary Ruth shook her head. "I sure wouldn't want her trying to do much of anything right now. Not till her back is feeling better. Even then, she'll have to be careful how she moves for a while."

He glanced around the room. "Is she still in bed?"

"Jah."

"Well, tell her I said hello and that I hope to see her later today."

"I surely will."

Jesse knelt on the floor and gave his daughter another kiss, then tickled her under the chin. "Be good for Mary Ruth."

Cindy looked up at him and giggled.

Chuckling, he stood. "I'll see you after work, Mary Ruth. I hope you have a good day and that my little one doesn't give you any trouble."

"I'm sure she won't. Cindy's always been a good girl for me."

Jesse said goodbye, and after he went out the front door, Mary Ruth moved over to the baby. "All right, little one, what shall we do while we're waiting for Lenore to get up?"

Cindy made some baby-talk sounds and stuck her thumb in her mouth.

Mary Ruth laughed. "I think we can find

something more exciting for you to do than that."

"How are you doing? What did the chiropractor say?" Grandma asked when Lenore limped through the front door later that afternoon.

"He took an X-ray, and there are no broken bones, so that's a relief." Lenore paused to take a breath. "He believes it's just a pulled muscle, and I have a pretty nasty bruise."

"What did he suggest you do for it?"

"Ice, alternating with heat. He also gave me a natural muscle relaxer and something for pain from the nutrition area of his clinic." Lenore took off her outer garments and hung them on the clothes tree in the hall. "He suggested that I rest and return to the clinic sometime next week."

Grandma tipped her head. "So no teaching for a while?"

"Not till the pain is better and I'm able to sit comfortably. My helper will have to be notified, and she may be on her own with the class if someone can't step in as the main teacher." Lenore grimaced. "This is not a good time for me to be away from school. The Christmas program the scholars will be putting on for their families is less than a month away. I would very much like to be at school so I can work with the children, helping them get their skits, recitations, and songs perfected."

"I am sure whoever fills in for you will work with the kinner."

"I suppose." Lenore glanced toward the living room. "How is Cindy doing? Has she been good for you today?"

Grandma nodded. "That boppli is so *siess.*"

"I think all babies are sweet." A pang of regret over not being a mother stabbed her heart. It was wrong to dwell on her desire to be married and raising a family, but she wasn't getting any younger, and the idea of having to remain single was never far from her thoughts.

"Where is Cindy now?" Lenore asked as she worked her way slowly to the living-room couch.

"She's taking a nap. I set up the playpen in my room so she could sleep undisturbed."

"That's good." As Grandma took a seat in her rocking chair, Lenore lowered herself to the couch. It was time to get off her feet.

"Would you like an ice pack or a warm compress for your back?" Grandma questioned.

"No, I just need to lie down and rest for a bit."

"Why don't you go into the guest room and take a nap? I'll call you when supper is ready."

Lenore reached around with one hand and rubbed the muscle spasm in her back. "I feel bad leaving you with all the work. I should be helping with supper."

"You need to rest your back, and I'm perfectly capable of fixing our evening meal by myself."

Lenore would have liked to argue the point, but Grandma was right. For now, at least, she needed to rest so her back would heal and she could return to teaching, in addition to all her other normal activities, just as soon as possible.

CHAPTER 27

"Would you mind if we stop by my grandma's before going back to Lancaster?" Sara asked as she and Brad traveled home Saturday morning. "I want to give Grandma an update on Kenny and see how Lenore is doing." Sara was glad her grandmother had told her about Lenore's fall on the ice so she could be praying for her.

Brad glanced over at Sara and smiled. "Sure, hon. In fact, I was going to suggest the very same thing."

They drove in silence awhile, until Sara asked another question. "Do you think I was too pushy, trying to convince Kenny he should come home with us to heal? He seemed kind of irritated when I brought it up again before we left the hospital."

With his eyes still on the road, Brad reached over and patted Sara's arm. "He's not your kid brother anymore; Kenny is almost twenty years old and has become pretty independent since he moved to Philadelphia to attend the music institute."

"I understand that, but how would staying with us for a few weeks hamper his independence?"

"He might feel as if you'd want to mother him."

Sara folded her arms. "That's ridiculous. I've never tried to do that to Kenny."

"Now don't get upset. I wasn't insinuating that you were mothering him." Brad spoke in a gentle tone. "I only mentioned it because sometimes when a person makes a suggestion, we take it the wrong way and assume they are trying to tell us what to do."

Sara felt heat behind her eyelids. "I only want what's best for him, but if he'd rather stay with Lynn's parents, then I guess that's okay. At least Kenny won't be by himself while he's recuperating from his injuries."

"Right. And you can keep in touch by phone to find out how he's doing."

Sara leaned against her headrest and tried to relax. *Maybe I'll feel better about things when we get to Grandma's and she's given me the hug I need.*

After breakfast, Mary Ruth headed to the basement to get some towels she'd hung on the inside line the night before. Lenore was resting on the living-room couch, so Mary Ruth figured it was also a good time to take a look inside the prayer jar that Sara, Michelle, and Lenore had found down there.

Going over to the step stool, she climbed up carefully and took down the jar. Taking a seat on a wooden stool, she opened the lid and pulled out a slip of paper near the top. A verse of scripture had been written on it. "The Lord is nigh unto them that are of a broken heart; and saveth such as be of a contrite spirit. Psalm 34:18."

Mary Ruth sighed. *My poor daughter's heart was broken, and that's why she chose this verse to put in her prayer jar. Oh Rhoda, if only you had talked to your daed and me — told us about the baby — we would have offered our love and support, even if we didn't approve of your actions. We loved you so much and would have worked things out if you'd let us.*

So many regrets, but they wouldn't change the past. *Now don't start wallowing in pity,* she chided herself. *Be thankful for the note Rhoda left in her Bible so you could get to know Sara.*

Mary Ruth put the piece of paper back in the jar and returned it to the shelf. Reading Rhoda's messages conjured up feelings of sadness, but at the same time Mary Ruth found comfort in learning what her daughter had written. For now, at least, she needed to concentrate on getting the towels off the clothesline, folding them, and taking them upstairs to put away.

Lenore had barely found a comfortable position on the couch when she heard a car pull into the yard. Thinking Grandma would see to whoever it was, she made no move to get up.

A short time later, a knock sounded on the front door. Lenore listened for Grandma's footsteps, but when they didn't come and the knock came again, she pulled herself off the couch. Limping across the room, she opened the door and was surprised to see Sara and Brad on the porch.

"How are you?" Sara asked.

"How's your brother?" Lenore queried at the same time.

"Kenny's still hurting but is out of the hospital now," Sara said. "We came by to see how you're doing and to give an update on his condition."

"We're anxious to hear. Grandma and I have been praying for him. Come on in." Lenore led the way to the living room, where she took a seat on the couch, placing a pillow behind her back. "Grandma went to the basement to get some clean towels, but I thought she'd be back up here by now."

"I should go check on her." Sara's brows drew together. "Those stairs are steep, and she might have fallen."

"In that case, I'd better go down to the basement. If she's hurt, I'll let you both know. Sara, why don't you stay here and visit with Lenore?" Brad suggested. He left before Sara could respond.

Sara lowered herself into Grandpa's recliner. "We heard about your fall on the ice. How are you doing, Lenore?"

"My back's still sore, but the X-ray at the chiropractor's office didn't show any broken bones. He thinks I just pulled a muscle, and of course my back and part of the hip area are bruised."

"Will you be able to teach on Monday?"

"I want to, but with the pain I'm feeling now, it's doubtful."

"I'm sorry to hear that. Slipping on ice can be so dangerous — same with stairs." Sara turned her gaze in the direction of the basement stairway. "I hope Grandma's okay. The last thing we need is someone else in the family getting hurt."

Lenore bobbed her head. "That's for sure."

A few minutes later, Brad entered the room carrying a laundry basket full of towels. Grandma was behind him.

Sara got up and gave Grandma a hug. "I was worried about you, and I'm glad you let Brad carry the laundry basket up. You shouldn't be going up and down those steps. An accident can happen when you least expect it — just ask Lenore."

Grandma patted Sara's arm. "I've been doing it for years, and I'm always careful on the stairs. Besides, the washing machine is down there, so how else am I supposed to get the laundry done?"

"True, but I often do the laundry," Lenore interjected.

"With your back hurting right now, you shouldn't try to do any chores." Shaking her finger, Grandma peered at Lenore over the top of her glasses. "Please try not to worry about me."

"Where should I put this?" Brad asked, nodding with his head toward the laundry basket he still held.

"You can set it in the hall by the bathroom door. The towels are folded. I just need to put them away."

"Okay, sure." When Brad left the room,

Grandma took a seat in her rocker. "How is Kenny doing?" she asked, looking at Sara. "I've been concerned since I first heard about his accident."

"He still has some pain from the concussion, but the broken ribs are causing the real discomfort." Sara frowned as she folded her arms. "I tried to talk him into coming home with us to recuperate, but he chose to stay with his girlfriend's parents instead."

"Maybe he wanted to be closer to his school so he could keep up with his classes," Grandma said.

"That could be, although we do have internet access and two computers, so he could do his schoolwork right in our home."

"At least he will have someone to keep an eye on him and make sure he doesn't overdo." Grandma got the rocking chair moving. "I'm thankful he wasn't seriously hurt."

Sara shuddered. "Same here. I was so scared when I got the call that he'd been involved in an accident. It felt like I was reliving Dean's accident when I found out he'd been seriously injured."

Brad returned to the living room and took a seat on the other end of the couch. "Is there anything Sara and I can do for either of you while we're here?" He looked at

Grandma and Lenore.

"Jesse will be coming over soon to take care of the chores in the barn." Grandma smiled. "That young man is so kind and helpful. He did several chores for us when he was here last evening, and he didn't hesitate to volunteer his help again today."

Tilting her head to one side, Sara looked over at Lenore with her lips slightly parted. "Are you still seeing Jesse socially?"

"I was, but thanks to my sore back, we probably won't be doing anything together for a while." Lenore grimaced. "Sure wish I had seen that patch of ice before it was too late. It was embarrassing enough to fall in front of Jesse and Peter, but when Jesse picked me up and carried me into the house, my face felt like it was on fire."

Brad chuckled. "Sounds like you've been bitten by the love bug."

Lenore kept quiet. No way was she about to admit that she'd allowed herself to fall in love with Jesse. Since he had not spoken any words of love or mentioned marriage, it wouldn't be right to blurt out her feelings.

"Once your back is doing better, maybe the four of us could get together and go bowling or out to supper at a nice restaurant," Sara suggested.

"That would be fun." Lenore repositioned

herself against the pillow. She hoped it wouldn't be too long before she was pain free and could function normally again. She also hoped Jesse would agree to go with Sara and Brad on what might be considered a double date.

CHAPTER 28

Clymer

Michelle glanced at the calendar on Ezekiel's desk. Today was Thursday, just a week after Thanksgiving. In another three weeks they'd be celebrating Christmas. Ezekiel had promised they could go to Strasburg for Christmas, and Michelle looked forward to that. They'd be taking Val with them, because Michelle couldn't stand the thought of someone else caring for the dog in her absence. Besides, Val probably missed Sadie and all the attention she used to get from family and friends in Strasburg.

Seeing everyone again would be a joy. Michelle missed them all terribly. Having Jack and Ernie visit for Thanksgiving had been wonderful, but they'd only been able to stay for a few days, and then loneliness had set in again.

She moved across the room to get breakfast started, nearly tripping on Val, who lay curled on a throw rug near the stove. The dog always wanted to be near Michelle and often slipped into the house as soon as the door would open.

Ezekiel would be in from doing chores soon, and he'd need to eat so he could get out to his shop and begin working on a new order for several bee boxes. He already had one employee working for him, but if business kept growing, he'd need to hire more help.

Michelle picked up a jar of honey and placed it on the table. Ezekiel liked to stir a heaping teaspoonful of honey into a glass of room-temperature water, along with a tablespoon of apple cider vinegar. He claimed it gave him extra energy and kept him from getting sick. Michelle had never tried the concoction, so she couldn't be sure what health benefits it offered. According to a book Ezekiel's mother gave them soon after they were married, drinking lukewarm water combined with pure, unfiltered honey and vinegar could be helpful for several ailments, including nausea.

Michelle was actually tempted to try some today, because she'd felt queasy ever since she'd gotten out of bed. "Sure hope I'm not coming down with the stomach bug that's been going around," she mumbled as she took out a slab of bacon and a carton of eggs. "If I get sick, I'll feel even more sorry for myself."

"Did I hear my fraa say she's feeling grank?"

Michelle whirled around. "Ach, you scared me, Ezekiel. I didn't hear you come in."

He wiggled his brows. "That's 'cause I'm so sneaky."

"I can't argue with that." Michelle took out the frying pan, placed four pieces of bacon in it, and turned on the gas burner. As it began to cook, her stomach rolled. "Eww . . . just the smell of this makes me feel sick. I must be coming down with the flu."

"Or you could be expecting our first boppli."

Her husband's hopeful tone caused Michelle to tear up. "If only it were true."

"It could be." Ezekiel slipped his arms around her waist. "You could get one of those home pregnancy tests at the pharmacy or make an appointment to see a doctor."

Michelle gave the hem of her apron a tug. "I suppose it wouldn't hurt to take a pregnancy test, although I'm sure it will be negative." Her chin jutted out. "I'm used to being disappointed."

"Are you disappointed in me, because I

wanted to move to New York?" Ezekiel rubbed his forehead with the palm of his hand. "You would have preferred to stay in Strasburg, right?"

"Yes, I would, but my place is with my husband, and if this is where you want to be, then I will learn to be content living here too."

Ezekiel kissed Michelle's forehead. "I love you so much."

"I love you too." She turned back toward the stove, being careful not to step on Val's tail. "Now I'd better get breakfast made or you'll never get out to your shop."

"Okay, but would you like me to go by the pharmacy sometime today and pick up a pregnancy test for you?"

Michelle shrugged. "Sure. Guess it can't hurt."

Strasburg

Lenore stood in front of the living-room window, staring out at the snow-covered yard. If the weather didn't change, they would definitely have a white Christmas.

Her shoulders drooped, and she sighed. The pain in her back had lessened, but she didn't feel good enough to begin teaching again. The healing process was taking longer than she'd expected, and it tried her patience. Staying home all day and not being able to do much was taking its toll on Lenore, as she'd never been one to sit around and do little or nothing.

"If you're up to it, I have a favor to ask."

Lenore turned at the sound of her grandmother's voice. "What is it?"

"Cindy just woke up, and I'm trying to finish the *frack* I started sewing for her yesterday."

"You want me to keep an eye on her?"

Grandma nodded. "I realize you have to be careful with your back, but perhaps you could sit on the couch with her in your lap and read the touch-and-feel book Jesse brought over the other day for his daughter to look at." Grandma clasped her hands together. "Hopefully you can keep her occupied until I finish the dress."

"Sure, no problem." Lenore took a seat on the couch, positioning a soft pillow behind her back. "If you'll bring Cindy and her little book to me, I'll do my best to keep her entertained."

Grandma smiled and left the room.

A lump formed in Lenore's throat as she looked at the quilt Grandma had made to drape over Grandpa's lap when he had been wheelchair-bound after his stroke. She closed her eyes, remembering Grandpa's satisfied expression as he sat in his wheelchair with the small quilt. The covering was about the size of a wall hanging and dropped from the middle of his chest all the way down to the floor. Grandma now kept it draped over the back of Grandpa's favorite chair.

Unwilling to give in to her tears, Lenore opened her eyes. It did no good to dwell on what could not be changed.

When Grandma brought Cindy out to Lenore a few minutes later, the little girl giggled and held out her arms. Lenore's heart nearly melted. What she wouldn't give to help Jesse raise this adorable child.

Grandma placed Cindy in Lenore's lap and handed her the book. "I'll just be in the next room, so if she gets squirmy and you need a break, please holler out to me and I'll come right away."

"Okay."

After Grandma left the room, Lenore began reading the story about the curious squirrel in the forest, searching for nuts and other good food. On each page was a picture of a little brown squirrel with fuzzy fur. The grass was also textured, and so were the fluffy clouds in the sky. Lenore took hold of Cindy's hand and rubbed it gently across each of the textures as she said the name of the item in Pennsylvania Dutch. "*Eechhaas* — squirrel. *Graas* — grass. *Wolke* — clouds."

Cindy giggled, tipping her head back to look up at Lenore and batting her feathery eyelashes.

Smiling, Lenore read through the story again. When she finished, Lenore sang one of her favorite Christmas songs while stroking Cindy's soft cheek with her thumb: "*Silent night, holy night . . . All is calm, all is bright.*"

Cindy sat still for several minutes but then grew restless. When she began to whimper and squirm, Lenore tried reading the book again, but the little girl had obviously lost interest. Realizing she wouldn't be able to keep the child entertained any longer, Lenore called out to Grandma. Maybe later today, if her back felt better, Lenore would try sitting in the rocking chair with Cindy. The child usually liked to be rocked, and sometimes that was all it took to put her to sleep.

With Christmas only a few weeks away, the flower shop was swamped with orders and lots of customers coming in to see what was available. Sara had put a small, beautifully decorated tree in the window display with pots of poinsettias sitting around it. All the plants had been purchased from the King family's greenhouse, but this year Ezekiel was not the one to deliver them. Instead, his brother Abe had brought the red, white, and pink blooming beauties into the shop.

Sighing as she took a seat behind the counter to look at the list of orders that had come in so far today, Sara thought about Michelle. She'd received a letter from her soon after she and Ezekiel moved to New York, but hadn't heard anything else from her in a while.

Sara leaned her elbows on the counter. *I wonder how Michelle's adjusting to her new home and how things are going with Ezekiel and his new business.*

There was a time when Sara would have been glad if Michelle had moved out of Strasburg. But the friendship they had eventually established changed all that, and now Sara truly missed Michelle. *I think Grandma and Lenore miss her too.*

Sara's musings were pushed aside when a customer entered the store. She was surprised to see Rick Osprey, whom she hadn't seen since their first night of Bible study.

As he approached the counter, his posture stiffened, and as he looked at Sara, Rick blinked a couple of times. "Say, aren't you

301

Pastor Fuller's wife?"

"Yes, I am. I met you at our first Bible study, but we haven't seen or heard from you since. Is everything all right?"

"It's fine. I had to quit the Bible study because I'm working nights now." He glanced down at his feet, then back at Sara again. "Guess I should have called and let the pastor know, but I've been super busy lately and sort of spaced it off."

"Oh, I see." Sara cleared her throat. "Umm . . . that night at the Bible study you attended, you said something about hanging out with some Amish young people when you were a teenager."

He nodded.

"You mentioned one of the girls and said you thought her name was Reba, or Rhoda. Was it Rhoda Lapp?"

He scratched the side of his head, and a flush crept across his cheeks. "Yeah, I think so."

"What did she look like? Did she have red hair?"

"Yeah, come to think of it, she sure did. It was real long and she wore it hanging down her back. But until one of the girls, whose name I don't remember, said something about Rhoda's heritage, I had no idea she'd been raised in an Amish home."

Sara shivered as a chill ran through her body. *Is this conversation making him uncomfortable? Could Rick be embarrassed because he'd been seeing an Amish girl? Could my mother have been secretly seeing him?* She gulped with the realization of what could be possible. *If Rick was seeing my mother, then he could be the man I've been searching for since I moved here to Pennsylvania. By some miracle, could my biological father be standing here before me? If so, did Mama tell him she was expecting a baby before she left?*

Sara licked her lips with cautious hope. "How well did you know Rhoda Lapp? Were the two of you close?"

While she waited for his answer, which seemed to be slow in coming, Sara studied the man carefully, trying to decide if she resembled him in any way. His eyes were blue, only a bit lighter than hers, but his hair was brown.

"Uh . . . I didn't know most of the Amish girls that well, except . . ." Rick paused and looked at his watch. "Oh boy, I didn't realize what time it is. There's someplace I need to go."

"Can I help you with anything before you leave?"

He shook his head. "Change of plans. I was going to order some flowers for my wife's birthday, but I can't do it right now."

Before Sara could respond, he rushed out the door. She bit the inside of her cheek. *Rick never finished answering my question, and he seemed in an awfully big hurry to get out of my store.* Goose bumps erupted on Sara's arms. *If Rick Osprey is my biological father, maybe he suspects that Mama told me, and he doesn't want anything to do with me. That could be why he rushed out the door and never fully responded to my question. If he does come back to order the flowers, should I mention that I'm Rhoda's daughter and see how he reacts to the news?*

CHAPTER 29

"How are things going with your new business, Son?" Ezekiel's father asked as the family sat around the dining-room table on Christmas Eve.

Ezekiel's eyes lit up. "Real good, Dad. I've been getting orders from several different states."

"Guess there must be plenty of people interested in raising bees for honey, huh?"

Ezekiel nodded enthusiastically, then looked at his brother Abe. "You takin' good care of the hives I left here?"

"Jah. Of course, there ain't much to do during the winter months other than to check on things."

Ezekiel's mother frowned as she shook her finger at Abe. "You know how I feel about that word *ain't.* Makes you sound like you've had no education at all."

Michelle glanced at Abe to see what his reaction would be, but without a word, he cut a piece of ham and popped it into his mouth.

As everyone continued to eat their food, Michelle wondered if Ezekiel was ever going to bring up the topic foremost on her mind. Finally, as their meal came to a close, he tapped his water glass with a spoon and said, "If I can have everyone's attention, Michelle and I have an announcement to make."

All heads turned in Michelle and Ezekiel's direction.

Ezekiel reached over and placed his hand on Michelle's shoulder. "The good news we have to share on this special Christmas Eve is that sometime toward the end of July, we're gonna become parents."

Belinda's face broke into a wide smile. "That's wonderful news, Son." She looked across the table at Michelle. "How are you feeling? Any problems at all?"

"I'm a little tired and have had some nausea in the mornings, but otherwise I'm doing okay." Michelle would never admit it — at least not to Ezekiel's folks — but despite her excitement over being pregnant, she had many concerns. Would she be able to carry the baby to full term? Could she bear the pains of labor? Would Ezekiel still think she was pretty when her stomach grew large? But what concerned her the most was whether she had what it took to be a mother. Her own mother had been abusive and neglected her three children. What if those tendencies were hereditary and Michelle ended up treating their child unfairly, the way her folks had treated her, Jack, and Ernie?

"Are you hoping for a *bu* or a *maedel*?" Ezekiel's sister Amy asked.

"I think Ezekiel would like a son, but it makes no difference to me," Michelle replied, after taking a drink of apple cider and setting her glass down.

Ezekiel shook his head. "I'm not set on having a boy. As long as the *boppli* is healthy, that's all that matters."

"Very true," Ezekiel's brother-in-law Toby spoke up. "When Sylvia and I found out she was in a family way eighteen months ago, the only thing we talked about and prayed for was that our child would be healthy." He glanced over at their nine-month-old son, Allen, sitting in his high chair with a big smile, and grinned. "We are ever so thankful for our little boy's good health."

Ezekiel's youngest brother, Henry, looked over at his dad. "Were you happy that I was a bu?"

Vernon bobbed his head. "But I'd have been equally glad if you were a maedel."

Henry rolled his eyes. "Sure glad I wasn't a girl. Can't imagine havin' to wear a dress and do all the things womenfolk do."

"Just what kind of things are you referring to?" his sister Amy asked.

"Uh, you know . . . cookin', cleanin', doin' dishes and laundry . . . that kind of stuff."

Amy bumped his arm with her elbow. "Those aren't just chores for women, little brother. You need to learn how to do most of them too."

His brows furrowed. "How come?"

"Because someday, when I get married and move out of the house, Mom might need extra help in the kitchen or doing other household chores, and she'll be counting on you."

Sylvia pointed at Henry. "Also, when you get married someday, your wife might need a hand with some chores."

Henry pressed a fist against his mouth as his cheeks puffed out. "I ain't . . . ." He paused and looked at his mother. "I mean, I'm not ever getting married."

Michelle chuckled at the seriousness in his tone.

"Never say never, little brother," Ezekiel put in. "When I was your age, I didn't think

I'd ever grow up and get married." He reached over and clasped Michelle's hand. "But look at me now. I'm not only a married man, but also a soon-to-be father."

Michelle stared at her plate of unfinished food. *I wish we could be here when I give birth to our baby, but it doesn't look like Ezekiel will change his mind and move back home.* In an effort not to give in to self-pity and ruin the evening, Michelle thought about the fun they would have when they went over to see Mary Ruth and Lenore sometime on Christmas Day.

"Where's Herschel?" Jesse asked when he and Cindy arrived at Vera and Milton's house for a Christmas Eve supper.

"He'll be here," Vera replied. "He's probably running behind because things were busy at the bulk-food store today. That does happen sometimes — especially when folks are out buying things at the last minute before Christmas Day." She looked at Cindy and clicked her tongue. "Goodness gracious, this little girl seems more grown up every time I see her." Her brows furrowed as she looked at Jesse. "Which isn't often enough, I might add."

"Sorry about that. Between work and running Cindy over to the Lapps' five days a week, there isn't much time for socializing."

"That's not what I heard," Milton put in as he joined them in the hallway where Jesse was removing Cindy's jacket.

Jesse looked at the older man. "What do you mean?"

"I've heard talk around that you're courting the schoolteacher, Lenore Lapp."

Vera looked at Jesse through her thick-lensed glasses. "Is it true?"

Jesse's ears burned. He hadn't told Esther's great-aunt and great-uncle that he'd begun courting Lenore because he was afraid of their reaction. They might think he was being untrue to his deceased wife. *And I am,* Jesse told himself. *Which is why I can't allow myself to fall in love with Lenore.* He shifted his weight from one foot to the other. *Should I tell them that the reason behind my decision to court Lenore is to give Cindy a mother? Would they understand or say I'm wrong to pursue a relationship where there is no love?* His jaw clenched. *No, it's best not to say anything — at least not right now.*

"Jesse, did you hear what I said?" Vera prompted.

He licked his lips. "Umm . . . jah, Lenore and I have been spending more time together." He moved into the living room and placed Cindy on the floor with a stuffed, floppy-eared puppy he'd brought along for her. It was a Christmas present, but he'd given it to her early. Of course, in order to avoid a lecture, he wouldn't mention it to Vera. She could be a stickler about certain things.

"It's hard to believe my daughter will be a year old so soon." Jesse hoped this new topic would take some pressure off him and get the conversation going in another direction.

"Jah, it sure is, and I'm surprised she's not walking yet." Vera took a seat in one of the overstuffed chairs. "Have you been working with her on that, Jesse?"

"She's getting close." Jesse tousled his daughter's hair, avoiding a direct answer to Vera's question. "She pulls herself up to things and walks when you're holding her hands, but she hasn't taken any steps on her own yet."

"All kinner walk at their own pace." Milton took a seat in the chair beside his wife. "Cindy will take off whenever she's ready."

Jesse had just settled himself on the couch when Herschel showed up. The poor man looked exhausted as he sagged into a chair.

"Sorry for showing up late, but it was busier than usual at the store all day. Everyone seemed to be shopping with a frenzy."

"It's okay. You're here now, Son, so that's all that matters." Vera rose from her chair. "I'll get supper on the table, and then we can eat."

Jesse jumped up and followed her to the kitchen. "What can I do to help?"

She waved her hand. "No need for that. You've been working most of the day too."

"It's okay. I'm more than happy to help." Jesse grabbed a potholder, took the kettle of green beans off the stove, drained off the water, and poured them into a serving bowl.

Vera smiled. "Danki. You're such a helpful young man."

"When I lived at home with my folks, I helped out with whatever needed to be done. 'Course, I never learned to cook that well, despite helping my mamm in the kitchen."

"It must be hard for you now, having to fend for yourself, plus take care of Cindy's needs."

"Jah, but on the days Mary Ruth watches Cindy, I usually stay for supper, so that helps a lot."

"You're welcome to eat with us here anytime, you know."

"I appreciate that." Seeing a kettle of cut-up potatoes cooking on the stove, Jesse grabbed a fork and gave them a poke. "These are done. Did you want me to mash them while you cut the ham, or would you prefer that I do the cutting?"

"I'll mash and you can cut. Milton likes his spuds fixed a certain way, so I'd better make sure they're just the way he likes them."

"Okay, no problem." Jesse took the ham from the oven, and while he sliced it, his thoughts went to Lenore. He and Cindy had been invited to eat with Mary Ruth and her family on Christmas Day, and he looked forward not only to the meal, but also to spending the day with them.

Lenore sat off to one side as her scholars presented the much anticipated Christmas program for their families and close friends. She was glad her back was feeling better and she'd been able to return to her teaching position a week ago. It had given her some time to work with the children, but Eva Riehl, the woman who had taken over for her, along with Lenore's assistant, Viola, had done most of the preparation for this special Christmas Eve event. Tonight, all three of them would prompt and support the students participating in the program with poems, songs, and skits.

The children's parents and other family members crowded into the schoolhouse, many doubling up and sitting at school desks. The overflow crowd sat on backless benches that had been set up at the back and sides of the room.

Lenore's heart swelled with joy when it came time for her older students to act out a short skit representing the birth of Jesus. *What a blessed event it must have been to witness God's Son being carefully laid in a manger and the glory of the Lord shining around the shepherds in the fields as the angels announced the Savior's birth.*

Lenore reflected on Luke 2:10–12, being quoted by the young boy playing the part of one of the shepherds. "And the angel said unto them, Fear not: for, behold, I bring you good tidings of great joy, which shall be to all people. For unto you is born this day in the city of David a Saviour, which is Christ the Lord. And this shall be a sign unto you; Ye shall find the babe wrapped in swaddling clothes, lying in a manger."

How wonderful it was to have the assurance that because Jesus came to die for the sins of the world, those who accepted Him and believed on His name would be saved.

Lenore thought once more about her dear grandfather and the many sermons he'd preached while ministering in their church. Grandpa was a strong believer in preaching God's Word in a way people understood. He often quoted verses on faith, hope, and spiritual blessings that would uplift hearts filled with despair and offer peace during difficult times. Grandpa also stressed the importance of being "filled with all the fulness of God" and remembering to praise and thank Him for all things.

As the program came to a close after the group sang several Christmas carols, Lenore closed her eyes and offered a brief prayer. *Heavenly Father, thank You for Your Son, Jesus, the Savior of the world. Please bless each of my students, as well as all those who came out tonight to share in the joy of the Christmas miracle.*

Lenore looked forward to spending Christmas Day with her family, along with seeing Jesse and Cindy again. Michelle and Ezekiel would also be dropping by for a short time, and she was eager to see them as well. But tonight Lenore's thoughts would be focused on the joy she saw on each scholar's face as they shared the good news of the Savior's birth with their family and friends.

CHAPTER 30

"The scholars did a good job with the program last night, don't you think?" Lenore asked as she and Mary Ruth began laying things out for their Christmas dinner.

"Uh-huh." Mary Ruth reached into the pantry for a stack of napkins and placed them on the counter next to the plates and silverware.

"I was so glad I could be there, because for a while I didn't think I would be up to going back to teach school in time to work with the kinner on their parts for the program."

Mary Ruth nodded slowly.

"Are you okay, Grandma?" Lenore touched Mary Ruth's arm. "You've been awfully quiet all morning."

"I'll be okay. I am just missing your grandpa more than ever today. This is the first Christmas since we got married that

I've spent without him." She sighed heavily. "It's ever so strange."

Lenore slipped her arms around Mary Ruth and gave her a hug. "I know, Grandma. I miss him too, and I'm sure the rest of the family does as well."

Mary Ruth sniffed, attempting to hold back tears. She'd been trying to remain strong since Willis's death, but the holidays made it harder. "I'll be all right. Just need to keep busy and focus on others today," she said. "When I'm feeling discouraged, I have to remind myself that there are so many other people in more difficult situations. I am grateful for each of my family members and friends, for without them I would be terribly lonely."

"Jah," Lenore agreed, gently patting Mary Ruth's back. "I can't imagine how it must be for people who have no one to spend the holidays with or be there to encourage them during times of distress."

Mary Ruth nodded as she slowly pulled away from her granddaughter's loving embrace. "Well, I need to get busy. There is still a lot to do before all our company arrives." She moved across the room. "Maybe you could get the potatoes cut up while I go down to the basement to get a few jars of pickled beets."

"Okay, but please be careful on the steps and make sure the battery-operated light at the top of the stairs is turned on before you head down," Lenore called.

"Don't worry. I'll make sure I have enough light, and I'll be extra cautious on the stairs." Mary Ruth had gone up and down her basement steps many times over the years and had never fallen, but she appreciated the reminder to be careful nonetheless. It was one more proof of how much her granddaughter cared about her.

Mary Ruth stepped into the hall and opened the basement door. After turning on the battery-operated light, she descended the stairs, making sure to hold on to the railing. When she reached the bottom, she turned on another lamp powered by batteries and went to the shelves where her home-canned fruits and vegetables were stored, along with all the empty, clean jars that would be used when they put up produce from their garden next summer.

Mary Ruth paused and stared up at the jar full of folded papers on the top shelf. *I wonder what the future holds for me. How long can I remain living in this house that Willis and I shared for so many years?*

She couldn't expect Lenore to live with her indefinitely. She'd be getting married someday — possibly to Jesse — and would want a home of her own.

Mary Ruth decided to take down the prayer jar and read some more of the messages her daughter had written before she'd run away. She thought somehow it might make her feel closer to Rhoda.

She positioned the step stool in front of the shelves and climbed up to retrieve the jar. *It's kind of silly to leave the jar way up here,* she told herself, *but since this is where Rhoda hid it, maybe it's best to keep it where it was originally found.*

After taking a seat on a folding chair, Mary Ruth reached inside the jar and pulled out a slip of paper with a prayer written on it: "Dear Lord, help me to trust You in all things."

"That's a good prayer for everyone," Mary Ruth whispered. "Sometimes we need to remind ourselves."

The second paper Mary Ruth pulled out contained the words of Philippians 4:19. "My God shall supply all your need according to his riches in glory by Christ Jesus."

Guess I need to stop fretting about what the future holds for me and trust the Lord with each new day. When the time comes for Lenore to move out, I may take Ivan up on his offer and move in with him and Yvonne.

With renewed determination to leave her future in God's hands, Mary Ruth put the prayer jar away and trudged back up the stairs.

A sense of peace came over Sara as soon as she and Brad, along with Brad's parents, stepped onto her grandmother's porch. She had hoped that Kenny could join them today, but he'd chosen to spend the holiday with his girlfriend and her parents.

As they entered the house, the delicious aroma of roasted turkey greeted them, along with Grandma's welcoming smile and hug.

"I'd like you to meet my parents, Clarence and Jean." Brad gestured to them as they all stood in the hallway entrance.

Grandma and Lenore shook both of their hands, welcoming them into their home. "Thank you for inviting us to join you today." Brad's mother smiled. "Clarence and I have heard so much about you."

"That's right," Brad's father agreed. "We feel like we know you already."

"We are so glad you could join us." Lenore took everyone's coats and hung them up while Grandma led the way to the living room and invited them all to take a seat. Lenore joined them a few minutes later. Jean and Clarence found seats on the couch, and Grandma sat in her rocker.

"How was your Christmas Eve?" Lenore asked, taking a seat next to Sara.

"Very nice. We held a beautiful Christmas Eve candlelight communion service at our church last night." Sara spoke in a bubbly tone. "We also sang Christmas carols, and Brad preached a short sermon, reflecting on scriptures from Luke."

Lenore placed her hand on Sara's arm. "In the skit some of my older students did during the school play last night, some verses from Luke were mentioned too."

"How did the program go?" Brad asked.

"Very well, and I'm thankful my back had healed enough that I could attend. As their teacher, I felt it was important for me to be there."

Jean leaned forward with her head tilted to one side, and Grandma explained about Lenore's accident that had kept her from the one-room schoolhouse until a week ago.

"I'm glad you're doing better." Sara clasped Lenore's hand and gave her fingers a gentle squeeze.

"Tell us about your role as teacher in a one-room schoolhouse." Jean looked at Lenore expectantly.

Sara was pleased to see how relaxed Brad's parents seemed to be, especially since this was their first time visiting an Amish home. They didn't appear to be the least bit uncomfortable talking to Grandma and Lenore, or sitting in a room with gas-generated lights and only basic furnishings. Of course her in-laws' home in Harrisburg, although lovely, wasn't overdone with a lot of expensive furniture or fancy decorations. She was thankful that Jean and Clarence were Christians and down-to-earth. Grandma and Lenore probably sensed that too.

While Lenore explained how she'd begun teaching, Sara caught Grandma's eye. "Is there something I can do to help you in the kitchen?" she asked.

"As a matter of fact, there is."

Sara left her seat and followed Grandma to the kitchen. "How are you doing? I'm sure you must be missing Grandpa today."

Grandma nodded. "But I'm thankful to have my family around me. You're all a blessing, and I appreciate each of you so much."

"We appreciate you too." Sara gave Grandma a hug. "Without your love and support, I wouldn't be where I am now, spiritually or emotionally." She swiped at a few tears trickling down her cheeks. "If it hadn't been for that letter in Mama's Bible,

I never would have met you."

"So true. And knowing you has brought great joy into my life, as it did your grandpa's." Grandma sniffed and reached under her glasses to blot at her tears. "I only wish Rhoda and Willis could be here today."

"I would have liked that too, but at least we have each other."

"Jah, and you know what?"

"What's that, Grandma?"

"I just heard a horse and buggy pulling in, so I'm guessing your uncle Ivan and his family have arrived."

When Lenore looked out the window and saw her parents' horse and buggy at the hitching rail, she got up and went to answer the door. Her youngest brother, Peter, was with them, but she didn't see any sign of Ben. Then she remembered that he'd been invited to spend Christmas with his girlfriend's family. Lenore figured it wouldn't be long before her brother would be getting married. She had always thought, since she was the oldest sibling, that she'd be the first one to get married. But from the way things were going with her and Jesse, it didn't seem likely. He hadn't mentioned marriage, and even though they were courting, he hadn't even held her hand.

Maybe we're not really courting, Lenore thought as she stood at the front door waiting for her parents and brother to make their way up to the house in the snow.

While there wasn't as much white stuff on the ground as there had been on Thanksgiving, it could be slippery in places. Early this morning, Lenore had gone outside and made sure the porch and walkway were free of ice and compacted snow. She didn't want anyone to fall and get injured, the way she had a month ago.

After Lenore's family had entered the house and taken off their outer garments, she invited them into the living room and made introductions. While everyone visited, she went to the kitchen to help Grandma and Sara get dinner on the table.

"I see your folks have arrived," Grandma said. "It's so nice to have our whole family here today."

"Jah, but no sign of Jesse and Cindy yet. I'm eager for them to get here, because today is Cindy's first birthday."

"I'm sure they will be along soon." Grandma gestured to the stack of plates and silverware on the counter. "Why don't you set the dining-room table while Sara and I finish mashing potatoes and making the gravy?"

"Sure, I can do that." Lenore picked up the plates. "If Jesse isn't here by the time everything is ready, are we going to eat without him?"

"I'd rather not, so we'll try to keep everything warm until they get here," Grandma replied.

"Okay." Lenore headed to the dining room. She couldn't help feeling concerned. What if they'd been in an accident on the way here? Or maybe Cindy had gotten sick and they weren't coming at all.

CHAPTER 31

"I'm sorry we're late," Jesse apologized after Lenore let him and Cindy into the house and he'd taken off their jackets. "We would have been here thirty minutes ago if this little schtinker hadn't messed her windel when we were getting ready to head out the door."

"Things like that can happen when it's least expected and most inconvenient." Mary Ruth chuckled as she joined them in the hall. "I may be old, but I still remember how it was when Willis and I were raising our two kinner."

Jesse smiled and sniffed the air. "The wonderful aromas in this home are enough to make my mouth water."

"Mine too." Mary Ruth placed her hands on Cindy's cheeks. "Happy birthday, sweet Cindy."

"It's hard to believe my baby girl is a year old already." Jesse felt a lump forming in his throat. "Seems like just yesterday that she was born."

"Babies don't stay babies long enough." Lenore gestured toward the doorway to their right. "Shall we go into the living room now? I'd like to introduce you to Brad's parents. They live up in Harrisburg, and we are happy they could join us today."

Jesse set Cindy's diaper bag on the floor, along with the bag containing gifts for Lenore and Mary Ruth. He would give them to the women privately so as not to offend anyone else here today, although he knew giving a gift to the others was not expected.

After Lenore introduced Jesse to Brad's parents, she excused herself to help get the meal on the table.

Jesse felt a bit uncomfortable visiting with people he didn't know, so he spoke only when a question was asked of him and let the others do most of the talking.

At one point, Lenore's mother got up and disappeared into the kitchen, and a short time later, Lenore came in and announced that Christmas dinner was ready and waiting on the dining-room table.

Carrying the birthday girl over his shoulder, Jesse followed the rest of the group into the other room. They all took their seats, with Lenore's father at the head of the table. Cindy sat in her high chair close to Lenore, as she had volunteered to oversee feeding Jesse's daughter.

Throughout their silent prayer and during the meal, Cindy babbled silly baby talk and pounded on her wooden tray whenever she wanted something more to eat.

Lenore seemed unaffected by the noise or interruption of her meal as she kept Cindy occupied and doled out her food. Her attentiveness to his daughter's needs impressed Jesse. *Lenore would truly be a good mother to my little girl.*

Once the meal was over, everyone returned to the living room to relax, sing Christmas carols, and visit. Jesse and Lenore sat on the couch with Cindy situated between them. When the child grew restless and started to squirm, Jesse set her on the floor in front of the coffee table. Within a matter of seconds, Cindy pulled herself up and stood grinning at everyone as she slapped her hands on top of the table. Fortunately, there was nothing on it that could get knocked off. Jesse's easily excited daughter had broken an empty cup the other evening when she pushed it off the coffee table in Jesse's living room.

Engrossed in their conversations, no one

seemed to pay Cindy's antics much attention, until she gripped the edge of the table, scooted around to the other side, and took a few wobbly steps. She teetered a bit but remained upright as she made her way across the room, stopping in front of where Mary Ruth sat in her rocking chair.

Mary Ruth laughed and held out her hands. Everyone else in the room clapped. Jesse was glad he'd been able to witness his daughter taking her first steps — and on Cindy's first birthday, no less. Squinting, he rubbed the bridge of his nose. *If only Esther could be here right now to see this milestone in our daughter's young life.*

Lenore felt such excitement seeing Cindy walk, she barely noticed the knock on their door. Grandma must have heard it right away, though, for she was up on her feet and heading to the hallway that led to the front door. A few minutes later, she returned to the living room with Ezekiel and Michelle. Brad's parents were introduced once more, and everyone gathered around the table again — this time for dessert. So many delicious pies had been set out: pumpkin, apple, chocolate cream, and Lenore's favorite, Pineapple Philly. Just looking at them made Lenore's mouth water.

"It's so good to see you both." Grandma looked over at Michelle and Ezekiel and smiled. "How are things going with your new business, Ezekiel?"

Michelle sat beside him quietly as he enthusiastically told all about making bee supplies and how much he enjoyed it. "I'm getting more customers all the time," he added.

"That's wunderbaar. And how about you?" Grandma asked, turning her gaze on Michelle. "Have you been keeping busy since you moved to New York?"

Michelle lowered her gaze to the table. "Not that much. It's kinda lonely being away from friends and family."

"Haven't you made any new friends yet?" The question came from Sara.

Michelle shook her head. "I know a few women from our church district, but I haven't developed a close relationship with any of them."

Lenore had a hunch Michelle might have closed herself off from establishing new friendships because she didn't really want to be in New York.

"We do have some exciting news, though." With a wide smile, Ezekiel spoke again. "We are expecting our first child. So sometime in July, my fraa will have more than enough

330

to keep her busy."

"That is exciting. I'm so happy for you." Sitting in a chair to Michelle's right, Lenore leaned over and hugged her friend.

"Thank you." Michelle pressed her lips together for a moment and then spoke. "I just hope everything goes okay with my pregnancy. I've suffered so many disappointments over the course of my life. I think I'd fall apart if I lost this boppli."

"What's a boppli?" Brad's mother asked.

"It's the Pennsylvania Dutch word for 'baby,' " Brad explained. He looked over at Mary Ruth and grinned. "Bet you didn't think I knew what it meant, huh?"

She shrugged. "I'm not really surprised. You have been around us so much you've probably picked up a lot of words from our everyday Amish language."

Brad nodded. "Not enough to understand whole sentences though — just a few words here and there."

"That's how it is with me too," Sara agreed. "Maybe someday I'll understand the language better."

"It took me a while to learn," Michelle interjected. "But Mary Ruth, Willis, and Ezekiel were good teachers. I may not say everything just right, but I'm quite comfortable with the Pennsylvania Dutch language now."

"Well, as you may have all noticed, there are more than enough pies on the table, so I say we should each take a piece or two, and as Daed used to say, 'let's eat ourselves full.' " Lenore's dad gave his belly a couple of thumps, just the way Grandpa used to do for emphasis.

The mention of Grandpa's name put a lump in Lenore's throat. From the way Grandma's shoulders drooped, Lenore figured she wasn't the only one at the table feeling the loss of Grandpa tonight.

By eight o'clock, everyone except Jesse and Cindy had gone home. He'd decided to stay a little longer to give Lenore and Mary Ruth their gifts and spend some more personal time with Lenore.

"I'll be right back. I have something for both of you," Jesse said, looking first at Lenore and then Mary Ruth.

He stepped into the hall to retrieve the sack he'd brought in earlier and took it to the living room where Mary Ruth and Lenore sat in chairs near the crackling fireplace. Cindy seemed quite content as she sat on the floor, playing with one of the toys she had received as a birthday present this evening.

"Here you go. Merry Christmas." Jesse handed one of the packages to Mary Ruth. "This is from me and Cindy."

Mary Ruth opened the gift and smiled when she removed the battery-operated candle Jesse had purchased at Herschel's store. "Danki for thinking of me. You can be sure this *inschlichlicht* will be put to good use."

"You're welcome." Jesse handed the other package to Lenore. "Merry Christmas. I hope you'll like what I got you as well."

Lenore removed the wrapping paper and withdrew a box of pretty stationery and a book filled with short devotionals. "Thank you, Jesse. These will also be useful." Lenore got up and left the room. When she came back, she handed him a package wrapped in red tissue paper.

Jesse tore it open and withdrew a dark gray knitted scarf. "This will keep my neck warm during our cold winter days. Did you make it, Lenore?"

"Jah. I knitted the scarf while I was waiting for my back to heal. Grandma's a good teacher. She taught me how to knit when I was around ten years old."

"Well, you did a fine job. Danki for thinking of me."

"You're most welcome."

Jesse sat toward the edge of the couch and shuffled his feet across the hardwood floor a few times. "Umm . . . I was wondering if you'd like to go outside with me and look at the moon. There's supposed to be a full one tonight."

Lenore looked at her grandmother as though asking for her approval.

Mary Ruth nodded. "You two go ahead. I'll keep an eye on Cindy. You'd better make sure you're dressed warmly though. It's bound to be nippy out there."

Jesse wrapped his new scarf around his neck and put on his jacket, hat, and gloves.

Lenore tied a woolen scarf over her white head covering, put a woolen shawl around her shoulders, and slipped on a pair of gloves. "I'm ready when you are, Jesse."

He opened the front door and held it for her. When she stepped out onto the porch, he followed. Then, closing the door behind him, Jesse walked up to the railing and pointed at the bright, full moon and the array of twinkling stars scattered across the dark sky. "Pretty awesome sight, isn't it?"

"Jah. Only God could have created such beauty."

They stood side by side, staring at the majestic display of lights, until Jesse managed to muster up his courage. "I have a question to ask you, Lenore, and if you say no, I'll understand."

When she turned her head in his direction, he saw a puff of warm breath emit from her slightly open mouth. "What is it?"

"Will you marry me?" There, it was out. Now he could breathe normally again. Jesse rubbed his hands down his pant legs, waiting nervously for her response.

Several seconds passed, then Lenore said in a near whisper, "Jah, Jesse, I would be honored to be your wife."

Jesse drew another breath and released it slowly. He wasn't sure if he felt relief or disappointment. Cindy needed a mother, and he needed someone to run his household, but how would Lenore feel if she knew he didn't love her?

CHAPTER 32

The weeks flew by, and before Lenore knew it, spring was in full blossom. Teaching school, helping Grandma with chores, and planning for her wedding kept her busy. She saw Jesse nearly every day and looked forward to becoming his wife on the last Thursday of May. It was hard to believe in just one month she would become Mrs. Jesse Smucker. While Jesse had never said he loved Lenore, she felt sure he did, or he wouldn't have asked her to marry him. Most Amish couples in their area got married in the fall, but Jesse had suggested May, since Lenore would be through teaching school by then.

Both she and Jesse had this Saturday off. Grandma had agreed to watch Cindy so they could go out to supper. It would give them an opportunity to be alone and talk more about the wedding.

Lenore checked her appearance in the

bedroom mirror and went downstairs to wait for Jesse. He would be dropping Cindy off soon, and they could be on their way to the Bird-in-Hand Family Restaurant, where Jesse had said he would like to go. Lenore had been there many times and always enjoyed their food. But the best part of the evening would be time spent with Jesse. The more Lenore was with him, the more convinced she was that he was the man God intended for her. Jesse was kind and soft-spoken, always willing to help out whenever Grandma or Lenore had a need. He was a good father to Cindy, and Lenore looked forward to raising more children with him. The thought of marrying Jesse sent shivers up her spine.

"You're shivering, dear girl. Are you cold?" Grandma asked from her chair across the room.

"Umm . . . no, not really. Just felt a little chill is all."

"Maybe you should move away from the window. When Jesse shows up, if he sees you standing there looking out, he might think you're *eiferich* to see him." Grandma spoke in a teasing voice.

Lenore moved over to the couch and took a seat. "I am eager to see him, as well as Cindy." She crossed her ankles and wiggled her feet. "I can hardly wait to be Cindy's mudder."

"What about Jesse? Are you eager to be his fraa?"

A warm flush crept across Lenore's cheeks. "Jah, I truly am."

Grandma set her knitting aside and looked directly at Lenore. "I hope the two of you will be as happy in your marriage as your grandpa and I were. And I hope the Lord gives you many good years to enjoy together."

Lenore smiled. "I want that too."

Jesse's muscles twitched as he guided his horse and buggy up the lane leading to Mary Ruth's house. Normally he wasn't this nervous about seeing Lenore, but tonight was different. He had something serious to discuss with her and hoped she would understand and accept what he said without becoming too upset. He'd already had a bad day that began when he climbed up a ladder to knock a yellow jacket nest off the house and received a nasty sting inside the collar of his shirt. The only good thing about it was he'd discovered how fast he could get down the ladder and pull off his shirt.

As the house came into view, Jesse's ten-

338

sion increased. *I have to tell Lenore I'm not in love with her. It wouldn't be fair to let her marry me thinking there will ever be anything more between us than friendship.* His jaw clenched so hard it spasmed. *She has the right to know before it's too late.*

He thought about his older brothers, Samuel, Noah, Moses, and Paul, and wondered if they had been in love with their wives when they got married. *I can only imagine what my family in Kentucky would have to say if they knew I was planning to marry Lenore only for convenience' sake.*

Jesse pulled up to the hitching rail and got out. After he'd secured his horse, he went around and got Cindy out of the buggy.

She clung to his neck and brushed her soft cheek against his.

"You deserve a mudder," Jesse whispered. "One who'll love you as much as I do. I only hope when Lenore hears my confession she'll still be willing to marry me."

Bird-in-Hand, Pennsylvania

"They're quite busy this evening." Lenore glanced around the restaurant. "Seems like a good many people had the same idea you had and decided to eat supper here."

Jesse took a bite of mashed potatoes and nodded. If he kept his mouth full, maybe he

339

wouldn't have to talk. *But I can't be rude and ignore her all night.* He struggled to come up with the right way to say what was on his mind. *Guess it'd be best to wait till I take Lenore home before I say anything. Sure don't want anyone to hear our conversation, or worse yet, what if Lenore doesn't take the news well and starts crying?*

Jesse had himself so worked up he could barely swallow the next bite of potatoes he put in his mouth. He wanted to make their meal as pleasant as possible, in hopes that it would put Lenore in an amicable mood.

Jesse swallowed his food, took a drink of water, and asked Lenore, "How did things go at school yesterday? Are the scholars getting anxious for their summer break?"

"I'm sure they are, although no one has come right out and said so." Lenore forked some noodles and ate them. "The other day when some of the older scholars were playing baseball, two of the boys crashed at first base. Gabe hit a ball toward right field, and the other boy, Delbert, jumped up to catch it. When he came down, Gabe was running onto the base and their heads collided. Both boys ended up getting stitches — one boy near his left ear, and the other close to his left eye." Lenore shook her head. "We teachers always have some rough-and-tumble boys to deal with."

"I was never that rough when I was a boy," Jesse said. "But I was good at playing ball."

Lenore smiled at Jesse from across the table. "I have always enjoyed playing ball too."

They ate in silence for several minutes, and then Lenore spoke again. "As you know, I've been working on my wedding dress."

Jesse nodded. He wished the topic of their wedding hadn't come up so soon.

"Well, I finished it earlier today, so that's one more item off my list of things to get done before our wedding."

Jesse couldn't think of what to say in response. He sure couldn't blurt out that she'd made the dress for nothing because he wasn't going to marry her after all. He clenched his fork so hard his knuckles whitened. *Get a grip on yourself. Just smile and nod.* Taking his own advice, he did just that.

"The wedding plans are coming together, and I'm pleased that I've been able to cross so many items off my list." Lenore's voice was light and bubbly, making it even more difficult for Jesse to carry on this conversation.

He felt like he was sinking in quicksand.

He desperately needed to change the subject. "I hope Cindy's being good for Mary Ruth. Now that she's learned to walk, she manages to get into a lot more things. Taking care of her might be more than your grandmother can handle now."

Lenore shook her head. "If I know Grandma, she's keeping Cindy well entertained."

"I hope so."

"I still need to find some appropriate gifts for my two witnesses." Lenore brought their conversation back to the wedding again. "Have you gotten anything for your witnesses?"

"Uh . . . no, not yet." Jesse reached under his shirt collar and scratched at the yellow jacket sting. He needed to come up with a new topic to talk about. He bit into a drumstick and wiped his mouth on a napkin. "This *hinkel* is sure moist and tasty."

Lenore nodded. "They've always served good chicken at this restaurant."

Desperate for something else to talk about lest the conversation turn to their wedding plans again, Jesse brought up the dessert bar. "Sure hope I'll have enough room for a piece of shoofly pie. Some vanilla ice cream to go with it would be mighty good too."

Lenore set her fork down and drank some

water. "The pies here are delicious, but in my opinion, no one makes shoofly pie better than my grandma."

"Your pineapple pie's hard to beat too."

Circles of pink erupted on Lenore's dimpled cheeks. "Danki."

As they finished eating their meal, Jesse kept the conversation rolling, talking mostly about food. He was willing to talk about nearly anything except the wedding that might not be happening. Everything depended on Lenore's reaction once he found the courage to tell her how he felt, and he needed to do it before their date ended.

When they left the restaurant and climbed into his buggy for the return trip home, Jesse's nervousness and apprehension took over again. It was good to be out of the restaurant and alone with Lenore, but he needed to choose the right moment to tell her the truth. Not that it mattered, because she would probably be upset regardless of how he put it.

"You're kind of quiet all of a sudden. Is everything all right?" Lenore broke into Jesse's thoughts.

It's now or never. I should just spit it out. He gripped his horse's reins a little tighter.

"Uh . . . there's something I need to tell you."

"What is it, Jesse? You sound so serious."

"It's about us getting married."

"Have you decided we should wait till fall?"

"No, I —" He paused and swallowed hard. "The thing is — I haven't been honest with you, Lenore."

"In . . . in what way?" Her voice quavered a bit.

"I never should have asked you to marry me."

"How come?" Lenore spoke so quietly, he could barely make out what she said.

"You're a good person, and I care about you as a friend, but I'm not in love with you, Lenore." Jesse paused and drew a quick breath. "Truth is, I'm still in *lieb* with Esther, and I think I'll always love her." He let go of the reins with one hand and touched his chest.

Lenore sat quietly beside him, breathing heavily.

What's she thinking? Why doesn't she say something? Jesse was tempted to reach for Lenore's hand to offer comfort but thought better of it. She might think he felt sorry for her, which of course, he did. Truthfully, he felt sorry for himself too. *How'd I ever get myself into this predicament?*

"I'm really sorry, Lenore, but unless you're willing to be a wife in name only, I can't marry you. It would be asking a lot, and would not be fair to you."

"So why did you ask me to be your wife?" Her tone was flat, almost devoid of emotion.

Before Jesse could respond, Lenore rushed on. "Was it so Cindy could have a mudder? Or was it because you need someone to cook, clean, and wash your dirty laundry?" Her voice had risen to a high pitch now.

Quietly Jesse choked out, "A little of both, but mostly it was for Cindy's benefit."

"Well, at least you told me the truth before it was too late, because I could not deal with a loveless marriage. I've waited a good many years to fall in love and get married, but I guess, for me, it's not meant to be."

Jesse didn't think he could possibly feel guiltier. His voice cracked as he repeated, "I'm sorry, Lenore."

She said nothing.

"Whew, I'm exhausted!" Gazing at Cindy sleeping peacefully on a blanket on the living-room floor, Mary Ruth lowered herself to the couch. How one little girl could have so much energy was beyond her.

Maybe I'm too old to be caring for a young child. After Cindy had knocked over a potted African violet and pulled the cat's tail several times, Mary Ruth had spent the rest of the evening chasing after Cindy to keep her from getting into anything else or bothering poor Precious the cat. And when she wasn't doing that, she was busy trying to occupy the child with toys, food, and the fuzzy-squirrel book.

Now that she finally had some quiet time to herself, Mary Ruth's thoughts went to Jesse and Lenore. She hoped they were having a nice evening together and didn't feel that they had to rush home. While Jesse came over regularly and spent time with Lenore, they didn't get the chance to be alone very often.

Mary Ruth had noticed how nervous Jesse seemed before he and Lenore left for their supper date. She hoped he wasn't having second thoughts about getting married.

She pinched the skin at her throat. *Or maybe he's just excited about making Lenore his bride.*

Lenore deserved to be happy, and Mary Ruth was eager to see her granddaughter married to a good man like Jesse. She pulled on her chin as a smile formed on her lips. *By this time next year, Lenore could be expecting a boppli. Now wouldn't that be excit-ing?*

Mary Ruth leaned her head against the back of the couch and closed her eyes. She was at the point of dozing off when the front door opened and Lenore and Jesse stepped in. Without saying a single word to Jesse or Mary Ruth, Lenore sprinted down the hall and dashed up the stairs.

Tipping her head, Mary Ruth looked at Jesse. "What's wrong? Did something happen to upset Lenore this evening?"

Jesse nodded. "I'm the reason Lenore is *umgerennt,* but it would be better if she tells you about it." He gathered up Cindy's things, lifted the still sleeping child in his arms, and went for the door. "Danki for taking care of my precious girl this evening," Jesse called over his shoulder before shutting the door.

Mary Ruth's gaze flitted around the room as though she might find the answer to her question there. Rising to her feet, she headed for the stairs, hoping Lenore would tell her what had happened.

CHAPTER 33

At the end of the school day Monday, Lenore remained at her desk a while, thinking about the past weekend and giving in to her tears.

Thankfully, yesterday had been an off-Sunday from attending church in their district, so Lenore hadn't had to endure the pain of seeing Jesse so soon after he'd called off the wedding. Besides, news traveled fast, and since her parents and brothers knew, they may have already begun to spread the word. Facing people's well-intentioned questions was something Lenore did not look forward to.

This morning she'd made sure to leave early so she wouldn't have to face Jesse when he dropped Cindy off. After Lenore left the schoolhouse, she planned to stop by the flower shop with more of her homemade greeting cards. She would wait at the shop until Sara was free to leave, and then the two of them planned to eat supper at one of the local restaurants in Strasburg. Sara had called last Friday to set it up, saying Brad wouldn't be able to join them because he had a meeting early Monday evening.

I wonder what Sara will say when I tell her I won't be getting married in May after all. Lenore took a tissue from the desk drawer and blew her nose. *Will she be as sympathetic as my family was when I told them what Jesse said?* Lenore's mother had been compassionate, of course, and Dad had made some negative comments about Jesse's deception in leading Lenore on all these months. "Doesn't that man have a conscience?" he'd said with a look of disdain. "I have half a notion to go over to Jesse's house some evening and give him a piece of my mind."

Lenore had pleaded with her father not to say anything to Jesse. It would be embarrassing and might make things worse. Dad had only grunted in response.

Lenore could still see the sadness in her grandmother's eyes as she listened and then offered counsel. "God will work things out in His time and in His way. Just trust Him with your future."

Lenore dabbed at the corners of her eyes with the tissue. She loved Jesse and his

349

daughter with her whole heart, but if he felt no love for her in return, their marriage would not have been a happy one — at least not for her. It wouldn't have been enough just to remain friends. Lenore needed more than friendship. She wanted a husband who would love her as much as she loved him, and if she had agreed to become a wife in name only, she'd never have felt complete. So as much as it hurt, Lenore had convinced herself that Jesse had done her a favor by calling off the wedding.

Pushing a stack of papers aside, Lenore slid her chair back and stood. All her tears and self-pity wouldn't change a thing. She needed to focus on something else. But what? When she'd thought she would soon be married, Lenore had given up her desire to teach school and had known she wouldn't miss it next year. Should she tell the school board she would be available to teach when school started up again in the fall, or would it be better to seek some other type of job?

Sara's floral designer, Misty, had left a short time ago for her yearly checkup with her doctor, and the young woman Sara had hired to do cleaning and odd jobs had the day off. That left Sara to answer the phone, wait on last-minute customers, and take care of any details needing to be addressed today. Fortunately, the young man in charge of deliveries had made them all earlier today, so it was one less thing she had to worry about this afternoon.

Since there were no customers at the moment, Sara went to the back room to be sure everything had been put away. Seeing a vase with a lovely floral arrangement in it, she picked it up and sniffed the pretty pink carnations. Feeling something wet on her foot, she looked down and saw water running off the counter and onto her feet. On close examination she realized the vase had a small crack in it. She would have to transfer the flowers to a new vase.

Sara had finished the transfer and was emptying the water from the leaky vase when the bell above the front door jingled. *Great. This is not a good time for a customer to show up. I should have put the Closed sign in the window.*

Sara hurried to finish her job, then moved quickly into the main part of the store. Lenore stood near the counter. "Oh, good, it's you. I was in the back room putting an arrangement in a vase, and when the bell jingled I was afraid a customer had come in and might leave before I could get back out here."

"Where's your floral designer?" Lenore asked.

"She left early for a doctor's appointment." Sara went on to explain about the cracked vase she'd discovered.

Lenore frowned. "Sorry to hear that. Sounds like I came at a bad time."

"No, you're fine. The carnations are in another vase now, and everything's good." Sara moved closer to Lenore. "Are you okay? Your usual smile is missing."

Lenore's chin trembled, and her eyes filled with tears. "Jesse called off our wedding."

"What?" Sara's brows lifted. "How come?"

"He doesn't love me, Sara. He's still in love with his deceased wife."

"Then why did he ask you to marry him?"

"He wanted a mother for Cindy and someone to keep house for him." Lenore placed the palm of her hand against her chest. "I'm in love with him, and it hurts so much to know he doesn't love me in return."

Sara drew Lenore into her arms and patted her back. "I'm really sorry Jesse did this to you. You deserve to be happy. You deserve to be loved, and not just used as a mother for his child."

Lenore's tears overflowed, dribbling down her cheeks and onto her dress. "I — I don't think I can ever trust another man not to hurt me again. I must learn to accept this and be content, because I am obviously meant to remain single for the rest of my life."

Paradise

"Peter, I thought I told you to unload that box of books and get them put on the shelf." Ivan gestured toward the offending box.

"I was gonna, Dad, but Mom asked me to take out the trash."

"So who do you get paid to listen to — her or me?"

Peter's cheeks reddened as he dropped his gaze to the floor. "Well . . . umm . . ."

Ivan sighed. "Never mind. Just get those books out as quick as you can. I have plenty of other things for both you and your brother to do yet today."

"Okay, Dad. I'll get on it right away." Peter hurried off toward the books.

"Are you a bit agitated today?" Yvonne asked, walking up to her husband.

"Jah, I suppose so. I still can't believe the nerve of Jesse Smucker asking our daughter to marry him, then tellin' Lenore he doesn't love her and that he only proposed so his daughter could have a mudder. There's no way she could ever marry him under those circumstances." Ivan breathed in a short, fast breath, then let it out with a groan. "I have half a mind to head over to that man's house after we close the store this evening and have a little man-to-man talk with him."

Yvonne placed her hand on his arm. "No, Ivan, you need to calm down. Nothing good could come from you going over to give Jesse a piece of your mind, and you might say things you'd regret."

Ivan scrubbed a hand over his face. *My wife is right, but it doesn't change the fact that Jesse broke Lenore's heart. The man should have had better sense than that.*

"There's no need to worry, Yvonne," Ivan reassured her. "I'm only blowing off a little steam that's been brewing inside me ever since Lenore told us that she won't be getting married in May."

Yvonne patted his arm. "I know, and I feel the same way. We just need to be thankful that Jesse admitted the truth to Lenore when he did. Can you imagine what it would have been like for our daughter if he'd married her and then she'd learned the truth?"

The muscles in Ivan's arms tightened. "I, for sure, would have gone over there and had a little heart-to-heart talk. I still have to wonder if that isn't what Jesse needs."

■ ■ ■ ■

Clymer

Michelle placed both hands against her ever-growing stomach and sat at the kitchen table to enjoy a cup of spearmint tea. Her nausea was gone, but she still enjoyed an afternoon cup of herbal tea now and then.

She had made a few friends from their church district, but no one she felt as close to as she was with Sara, Lenore, or Mary Ruth. Letters and phone calls didn't ease the loneliness she felt or the desire to move back home.

Maybe I'll feel better once our boppli is born, she told herself. *At least motherhood will keep me busy, and maybe I won't have time to feel sorry for myself because we're not living in Strasburg anymore.*

She thought about the prayer jars she'd discovered at the Lapps'. So many of the notes inside the jars had spoken to her heart and helped her through a difficult time. Some of those notes contained scripture verses.

Michelle got up from the table and went to get her Bible, lying on Ezekiel's desk. She'd placed it there last night after they'd had devotions.

355

She opened the book randomly, her gaze coming to rest on Philippians 4:11, a verse she had underlined some time ago. "I have learned, in whatsoever state I am, therewith to be content."

Michelle's cheeks burned hot, and her throat tightened. "Forgive me, Lord. How could I have forgotten that special verse? I have much to be thankful for — a loving husband who enjoys his new job, a cozy home" — she touched her stomach — "and a sweet boppli on the way."

At that moment, Michelle decided she would start a prayer jar of her own, filling it with scriptures, prayers, and reminders of all the ways God had blessed her.

CHAPTER 34

Strasburg

Mary Ruth looked down at Cindy and smiled. The little girl sat on the kitchen floor with a wooden spoon and a set of mixing bowls. Cindy held the spoon in one hand and stirred it around inside the smallest bowl, the way Mary Ruth had done earlier when she'd made a batch of brownies. The second bowl was turned upside down, and every few seconds Cindy would take the spoon and hit the bottom of the bowl like it was a drum. The third and largest bowl was on the little girl's head.

"What a sight you are, Cindy." Mary Ruth chuckled. Having this delightful child around had made such a difference in Mary Ruth's life. While she still thought about Willis often and continued to miss him, the raw pain of losing her husband had lessened some, thanks to the joy of caring for Jesse's daughter.

As Mary Ruth sat at the table, drinking a glass of water with a slice of lemon, she thought about the situation with Jesse and Lenore, comparing it to when she and Willis had been courting. Willis had proclaimed his love for Mary Ruth long before she could admit her love for him. They'd established a friendship though — and a strong one at that. But love came later. If Jesse had given it more time, he might have eventually fallen in love with Lenore. *Then again,* she reasoned, *perhaps he might never stop pining for Cindy's mother, in which case Jesse would never be able to commit to another woman with unconditional love.*

Cindy banged on the overturned bowl again, jolting Mary Ruth out of her contemplations.

"Where do you get all that energy, little one? If I had even half your energy, I could get so much more done." Mary Ruth smiled, and Cindy grinned back at her.

A knock sounded on the front door, and Mary Ruth went to answer it. *I bet that's Jesse, come to pick up his daughter.*

When Jesse entered Mary Ruth's house, his nose twitched. He recognized the smell of chocolate and knew someone had been doing some baking today. "The house smells mighty nice. Have you or Lenore done some baking today?"

"It was me," Mary Ruth replied. "I made a batch of brownies. Would you like to try one?"

He nodded eagerly. "Jah, I sure would."

"Well then, please follow me." Mary Ruth headed down the hall, and Jesse was close behind. Upon entering the kitchen, he spotted Cindy on the floor with a plastic mixing bowl on her head. He laughed and pointed at her. "Is my little girl learning how to cook?"

"Well, I have a hunch that's exactly what she thinks. She helped me bake brownies today — or more to the point, she watched from her high chair while I made the brownies." Mary Ruth gestured to a plastic container on the counter. "Help yourself to one if you like."

"Would it be all right if I take a few home?"

"Certainly. I'll put them in a container before you leave."

"Danki. That's so nice of you." Jesse crossed and uncrossed his arms, then gave a sidelong glance toward the door leading from the kitchen out to the hallway. "Is Lenore here? I'd like to speak to her."

Mary Ruth shook her head. "Afraid not.

She made plans to meet up with Sara after school let out today, and then they were going to eat supper out."

Jesse had a hunch Lenore was avoiding him, since she wasn't here this morning when he'd dropped Cindy off. He guessed he couldn't blame her for that, but he did want the opportunity to speak with her again and apologize once more.

"I'm sure Lenore told you that we won't be getting married." Jesse rolled his shoulders to get the kinks out.

"Yes, she explained everything to me." Mary Ruth's forehead wrinkled. "I understand your reason, but you should have been honest with Lenore from the beginning, then let her decide if she'd be willing to enter into a marriage without love."

"I agree, but since I'm not free to give her the kind of love she deserves, the only logical thing was to call off the wedding." Jesse leaned his weight against the counter. "I wonder if it would be better all the way around if I asked Vera to watch Cindy again so it won't be uncomfortable for Lenore to see me every day."

Mary Ruth pursed her lips. "We would miss Cindy, of course, but it's your decision, so please do as you wish."

"Okay, and in the meantime, I will look

for someone who'd be willing to come to my place and watch Cindy while I'm at work. I probably should have pursued that option a little harder before Lenore began watching Cindy."

Mary Ruth nodded.

"Guess I'd better gather up my daughter and her things now so we can be on our way."

"And don't forget the brownies."

"Right."

When Jesse headed for his horse and buggy several minutes later, he felt unsure of what he should do. Mary Ruth was so good with Cindy, and Cindy seemed content being there. But it was unfair to expect Lenore to see him each day and not be upset. She sure couldn't have supper away from home every night or hide out in her room until he left with Cindy. There was no question about it: finding someone else to watch his little girl would be the best thing for all.

"Are you sure you don't mind eating here?" Sara asked as she and Lenore entered a restaurant down the street from the flower shop.

Lenore shook her head. "I always enjoy pizza."

Sara smiled. "Same here. Brad and I have eaten at this place several times and never been disappointed."

Once they were seated, a waitress came and gave them menus. They both ordered personal-sized pepperoni pizzas and glasses of iced tea.

"This whole situation with Jesse is such a shock," Sara said. "Have you had a chance to develop any strategies for dealing with him and Cindy still being in our community?"

"I try not to dwell on it, because there is nothing I can do to change what happened." Lenore glanced out the window at a horse and buggy passing by. The distinctive *clippity-clop* sound of the horse's hooves could be heard inside the restaurant. "I've been avoiding Jesse whenever I can because seeing him and Cindy hurts so much and is just a reminder of what will never be."

"This too will pass, Lenore." Sara fingered her beaded necklace. "Someday, when the right man has come along and you're happily married, you'll look back at this time in your life and realize that what happened was for the best."

Lenore was about to respond, when a clean-shaven young Amish man with thick blond hair approached their table.

"Sorry to interrupt," he said, looking at Lenore, "but aren't you Lenore Lapp?"

"Yes, I am." Lenore had no idea who the man was or how he knew her name. She was about to ask when he said, "I'm Mark Zook. We knew each other in school, but my family moved away when I was in the fifth grade."

Lenore tapped her chin. "Oh, yes, I remember. It's nice to see you again, Mark." She extended her hand. When he clasped her hand and shook it, Lenore noticed that it felt warm and sweaty. "What brings you back to this area?"

"I'm here helping my uncle with his woodworking business." His blue eyes held no sparkle. Lenore wondered if Mark might not like his job.

"I see." She gestured to Sara. "This is my cousin, Sara Fuller. She owns the flower shop here in Strasburg, and she and her husband, Brad, live in Lancaster."

"It's nice to meet you, Sara." Mark shook her hand.

Sara smiled. "It's good to meet you too."

Fiddling with her napkin, Lenore couldn't think of anything else to say. She hadn't known Mark very well in school and knew even less about him now.

Mark's gaze went back to Lenore. "Maybe

we can get together sometime and catch up with each other's lives."

When the waitress came with Lenore and Sara's pizzas, Mark backed slowly away from their table. "Well, guess I'd better get going."

"It was nice seeing you." Lenore couldn't bring herself to respond to his suggestion about getting together sometime. If Mark was looking to establish a relationship with her, she had no interest whatsoever. Lenore couldn't afford to get involved with another man right now — if that was even what Mark had in mind. Maybe he was only trying to be friendly, and since he had been gone for so long, he might need someone to talk to. Either way, the only thing Lenore needed right now was to find a way to heal the deep ache in her heart.

"Mark seems nice," Sara whispered after he'd walked away. "Maybe you should get together with him sometime and catch up. It would take your mind off the situation with Jesse."

Lenore gave a noncommittal shrug.

"And you and I need to get together more often too," Sara added. "With us both working full-time, we don't see each other nearly enough."

"True." Lenore drank some of her beverage. "I haven't told anyone this, but it's getting harder for me to teach school."

"Oh, why's that?"

"I had so looked forward to getting married and having a family to care for, and I was prepared to give up teaching."

"But you still enjoy your job, don't you?"

"To some extent, yes, but I'd much rather be a wife and homemaker." Lenore dropped her gaze to the pizza before her. It didn't hold nearly the appeal as it had before this conversation began.

"I'm sorry, Lenore. You deserve better than this. I wish there was something I could do to alleviate your pain from losing out on a relationship you believed was for keeps." Sara's tone was soothing.

"There's really nothing anyone can do about my situation, but I appreciate your words and emotional support." Lenore heaved a sigh. "I'm so thankful your mother left you that note in her Bible and told you about our grandparents. Because if she hadn't, you never would have come here to Strasburg to meet Grandma and Grandpa, and I never would have had the privilege of knowing you."

Sara smiled. "I feel the same as you. It's been wonderful to have a cousin I can visit with and share my thoughts and concerns with, as well as the joys in my life. I hope we will always be close — not just in where we live, but in the bond that ties our family together."

CHAPTER 35

Gordonville

The following Saturday, Lenore decided to attend a mud sale sponsored by the Gordonville Fire Company. Mud sales, so named because of the condition of the thawing ground in the spring, were major fundraisers for the volunteer fire companies. All the mud sales Lenore had previously attended drew huge crowds, and up for bid were things like hand-stitched Amish quilts, locally made crafts, livestock, baked goods, and all kinds of housewares. Six or more auctions were conducted at the same time as Amish and English folks milled around.

Grandma had come down with a cold and didn't feel like going out, so Lenore went to Gordonville alone. As she wandered around, perusing various items for sale and smelling the tantalizing aroma of sticky buns and funnel cakes, Lenore caught a glimpse of Mark Zook standing in a crowd of people near one of the food vendors. He must have seen Lenore at the same time, for he waved and headed her way.

"Hey, it's good to see you again," Mark said as he reached her. "Have you been here long?"

"About half an hour or so."

"Did you come to buy or just look around?"

"A little of both. If something catches my eye and I think I can't live without it, I may place a bid." Lenore smiled. "How about you? What brought you to the mud sale today?"

"I'm actually looking for a good used buggy. I lost the one I had before moving here. It got demolished when a driver who was talking on his cell phone rear-ended it. My buggy was parked near the hitching rail in the parking lot."

"What a shame. Were you hurt?"

"No, I was in the store when it happened. Thankfully, my horse was okay."

"That's a blessing. So have you seen any buggies here today that you like?"

He shook his head. "Unfortunately, there are only two up for bids. One is a large family buggy, which I have no use for at this time. The other is pretty old, and it probably won't be long before the rig needs to be replaced or have some major repairs done to it."

"So what have you been doing for transportation since you moved back here?" she asked.

"Borrowing my uncle's open buggy, but I need something of my own, and soon."

"Have you checked with one of our local buggy shops to see if they have any used buggies for sale?"

"Not yet, but since I didn't have any luck finding one today, I plan to check with one or more of the buggy shops next week." Mark removed his straw hat and pulled his fingers through his thick blond hair. "When I get a new one, would you wanna go for a ride with me to test out the seats?"

Before Lenore had a chance to really think his request through, she smiled and nodded. "Sure. I'll give you my grandma's phone number so you can let me know when."

Mark offered Lenore a boyish grin and gave her arm a light tap. "Great. I'll look forward to that."

The tantalizing aromas from food vendors scattered around the mud sale beckoned to Jesse as he stepped out of his buggy. In a hurry to drop Cindy off at Vera's so he could get an early start to the mud sale, he hadn't taken the time to eat breakfast this morning.

After making sure his horse was secured, Jesse strode across the parking area and blended into the crowd. He had a few things on his mind he would like to see. Jesse thought about getting a rocking chair for his place, but the smell of food was rising to the top of his to-do list.

Jesse noticed a place farther down from where he was and started in that direction. He'd only gone a short ways when he spotted Lenore talking to a tall, blond Amish man. He had no beard, so Jesse could only assume the man was not married. Seeing the two of them together caught him off guard so much that he bumped into a kid ahead of him. "Oh, I'm sorry," Jesse apologized. "I should have been watching where I was going."

The boy turned around and gave Jesse an amused-looking grin, then moved on with his family. Jesse decided to step out of the way to avoid running into someone else. He moved to the side of the crowd and kept a close watch on Lenore and the blond man as they chatted.

Fists clenched, he took a few steps closer, hoping to get a better look. He'd never seen this fellow before, although he could be from another district in Lancaster County, or even an Amish community in some other state.

When the man touched Lenore's arm, Jesse felt a burning sensation in his chest. *What is wrong with me?* He took a few breaths and tried to refocus. *There's not a single reason for me to feel jealous. I have no claim on Mary Ruth's granddaughter. I told Lenore I don't love her, so she's free to see whomever she chooses.*

Hoping Lenore hadn't seen him, Jesse quickly moved on.

Lancaster

Sara and Brad had spent most of the morning shopping at several of the stores at the Rockvale outlet mall. Now, tired and hungry, Sara felt ready to stop somewhere for lunch. "Are you hungry yet, Brad?"

"Sure, anytime you are."

"How about we go in there and get something to eat?" Sara pointed to a Ruby Tuesday restaurant. Since the first time she had visited the establishment, she'd been hooked on the salad bar, offering so many choices. Brad enjoyed the burgers there, so Sara figured he'd be more than willing to go along with her suggestion.

"Sounds good to me." Brad put his arm around Sara's waist as they headed in that direction.

The restaurant wasn't too busy, so they were shown to a table right away. After Brad placed his hamburger order, he told Sara to go ahead to the salad bar.

When she returned to the table with a plate full of her favorite salad items, they bowed their heads for silent prayer. When Sara finished praying and looked up, she was surprised to see Rick Osprey standing quietly at their table.

"I don't mean to interrupt, Pastor Fuller, but I saw you and your wife sitting here and wanted to come over and let you know that I won't be coming to your church anymore, or attending the Bible study for new believers."

Brad tipped his head. "I'm sorry to hear that." He glanced at Sara, then back at Rick. "Is there a problem — something you'd like to talk about?"

"No, not at all. I won't be back because I have a new job opportunity in Cincinnati. Me, my wife, Tammy, and our two boys will be moving to Ohio next week."

Sara's fingers twitched as she rolled her spoon back and forth next to her plate. A desperate need to know if Rick might be her father gave Sara the boldness to ask him a few questions.

"When we spoke at my flower shop, Mr. Osprey, you mentioned that you had known a young Amish woman named Rhoda Lapp when you were a teenager."

He nodded.

"When I asked how well you knew her, you said you didn't know most of the Amish girls that well, and you started to say something more, but then you never finished your sentence because you looked at your watch and realized you had to go somewhere."

"Yeah, that's right, but what's that got to do with anything? I mean, since you're obviously not Amish, why would you care about an Amish woman who was about the same age as me?"

"Was she your girlfriend?" Sara asked, without answering his question.

Rick shook his head, and his posture stiffened as he continued to remain next to their table. Sara wondered if she had touched a nerve. "No, of course not. I was dating Tammy Cantrell at the time, and I ended up marrying her." He squinted at Sara. "You never answered my question: Why all this interest in an Amish woman named Rhoda?"

"She was my mother." Sara's face heated as she averted her gaze. "But I've never known who my biological father was."

"That's a shame. If I had a daughter like you, I'd want her to know who I was. Tammy and I have two boys, but she's always wanted a girl."

"About Rhoda . . . Did she have a boyfriend — someone who hung out with your group?" Brad spoke the words Sara was about to ask.

"Sorry to disappoint you, but I barely knew the young woman, and she showed no interest in me — although I did see her talking to a couple of other guys in our group once. I suppose she could have been involved with one of them."

"Do you remember any of their names?" Sara felt that the truth was at her fingertips, yet she couldn't quite reach it.

"Sorry, I don't." Rick gave his ear a tug. " 'Course, Tammy had me so mesmerized, I didn't pay attention to much else going on."

"I understand. Thanks for taking the time to talk to us." Sara spoke quietly, hoping she wouldn't break down. Rick Osprey was her last shred of hope, and since she didn't know the name of the other young men in the group, there was no one else to ask.

Brad stood and shook Rick's hand. "I

enjoyed the opportunity to meet you, and you'll certainly be missed at church."

"Yeah, I'll miss attending there too, but I can't pass up this new job opportunity."

"I understand." Brad reached in his pocket and pulled out one of his business cards. "Once you're moved and settled in your new home in Cincinnati, give me a call. I know a pastor in that area, and you might consider trying out his church."

"I'll do that." Rick smiled. "My two youngest boys are teenagers, so it would be good for them to attend church and get to know some other young people their age." He reached out and shook Sara's hand. "It's been nice meeting you too, Sara."

She nodded and smiled. As much as it pained her, Sara resolved to drop the search she'd started a few years ago and learn to live with the knowledge that it must not be meant for her to find her father.

CHAPTER 36

Gordonville

When Jesse entered Vera and Milton's house to pick up Cindy, he discovered her sitting on Milton's lap in the living room. Since they were both asleep, Jesse went to the kitchen, where he found Vera at the table with a crossword puzzle.

"How did things go at the mud sale?" she asked, looking up at Jesse. "Did you find anything interesting?"

"There were plenty of interesting things to see, but nothing I needed or wanted." Jesse pulled out a chair at the table and sat down with a heavy sigh.

"Is something wrong? You look unhappy."

"Nothing's wrong exactly; I just saw something that kind of disturbed me."

"What was it?"

"Lenore was at the mud sale with some tall, blond-haired fellow, and he had his hand on her arm. I had a feeling that they

376

came there together. Just thinking that the young man she was with might be interested in her made me feel a twinge of jealousy."

"First of all, how do you know they were together? Maybe he's simply someone she knows and they were having a casual conversation." Vera shrugged. "Besides, even if there is something going on between Lenore and this fellow, why should it bother you? You're not going to marry her, and you admitted that you don't love her. So you shouldn't be jealous, and seeing her with another man shouldn't bother you one iota."

Vera was right, but even though it didn't make any sense, Jesse was more than a little bothered by the idea that Lenore might have a new love interest.

"Maybe you care more for Lenore than you're willing to admit."

Jesse shook his head. "It's just the idea that a few weeks ago Lenore and I were planning to be married. It was a bit upsetting to see her with someone so soon after our breakup."

Vera reached over and gave his shirtsleeve a tug. "Don't you think it's time to move on, Jesse?"

"What do you mean? I moved here to start over after Esther died. Isn't that moving on?"

"It's a beginning all right." Her forehead creased. "But I have a hunch you've been fighting your feelings for Lenore."

Jesse shook his head. "I don't think so, Vera. I only see her as a friend."

"Would you like some advice from a woman who's lived a good many years?"

Jesse nodded slowly. What else could he do? It wouldn't be right to tell Vera he didn't want her advice.

"Don't be like my son, Herschel, and live the rest of your life alone, pining for a wife who is gone and will never return to you." She paused and drew in a breath. After releasing it slowly, Vera spoke again. "My husband and I have had to sit back all this time and watch our son refuse to let go of his grief. I'm not saying he should have gotten married again, mind you. But Herschel has never given himself a chance to really enjoy life since Mattie died. And if the opportunity to love another woman had come along, I am almost certain he would not have taken it, because he didn't want to be untrue to Mattie's memory." She placed her hand on his arm. "Your dear wife is gone, Jesse, but you're still here with the responsibility of raising your daughter."

"I'm doing the best I can for Cindy."

"Of course you are, but you need to think

of your own needs too."

Jesse dropped his gaze. "I was. When I asked Lenore to marry me, I was selfishly thinking how nice it would be to have someone to run the household for me." His eyebrows gathered in. "I regret having asked her now. It wasn't fair to let Lenore believe I was in love with her."

Vera placed both hands on her hips. "How do you know your friendship couldn't have developed into love? Most relationships between a man and woman start out that way. Weren't you and Esther friends before you fell in love?"

"Jah."

"And don't you think Esther would want you to find love again?"

"I'm not sure."

"Of course she would. And I believe Esther would approve of Lenore. If Lenore is willing, maybe you should begin courting her again and see where things lead."

Jesse leaned heavily against the back of his chair. "I'm not sure my feelings for Lenore will change, but I'll think seriously about what you've said."

"There's one more thing I'd like to say on the matter." Vera leaned slightly forward.

"What's that?"

"If your feelings for Lenore aren't changing, then why are you jealous of the man you saw her talking to at the mud sale?"

Jesse's only response was a brief shrug, because he had no answer to Vera's question.

Strasburg

"I'm home!" Lenore called when she came in the back door.

"Welcome back. I'm in here!"

When Lenore entered the kitchen, she found Grandma at the stove, stirring something in a kettle.

Lenore sniffed. "Are you making baked potato soup for lunch?"

Grandma turned to look at Lenore and grinned. "You have a good sniffer."

Lenore laughed.

"How did things go at the mud sale? Were there a lot of people?"

"Jah, and I ran into Mark Zook while I was there."

Grandma tipped her head. "Oh? He's the young man you mentioned who recently moved back to our area, right?"

Lenore nodded. "He came to work for his uncle in the woodworking trade."

Grandma turned back to the stove. "Was he looking for woodworking tools at the sale?"

"He said he came there to see if he could find a used buggy."

"And did he?"

"No. I suggested he check with one of the local buggy makers who often have used carriages to sell." Lenore went to the kitchen sink and washed her hands. "He said he'd like to take me for a ride when he gets his own buggy."

"Hmm . . . sounds like this young man might be interested in you."

"I doubt it. I'm sure he just needs a friend." Lenore finished washing her hands and dried them on a clean towel. "Now what can I do to help with lunch?"

"If you don't mind, I'd appreciate you going down to the basement for a jar of canned peaches. I thought I'd make a cobbler for dessert this evening."

"I'd be happy to do that. Anything else?"

"Maybe a jar of green beans. We can have them as our vegetable to go with the chicken I'll be roasting later this afternoon."

"Okay, I'll be up with the beans and peaches soon." Lenore headed for the basement stairs and turned on the battery-operated light to guide her down. When she reached the bottom, a thought popped into her head. *Think I'll take a few minutes to read some of the notes in the prayer jar. I haven't looked at it in a while, and I might read something that will inspire me today.*

Lenore got the jar down, and the first note she pulled out was a prayer: *Dear Lord, please heal the hurt in my heart, for right now I feel that it will never go away.*

Lenore could relate to the feeling of hurt that had been in her heart since Jesse called off the wedding. It pained her even more whenever she met someone from their community and was asked why she and Jesse weren't seeing each other anymore or why the wedding had been called off. Every time she had to explain, it was like opening a wound that had never fully healed.

The biggest question for Lenore was why she had allowed herself to fall in love with Jesse. She squeezed her eyes shut. *And my precious little Cindy — I love her so much too.*

Feeling weighed down and wishing she could sleep, Lenore forced her eyes to open. Reaching into the jar again, she pulled out another slip of paper. Proverbs 3:5–6 had been written on this one: "Trust in the Lord with all thine heart; and lean not unto thine own understanding. In all thy ways acknowledge him, and he shall direct thy paths."

Lenore contemplated her need to trust God with her future and quit fretting over what might have been. She needed to move forward with her life and pray for wisdom and direction in the days ahead.

Before going home, Sara asked Brad if he would mind stopping by her grandmother's house for a short visit.

"Sure, that's fine. It's good to check on her regularly, in case she needs something."

"Agreed." Once more, Sara thanked the Lord for her thoughtful, caring husband.

When they arrived at their destination, Sara got out of the car and headed for the house while Brad played chase-the-stick with Sadie. The poor dog always acted starved for attention, although Sara felt sure the collie wasn't ignored by Grandma or Lenore. No doubt Sadie missed Grandpa. He'd spent a lot of time with her. Even when he did his chores, the dog tagged along. Pets often grieved when they lost someone close to them.

Sara pressed a palm against her chest. When Sara's mother died, she felt like an empty vessel — unable to cope with her feelings of abandonment and despair. Sara had also grieved when her stepfather died and again when Grandpa passed on. Unfortunately, dying was part of everyone's life, and oh, how deeply it hurt when a loved one departed this earth. Sara's only comfort was the knowledge that if they all made it to heaven, she would be reunited with them someday.

Determined to set aside her thoughts about death, Sara stepped onto the porch and knocked on the door. A few minutes passed before Grandma opened the door and greeted her.

"This is a nice surprise." Grandma's face broke into a wide smile. "Is your husband with you?"

"Yes. Brad's occupied with Sadie outside. I'm sure he will join us as soon as she gets tired of running after the stick that he keeps throwing." Sara giggled and entered the house. She paused in the entry and set her purse on the floor.

"What have you two been up to today?" Grandma asked, leading the way to the kitchen.

"We did a little shopping at the Rockvale outlet and then went to lunch." Sara pulled out a chair at the table and sat down.

"Would you like a cup of tea?" Grandma asked. "Lenore and I had some earlier, and the water's still warm in the teakettle."

"That sounds nice. Where is Lenore any-way?"

"She developed a headache and went upstairs to her room to rest awhile."

"Sorry to hear that. If she doesn't come down before we leave, please tell her I hope she feels better soon."

"I certainly will." Grandma got out two cups and poured them both some tea. "How are things going at the flower shop?" she asked, taking a seat across from Sara.

"Fairly well. I'm having the walls in the main part of the store painted today, so the store is closed until Monday." Sara blew on her tea and took a cautious sip. "Can I ask you something, Grandma?"

"Of course you may."

Sara told her grandmother about meeting Rick Osprey at the restaurant and how disappointed she felt when she realized he was not her father and that he didn't have any idea who her mother had been seeing. "I believe I should give up looking, because if God wanted me to know who my biological father is, it would have happened by now." Sara looked directly at Grandma. "Do you agree?"

"That all depends."

"On what?"

"Can you put the question of who your father is out of your mind?"

Sara pushed a lock of hair out of her face. "I — I honestly don't know, but I'm going to try, because every time I think about it, I just get more upset."

CHAPTER 37

Sara entered the flower shop early the first Monday of May. This would be a busy month, with Mother's Day just weeks away and many people placing orders.

Sara turned on all the lights, put away her purse, and went to check the big cooler in the back room as she did each day upon arrival. She was stunned to discover the temperature was at fifty-five degrees, despite having been set at thirty-eight degrees, which Misty had said was the temperature she felt was best for the flowers.

"This is not a good way to begin a new week," Sara muttered. "I need a repairman to take a look at the cooler — and fast."

She hurried to remove as many flowers as she could from the big cooler to the display cooler. Since the roses were the most important to move, she began with those. Hopefully this would keep her losses down. No telling when the heat had begun to rise. The flowers Sara couldn't fit into the display cooler would have to sit out until the other cooler got fixed, which meant she'd have to either mark them down for a quick sale or suffer the loss if they went bad.

Sara was still in the process of removing the flowers from the larger cooler when her designer showed up.

"What's going on?" Misty asked, gesturing to the flowers on the counter. "Why are all of these sitting out?"

Sara explained about the temperature malfunction and said she still needed to call a repairman.

"I know just who to call, so I'll take care of it for you."

"Thanks." While Misty made the phone call, Sara finished the job of finding places to set all the flowers. When she returned from the back room with the last bunch, Misty was off the phone.

"Did the repairman agree to come over soon?"

Misty shook her head. "Unfortunately, he's tied up all morning and probably won't get here until sometime this afternoon."

Sara lifted her gaze to the ceiling. "Oh, great. I hope all the flowers will be okay until then. I have no idea how long they've been sitting inside the big cooler in fifty-five-degree heat."

"They should be okay, but I'll keep an eye on them. In the meantime, I need to get to work on the orders that need to be done today." Misty headed for the back room.

Sara sank into a chair at her desk. Last week hadn't gone well, as they'd dealt with several difficult customers they couldn't seem to satisfy. Then there was the cat that got into the store and knocked over a vase of flowers an elderly woman was about to purchase. The week had ended on a negative note when her delivery boy got sick and had to leave early, leaving Sara to deliver the flowers while Misty finished two last-minute bouquets.

Sara didn't mind making deliveries when she had to, but when she was faced with barking dogs in a customer's yard that looked like they might take a bite out of her leg, stress always took over. One time when she was heading to the delivery van with a pretty bouquet, a man walking a dog came by and told her not to worry, that his dog wouldn't bite. Sara quickly realized his statement wasn't true when she wound up with a Jack Russell terrier hanging off the corner of her jacket. Another time when she made a delivery, Sara had to walk up a grassy hill to get to the front door. She ended up slipping on the grass and falling but somehow managed to save the floral arrangement. Unfortunately her slacks sustained a bad grass stain and she never was able to remove the marks.

Sara hoped this week would go better, but things weren't off to a great start. At moments like this Sara wondered if she should sell the shop and concentrate fully on helping Brad in his ministry.

She exhaled noisily. *But I probably wouldn't be happy if I gave up something I really enjoy doing that's outside of the church.*

Mary Ruth hadn't said anything to Lenore because she didn't want to bring up the topic of Jesse, but she greatly missed spending time with Cindy. Having the little girl to care for had given her something meaningful to do. She used to look forward to the little girl's arrival on the days Jesse had to work. The child's cute antics and contagious belly laugh had given Mary Ruth a reason to smile. But with no one in the house except herself during the day, Mary Ruth felt lonely. It seemed as if her life no longer had a purpose. She tried to keep busy, as she was doing now, weeding and watering her flower and vegetable garden, but it wasn't the same as having a child to nurture and love. Even Sadie, who followed Mary Ruth nearly everywhere these days, seemed despondent. Perhaps she too missed all the activity of having a small child around.

Mary Ruth weeded thoroughly around the front border of her flower garden, where she'd planted red and white geraniums. Willis had liked those flowers and often commented on how nice they looked in the flower bed. She wanted to keep that theme in place as though nothing had changed.

I'll need to do one more thing. Mary Ruth got up and walked out to the shed to get her watering can and the plant food for the flowers. "Hmm . . . there's the food, but where is my watering can?" She dug around inside the shed, but the item wasn't there.

Mary Ruth grabbed the food and a nearby bucket and then got to work feeding the favored flowers. When she'd finished with that chore, she put things away. Then she went back to the garden to decide on the next spot to weed.

She walked slowly, eyeing the flower beds close to the house, and found that the pretty purple-and-white petunias needed some attention. As Mary Ruth weeded, she remembered about the watering can. The plastic container had a split and leaked a lot. So she had thrown it out and forgotten to buy a replacement.

"My old brain isn't working well these days," Mary Ruth muttered. She piled up the weeds as she cleaned out the bed. Once that chore was done, she stopped to watch her neighbors walking down the road and waved as they went by. The weather was lovely today, and working outside gave her a sense of accomplishment.

Mary Ruth continued to weed until each flower bed looked just right. She wished she had another bag of compost to add around the just-weeded spots. It would discourage more weeds from sprouting, making the weeding easier on the next go-round.

Mary Ruth noticed one of the barn cats out sunning itself, looking as though it was asleep. *That actually looks like a good plan. Maybe I should go inside and take a nap.* She rose from her kneeling position and reached around to rub a sore spot on the right side of her back. In a few weeks school would be out and Lenore would be home again for the summer. Mary Ruth looked forward to her granddaughter's companionship, as well as the extra help Lenore would offer with the yard and household chores. Having someone to talk to while doing one's chores was always more pleasurable than doing them alone.

Mary Ruth stared down at her hands, soiled from tugging at weeds. She should have worn a pair of gardening gloves but had always felt she could do a better job with her bare hands. *If I'm not careful, I'll sink into depression, and I can't allow that to happen. If Willis were here, he would shake his finger at me and say, "Count your blessings, Fraa. Do not give in to despair."*

She moved around to the other side of the house and stood looking at the lovely flowers in bloom. *Guess there's always something to be thankful for; I just need to look for it and try to keep a positive attitude.*

But her soul felt empty this afternoon. In addition to missing Willis every single day, she only got to see Cindy on Sundays, and seeing the little girl's eyes light up whenever she approached only made it that much harder.

Mary Ruth also felt a burden for both of her granddaughters. Although Lenore didn't say so, Mary Ruth was certain the somber expression on Lenore's face proved that she still loved Jesse and hurt because he didn't return her love.

Then there was Sara, still burdened over not knowing who her biological father was. Mary Ruth wished she had an answer for her English granddaughter. *If only Rhoda had confided in her father or me and admitted she was pregnant and told us the name of her baby's father.*

"Enough weeding for today." Mary Ruth ended her introspections and set her gardening tools on the porch. Nothing could be gained by rehashing the past when it couldn't be changed. "Think I'll go inside now, read some scripture and pray, and then take a nap."

Lenore sat at her desk, rubbing her tired eyes. The scholars had left for the day, and she had some papers to go over before tomorrow's lessons. *If I could be anywhere else right now, where would it be? Maybe on a two-week trip to Sarasota with Grandma,* she mused. *A getaway would be a nice change but not practical at this time.*

Lenore picked up a paper and began to review it. The student had done a fine job, and she wrote the grade at the top of the page. Lenore hoped every paper in the pile would be like the first one. It was hard to believe the school term was almost over. Lenore would spend the summer months helping Grandma with the garden and all the chores that needed to be done around the house. Either Dad or one of her brothers would continue to do most of the heavy outdoor chores, as well as anything Lenore and Grandma couldn't do inside the house.

Last Saturday, Ben and Peter had come over to patch a few places on the roof where some shingles had come loose. A few days before that Dad had come by to fix a leaky toilet upstairs. Lenore's mother came as often as she could to help with some of the easier chores. She would no doubt be available when it was time to pick produce from the garden and can some of it in the pressure cooker.

Lenore tapped her fingers on the desk. *Wish I could be home with Grandma all the time and didn't have to teach school anymore. If Jesse hadn't called off our wedding, we'd be getting married the last Thursday of this month, and then my only job would be taking care of Cindy and being a good wife.*

Despite her sorrow over the way things had transpired, it was better than finding out he didn't love her after they were married. That would have been a crushing blow. It was hard to imagine living with a man she called *husband* but not truly being his wife in every sense of the word. *Could I have done it for Cindy's sake?* Lenore asked herself for the umpteenth time. *Should I have agreed to marry Jesse anyway, in hopes that he might love me someday?*

The schoolhouse door opened and Mark stepped inside. "I was hoping you'd still be here. Are you busy?" he called.

"Just going over some papers." She smiled as he approached her desk. "What brings you by the schoolhouse this afternoon?"

"Came to let you know I finally got myself a new *waegli*."

"That's good. I'm sure you're glad to have found a buggy that will work for you."

"I am, and now the rig I'd been borrowing is back with its owner. It's nice having a closed-in buggy."

Lenore laid down her pen. "So where did you get it?"

"The buggy maker closest to here mentioned an Amish man who wanted to sell his used buggy. So I went to the address, and the man showed me the one I'm driving now."

"It sounds like you're happy with it."

"Jah, and I was hoping you'd have the time to go for a ride with me. I'd like to show you how nice it rides."

She motioned to the stack of papers on her desk. "Sorry, Mark, I can't go right now, but maybe some evening this week." Lenore could tell he really wanted her to go with him today, and she felt bad for turning him down.

Mark's smile faded as he remained next to her desk. Then his grin returned before he spoke. "How about Friday? Would that work for you?" He popped the knuckles on his right hand.

Lenore had a flashback, remembering that she'd seen him do that several times when they attended school together. As she recalled, the finger popping had taken place whenever Mark seemed apprehensive about something. Perhaps he'd been nervous about asking her to take a ride in his buggy.

With only a slight hesitation, Lenore nodded. Maybe a few hours with Mark would take her mind off other things.

CHAPTER 38

Clymer

Michelle listened intently as one of their elderly ministers read Romans 8:28: "We know that all things work together for good to them that love God, to them who are the called according to his purpose." The minister delivering the message was the easiest to understand. He tended to use more English words in his address to the congregation than the bishop and other preachers did.

Michelle was still getting used to deciphering the German words spoken during Amish church, but her language skills were coming along. At least she understood most of the Pennsylvania Dutch words the Amish spoke as their everyday language.

She'd gotten used to doing without TV and other modern electronic conveniences. She no longer needed those forms of stimulation. The simple life was what Michelle thought was important.

As she sat with the other women on wooden benches, Michelle appreciated the pillow she'd been offered to sit on today. Another young woman also sat on a pillow. She was expecting a baby too, only she wasn't as far along as Michelle.

Michelle rested both hands on her stomach. In a little over two months she would give birth, and since she'd finally set her fears aside, she could hardly wait for the big day. Michelle felt certain that Ezekiel would be a good father, and hoped she'd be a good mother as well. Ezekiel's mother planned to come and stay with them for a while after the baby was born, and Michelle looked forward to that. Even though Belinda hadn't accepted her at first, as time went on and Michelle became a member of the Amish church, their relationship had improved.

Michelle glanced at her new friend, Anita Beiler, who was also new to the area. Anita and her husband, Nate, were expecting a baby in August. The two couples had gotten together a few times to visit and play board games. Michelle and Anita had also spent some time together, sewing clothes for their babies and helping each other with their gardens. It was nice to have someone to talk to who was about her age, and Michelle had finally reached the point where she felt like

Clymer was her home.

She gave her belly a gentle tap, and as if in response, the baby kicked. *It will be your home too, little one.* As the Bible verse said, all things were working out for her good.

Michelle glanced at her husband from across the room. Ezekiel's relaxed expression let her know that he too felt content.

Strasburg

As Lenore sat in church, listening to the second message of the morning, she glanced at the men's side and noticed Mark looking at her. She quickly dropped her gaze, hoping no one had noticed them making eye contact, which would be inappropriate in church.

Lenore wondered why he hadn't picked her up for a buggy ride on Friday evening as they'd planned. He hadn't even bothered to call. Had he forgotten about it or simply changed his mind? Either way, it was inconsiderate of him not to let her know.

Lenore kept her gaze focused on her folded hands. *Since I have no expectations of us establishing a relationship and apparently neither does Mark, I suppose it doesn't really matter that he didn't show up on Friday evening. He's just an acquaintance — not even a close friend, because a friend would have the courtesy to let the other person know if they had to cancel their plans.*

As the next song began, Lenore looked up from her hymnal and saw Jesse holding Cindy. The child looked so cute sitting on her daddy's lap with a wide-eyed expression. Drawing her arms close to her body and gripping the Amish hymnal tightly, Lenore dropped her gaze once more. *Some men can't be trusted. At least that's how it appears to be with Jesse and Mark. They say one thing and then go back on their word.*

When church was over and everyone had been served a light lunch, some people went home while others lingered, gathering in groups to visit. Since Cindy had become fussy and needed her diaper changed, Jesse decided it was time to head for home. Hopefully she would sleep after he'd changed her diaper, and then Jesse would try to do some reading, or he might even take a nap himself.

As Jesse headed for his buggy, carrying Cindy as well as her diaper bag, he thought about how things were when he'd been courting Lenore. He reflected on the advice Vera had given him a few weeks ago and wondered if he'd been too hasty breaking things off with Lenore. Maybe he did have some feelings for her. It could be that if they had gotten married those feelings would have turned to love. Jesse wondered if he should see if Lenore might be willing to let him court her again.

Almost every Sunday that their district held church services, he and Cindy had gone over to Mary Ruth's house and spent the afternoon and evening hours with her and Lenore. They'd often played board games or just sat and visited. And of course, the women would always fix something tasty to eat. Jesse missed those times. Truth was, he also missed conversing with Lenore. But the question was — did he love her? If he did, he had been pushing his feelings down to keep from being untrue to Esther's memory.

Jesse approached his buggy and got Cindy settled inside. As he turned toward his horse, waiting patiently to go, he caught sight of Lenore over by the fence, talking to Mark Zook, whom he'd finally met.

Jesse tried not to gawk at the two of them as they visited. Instead, he turned his head to look inside the buggy at Cindy, yawning in her car seat. When Jesse looked back, he noticed Lenore's buggy. Mary Ruth stood outside the buggy with her arms folded, no doubt waiting for Lenore. Jesse caught sight of her looking in the couple's direction. He couldn't see her expression from here but wondered if Mary Ruth approved of Lenore's new friend.

The skin under Jesse's eyes tightened as a pang of jealousy shot through him. His teeth clenched. *I bet something is going on between those two. Guess I waited too long,* he berated himself. *So now what do I do? Should I forget about Lenore and move on with my life, or see if there's a possibility of pursuing a relationship again?*

"I'm sorry about not coming by to pick you up on Friday for a ride in my buggy." Mark reached out his hand as if to touch Lenore, but quickly pulled it away. "If you're willing to listen, I'd like to explain what happened."

Lenore leaned against the fence and looked up at him. "I'm willing to listen."

"I had to work later than normal Friday evening, and by the time I got back to my uncle's place, I'd developed a *koppweh.*" Mark leaned on the fence too, and when he smiled, she caught a whiff of his minty breath.

"It's too bad about your headache. I understand how miserable those can be. What I don't understand, though, is why you didn't call and let me know you weren't

403

coming."

"I did call, but the voice mail on your answering machine must have been nearly full, because it cut off before I could even say who I was." He popped a few knuckles on his left hand.

"Oh, I see." Lenore had no choice but to give him the benefit of the doubt — especially because she had discovered that their answering machine was full when she'd checked it last evening.

"Am I forgiven?" Mark's arms hung loosely at his sides, but his tender gaze remained on her.

"Jah." Lenore looked over toward her buggy and saw Grandma waiting. She appeared to be looking their way. Lenore's face warmed, and Mark's proximity wasn't helping. *I wonder what Grandma is thinking right now. Am I moving on too soon?*

Mark cleared his throat. "Lenore, are you okay? Your cheeks look mighty red all of a sudden."

"I'm fine. Uh, sorry, what did you say?" She stepped from Grandma's view.

"I'd like another chance, and I was thinking if you're not busy, I could come by your grandma's place this evening and take you for a ride." Mark's sincere expression made it difficult to say no.

Lenore managed a weak smile. "I have no special plans for this evening, so jah, I'm willing to go for a ride."

Mark's lips stretched into a pleasant smile. "Okay, good. I'll see you around seven."

As Mark walked away, Lenore turned toward her buggy, where Grandma sat waiting. *Sure hope I didn't make a mistake saying I would go.*

That evening, Lenore's parents came by to see how she and Grandma were doing. Mom brought along some cold fried chicken and potato salad, and Lenore took coleslaw from the refrigerator that she'd made yesterday, along with some pickled beets and chow-chow.

"Danki for helping me get supper on," Lenore said to her mother. "It's nice for Grandma to just sit and relax for a change while she visits with Dad."

Mom nodded. "Jah, it's good for them to have a little mother-son time."

"I agree. It's been awfully quiet around the house ever since Jesse found someone else to watch Cindy, and Grandma misses the little girl."

"I figured as much. She's not as cheerful as she was when she kept busy taking care of Cindy," Mom observed. "So how are things going with you?"

Lenore shrugged as she placed the bowl of coleslaw on the table. "Okay, I guess. I'm getting a bit bored with teaching though, and I've been praying that God will show me what He has in store for me down the road."

"I'll be praying for you too." Mom hugged Lenore. "Now your grandma mentioned when we first arrived that you were talking to a nice-looking Amish man after church this afternoon."

"It was Mark Zook. He and his folks used to live in the area, and he went to school with me."

"So are he and his family here for a visit?"

"No, I believe Mark plans to stay here. He's working for his uncle John in his woodworking business."

"I see." Mom tipped her head. "Do you mind me asking what the two of you were talking about today?"

"Nothing much. Mark was just asking if he could take me for a buggy ride."

A wide smile spread across Mom's face. "I'm glad to hear that. It'll be good for you to start courting again."

Lenore released an exasperated sigh. "Mom, Mark and I are not courting. We're just renewing our acquaintance, and he probably needs a friend."

"Well, you just never know — your friendship with Mark might lead to something else." Mom's tone sounded hopeful. No doubt she was as eager to see Lenore married off as Lenore was herself. Well, it remained to be seen what her future held. The main thing, Lenore kept reminding herself, was to keep her focus on God and live a good Christian life. And as long as she was teaching, she needed to be a good example to her students, even if she no longer felt that teaching was her true calling.

CHAPTER 39

Lancaster

As the last few parishioners headed out the door after the church service had ended, Charlene Givens, a young woman who had recently started attending Brad's Friday night Bible study, paused at the door and smiled at Sara. "My husband and I are looking forward to the barbecue you and the pastor are hosting this coming Saturday. Is there anything I can bring?"

Stunned and barely able to form any words, Sara stammered, "Uh, no, I — I don't think so."

Charlene smiled. "Okay, we'll see you Saturday evening then. And if you change your mind and would like me to bring something, please give me a call."

Sara watched as the young woman walked away and got into the car where her husband, Roger, waited. Sara's forehead creased. *Now what was that all about?* This was the first she'd heard anything about a barbecue at their house. *Could Charlene be misinformed, or did Brad plan the event without telling me? Should I have told her I didn't know about the barbecue?*

She turned toward her husband, who had moments ago been talking with the head deacon. *Should I say something to Brad now or wait till we get home?*

"You okay, hon?" Brad asked, stepping up to her. "You look perplexed."

"I am. Did you invite Charlene and Roger Givens to our house for a barbecue this coming Saturday?"

He nodded.

Sara frowned, clamping one hand firmly against her hip. "Without telling me or asking if I approved?"

Brad blinked rapidly. "I did tell you. We discussed it one night last week after you got home from work."

Sara shook her head. "I'm sure I'd remember if we had such a discussion. You can imagine how surprised I was when Charlene brought it up and asked if there was anything she could bring."

"Can we discuss this after we get home?" Brad glanced to his right, and Sara noticed that the deacon stood nearby, looking at the church guest book. *Or maybe he's listening*

409

to our conversation so he can tell others what we're saying.

Knowing Brad was right about waiting until they got home to finish their discussion, Sara gave a brief nod. The last thing they needed was a round of gossip about the pastor and his wife having a disagreement right here in the church.

Brad said a few words to the deacon, then followed Sara out the door. They walked across the parking lot and into the yard of the parsonage, which was next to the church. As soon as they entered the house, Sara turned to face Brad. "I am almost one-hundred percent sure you did not mention anything about a barbecue to me."

A muscle quivered in his jaw. "And I'm equally sure I did, Sara. You were probably preoccupied and didn't listen to what I said. However, when I mentioned it, you did nod your head, so I assumed you were fine with the idea of having a few people over for food and fellowship."

Sara tapped her foot impatiently. "I'm certain I would remember something as important as you expecting me to host a barbecue — and during one of the busiest times for the flower shop, no less." She looked at Brad through half-closed lids. "Have you forgotten that next Sunday is

410

Mother's Day? Saturday will be a zoo at the shop all day, and I may even have to work late."

"No, I haven't forgotten about Mother's Day. I just thought with the barbecue taking place at seven o'clock, you'd have plenty of time to get home from work."

"As I said before . . . I may be working late."

He placed his hand on her shoulder. "I'm sorry, but the plans have already been made and I don't want to disappoint the people I've invited."

Her jaw clenched as she looked up at him. "Just how many people did you invite?"

"There will be eight, counting us."

"Well, that's just great. The next time you decide to plan an event at our house, please send me a memo." Sara dropped her Bible on the entry table and tromped down the hall to their bedroom. This was the first real disagreement between her and Brad, and it hurt to know he hadn't put her needs above others'. The worst part of all was that he hadn't even told her about it.

Strasburg

"Your new buggy is very nice," Lenore said as she and Mark traveled down the road.

"Danki, I like it too, and I'm real pleased

411

with how well it rides." He ran his hand across the upholstered seat in the area between them. "The interior is in good shape too. Sure am glad I found this rig and was able to get it for a reasonable price." Mark's tone was enthusiastic.

"How long do you plan to stay in Lancaster County?" Lenore asked.

"I'm here to stay." Mark's brows lowered as he turned his head to look at her. "Thought I told you that when we met the first time after I came back here." He gestured to the front of the buggy. "Why else would I have invested in this?"

Lenore's ears burned. "Oh, sorry. I must have forgotten."

"No problem. Maybe I just didn't make myself clear." He reached across the seat and gave her arm a light tap. "I don't plan to stay at my uncle's place indefinitely, though. If things work out as I hope, I plan to either rent or buy a home of my own."

"I see."

"How long do you plan on teaching school?" Mark asked.

"Until the Lord guides me in a different direction. I hope to have a home and family someday. But for now I'm content to live with my grandma and teach school."

"I'd like to get married and have a family

too. Just waitin' for the right woman to make me fall in love." He gave her another sidelong glance, then focused on the road again.

Lenore remained quiet, and they rode without talking for a while.

"Say, next Saturday is my birthday," Mark said, breaking the silence. "My aunt and uncle are planning a birthday dinner for me. Would you like to come? We'll be making homemade ice cream," he added with a grin.

"That sounds yummy. Sure, I'd like to come to your birthday celebration."

Mark's horse picked up speed, and he pulled back on the reins. "Slow down, Clipper. No need to hurry, boy." He looked at Lenore once more. "Unless you need to get home soon, that is."

She shook her head and relaxed against the seat. It was nice to spend time with a man who seemed genuinely interested in her. The fact that Mark had invited Lenore to his birthday party let her know that he might have more than a passing interest in her.

"I don't think you've ever said, but I'm curious as to the reason you decided to move back here without any of your family coming along." Lenore sat quietly, waiting for his response.

Mark's lips drew into a straight line as he kept his focus on the road. Several seconds passed before he answered her question. "I . . . uh . . . just needed a new start."

Was Mark reluctant to answer her question? She felt it wouldn't be right to prod him further, so she changed the subject. "It's a nice evening, jah?"

He nodded. Lenore couldn't figure out why he'd gone quiet all of a sudden. Mark had been plenty talkative until she'd brought up the subject of why he'd moved back to Strasburg. Could Mark have had a falling out with his parents? Or maybe he was trying to get over a broken relationship with a young woman. Many reasons could cause someone to want to start over, but Lenore wouldn't press Mark for the details. If he wanted to talk about it in his own time, she'd be willing to listen.

Holding tight to his fidgety daughter in his arms, Jesse stepped onto Mary Ruth's porch and knocked on the door. All the way here he'd thought about Lenore and what he would say to her. *Sure hope she's willing to give me another chance at courting her. How else can I ever really know what my true feelings are for her if I don't give it more time? I was stupid to just break things off like I did.*

Should have told her the truth and then asked if she'd be willing to postpone the wedding and give us more time to court and get to know each other better. With a little more time, maybe my feelings for Lenore would have changed.

A few minutes passed before the door opened. Mary Ruth stood inside with her head covering askew. "Ach, Jesse! It's nice to see you." She reached up to adjust her kapp. "And you too, sweet girl." Mary Ruth touched the end of Cindy's nose, which caused the child to giggle. "Please, come inside."

When Jesse entered the house, Mary Ruth held out her arms. "May I hold her?"

"Of course, but she's getting heavy. Not fat, just solid." Jesse gave a nervous laugh as he glanced around, hoping Lenore would make an appearance. "Maybe I should put her down and you can walk with her out to the living room."

Mary Ruth bobbed her head. "Good idea."

Once Jesse set his daughter on her feet, Mary Ruth clasped Cindy's chubby little hand, and they all went to the living room.

After Mary Ruth was seated in her rocking chair, she lifted Cindy into her lap and got the chair moving at a slow and gentle pace. "I've missed this precious little girl something awful." She brought Cindy's hand up to her lips and gave it a kiss. "I've missed seeing you too, Jesse. We don't really get the chance to converse at church, and I've only seen you there a few times since I quit watching Cindy. How have the two of you been?"

"Doing okay, but Cindy and I both miss you as well. She did much better with you watching her than she does with Vera."

"I wish I could offer to watch her again, but with you and my granddaughter breaking up, it might be too awkward. Especially since Lenore will be done teaching school for the summer soon. She'll be here most of the time, so it would be hard for you to avoid seeing her."

I don't want to avoid seeing Lenore. I want to spend more time with her. Jesse kept his thoughts to himself.

Crossing and then uncrossing his arms, Jesse shifted on the couch. "Speaking of Lenore, is she here right now?"

Mary Ruth shook her head. "No need to worry. Mark Zook came by a while ago to take Lenore for a ride in his new buggy."

"Oh, I see." Jesse weaved his fingers through his beard. "Well, would you please tell her I stopped by, and that I said hello?"

"Of course." Mary Ruth set Cindy on the floor again. "Now how about I go into the kitchen and fetch us all some *millich un kichlin*? Maybe by the time we're done eating, Lenore will be home."

Jesse lifted a hand. "No, that's okay. Don't trouble yourself. I just dropped by to say hello, but we really should get home now."

Mary Ruth's shoulders slumped a bit, but she did offer him a smile. "Whatever you think is best."

Jesse got up, scooped Cindy into his arms, and moved toward the front door. Apparently renewing his relationship with Lenore was not meant to be. *I'm too late. Lenore is already being courted by someone else.*

Mary Ruth stood at the door, waving as Jesse guided his horse and buggy out of her yard. *I wish he'd stayed a while longer.* In addition to wanting to spend more time with Cindy, Mary Ruth hoped if Jesse and Lenore could spend a little time visiting, they might get back together. "Maybe it's just my silly wishful thinking again," she murmured. "Guess I'm a romantic at heart."

Mary Ruth went to the kitchen and heated hot water for tea. She'd no more than sat down with her cup when Lenore showed up.

"You just missed Jesse and Cindy," she said after Lenore entered the kitchen.

Lenore blinked a couple of times. "They were here?"

"Jah. Came by to say hello, but they didn't stay long."

Lenore hung her lightweight shawl over the back of a chair and took a seat at the table. "I bet you enjoyed seeing Cindy. When I saw her in church this morning, I was surprised to see how much she's grown. I think Jesse's been going to Vera and Milton's church district the last few weeks, because today is the first time I've seen him and Cindy in a while."

"Jah, that could be." Mary Ruth took a sip of her tea. "Jesse asked about you. He seemed disappointed when I told him you weren't here."

"I'm sorry I missed them." Lenore fiddled with the basket of napkins on the table, wishing they weren't having this conversation. "It would have been nice to spend a little time with Cindy again."

"What about Jesse? Wouldn't you have enjoyed visiting with him?"

She shrugged. "I suppose so, but it would have been kind of awkward for both of us.

Since Jesse broke things off with me, we've only spoken a few times, and I could feel the tension between us."

"Maybe he's having second thoughts."

Lenore gave a deep, weighted sigh. "I doubt that Jesse misses me." She yawned and stretched her arms over her head. "I'm kind of tired, Grandma. If you don't mind, I'm going upstairs to bed."

"That's fine," Mary Ruth said, trying to hide her disappointment. She'd hoped the two of them might sit and visit awhile before retiring for the evening. Mary Ruth wanted to hear how things had gone with Mark and maybe say a few more things about Jesse.

She stood and gave Lenore a hug. "Good night, dear one. I hope you sleep well."

"You too, Grandma." Lenore smiled, but there was an unmistakable sadness in her eyes.

Lenore may not be willing to admit it, but I am convinced that she still misses Jesse, Mary Ruth thought as her granddaughter left the room. Tapping her chin with her knuckles, she tipped her head to one side. *There must be some way to get those two back together. I just need to figure out what.*

CHAPTER 40

Lenore finished her cup of coffee and set it in the sink. "Oh Grandma, before I leave for school, I wanted to let you know that I won't be here for supper Saturday night."

"Oh, why's that?"

"Last night on our buggy ride, Mark invited me to attend his birthday supper at his aunt and uncle's place. I should have told you after I got home, but I had other things on my mind and forgot to mention it."

"Danki for letting me know. Guess I'll plan something small for my supper that evening, or maybe I'll hitch my horse to the buggy and go out somewhere to eat."

Lenore's brows lifted. "By yourself?"

"Of course. I'm not so old that I can't take the horse and buggy out by myself, and I don't mind eating alone once in a while."

Lenore blew out a quick breath. Now, in addition to being a bit nervous about going to Mark's party, she'd have to worry about Grandma all evening.

Grandma waved her hand. "I know what you're thinking, and I'll be fine, so there's no need to *druwwle* about me."

"Okay, I'll try not to worry." Lenore managed to smile. "Oh, and one more thing before I forget . . . After school lets out today, I'm going shopping to get a birthday present for Mark. Any suggestions for what I should get?"

Grandma shook her head. "You know the young man better than I do. What kinds of things does he like?"

Lenore shrugged. "To tell you the truth, I'm not really sure. Mark works in his uncle's woodworking shop, but that's his job. I don't know what kinds of things he enjoys doing when he's not working."

Grandma tapped her fingers along the edge of the table. "How about a *buch*? Most people enjoy reading."

"A book would make a nice gift if I knew what type of subject Mark likes to read about."

"How about a book on railroads or Pennsylvania history? I would think he might enjoy reading either of those topics," Grandma suggested. "You could go to Moyer's Book Barn here in Strasburg and see what they have."

Lenore wrinkled her nose. "I would feel kind of funny about getting him a used book, which is mostly what they have there in the old barn."

"Guess you could try Gordonville Bookstore. There's also the Ridgeview Bookstore if you're looking for someplace closer than Lancaster."

"Okay, thanks for the ideas." Lenore leaned over and kissed her grandmother's cheek. "I'd better get going or the scholars will be at the schoolhouse before I am. I'll try to be home in time to help you fix supper."

Grandma lifted both hands. "No worries. I can fix the evening meal without your help once in a while."

Lenore smiled and hurried out the door. It was a blessing and a privilege to be living here with Grandma. Something she may not be able to do if she ever got married, since her husband might want a place of their own. If a marriage were to happen, which Lenore thought was doubtful, she would join forces with her parents to convince Grandma to move in with them.

After Lenore went out the door, Mary Ruth remained at the kitchen table with a cup of cinnamon tea, pondering what Lenore said about being invited to Mark's birthday celebration. She couldn't help feeling some concern that Lenore might end up getting serious about Mark. He was obviously trying to develop a relationship with her or he wouldn't have invited her to take a ride in his buggy last evening, not to mention asking her to attend his birthday supper.

Mary Ruth took a sip of tea and set the cup on the table with renewed determination. "I have to come up with some way to get Lenore and Jesse together again. If I were to invite him and Cindy to join us for supper some evening, that might seem too obvious to both Lenore and Jesse. Maybe I should enlist someone's help with this." She tipped her head from side to side, weighing her choices. "Now who could I ask that's had some experience in matchmaking?"

As Sara wrapped a gift for a customer, she tried to keep her focus on making the package look as nice as possible. It was hard to keep her focus on anything other than the unresolved disagreement she and Brad were having.

We should have talked things through before going to bed, Sara thought as she handed her customer the wrapped item.

"Thank you." The young woman smiled. "I'm sure my mother will like the pretty beaded necklace and matching earrings. Mom's allergic to most flowers, so I appreciate that you sell other things here besides floral arrangements."

"You're welcome." Sara did her best to offer a friendly smile. "I make the beaded items whenever I have some free time."

"This is my first time in your shop, but it won't be the last," the woman called over her shoulder as she headed for the door.

Sara was pleased by the customer's comment, but her heart still felt heavy. When she went home this evening she planned to air things out with Brad and say she was sorry for anything she'd said yesterday that may have hurt him. *And I need to give him the benefit of the doubt. With all the busyness in the shop the past week or so, maybe he did mention plans for a barbecue and I just forgot.*

Since no other customers were in the store for the moment, Sara stepped into the back room to see if Misty needed her help with anything.

Sara's nose twitched and she sneezed a couple of times. She was surprised to see Misty putting bleach in a bucket with the grate for the Gerbera daisies.

"How come you're adding bleach in there?" Sara asked, stepping up to her talented designer.

Misty gestured to the daisies. "It may seem strange, but Gerbs like the bleach. It actually helps them stay fresh longer."

Sara's eyes widened. "How interesting. I never would have guessed that any flower would do well in bleach."

"Would you like another tip — only this one's for tulips?"

"Sure."

"Putting a couple of pennies in the bottom of the vase helps tulips stand up straight."

Sara tipped her head. "Seriously?"

"Yes, and did you know tulips are the only flowers that continue to grow after they are cut? They can grow up to an inch." There was a gleam in Misty's eyes. "Here's another one for you. Hydrangeas can be a difficult flower to keep alive once they're cut, as they wilt easily. So the trick is after you cut them, you should dip them in alum before adding them to an arrangement. Some florists turn them upside down in the water for a while and then turn them over, cut the stems, and put them upright in the bucket. Oh, and spritzing the hydrangea can help some too."

Sara gave a slow, disbelieving shake of her

head. "You are amazing, Misty — so full of information the average person would not know."

Misty grinned. "It's my job as a floral designer to know lots of things about flowers."

Sara patted Misty's arm. "I'm glad you're here working for me. I'd be lost without you."

The bell on the front door jingled, signaling a customer had come into the store. "I'd better get out there. Talk to you later, Misty."

Misty gave a nod. "Sure thing."

When Sara stepped into the front of her flower shop, she was surprised to see Brad standing in front of the counter, holding one hand against his chest. "I came to apologize to my beautiful wife. If I did plan the barbecue without telling you, I was wrong, and I shouldn't have gone to bed last night without saying I'm sorry."

Sara rushed into his arms. "I'm just as much at fault as you for the disagreement and not resolving it then. Will you forgive me, Brad?"

"Of course." He gently patted her back. "If you want me to cancel the barbecue, I'll call everyone and ask if we can make it for some other time. It was inconsiderate of me to plan something like that so close to Mother's Day, knowing how busy you've been."

A few tears leaked out from under Sara's lashes. "You don't have to cancel, but maybe you could ask everyone if they would mind bringing a salad, chips, or dessert to accompany the meat you'll barbecue. That would help, and I wouldn't have to do any major preparation."

"Sounds good to me." When Brad lifted Sara's chin and gave her a kiss, the ache in her heart she'd felt earlier melted like ice on a hot summer day.

By the end of the school day Lenore was more than ready to head for Moyer's Book Barn. She'd changed her mind and decided to go there and see if any of their used books about the history of Pennsylvania were in good enough condition to buy. If she couldn't find anything to her liking, she would go to Gordonville. Lenore also planned to give Mark one of her homemade greeting cards to go with whatever present she found.

As Lenore headed down the road a short time later, keeping her horse at a steady pace, her thoughts went to Jesse. Had he really asked about her when he'd stopped to see Grandma yesterday evening?

What would I have said to him if I had been home? Lenore kept a firm grip on the reins. *I probably would have kept my focus mainly on Cindy and said very little to Jesse. After all, how does a woman make small talk with a man who broke their engagement? What would there be to converse about?*

Lenore swatted at the annoying fly that had found its way into her buggy before she left the schoolyard. *I suppose I could have mentioned the lovely spring weather we're having. Or maybe asked how Cindy's been doing in the care of his wife's great-aunt.*

Lenore was fully aware of how much Grandma missed taking care of Jesse's little girl. It was obvious whenever she looked longingly at the toys she'd gotten out for Cindy to play with, kept in a wooden box Grandpa had made when Lenore and her brothers were children.

Maybe I should speak to Grandma about this. I could suggest that she talk to Jesse and volunteer to watch Cindy again. I'll just make myself scarce whenever he drops Cindy off or picks her up. That way, at least Grandma will be happy.

As the old book barn came into view, Lenore quieted her thoughts and focused on the task of finding Mark an appropriate gift.

CHAPTER 41

"I'm glad you could help us celebrate our nephew's twenty-eighth birthday this evening." Mark's aunt Martha smiled at Lenore as they gathered up supplies to take outside for their meal. "My husband and I are glad Mark's courting again. He took it hard when his girlfriend back home broke up with him."

No wonder Mark didn't want to talk about the reason he decided to move here when I asked him.

Then another thought popped into Lenore's head. "Did Mark tell you he and I are courting?"

Martha bobbed her head. "And just from the short time we've spent together this evening, I can see why he chose you."

"Thank you." Lenore's face heated. She was tempted to tell Mark's aunt that she and Mark were not courting. If they were, it was only in Mark's mind, because he'd never asked if Lenore wanted him to court her.

What would I say if he did ask? she wondered. *Do I like Mark well enough to be in a relationship that could eventually result in a marriage proposal?*

Lenore pushed her considerations aside and picked up the tray full of paper plates, napkins, and silverware. "Should I take these out to the picnic table now?"

"Jah, that would be fine, but be sure you weigh the plates and napkins down with the silverware. It's a little breezy this evening, and we don't need our supper plates blowing all over the yard."

"No problem. I'll make certain each plate is held fast."

Lenore left the house and went straight to the oversized picnic table. She'd finished setting everything out when Mark came alongside her.

"Sure am glad you could be here tonight." His face seemed to shine as he popped his knuckles and grinned at her.

Lenore fought the urge to ask Mark right then if he'd told his aunt they were courting. She would wait for a more appropriate time. "It's nice to be here," she replied. "I enjoyed visiting with your aunt Martha in the kitchen. She seems like a nice person."

431

"Jah. She and my Uncle are great." Mark sniffed the air. "Don't you just love the smoky aroma of meat cooking on the grill?"

"It does smell good." Lenore glanced toward the house and saw Martha carrying a cardboard box. "I should go see if your aunt needs any more help."

"I'm sure if she does, she'll ask for it." Mark put his hand against the small of Lenore's back. "Why don't the two of us take a walk? It'll be a while before the chicken is done."

Lenore hesitated but finally nodded. "Let's not be gone very long though. I want to be here to help with any last-minute things that might need to be brought out to the picnic table."

"We'll be back in plenty of time before we're called to eat." Before Lenore could offer a response, Mark grabbed hold of her hand and began walking in the direction of the barn. Lenore assumed he might want to show her some special animal inside.

"Let's go in here," Mark said. "There's something I want to ask you in private."

Lenore's heartbeat picked up speed again. Was Mark going to ask if he could court her? If so, would he expect an immediate answer?

When they entered the barn, the distinctive aroma of dried hay and sweaty horse-flesh wafted up to Lenore's nose, causing her to sneeze. *Achoo! Achoo!* She removed a tissue she'd tucked inside one of her dress sleeves.

"Bless you." Mark led Lenore over to a bale of straw and asked her to take a seat. After Lenore sat down, he seated himself beside her. Mark was so close to Lenore, she could smell the musky fragrance of his aftershave — or maybe it was whatever shampoo he'd used to wash his hair.

"I really like you, Lenore, and I think we should start courting." He leaned even closer, so his mouth nearly rested against her ear. "Are you okay with that?"

Swallowing hard, she shifted on the bale of straw. Did she want Mark to court her? Did they have enough in common to begin a relationship? Lenore wasn't sure how she felt about Mark. He seemed nice enough, but her stomach didn't flutter in his presence, the way it had whenever she'd been with Jesse. Still, it was nice to have someone to do things with, and Mark seemed to have a pleasant personality.

A light nudge brought Lenore's contemplations to a halt. "So what do you say, Lenore? Are you willing to let me court you?"

She moistened her lips with the tip of her tongue. "I . . . I suppose it would be okay."

"That's great. I look forward to spending more time with you." Mark reached for Lenore's hand and gave her fingers a squeeze. His hand seemed chilly and a bit sweaty too. *He's probably as nervous as I am right now.*

Lenore let go of Mark's hand and stood. "We should go back to the picnic area now. Your aunt and uncle might wonder where we are, and as I mentioned before, I want to offer my help if needed."

His brows gathered in. "Okay, if you say so."

As they left the barn, Lenore couldn't help wondering if she'd done the right thing by agreeing to let Mark court her. Well, it was too late to take back her words. She would just go through the courting procedure and see how things went. Maybe in time she would develop strong feelings for Mark. If not, then she would have to tell him they could only be friends. *One thing's for sure,* Lenore decided, *I will never agree to marry Mark if I don't love him. And if Mark and I should ever become engaged, I will not break it off the way Jesse did to me.*

"Well, I think all the meat and vegetables

are about ready for our barbecue," Brad announced after he'd cut up the onions and tomatoes and placed them on the table.

"I have all the eating utensils ready to set out on the picnic table too." Sara pointed to the stack of paper plates, cups, silverware, and napkins on the counter.

"While we're waiting for our guests to arrive, I'm going to give my mom a call." Brad pulled out his cell phone. "Since she and Dad will be leaving on a cruise to the Bahamas tomorrow morning, I want to wish her a happy Mother's Day now."

"Good idea." Sara took a seat at the table while Brad made the call. Once he had his mother on the phone, he put it on speaker so Sara could hear what was being said and join the conversation.

"Happy Mother's Day," Sara and Brad said in unison.

"Thank you," his mother replied. "And thanks for the lovely African violet you had sent to me."

"You're welcome," Sara said. "I hope the plant will be okay while you're away on vacation. I should have thought about that before I had it sent to you."

"I'm sure it'll be fine. A friend of mine will be housesitting for us while we're gone, and I'll make sure to leave instructions on

435

watering and fertilizing the violet."

"Sounds good. Well, I'll let you finish up with Brad," Sara said. "We have company coming soon, so I need to double-check on things and make sure everything is ready."

"You go right ahead, Sara. And thanks again for the lovely plant."

Sara wished Jean a good trip, said good-bye, and went to the refrigerator to take out a pitcher of iced tea.

As Brad continued the conversation with his mother, Sara's mind wandered. With tomorrow being Mother's Day, she couldn't help thinking about her own mother and how much she still missed her.

She rubbed a hand over her face. *All the years I spent with Mama before she died, I took so much for granted, never expecting she would be gone so unexpectedly. What I wouldn't give to spend tomorrow with my mother.*

Changing her focus, Sara looked forward to going over to see her grandmother after church tomorrow. She had a plant for Grandma too, and it would be great just to sit and visit awhile. No doubt there would be food and beverages. Sara almost laughed out loud. No one could visit Grandma's house and not be invited to partake of a meal or at least some tasty refreshments.

By the time Brad ended the phone call with his mother, their first few guests had arrived. Making sure she was wearing a pleasant smile, Sara left the kitchen and went to greet them.

Clymer

"It's time to get up, *schlofkopp*."

Michelle rolled onto her side and groaned. "You're right, Ezekiel, I am a sleepyhead this morning, and I have every right to be. Our boppli kept me awake most of the night, kicking and moving around in my belly."

Ezekiel smiled. "He must be eager to make his appearance."

"Well, *he* or *she* will have to wait a little longer. I want our first child to be born right on schedule."

"Same here." Ezekiel climbed out of bed. "We need to eat and get ready for church."

She yawned and stretched her arms over her head. "Okay, I can take a hint. You want me to fix breakfast."

Ezekiel chuckled. "You know me too well."

She smiled.

"I hope my mamm got her Mother's Day card yesterday."

"Are you planning to call her?"

"I did that last night. Had to leave a message, of course, because no one was in the phone shack. Since my folks don't usually check messages on Sundays, Mom probably won't hear what I had to say till Monday."

Michelle pulled herself to a sitting position. "At least you have a mother to send a card to and leave a phone message for. I, on the other hand, don't even know where my mom is. For all I know, she might not even be alive." Michelle placed both hands across her stomach, rubbing in a circular motion. "I am determined to be a better mother to our baby than my mother was to me, Jack, and Ernie."

"You will be. I'm certain of it." Ezekiel's reassuring tone comforted Michelle. She rarely thought about her abusive mother anymore, but with today being Mother's Day, it was hard not to think about the past and what she and her brothers had been through.

She closed her eyes and said a silent prayer. *Dear Lord, even though I have no idea where my mom and dad are living these days, You do. You know everything about them. If Mom and Dad are still alive, would You please send someone into their lives to light the way so they can know You personally, the way I do?*

When Michelle's prayer ended, she felt a

bit better. She could honestly say she no longer hated her parents. Now all she wanted was for them to find the same sense of peace she had found since she'd accepted Christ as her Savior.

Strasburg

"Thank you all for the lovely gifts and cards you gave me today." Mary Ruth sniffed as she made an effort to hold back tears. What a joy it was to have her family around her right now — Sara, Brad, Lenore, Ivan, Yvonne, Peter, and Ben — all gathered in her living room to wish her a happy Mother's Day.

"I'm a fortunate woman to have you all as my family." Mary Ruth nearly choked on the words as she expressed her gratitude. "I can't imagine what I would do without all of you."

"We love you, Grandma," Lenore spoke up. "And there isn't anything we wouldn't do for you."

All heads nodded in agreement.

"Danki. Danki so much."

Lenore cleared her throat a few times, and all heads turned in her direction. "I have an announcement to make."

"What is it, dear one?" Mary Ruth asked. She couldn't help noticing her granddaughter's rosy cheeks.

"Last night at Mark's birthday party, he asked if he could begin courting me."

"That's wunderbaar, Daughter." Lenore's mother reached across the couch where she sat and clasped Lenore's hand. "I hope Mark is the right man for you."

"I hope so too, but I'll have to wait and see how it goes after we've spent more time together and gotten better acquainted."

Mary Ruth cringed inside, but she tried to hide her feelings by putting a smile on her face. *If Mark begins courting Lenore, then how in the world am I ever going to get Lenore and Jesse back together?*

CHAPTER 42

The months of June and July were hot and muggy, but that didn't keep Lenore from helping Grandma in the garden or doing all the necessary chores around the place. Lenore's father or one of her brothers still came over regularly to take care of the larger tasks, but for the most part, Lenore managed to get things done on her own and still squeeze in some time to spend with Mark. It surprised her, though, that Mark never volunteered to help out at Grandma's place. Even though he worked five days a week in his uncle's shop, Lenore figured he would at least be willing to offer his help to do some things for Grandma.

For the most part, Lenore enjoyed Mark's company, but she couldn't see herself in a permanent relationship with him. She hoped he felt the same, because she didn't want to hurt his feelings by turning down a prospective marriage proposal.

Maybe Mark will never ask me to marry him. He might only see me as a friend, Lenore told herself as she got out the gardening tools in readiness for her cousin's arrival.

Sara had been closing the flower shop on Mondays lately so she could work Saturdays, which seemed to be one of the busiest days for her business. They'd reached the last Monday in July, and Sara should be arriving soon. Lenore looked forward to this time of working together and getting caught up with each other's lives. Between Sara's full-time business and her involvement in the church Brad pastored, they didn't get to see each other as often as Lenore would like.

Grandma had wanted to help out in the garden today, but she'd pulled a muscle in her back a few days ago, so pulling weeds was out of the question. That was okay; she deserved some time to rest.

"Guess there's no point in waiting for Sara to get here. I may as well get started on these weeds." Lenore spoke out loud. She went down on her knees next to a row of bush beans and stuck her hand shovel in the ground. Normally, she was able to keep up with the weeds, but this summer they'd gotten away from her, as she'd spent too much time doing other things. Today, however, Lenore was determined to get all of the weeding done.

Clymer

Michelle sat in a chair on the front porch, rubbing her stomach. It was so hot and humid this morning she could hardly breathe. The flower and vegetable gardens needed watering, and another batch of laundry waited to be washed. She couldn't muster up the strength, though. Even if she weren't pregnant, the exceptionally warm, muggy weather would have pulled her down. In Michelle's condition, it seemed almost unbearable.

Michelle continued to rub her stomach, as though in doing so, she might create some action. "Come on, sweet baby, when are you going to be ready to make your appearance into this world?"

Whimpering, Val, who'd been lying on the porch near her chair, got up and put her head in Michelle's lap.

She stroked the dog's head. "Are you sympathizing with me, girl, or do you just need some attention?"

With another whimper, Val nuzzled Michelle's hand.

"Oh, you're such a big boppli. I wonder how you'll act when my real baby is here."

Michelle hoped the dog wouldn't be too jealous or become aggressive. It would be a blessing if Val got along with the baby, and even acted as a protector should the child ever be put in a dangerous situation.

Michelle had heard about dogs rescuing people who were in peril, or even alerting a person when something like a fire got started in their home. She felt sure her dog was smart enough to alert them of any danger.

"Would you like to take a walk to the mailbox with me, girl?" Michelle rose from her chair. As she stepped off the porch, Val followed. Walking down the driveway, the dog stayed close to Michelle's side.

Michelle looked down at Val and smiled. "You're my protector, aren't you?"

Val wagged her tail.

When they reached the mailbox, the Irish setter stood beside Michelle, waiting patiently while she retrieved the mail. As they turned to walk back to the house, Michelle felt her stomach contract. She paused and waited for it to subside. It wasn't a strong contraction, but it could mean the beginning of labor. She certainly hoped so, because she was more than ready to become a mother. As far as she was concerned, it couldn't happen soon enough. Ezekiel was out in his shop, and if the contractions continued, she would let him know.

Strasburg

Mary Ruth repositioned a small pillow behind her back, trying to find a more comfortable position. She felt useless, sitting around unable to do all the normal things. Worse yet, the muscle relaxers the doctor had prescribed made her sleepy. So for the last few days she hadn't even gotten much knitting or mending done. Her diminished vigor frustrated her. Mary Ruth liked lots of action around her — people to talk with and plenty to do.

It's probably for the best that Jesse turned down my offer to watch Cindy again. Mary Ruth frowned. She had asked Jesse about the possibility several weeks ago when she'd seen him at the grocery store. That's when he informed Mary Ruth that he had recently hired a fifteen-year-old girl from outside their church district who'd been coming over to his house to watch Cindy when he was at work.

Mary Ruth felt disappointed and still hadn't come up with a way to get Lenore and Jesse together again. It didn't help that Mark monopolized so much of Lenore's time these days. Mary Ruth was convinced that he was not the right man for Lenore, but she didn't feel right about saying anything.

She released a heavy sigh. *Guess the best thing to do is give my concerns and desires for Lenore over to God and try not to meddle.*

Mary Ruth heard a car pull into the yard and assumed it must be Sara. She would rest a while longer, then go out to see how her granddaughters were doing in the garden. She chuckled. *And if they need any advice on weed pulling, I can give that too.*

"Sorry I'm late, Lenore. I see you started without me." Sara gestured to the row where Lenore worked, then slipped on a pair of gardening gloves and knelt beside a line of tomato plants.

"It's all right. I didn't want to sit here wasting time, so I decided to get busy pulling these stubborn weeds."

"There does seem to be a lot of them." Sara clicked her tongue against the roof of her mouth as she shook her head. "The abundance of harvest from the tiny seeds we plant is awesome, but weeding is the only part of growing a garden I don't like."

"How are the little pots of tomatoes you set out on your patio doing?" Lenore asked.

"Not bad, thanks to Brad. He keeps them

446

watered, and of course since they are in pots, there are very few weeds to worry about."

"Did you plant anything besides tomatoes?"

"Just a pot of chives. They grow well, and it's handy to go out back and cut some whenever we have baked potatoes or some other food that chives go well with."

"Yes, and unless you don't care about them spreading all over the garden, chives do best contained in pots. The same holds true for mint and most other herbs."

"You seem to know a lot about gardening."

"I suppose so — enough to know that these weeds are not giving way easily this morning." Lenore dug her shovel deep into the ground and lifted out a hunk of weeds. She repeated the process, only this time the shovel went deeper.

Sara tipped her head. "What was that? I heard a clink. You must have hit a rock or something."

Lenore's sweaty forehead wrinkled. "I don't know. It sounded like glass, not a rock." Lenore reached her hand into the hole she'd created.

Sara dropped her shovel and moved closer to her cousin. "Be careful. If it's broken glass, you might cut yourself."

"I don't think it's broken." Lenore moved her hand around inside the hole. "It feels like one of Grandma's canning jars."

"Why would a canning jar be buried in the garden?" Sara craned her neck forward.

"I'm not sure. Maybe for the same reason those secret canning jars were found in the basement and barn."

"You think it's another prayer jar?"

"We'll soon see." Lenore continued to dig and pull, until at last she held the glass jar in her hand.

"Look!" Sara pointed. "There are strips of paper inside."

"The glass lid is on pretty tight, but I think I can get it off." Lenore pried on the metal wire holding the lid in place; after a few seconds it loosened, and she removed the lid.

"Reach inside and let's see what one of the notes has to say. Maybe it's a few words of encouragement that will brighten our day." Sara scooted closer to Lenore.

Lenore brushed off her hands, then reached in and removed the paper nearest the top. She spread it out and read 2 Corinthians 12:9: " 'My grace is sufficient for thee: for my strength is made perfect in weakness.' "

Sara drew in a sharp breath. "This has to be another jar filled with notes from my mother. But why would Mama hide it in the ground?"

Lenore shrugged. "Should we see what some of the other notes say?"

"Yes. Let's dump them out on the grass, and then we'll each pick a note to read." This wasn't getting the weeding done, but Sara felt a strong need to see what her mother had written in secret.

Lenore held the jar upside down, allowing the scraps of paper to fall onto the grass. "Do you want to go first, or shall I?"

Sara hesitated a moment, then reached out her hand. "I'll choose one randomly." She chose one of the larger pieces of paper lying closest to her knees.

As she read the note silently to herself, Sara's mouth gaped open. "Th–that's impossible."

"What is? What does the note say?" Lenore's voice rose a notch, but Sara barely took notice.

Sara's stomached clenched, and her breathing felt restricted. She wasn't sure she could even speak. "Here, read this." She handed the slip of paper to Lenore.

"This is my final note before I leave home, carrying the shame of what I've done. For the past year I've been sneaking out at night or whenever my folks are away to meet Herschel Fisher from a neighboring community. I've never told anyone about him, because he's kind of wild, and Mom and Dad would not approve. I found out the other day that Herschel has been seeing someone else — a young woman named Mattie, and they are planning to get married. There is no point in me telling Herschel now and ruining his chance at happiness with Mattie. I love Herschel and would not want him to marry me out of obligation when he doesn't love me in return, so Herschel must never know I am carrying his baby."

Lenore reached over and clasped Sara's trembling hand. "Jesse's late wife had an uncle named Herschel Fisher. Could he be the same man your mother wrote about?"

Sara's skin tingled as her fingers touched her parted lips. "Oh my! Wouldn't it be something if he was? All those times Herschel came into the flower shop, and the thought that he could be my father never entered my mind."

"What are you going to do about this?" Lenore asked.

"I . . . I don't know." Sara's voice trembled as a flush of adrenaline zipped through her body. She'd waited so many years to learn the truth of who her father was, and now she didn't know what to do. If she approached Herschel and asked if he'd known her mother, would she have the nerve to tell him that she was his daughter, whom he'd never known anything about? Would he be happy to meet her? Or could this unexpected news be too much for him to accept?

CHAPTER 43

"Are you going to talk to Jesse and get Herschel's address so you can tell him what you found out?" Lenore asked Sara.

Sara sucked in her bottom lip. "I'm not sure what to do. What if Herschel isn't my father? Or what if he is, and he doesn't want anything to do with me? Herschel has already been through a lot, what with losing his wife and grieving for her for so many years. I don't want to put any more stress on him."

Lenore looked at the piece of paper Sara still held. "Jesse mentioned once that his wife's uncle has no children, so he might be happy to learn that he has a daughter."

Sara moaned. "Oh, why does this have to be so difficult?"

"Maybe you should talk to Grandma about it. She deserves to know we've found another prayer jar, and don't you think she should read what your mother wrote in that note?"

"You're right. Let's go talk to her now." Sara scooped all the notes back into the jar and picked it up. "Grandma might want to read the rest of these messages too."

When they entered the house, Grandma greeted them in the entryway. "I was about to come outside and see how much progress you two have made in the garden. Is everything going well out there?"

"We haven't pulled even half the weeds yet because we found this." Sara held up the glass jar.

Grandma squinted over the top of her glasses. "Is that another prayer jar?"

Lenore nodded. "I found it buried in the dirt when I was trying to dig up some really tough weeds."

"As you can see," Sara interjected, "there are slips of paper inside the jar, just like the ones we found in the basement and barn." She held out the slip of paper naming Herschel as her father and handed it to Grandma. "I'm curious to know what you think of this."

Grandma's lips moved slowly as she read the message to herself. "Oh Sara, I can't believe your mother wrote down the name of your father. And now we know why she

453

left without telling anyone who had fathered her child."

"Did you have any idea my mother was seeing a man named Herschel Fisher?" Sara's lips quivered.

Grandma shook her head. "I never heard that name until we met Jesse." Her mouth opened as she let out a gasp. "Could his wife's uncle be your father, Sara?"

"I'm not completely sure, but I believe so."

"Then he needs to see this confession your mother wrote."

"I'm not sure that's a good idea."

"Why not?"

Sara explained her reasons and ended by saying she wanted to go home and talk to Brad before making a decision about whether to confront Herschel or not.

"That's a good idea." Grandma gave Sara a hug. "Prayer is always the first thing we should do when faced with a problem or an unanswered question."

"I agree with Grandma," Lenore put in. "And we'll be praying that you make the right decision."

Lancaster

Sara paced the living-room floor, waiting for Brad to get home. He'd had a lunch meeting with some pastors from other churches in the area at noon. Following that, he was supposed to call on a few people from their congregation who were living in nursing homes. Sara could have called and asked him to come home right away, but she didn't feel right about taking him away from his pastoral duties for something that was not an emergency.

She looked out the front window. *Even though it's not critical, I sure wish my husband would hurry and get here. I need to talk with him about the note Lenore and I found in the buried prayer jar this morning, and I can't make a decision on my own.*

Sara's thoughts ran wild as she continued to pace and try to analyze things. She was filled with mixed emotions concerning her mother's confession. She understood Mama's decision to keep the identity of Sara's father a secret, but at the same time, Sara felt cheated and more confused than ever.

She stopped pacing and blotted the tears on her hot cheeks with a tissue. So many times in the past Sara had asked who her father was, but Mama always changed the subject or said it didn't matter. Well, it mattered to Sara. All the years of not knowing who her biological father was had left an empty place in Sara's heart.

At the sound of Brad's van coming up the drive, Sara hurried to the front door. When Brad entered the house a short time later, she threw herself into his arms. "Oh, I'm so glad you're home."

He leaned down and gave her a kiss. "Now this is the kind of greeting that melts a man's heart."

More tears sprang to Sara's eyes, and she nearly choked on the sob rising in her throat.

"Honey, what's wrong? Why are you crying?"

"I believe I know who my biological father is."

Brad's eyes opened wide. "You do?"

"Yes. He lives right here in Lancaster County." Sara could barely speak the words without shouting.

Brad guided her into the living room and onto the couch. "Who is it, and how did you find out?"

Bringing a trembling hand to her forehead, Sara explained about the note she and Lenore had discovered. "And now that I've learned the name of my father, I don't know what to do. Lenore said she could find out from Jesse where Herschel lives, but I can't just barge over to his house and tell him about Mama's note." She paused and drew in a shaky breath. "What if he truly is my father, and he doesn't want anything to do with me? After all, he chose some other woman to marry and dropped my mother flat."

Brad began to open his mouth, but Sara cut him off.

"I can't even imagine the horrible pain Mama must have felt when she found out she was carrying Herschel's child and then learned he was planning to marry someone else. It's no wonder she ran away without telling anyone where she was going. Mama obviously did not want anyone — especially Herschel — to know her whereabouts."

Brad shook his head. "She could have told her parents. From the time I first met the Lapps, I realized what good people they were. I think they would have understood and tried to help their daughter through her difficult time."

Sara sniffed and swiped at a few more tears that had fallen. "I believe you're right, but poor Mama probably didn't realize it back then. She was running on emotion and not thinking things through. No doubt she thought they would be embarrassed by their daughter's mistake. And also," Sara continued, "Grandma and Grandpa most likely would have insisted that Mama tell them who the father of her baby was."

"You may be right."

"Don't you see, Brad, if my mother had revealed the father's name, Grandpa would have gone to Herschel and tried to convince him to do the right thing and marry his daughter, regardless of whether Herschel cared anything about her or not."

Brad slowly nodded. "That may also be true, but we can't change the past, honey. The question now is, do you want to speak with Herschel and let him know who you are — find out for sure if he is your father?"

Sara rolled her neck from side to side. "I'm not sure. What do you think I should do?"

Brad took hold of her hand. "The first thing we should do is pray and ask God to help you make the right decision and give you a sense of peace about whatever you decide."

"Okay."

As Brad prayed out loud on Sara's behalf, a little voice in her head seemed to be saying she should wait to speak to Herschel, at least for now, and that if it was meant for her to do so, she would know when the time was right.

■ ■ ■ ■

Clymer

Michelle's contractions were stronger and more regular. It was time to alert Ezekiel. Despite the oppressing heat, she felt a chill as she headed out to his shop. *What if giving birth is too painful and I never want to have another child? What if our baby is born with a birth defect? Would I have the strength to deal with it?* Negative thoughts continued to swirl through Michelle's head, each one making her more apprehensive. By the time she reached Ezekiel's shop, Michelle was so worked up she felt light-headed.

"What's wrong?" Ezekiel asked as she approached his workbench. "Your face is so pale."

"I'm in labor," she panted. "The pains are becoming more intense and closer together. I can't believe how quickly they came on. This morning I had a few, and they weren't regular or very painful."

Eyes wide, Ezekiel jumped up from his chair. "You'd better sit down right here and rest while I run out to the phone shack and call one of our drivers to bring the midwife and stand by in case there are any problems during the delivery and we end up having to make a trip to the hospital." Ezekiel talked so fast, Michelle could hardly keep up with him. "I may have a lot of knowledge about bees, but I have no idea how to deliver a boppli!" He turned and raced out the door.

As Michelle sat in her husband's chair, trying to calm herself, she whispered a heartfelt prayer. "Heavenly Father, please help me not to be afraid, and" — she placed both hands on her stomach — "and may this child of ours be born without complications."

CHAPTER 44

Strasburg

When Mary Ruth woke up the next morning, she was pleased to discover that her back hurt less than it had the previous day. But she hadn't slept well the night before. While lying in bed awake, all she could think about was the note inside the prayer jar that her granddaughters had discovered beneath the garden soil. How many times had she dug around in that plot and never found the old jar?

Mary Ruth stood in front of her bedroom window, staring out into the yard but barely taking notice of anything. *If Willis were here right now, I wonder what he would say about all of this.*

She reached around and rubbed the small of her back. If she wasn't careful, the stress of her conflicting emotions over Rhoda's note might cause her back to spasm again. The idea that the uncle of Jesse Smucker's

461

late wife could actually be Sara's father was hard to accept.

Mary Ruth tapped her bare foot. *I hope Sara decides to speak to Herschel Fisher about this, because we all need to know the truth. I have half a notion to seek him out myself and ask about his relationship with Rhoda.* She shook her head. *But that wouldn't be right. I can't go sticking my nose into this. It has to be Sara's decision.*

Mary Ruth crossed her arms over her chest and hugged herself. *If he did father my daughter's child, then we need to know why he became intimate with Rhoda and then moved on to someone else, as though his relationship with Rhoda meant nothing at all.*

She moved away from the window, took her clothes out of the closet, and placed them on the bed. Picking up her hairbrush, Mary Ruth gripped the handle tightly. *Oh Rhoda, why couldn't you have remained true to our biblical teachings and kept yourself pure?*

"Would you like me to go out and check the mail and then listen to any messages that might be on our answering machine in the phone shack?" Lenore asked after she'd finished drying the breakfast dishes

Grandma had washed.

Grandma nodded and pointed at the grocery list she had started before breakfast. "Danki for offering. I need to finish this so we can go to the store sometime today."

"I can do the shopping by myself," Lenore offered. "There's no reason for you to go out — unless you want to, that is."

"Maybe it would be best if I stayed home and rested. My back's doing some better, but the bumpy ride to the store might be pushing my luck." Grandma smiled. "Not that I believe in luck, mind you. It was just a figure of speech."

"I understand." Lenore grabbed a plastic bag to put the mail in and headed out the back door. She was glad Grandma felt a little better today, but hoped she wouldn't push herself and end up hurting her back again.

Outside, Lenore stopped to pet Sadie and then threw a stick to divert the dog's attention before walking down the driveway without interruption.

After checking the mailbox and finding it empty, Lenore headed for the phone shack. The light blinked on the answering machine, so they had at least one message.

She took a seat and clicked the button. The first message was from their driver,

Stan, saying he'd found an unopened bag of cough drops in the back seat of his van and wondered if Grandma might have left it there when he'd taken her to see the doctor last week. Lenore didn't think the cough drops were Grandma's, but she would check with her first before calling Stan back.

The second message was from Mark, letting Lenore know that he'd hired a driver and made plans for them to go up to Hersheypark next Saturday. He also mentioned that he wanted to go on as many rides as possible, and said it was bound to be a fun adventure.

Hitting the Stop button on the answering machine, Lenore sucked in her bottom lip and frowned. *He didn't even have the courtesy to ask if I wanted to go there.*

This kind of thing had been happening a lot lately, with Mark making plans for them to do certain things without getting Lenore's input. She'd gone along with it, even though it was upsetting, but this was the last straw. No way did Lenore want to go on any crazy rides at Hersheypark. When she was a teenager Lenore had gone up there with a group of her friends. After getting off most of the wild rides, she'd gotten sick to her stomach, not to mention so dizzy she could hardly stand up. So this kind of adventure was not her idea of having fun.

Lenore leaned on the counter where the phone and answering machine sat. *I need to find the courage to break things off with Mark. He's not the right man for me, and I'm not right for him either.* She was tempted to pick up the phone and call Mark to let him know that she wouldn't be going to Hersheypark or seeing him socially anymore. But that would be a coward's way out, and it might hurt him too, which she did not want to do. So she would wait to tell Mark how she felt about their relationship until she saw him face-to-face and could try to break it to him in a kind and gentle way.

But it had better be soon, she told herself. *I need to let him know before next Saturday so he doesn't come by with his driver expecting me to go up to Hershey with him.*

Turning back to the answering machine, Lenore punched the message button again. The last communication was from Ezekiel. Lenore got so excited when she heard what he said, she let out a whoop. Michelle had delivered a six-pound, two-ounce baby girl last night, shortly before ten o'clock. The baby appeared to be healthy, and Michelle was doing quite well. They'd decided to call their daughter Angela Mary.

"Angela," Lenore repeated. "What a sweet

name. And I bet they chose Mary for their daughter's middle name in honor of Grandma."

Lenore figured by now Ezekiel's parents had also heard the news and no doubt were happy about having another grandchild to love and fuss over. They'd probably head up to New York to see the baby girl as soon as possible. Most likely Michelle's brothers had also been notified and would probably show up at Michelle and Ezekiel's place soon to see their new niece. Lenore wished she and Grandma could make a trip to New York, but right now would not be a good time for them or for Michelle and Ezekiel, since they would no doubt have other company there soon. Hopefully Ezekiel and Michelle would make a trip to Lancaster County when the baby was able to travel, and she and Grandma could see the baby then.

Since there were no other messages, Lenore left the phone shack and raced back to the house, eager to share Ezekiel's message with Grandma. After the shock of finding the third prayer jar yesterday, they needed some news that didn't involve hidden secrets.

Sara had been working in the flower shop

about an hour when a headache developed. She'd had very little sleep last night, thinking about her current situation and trying to discern what God wanted her to do. Part of Sara wanted to seek Herschel out and announce that she believed she was his daughter, but the other part said it might be best to leave well enough alone and be satisfied with simply knowing the name of her father.

She picked up the invoice book and tried to focus on the latest orders, but her mind kept replaying the what-ifs.

Remembering the times Herschel had come into her shop to buy flowers, Sara had thought he was such a nice man for wanting to give his wife special bouquets. Then she'd learned from Herschel's mother, Vera, that her son's wife had died, and the flowers he'd purchased were to put on her grave. Placing flowers on graves in an Amish cemetery went against the Amish way. Apparently Herschel's love for his wife went so deep he didn't care if his actions were acceptable or whether he might be in trouble with his church ministers for doing something controversial. When Sara had heard about this from Vera, she'd felt sorry for Herschel.

Sara's mouth twisted as the bitter taste of

bile rose in her throat. *Why couldn't he have loved Mama as much as he loved his wife? How could Herschel have taken advantage of an innocent young woman and then dropped her for someone else? Poor Mama — her heart must have been broken when she heard he planned to marry another woman.*

The more Sara thought about it, the angrier she became. For this reason alone, she figured it would be best if she didn't reveal her identity to Mr. Fisher. *If he could treat Mama in such a hurtful way, he most likely wouldn't want anything to do with me, and I'm not sure I want any kind of a relationship with him either.*

The bell above the door jingled, pushing Sara's thoughts aside. She looked up from her work to see who'd come in and was shocked to see Herschel standing a few feet from the front door.

Sara's mouth went dry, and her heart pounded so hard she felt it might burst. Why was Herschel here at this very moment? Had he come to buy flowers for someone, or had Herschel somehow found out about the note in her mother's prayer jar? Could Grandma or Lenore have told him?

CHAPTER 45

Sara sucked in her breath, trying to steady her nerves. *Could Herschel's showing up at the flower shop today be a sign that I should tell him about Mama's note?* She stood frozen to the spot, unable to form any words.

Herschel moved closer to the counter. "It's been a while since I've visited your shop, and since I had some errands in Strasburg today, I thought I'd drop by to see what summer flowers you have available."

Sara swallowed hard, hoping she could speak. "Umm . . . what kind of flowers are you looking for?"

"Nothing in particular. I'll know when something catches my eye." He tilted his head, looking at her with a curious expression. "I've never mentioned it before, but you remind me of someone."

"Oh?"

"A young woman I used to know. Her hair

469

wasn't blond like yours. It was red, and she had the prettiest hazel eyes." Herschel stared off into space, as though he'd been transported to another world. Then looking quickly back at Sara, he said, "It's your facial features that remind me of Rhoda."

"Rhoda?" Sara touched her swollen throat. "Did you say Rhoda?"

Herschel moved his had slowly up and down. "Her name was Rhoda Lapp, and I had hoped she would be my wife someday."

"Oh, really? Then why did you marry someone else? Mattie — wasn't that her name?"

"For a long time Mattie and I were just friends. We'd known each other since we were babies." Herschel got that faraway look in his eyes again, and to Sara's surprise, he even teared up. "But I never had any interest in her as a potential wife until Rhoda broke up with me and ran away."

Since there were no other customers in the store at the moment, and Misty wasn't here to tend the store, Sara walked to the front of the building and put the Closed sign in the window. "We need to talk, Herschel."

He reached under his straw hat and scratched his head. "I thought that's what we were doing."

"Mostly you were talking, and I was listening, but now I have something important to say. Please, go over to my desk and take a seat." Sara pointed in that direction.

Herschel did as she asked, and once he had taken a chair, she grabbed the stool that sat behind the counter and seated herself on it.

Herschel leaned forward slightly with one hand on his knee. "What did you want to talk about?"

"Rhoda Lapp was my mother."

"She . . . she was?"

"Yes, but she passed away a few years ago."

"I'm so sorry for your loss." Herschel put his hands on Sara's desk and folded them, looking at her with a grave expression. "If you're Rhoda's daughter, then it's no wonder that you remind me of her."

Sara now knew without a shadow of a doubt that Herschel Fisher was her father. It was time to tell him the truth, no matter how he reacted.

She cleared her throat and swallowed. "There is something you need to know, and I may as well start at the beginning."

Herschel sat quietly, his gaze focused on her.

"Shortly before my mother died, she said there was a note she'd written for me inside her old Bible." Sara paused a few seconds to collect her thoughts and make sure she didn't leave anything important out.

"But it wasn't until after Mama passed away that I found the note." Her eyes began to water, and she sniffed a couple of times. "Mama's note said her maiden name was Lapp, and that when she was eighteen, she left home and changed her last name. She also stated that her parents lived in Strasburg, and she included their address."

Sara shifted on the stool and continued. "Mama said she hoped I would get the chance to meet them and asked me to let her parents know that she loved them and was sorry for the things she said and did to hurt them." Sara paused to steady her nerves. "My mother's note said that she was too ashamed to let her parents know about me, and that she was concerned about what they would think of her being unmarried and pregnant. So several months later I came here to Strasburg to meet my grandparents for the first time. I was surprised to discover that they were Amish. Mama had never told me of her Pennsylvania Dutch heritage."

Herschel continued to listen as Sara went on to tell him how, during the time she'd visited her grandparents, she had discovered two old jars filled with slips of paper. "At first I had no idea who had written the Bible verses, prayers, and notes that the jars contained. Then, after my cousin Lenore found one of the jars, she showed it to our grandmother and —"

"Lenore Lapp?"

"Yes."

"Is she the same Lenore who was courted by my niece's husband, Jesse, for a while?"

Sara nodded. "But that's beside the point. The issue is that until Grandma saw the notes and recognized the handwriting, we had no idea who had written the messages and put them inside the jars."

Herschel pulled his fingers through the ends of his thick beard. "Was it Rhoda?"

"Yes, my mother obviously wrote all the notes." Sara stopped talking again and rubbed the bridge of her nose. The headache that had begun earlier had increased. Talking about this was stressful, but the fear of Herschel's reaction to what Sara was on the verge of revealing was nearly her undoing.

"I suspect there is more you wish to tell me." Herschel tipped his head.

All Sara could do was nod. The words she wanted to say seemed lodged in her throat.

"Go ahead. I'm listening."

Sara sucked in a deep breath and forced

herself to continue. "Yesterday, when Lenore and I were pulling weeds in Grandma's garden, we found a third jar buried in the dirt."

"More notes from Rhoda?"

"Uh-huh." Sara reached for her purse, sitting on one corner of the desk. She unzipped it, slipped her hand inside, and pulled out the all-important note. "I think you should read this."

Herschel put on his reading glasses and squinted as he read Mama's message. When he finished reading and looked at Sara again, his head jerked back as he slapped both hands against his cheeks. "I'm your father?"

"According to Mama's note, the answer is yes, and I see no reason why she would lie about it."

"But . . . but — I don't see how. I mean . . . if Rhoda was carrying my baby, then why didn't she tell me about it?"

"Because she found out from someone that you didn't care about her and had made plans to marry another woman." Sara's hand trembled as she pointed to the note. "Did you not read that part?" At this point she felt like shaking Herschel. Was he going to deny what he'd done to her mother?

Herschel's mouth twisted grimly. "I had no idea. If I'd known . . ."

"What? If you'd known about the baby, you would have broken up with the other girl and married my mother? Is that what you're trying to tell me?" Sara was one step away from shouting at the top of her lungs. She wasn't setting a Christian example, but she couldn't get control of her emotions.

He shook his head vigorously. "I wasn't going with Mattie at the time. I loved Rhoda and only had eyes for her."

"Then why did she think otherwise? What made Mama decide to keep the truth of my existence from you and her parents?"

"You already answered that question. Someone, and I believe I know who, lied to your mother about my feelings for her."

Sara jumped when Herschel pounded his fist on the desk. "It was Emanuel's fault! He told me Rhoda was seeing someone else and that she wanted nothing more to do with me." His face flamed. "And later, after Rhoda went missing and didn't return, Emanuel confessed that he had wanted Rhoda himself so he'd told her I was planning to break up with her because I was in love with Mattie."

Sara rubbed her forehead, trying to take in everything Herschel had said. "If all of that is true, then it's no wonder Mama left. She felt hopeless, thinking you didn't love her and believing her parents would turn their backs on her if they knew she was carrying an illegitimate child."

Tears slipped from Herschel's eyes and coursed down his cheeks. "I honestly did not know your mother was with child, but one thing I do know — and did back then — is that I loved Rhoda and planned to ask her to be my wife after we finished our crazy rumspringa and joined the Amish church."

Sara felt some measure of comfort knowing Herschel had loved her mother and planned to marry her. But she still did not know how he felt about her being his daughter. Was he embarrassed by this? Did he want to keep it a secret so as not to bring shame on him or his family?

Herschel got up and came over to where she sat on the stool. He placed his hands on her flushed cheeks and said, "Mattie and I were not able to have any children, and I always wished for a son or daughter. Now my deepest desire and prayer has come true. Although I can hardly believe it, this is truly a miracle from God."

"I think so too." She leaned in and gave him a hug. "I've waited and prayed for many years that I would find my biological father.

And now an empty place in my heart has been filled."

Herschel rubbed Sara's back between her shoulders. "It just goes to show that even when people make terrible mistakes, God can take a negative situation and turn it into something good."

"You are so right about that." Her eyes misted. "I'm sorry for shouting earlier. I let my temper and emotions take over because I was upset, but it's no excuse."

"It's okay. I understand." Herschel pulled away slightly, looking lovingly at Sara. "I can hardly wait to introduce you to my mom and dad. They will be surprised to learn that they have a granddaughter they knew nothing about, who lives right here in Lancaster County."

Sara's whole body tingled with anticipation. She hoped Herschel's parents would accept her as easily as he had.

Lenore shook her horse's reins. Dolly was being a slowpoke today, and she needed to get to the store soon so she could go home and help Grandma do some baking.

Lenore thought about the news they'd received from Ezekiel this morning. How exciting to know Michelle and Ezekiel were now the happy parents of a baby girl.

With the way things were going, it was doubtful she would ever have the joy of being a wife or mother. Lenore didn't want to sink into self-pity, especially when she truly was happy for Michelle and Ezekiel. But the hole in her heart left from Jesse's rejection made Lenore wonder if that wound would ever be healed.

The words of Psalm 147:3 came to mind: "He healeth the broken in heart, and bindeth up their wounds."

Dear Lord, please heal my broken heart and bind up my wounds. Help me to focus on other things, like helping Grandma and being a good schoolteacher. If it's not meant for me to get married, then take away my desire for a husband and family.

When Lenore reached the grocery store, she secured her horse to the hitching rail, grabbed her purse, and went inside. She'd only been shopping a few minutes when she spotted Mark. She wasn't ready to talk to him yet and hoped he hadn't seen her, but it was too late — Mark was heading her way.

"Did you get my phone message?" he asked, pushing his grocery cart next to hers.

"Yes, I did, but I was waiting to talk to you in person."

His forehead wrinkled. "How come?

Couldn't you have called and left me a message?"

Lenore shook her head. "I'm sorry, Mark, but I don't want to go up to Hersheypark."

"Why not? It'll be fun. You'll see when we get there."

"Maybe for you, but not for me. I wouldn't enjoy going on all those rides."

"Well, okay then. I guess we could do something else."

Lenore looked around to be sure no one was close and could hear their conversation. "The thing is, Mark, I don't think we should see each other socially anymore."

"What?" His eyebrows rose. "Why would you say that? We've been courting a few months now, and I thought we were getting along pretty well."

Lenore made sure to keep her voice low. This was not the place she would have chosen to have this conversation. "We don't have much in common, Mark, and —"

"Sure we do. We've done several fun things together, right?"

"True, but they were things you wanted to do, and I went along with them, thinking I might enjoy them myself."

"And you didn't?"

"Not really."

"I see." Mark folded his arms and scowled

479

at her. "You're just like my ex-girlfriend, Debra. Nothing I did was ever good enough for her. She accused me of being too pushy and always wanting things my way. That's why, when she broke up with me, I decided to move back here and start over. I thought you and I were getting close and that my future was going to be with you."

Lenore reached her hand toward him, then pulled it away. "I'm sorry, but I think we should go our separate ways. I should have said something sooner, but I kept hoping things might be different and that —"

His eyes flashed angrily. "Fine then, I'll look for someone else who will appreciate me for the fun-loving guy I truly am." Before Lenore could say anything more, Mark grabbed the handle of his cart and practically ran down the aisle toward the checkout counter.

She stood watching him go, wondering if she'd made a mistake. It wasn't in Lenore's nature to say unkind things or intentionally hurt someone, but that was exactly what she had done. *It's my fault for allowing Mark to court me. I should have said no in the first place. Now he'll probably never speak to me again, and who knows what he will say to others about me?*

Chapter 46

Clymer

"She's a beautiful boppli, and we're glad you are both doing well." Belinda smiled at Michelle as she caressed the baby's cheek. "My only regret is that you don't live closer so we can spend more time together and watch little Angela grow."

"Don't worry, Mom," Ezekiel spoke up. "We'll come down to Strasburg as often as we can. That way, everyone else will have a chance to see the baby too."

"And you're welcome to come here whenever you like," Michelle interjected.

Ezekiel's parents had arrived three days ago, but his dad would be heading back home tomorrow morning, leaving Belinda to stay for another two weeks to help out. Michelle was grateful for her mother-in-law's assistance. Still weak from having given birth, Michelle needed to rest more than she usually would. Also, being a new mother, she was unsure of herself, and it was a comfort to have Belinda there to answer questions and respond to any of Michelle's concerns about newborn babies. The only downside was that having her inlaws there caused Michelle to feel a bit of homesickness. Although she no longer dwelled on it, Michelle realized that her desire to move back to Lancaster County had never completely vanished. But she'd learned to accept that Clymer was their home now, and she would not ask Ezekiel to relocate again.

Michelle had heard from Ernie and Jack yesterday, both saying they would try to get by to see the baby sometime next week. She looked forward to seeing them again and of course showing her brothers their niece, Angela Mary.

She leaned against the sofa pillows and looked at her husband as she caressed her infant daughter's silky hair. "Hopefully we'll make it down to Strasburg before the summer is over. I'd like the rest of your family, as well as Mary Ruth, Lenore, and Sara, to see the boppli."

Ezekiel smiled. "We'll go as soon as you're strong enough."

She reached for his hand. "I can hardly wait."

■ ■ ■

Gordonville

Jesse sat with his mouth gaping open. He could hardly believe all that Herschel had just told him. He'd stopped by after work to get a few things from Herschel's store but had never expected to be told surprising news like this. "Lenore's cousin Sara is your daughter?" Jesse asked when he'd found his voice.

"Jah, it's true. Sara and her husband are going over to my folks' place with me this evening so Mom and Dad can meet the granddaughter they never knew anything about."

"Since this all came to light with Sara a few days ago, have you already told your parents how you discovered she is your daughter?" Jesse asked.

"Of course. I wanted to explain things and prepare them for meeting her."

Herschel gave Jesse the biggest smile he'd ever seen on the man's normally placid face. It was clear how happy his wife's uncle was to learn that he had a daughter. It was wonderful to see things working out well for Herschel. He'd been unhappy for as long as Jesse had known him. Jesse had always as-

483

sumed Herschel's grief was because of his wife's death, but apparently it went even deeper than that.

I guess it's possible for a man to love more than one woman during the course of his life. Jesse twirled his straw hat in his hands. *Could it be possible for me if I give myself a chance?* The trouble was, Jesse still wasn't sure how he felt about Lenore. Some days when he thought about her, his heart beat a little faster. Other times when Jesse compared his feelings for Lenore to the way he'd felt for his wife, he convinced himself that he could never love anyone as much as he had loved Esther. So unless and until it became clear to him, he would continue on with the way things were. *Besides, what good would it do me even if I did get in touch with my feelings and declare them to Lenore? She's already moved on with her life.*

Jesse had prayed last night, asking God to teach him how to trust his own heart, mind, and intuition. Now he simply needed to listen to the Lord's still, small voice guiding him in the days ahead.

Strasburg

"It's hard to believe school will be starting again in a few weeks." Lenore leaned her head against the back of the porch swing and drew in a few deep breaths. Today had been muggy, and it was good to sit outside next to her grandmother and breathe in some air that finally felt fresh.

"Are you sorry you agreed to teach again this year?" Grandma asked.

"Not really. What else would I do with my time? I've never worked at any job away from home other than teaching."

"Is there something else you might enjoy doing more?"

Lenore shrugged. "I'm not sure." She wouldn't say it out loud, but the only thing besides teaching that appealed to her was being a full-time wife and mother.

She clutched the folds in her dress, then let go and smoothed out the wrinkles she'd created. *I can't allow myself to dwell on that.*

"I hope things go well with Sara this evening as she meets her other grandparents," Grandma said. "The Fishers should feel as blessed to have Sara be a part of their life as you and I do."

Lenore agreed. Growing up, she'd had no idea if her aunt Rhoda, whom she'd never met, had any children, but she'd wondered sometimes if she would ever get the chance to meet her aunt and any family she might have. Even though Lenore had never met Grandma and Grandpa Lapp's daughter,

485

she felt fortunate to have met their grand-daughter, Sara, as well as Sara's half brother, Kenny. They had become such an important part of her family.

Gordonville

As Sara sat in the front passenger seat of her husband's van, she picked at her clear nail polish. It was a nervous habit whenever she felt full of apprehension.

Sara's newly discovered father sat quietly in the back seat. Did he feel as nervous as Sara about her meeting his parents?

While Sara had always wanted to find out who her biological father was, she had never imagined meeting him or his parents. Since the Fishers didn't live far from Grandma Lapp, Sara would be able to visit them regularly.

If they want me to, that is. Sara flipped the visor down and checked her appearance in the mirror. *Even though they agreed to see me, maybe Herschel's parents won't accept me as their granddaughter. They may only want to ask me a bunch of questions about what my mother wrote concerning her relationship with their son.*

At the moment, Sara understood exactly how Mama must have felt when she'd convinced herself that her family and others in their community would sit in judgment on her. *Maybe because I'm Rhoda and Herschel's illegitimate daughter, they will turn their backs on me. For that matter, they might be equally upset with their son for taking advantage of a young woman during her time of rumspringa.*

Sara's thoughts ran wild until she realized she was probably blowing things out of proportion. For all she knew, the Fishers might welcome her into their home with open arms.

As though sensing her apprehension, Brad reached over and clasped Sara's hand. "We're almost there, hon, and everything's going to be okay. Now please take a deep breath and try to relax."

That's easy enough for you to say, Sara thought. *It's not you who's about to step into the unknown.* Well, in a way he was, because Brad had never met Herschel's parents, and he couldn't predict whether they would accept Sara or not. But Sara appreciated her husband's positive tone and encouragement.

"No need to be nervous," Herschel interjected. "My folks are looking forward to meeting you."

When Brad turned in where Herschel instructed, Sara's anxiety increased. Her hands were so sweaty she could hardly open the van door. *Relax. Relax. Breathe deep like Brad said.*

After they exited the vehicle, Herschel walked beside Sara, and Brad followed. Stepping onto the front porch, Sara said a prayer. *Heavenly Father, please calm my nerves and my father's as well.*

Herschel opened the door and hollered: "Mom! Dad! We're here!"

His parents joined them in the entryway. "Sara, these are my folks — Milton and Vera." Herschel gestured to Sara. "Mom . . . Dad . . . this is my daughter, Sara, and her husband, Brad. He's a minister at a church in Lancaster."

All Sara's fears and doubts vanished like vapor when her paternal grandparents enveloped her with hugs. Following that, they shook Brad's hand.

"Welcome, Sara. Milton and I are so happy our son has found you — or maybe it was the other way around." Vera's eyes filled with tears. "When I came into your flower shop some time ago, if I'd had any idea you were our granddaughter, I would have welcomed you then."

"Thank you. Thank you so much." Sara turned to face Herschel. "God has truly given us a miracle, jah?"

488

His eyes glistened as he chuckled and gave a hearty nod. "And now we can spend the rest of our days getting better acquainted." He looked over at Brad. "We welcome you into our family as well."

Sara felt like singing, dancing, and shouting. *I'm so blessed! If only Mama could be here to share in my joy.*

CHAPTER 47

Strasburg

Cooler days had finally arrived in Lancaster County, and Lenore had begun the routine of teaching school three weeks ago. This year she had two difficult students — Andy, a second grader, and his brother, Dennis, who was in fourth grade. The boys were new to the area, and Lenore had to make sure they understood the rules and realized they were not allowed to talk out of turn. It had been a few years since any students had challenged her the way these two did, but she'd let them know early on what their boundaries were. Lenore did her best to keep an eye on Andy and Dennis when they went outside for recess too, because often one or both of them would get into a mischievous mode and find some vulnerable girl to tease.

Lenore had a different assistant this year, named Caroline. Unfortunately, she was not as good about making the children behave as last year's helper was. The important thing, from Lenore's point of view, was to mold positive attitudes and cooperation in each of her pupils that would be helpful to them throughout their lives.

As Lenore sat at her teacher's desk looking over some test papers, she checked the time. It was two o'clock — time for the final recess of the day. She rang the bell on her desk and dismissed the scholars to go outside. Caroline went with them while Lenore took care of a few things inside.

Lenore smiled as the sound of excited chatter and laughter floated into the building through the open windows. She remembered her own school days, and how she and her friend Nancy had enjoyed looking for unusual things around the school, while most of the other children played baseball, jumped rope, or took turns pushing each other on the swings.

Lenore reflected on the time she'd found a heart-shaped rock near the teeter-totters. Someone teasingly said if a person found a heart-shaped rock, it meant they were going to fall in love and marry the first person they showed the rock to. Since, at the tender age of nine, Lenore had no interest in boys and didn't want to be teased, she'd hidden the rock under the schoolhouse porch. Later, after school let out and everyone else had gone home, Lenore returned for the unusual stone. She took it home and put it in a box inside her closet with all the other collectibles she'd found.

"Maybe I should have gotten out the old rock and showed it to Jesse." She lifted her gaze toward the ceiling. *Now, what a silly notion. I seriously doubt showing the heart-shaped rock to Jesse would have made him fall in love with me.*

Last week Lenore had seen Mark at the bank, but he'd barely mumbled a greeting. She'd heard through the grapevine that he'd begun seeing someone else, so she didn't understand why he couldn't have been a bit friendlier. Mark was definitely not the right man for her.

Lydia Ann, a fifth grader, rushed into the room, capturing Lenore's attention. "Recess isn't over yet, Lydia. You still have five more minutes." Lenore pointed to the battery-operated clock on the far wall.

"I'm not supposed to be a tattletale, but there's something going on that you might wanna know about."

"What is it?"

"Those new boys, Dennis and Andy, left the schoolyard a while ago. They're playin'

492

in that empty field on the other side of the fence." Lydia came closer and placed her hands on Lenore's desk. "I told 'em to get outta there, but they wouldn't listen. Dennis even stuck his tongue out at me."

"Thank you for telling me. I'll take care of this right now." Lenore rose from her chair and headed out the door. When she stepped outside, she saw the two boys in question laughing and running back and forth along the fence line, while some other children urged them to get back in the schoolyard before the teacher saw them. Caroline was busy pushing one of the first-grade girls on the swings, so Lenore headed out of the schoolyard to deal with the situation.

Walking quickly, Lenore went down the road a ways until she came to a place where the fence had been broken. Stepping through the opening, she hollered at the boys. "You are not supposed to be here. Recess is over, and you need to return to the schoolyard now."

Dennis and Andy ignored her and kept running.

Lenore's muscles tensed. *If these two don't come now, their parents are going to hear about this.* She called to them again, but when they continued to run in the opposite direction, Lenore took off after the disobedient brothers. She was a fast runner — had been since she was a child — so it didn't take her long to gain on them.

Lenore had instructed her class several times not to leave the premises of the schoolyard, not even for a wayward ball, and no one until now had challenged her on this rule.

She was gaining on them, but as Lenore drew close to the youngest boy, she stepped on a decaying board and fell into a hole.

Darkness shrouded Lenore as she lay at the bottom of what she believed to be a dry well. She felt gravel underneath her, and from what she could tell, the walls were made of corrugated steel.

Lenore tried to stand up, but a searing pain in her right leg, in addition to a pulsating throb at the back of her head, kept her from moving. Cupping her trembling hands around her mouth, she shouted, "Help! Help! Somebody help me, please!"

A swirling sensation overtook Lenore, and then her world faded into darkness.

Jesse had gotten off work early for another dental appointment — this time just a cleaning — and was on his way home. He was approaching the schoolhouse where

Lenore taught when he noticed a group of children gathered around an area on the other side of the fence separating the schoolyard and an empty field. Some of the children pointed downward, and a few of the younger ones appeared to be crying.

Concerned, Jesse pulled his horse and buggy into the schoolyard, jumped down, and secured Restless to the hitching rail. It didn't take much for him to leap over the wire fence. When he approached the children and saw their worried expressions, Jesse knew something horrible must have happened.

"What's going on? Why are you all over here?"

"It's my fault." A young boy with a thick head of dark brown hair pointed at a gaping hole. "Our teacher was chasin' after me and my *bruder,* and she fell in a hole."

Jesse's muscles jumped beneath his skin as he moved closer and tried to look down the well. "Lenore! Can you hear me?"

All was quiet.

"I heard her hollering before you got here," a blond-haired girl said tearfully. Her chin quivered as she looked up at Jesse. "Sure hope she's not dead."

"I have a cell phone. I'll call for help." Trying to ignore the young girl's negative comment, Jesse pulled the phone he used for work only out of his pocket and dialed 911. As he knelt in front of the hole, praying and waiting for help to arrive, his heart hammered in his chest. Jesse had lost one woman he loved; he couldn't lose another.

CHAPTER 48

Lancaster

Mary Ruth's skin tingled as she sat in the hospital waiting room with Jesse on one side of her and Lenore's parents on the other side. It was hard not to think about the last time she and her family were here. She looked up toward the ceiling as though seeking some answers. There'd been too many tragedies and accidents this past year — Willis, Sara's brother, and now Lenore. It was difficult not to question God.

Mary Ruth closed her eyes briefly, rubbing her eyelids as she reflected on the events of the afternoon. As soon as Lenore had been transported to the hospital by ambulance, Jesse had come by Mary Ruth's place, since she lived the closest. Then they'd called one of her drivers and asked him to drive them over to Paradise to tell Ivan and Yvonne what had happened. After that, they had all ridden in Stan's vehicle to

497

the hospital.

Soon after they got there, Mary Ruth called Sara at the flower shop. Sara said she would let Brad know about the accident and they would be there as soon as possible.

"I can't stand the waiting." Yvonne got up and began to pace. "I need to know how our daughter is doing."

Ivan patted the seat beside him. "We know her leg is broken and that she has multiple lacerations and a head injury. All we can do now is pray that she wakes up soon and doesn't have a serious concussion."

"I don't see why we have to wait here when we should be in Lenore's hospital room, but if it makes you feel any better, I'll sit down." Yvonne lifted her hands as if in defeat and sank into the chair with a huff.

Mary Ruth glanced at Jesse. He sat with his hands clasped together, staring at the floor. She wished she knew what thoughts were going through his head right now. He was obviously concerned about Lenore, although he hadn't vocalized it. When he'd stopped at the house to tell Mary Ruth what happened to Lenore and explained how the fire department came and rescued her, Jesse's voice had been thick with emotion.

Mary Ruth had seen Jesse make a call on his cell phone and heard him leave a message for the girl who watched Cindy, explaining what had happened and asking her to stay with his daughter a little longer than usual today. Mary Ruth took it to mean he was in no hurry to rush home, and that he too wanted to be at the hospital to see how Lenore was doing.

He's in love with her. I'm certain of it. Why else would his expression be so somber right now?

Ivan watched Jesse closely as the young man sat with his head down and eyes closed, as though praying. *Did I misjudge this fellow? Could he have strong feelings for my daughter after all? Why else did Jesse seem so distraught when he sent a driver to our store to let us know what happened to Lenore and offer us a ride to the hospital?*

When Jesse opened his eyes, Ivan saw tears on his reddened cheeks. *A man doesn't cry over a woman unless he cares deeply for her. When I'm wrong about someone, I need to say I'm wrong.*

Ivan moved over to the chair next to Jesse and placed his hand on the young man's shoulder. "I wanna thank you again for getting Lenore out of that well. It's a miracle that you came along when you did. The call you made for help may have saved our daughter's life."

"I do believe it was God's timing, but I'm sure someone else would have come along if I hadn't." Jesse ran a jerky hand through his dark hair. "It scared me really bad when I found out she'd fallen into an abandoned well, and I sure hope she's going to be okay. Lenore's a wonderful person, and . . ." His voice trailed off.

And you're in lieb with her. Ivan didn't voice his thoughts or make an attempt to finish Jesse's sentence. There was no mistaking the look of love on Jesse's face.

Everyone remained quiet for a while, reading a magazine or looking out one of the windows in the room. The longer they waited, the harder it was to relax.

Ivan was on the verge of going to the nurses' station and asking if there had been any news, when Sara and Brad showed up. As soon as they entered the room, Sara hugged Mary Ruth and Yvonne, and then she asked Jesse to explain how Lenore had fallen into the old abandoned well.

After Jesse shared the details, Brad visited with Lenore's parents a bit before offering a prayer on Lenore's behalf.

A short time later, a nurse came in and said Lenore was awake and able to receive visitors. However, she said they would need to go in two at a time. It was decided that Ivan and Yvonne would go first, but after seeing the lines of worry on Jesse's face, Ivan suggested he go in to see Lenore after them, and that his mother and Sara would be last. Brad could go too, of course, since he was an ordained minister and had hospital visiting privileges.

Jesse sagged in his chair. "Danki. I'm anxious to see how Lenore is doing." He looked at Ivan with a sober expression. "If I could have gone down into that well myself to rescue her, I surely would."

"I'm going to be fine, Mom and Dad, so there's no need to worry. The doctor assured me that my concussion isn't serious, and it's just going to take some time for my leg to heal."

Mom took Lenore's hand. "We're so glad your injuries weren't any worse."

"That old well needs to be boarded up for good," Dad said. "And I, along with some men in your community, will see that it happens." Deep wrinkles formed across his forehead. "It was an accident that never should have occurred."

"What were you doing over in that field anyway?" Mom asked.

Lenore explained about the new boys leaving the schoolyard during afternoon recess. "When I called for them to come, they ran the other way."

Dad's face tightened as his eyes narrowed. "I'll make sure their parents find out about this. That kind of behavior cannot be tolerated — especially at school where younger ones observe. It might lead them to believe they can also break the rules."

"I'll need a substitute teacher for a while. At least until I can get around well enough on my leg."

"No need to worry about that right now." Mom patted Lenore's arm. "We're going to go now and let you visit with some of the others who are in the waiting room." She gestured to the call button connected to a long cord, lying on one side of Lenore's bed. "Be sure to let the nurses know when you need more pain medicine."

"I will."

After her parents left the room, Lenore closed her eyes. She was almost at the point of dozing off when she heard heavy footsteps moving across the floor. She opened her eyes and was surprised to see Jesse standing next to her bed.

"I heard you were the one who got help for me," she said, looking up at him with a heart full of gratitude. "Danki."

"You're welcome. I only wish I would have been there sooner and could have prevented you from falling into the well." He lowered himself into the nearby chair.

"I was upset when those boys ran off, so that was probably the reason I wasn't watching where I was going."

"They shouldn't have been over in the field at all, and whoever owns that property should have made sure the well was properly covered."

"I agree, and so does my daed. He's going to speak with the members of the school board and make sure they tend to the matter of the uncovered well."

"I'm certain those boys' parents will be displeased and take proper action when they hear what their sons were up to."

Lenore heard the concern in Jesse's voice, and also noticed the lines of worry on his handsome face. For one second, she thought he might have deep feelings for her, but she quickly dismissed that idea as clouded thinking caused by the pain medicine she'd been given.

He reached over and gently placed his hand on hers. "There's something I need to tell you, Lenore."

"What is it?"

"I told you once that I still loved my wife,

and that we couldn't get married because I didn't feel that kind of love for you."

Lenore barely looked at him. It hurt to be reminded of his rejection.

"Well, I don't feel that way anymore."

"You . . . you don't?"

"No, not at all." Jesse slid his finger gently across the top of her hand, causing goose bumps to erupt on Lenore's arm. "It took me a while to realize it, but for some time now I've been fighting my attraction to you."

"You have?"

"Discovering you were down in that well and not knowing if you were seriously hurt made me realize how I would feel if you were to die, like Esther."

"How would you feel, Jesse?"

"I'd feel sad and empty inside." His voice lowered to a near whisper. "I care deeply for you, Lenore, and if you'll give me a second chance, I'd like the opportunity to prove my love to you."

Lenore gazed into his dark eyes and smiled. "Of course I'm willing to give you another chance, because I love you too, Jesse Smucker." She swallowed hard and brushed at the tears on her cheeks. "And I love that precious daughter of yours."

Lenore smiled as she thought of the heart-shaped rock again. *I think I may show that unusual stone to Jesse the first time he comes to call on me.*

EPILOGUE

Six months later

Lenore's heart swelled with joy as she and Jesse stood before their bishop in preparation for taking their marriage vows. Thankfully, her broken leg had healed well and she didn't have a limp.

In a solemn tone of voice, the bishop looked at Jesse and said, "Can you confess, brother, that you accept this our sister as your wife, and that you will not leave her until death separates you? And do you believe that this is from the Lord and that you have come thus far by your faith and prayers?"

Jesse replied, "Yes."

The bishop directed the next question to Lenore. "Can you confess, sister, that you accept this our brother as your husband, and that you will not leave him until death separates you? And do you believe that this is from the Lord and that you have come thus far by your faith and prayers?"

Swallowing against the sob rising in her throat, Lenore answered affirmatively.

Bishop John asked a few more well-chosen questions, then placed Lenore's right hand in Jesse's right hand, putting his own hands above and beneath their hands. "The God of Abraham, the God of Isaac, and the God of Jacob be with you together and give His rich blessing upon you and be merciful to you. I wish you the blessings of God for a good beginning, a steadfast middle time of your marriage, and may you hold out until a blessed end, through Jesus Christ. Amen."

Jesse, Lenore, and the bishop bowed their knees, and then he spoke again. "Go forth in the name of the Lord. You are now man and wife."

Before returning to their seats, Lenore glanced at the women's side of the room, where female members of her and Jesse's family were seated. Grandma, smiling widely while holding Cindy in her lap, sat between Lenore's mother and Sara. Jesse's parents and brothers had come down from Kentucky, and his mother sat next to Lenore's mom. Michelle, although not related by blood, sat on the other side of Sara, holding her and Ezekiel's baby girl.

On the other end of the room, several men

were representative of both the bride's and groom's families — Jesse's father and four brothers as well as Lenore's dad and her two brothers.

Herschel, Sara's father, and his parents were also in attendance, as were all of Ezekiel's family and many other friends Lenore had known since she was a girl. This day was the most joyous occasion of her life — one she would remember for the rest of her days.

After the wedding — which was being held inside a large tent in Grandma's yard — Lenore, Jesse, and Cindy would take up residence in Grandma's house. It was the perfect arrangement for all concerned. Grandma had told Lenore this morning during breakfast that someday after she was gone, the house would belong to her and Jesse.

For a few moments, Lenore felt a sense of heaviness in her chest. *What a shame Grandpa couldn't be here today to witness my marriage. Grandpa always said someday the right man would come along, and he was correct.* Lenore felt sure Jesse was the husband God had chosen for her.

She smiled inwardly, thinking about the heart-shaped rock she'd placed in the center of the corner table, known as the *Eck,* where she and Jesse would sit during the wedding meal today. She'd shown it to him a few days after she'd gotten out of the hospital, when he and Cindy came to Grandma's house to visit Lenore. When she'd explained about what she'd heard concerning finding a heart-shaped rock, Jesse smiled and said, "I think you should have shown it to me sooner."

Including the rock as part of their table decorations would be a reminder of their undying love.

As they took their seats again, Jesse offered Lenore a heart-melting smile, and she gave him one in return. They listened to the other ministers speak, and one of them quoted Psalm 147:3: " 'He healeth the broken in heart, and bindeth up their wounds.' "

Lenore closed her eyes briefly and prayed, *Dear Lord, thank You for the prayer jars Michelle, Sara, and I discovered. The scriptures, prayers, and personal notes my aunt Rhoda wrote helped all three of us in some way, and they drew us closer to You. Thank You for Your healing touch during the times we were hurting. Please guide and direct me in the days ahead, and may all that I say and do be pleasing unto You. And I thank You for the privilege of becoming Jesse's wife and the joy*

509

of being Cindy's new mother.

When Lenore's prayer ended, she opened her eyes, keeping her focus on the man who had just become her husband for life. Although they would no doubt be faced with various trials over the years, there would be plenty of good times too. Together, and with God's help, Lenore and Jesse would deal joyfully with whatever might come their way.

RECIPE FOR LENORE'S PINEAPPLE PHILLY PIE

Ingredients:
1 (20 ounce) can pineapple pie filling
1 (9 inch) unbaked pastry shell
1 (8 ounce) package cream cheese
1/2 cup sugar
1/2 teaspoon salt
2 eggs
1/2 cup milk
1/2 teaspoon vanilla

Preheat oven to 400 degrees. Spread pineapple mixture over bottom of unbaked pastry shell. Put cream cheese in bowl and cream until soft and smooth. Slowly add sugar and salt. Mix in eggs one at a time, stirring well after each addition. Blend in milk and vanilla. Pour cream cheese mixture over pineapple and bake for 10 minutes. Reduce heat to 325 degrees and bake for an additional 40 minutes. Cool before serving.

DISCUSSION QUESTIONS

1. Lenore became discouraged and began to feel frustrated about her future and her desire to be married and have a family of her own. Have you ever become impatient with God's timing and plan for your life and tried to work things out your own way?

2. Michelle faced a number of major changes in her life, including becoming Amish, getting established in the Plain community, and, later, moving to New York where she didn't know anyone. Have you had to move a lot or dealt with numerous life changes? How did you grow or adjust to each situation?

3. Jesse suffered a great loss and had trouble moving on. Although he still loved his deceased wife and was not in love with Lenore, Jesse saw the need to move on for

his daughter, Cindy's, sake because he felt that she needed a mother to care for her. Jesse also needed someone to cook and keep house for him. Can you understand his indecision about marrying Lenore? Have you or someone you know been in a similar situation? How did you handle it? Would you marry someone for the sake of convenience if you did not feel any love for them?

4. Lenore's father, Ivan, was frustrated with Jesse after he broke his engagement to Lenore. He felt that Jesse should have been honest with her about his feelings from the beginning and not led Lenore to believe he was in love with her. As parents, we don't like seeing our children, even as adults, be rejected by someone. What are some ways we can help our children deal with the hurts they face in life?

5. Although devastated by the loss of Willis, Mary Ruth felt assured that she would see him again. She also took comfort in knowing her beloved husband was with the Lord and no longer suffering. Have you lost someone dear to you? Are you assured you will see them again? Do you know the Lord personally and have confidence that

you'll be with Him when you pass from this world?

6. Brad was a pastor, dedicated to preaching God's Word and helping others. Sara had taken on the role of a pastor's wife. Can you think of ways these responsibilities are fulfilling as well as stressful? Have you been praying for your pastor and pastor's family? What are some things you can do to show your love and appreciation of the clergy and their families in the church you attend?

7. Lenore was confused by her feelings for Jesse after he admitted he was not in love with her. She enjoyed spending time with Mark, but her heart continued to lean toward Jesse. How did she figure out what to do? Have you ever been in a situation where you couldn't see clearly which direction the Lord was leading? What did you do about it?

8. Ezekiel had to confront his parents with his decision to move to New York and begin a new vocation. He needed to tell his dad he wasn't happy working in the greenhouse and wanted to pursue his own interests. Have you ever been in Ezekiel's

situation or in his parents' situation? Should parents dictate what grown children should do with their lives or expect them to live where they want them to?

9. Michelle was separated from her bothers at an early age. Can you imagine her feeling of loss and separation and the desire to see them again? Have you experienced anything like that? How did you cope?

10. Lenore loved to teach, but it became harder for her as time went on. The stress seemed more difficult to handle as she grew older and dreamed of becoming a wife and mother. Do you have a job you are dissatisfied with? Is the Lord leading you in a new direction or wanting you to learn some valuable lessons along the way?

11. Jesse was a single parent. That seems to be much more common than it used to be. Do you know a single parent you could lend a hand to or encourage? Are you a single parent? What could you use the most help with in your situation?

12. When Mary Ruth became a widow, at first she felt as if her life had no meaning. Having Lenore and Cindy around helped

to fill her lonely days, but she still grieved the loss of her husband. What can be done for a person who has suffered such bereavement? If you have lost someone close to you, what helped the most as you moved forward?

13. Why do you think Rhoda put the verses and sayings in the old jars? Do you have a collection of verses and sayings that have helped you during difficult times? If so, you may want to review them and then share them with someone who might need encouragement.

14. Did you learn anything new about the Amish way of living while reading *The Healing Jar*? If so, what did you learn, and what are your thoughts about people who have chosen to live the Plain way of life?

15. What have you learned from this book, as well as the others in the Prayer Jars series? Were there any particular Bible verses that spoke to your heart? Spend some time thinking about new insights and scriptures and consider how to incorporate them into your life.

ABOUT THE AUTHOR

New York Times bestselling and award-winning author **Wanda E. Brunstetter** is one of the founders of the Amish fiction genre. She has written over 100 books translated into four languages. With over 11 million copies sold, Wanda's stories consistently earn spots on the nation's most prestigious bestseller lists and have received numerous awards.

Wanda's ancestors were part of the Anabaptist faith, and her novels are based on personal research intended to accurately portray the Amish way of life. Her books are well read and trusted by many Amish, who credit her for giving readers a deeper understanding of the people and their customs.

When Wanda visits her Amish friends, she finds herself drawn to their peaceful lifestyle, sincerity, and close family ties. Wanda enjoys photography, ventriloquism, gardening, bird-watching, beach-combing, and spending time with her family. She and her husband, Richard, have been blessed with two grown children, six grandchildren, and two great-grandchildren.

To learn more about Wanda, visit her website at www.wandabrunstetter.com.

The employees of Thorndike Press hope you have enjoyed this Large Print book. All our Thorndike, Wheeler, and Kennebec Large Print titles are designed for easy reading, and all our books are made to last. Other Thorndike Press Large Print books are available at your library, through selected bookstores, or directly from us.

For information about titles, please call:
  (800) 223-1244

or visit our website at:
  gale.com/thorndike

To share your comments, please write:
  Publisher
  Thorndike Press
  10 Water St., Suite 310
  Waterville, ME 04901